This Here Is Love

This Here Is Love

A Novel

Princess Joy L. Perry

W. W. NORTON & COMPANY

Independent Publishers Since 1923

For information about permission to reproduce selections from this book, write to
Permissions, W. W. Norton & Company, Inc., 500 Fifth Avenue, New York, NY 10110

For information about special discounts for bulk purchases, please contact
W. W. Norton Special Sales at specialsales@wwnorton.com or 800-233-4830

Manufacturing by Lake Book Manufacturing
Book design by Buckley Design
Production manager: Lauren Abbate

ISBN 978-1-324-10597-8

W. W. Norton & Company, Inc., 500 Fifth Avenue, New York, NY 10110
www.wwnorton.com

W. W. Norton & Company Ltd., 15 Carlisle Street, London W1D 3BS

1 2 3 4 5 6 7 8 9 0

For Annie Gaskins Perry and Ruth Slade Gaskins

Contents

PART ONE • 1

PART TWO • 191

PART THREE • 293

ACKNOWLEDGMENTS • 371

This Here Is Love

PART
ONE

Odofoley and Bless

Willow Oaks Plantation
Kecoughtan Settlement, Elizabeth City Shire
Colony of Virginia, 1692

Twenty years had passed, and still sometimes Odofoley expected to wake elsewhere. She awoke in motion, heels thrashing against the side of the bed, hands grasping. She had dreamed of home, of running along the paths toward the center of the small village, toward the sounds of the women pounding millet at the communal grinding stone; her mother stood among them, waiting for her daughter to leave her play and help her carry home the grain, but Odofoley was in no hurry. There was so much to peek and peer at along the way.

On swift legs, she caught glimpses of her future. Girls older than her ten years learned to throw water pots. From hut to hut, they sat beside their mothers coiling and shaping the rings of clay. The oldest boys had also been corralled. The clanging of tools, an unexpected waft of heat from the bellows, and she did not have to look to know they were gathered with the old men, crafting out of metal the hoes and weapons that sustained them. She glimpsed her gangly brother as she dashed by the meeting ground. Two years older than her, he and a troupe of boys were learning the movements mastered just a few seasons ago by their big brothers, years ago by their fathers and grandfathers, practicing the leaps and spins and undulations that would dance them over the threshold of manhood. Within that cohort of boys was the man she would marry.

But for yet a little while, Odo remained free. Too young to be trusted with pounding the leaves for supper sauce, too young to shape the pots or do anything but snicker at the dance that would ceremonially convert playmates into men, she remained a child running to the heart of the village where her mother waited—the newest baby tied to her back—pounding millet with her own sugar-loaf-sized stone. With the work complete, she would hand the stone to Odo who would try to fit her fingers into the indentations pressed there by the grandmothers, women who left their mark in stone. Odo ran toward the chatter of the mothers, the aunts. They had been blessed with much to grind. They sang a song to give thanks and make the work go faster. She glimpsed her mother's profile, full cheeks raised to make room for her loud laugh and wide smile. Odo hurled herself against the strong and plentiful flesh of her mother's hip.

"Mama!"

The warm clay path beneath Odo's feet turned clammy. Her ankle bone cracked hard against the bed timber, and she was not a child calling but a woman summoned out of a dream.

"Mama?" Odo, the girl within her, receded, became smaller than the small hand on her shoulder. "Mama?" Cassie, the woman, woke to the voice of her child.

She pretended not to be pained and confused. "What, Bless?"

"You was getting up again."

"I was?"

"Talking too."

"I'm woke now. Go back to sleep."

Bless crawled to the side of the bed. She knelt beside her mother. The child's eyes were wide open and full of disquiet. "Will you hold me?"

Cassie wanted to say no. She wanted to curl onto her side and return to the refuge of memory. She wanted the last twenty years—all that those years brought and took, the walls of the cabin, the damp cold floor, even the child pressing into her embrace—to be the dream from which she awoke. It was not to be. The child who had been Odofoley had been stolen by the flesh-traders. She had been marched and shipped and sold into the life of a slave named Cassie.

She drew her feet from the cold floor and into the warmth of the narrow rail bed. She settled on her back and took the weight of her child upon her breasts. The rocking embrace of her own mother was only a memory. Cassie should be glad to have even that. Though her other children were gone, she still had one child to love. That was more than some possessed. Cassie tried to be grateful. She would not have this daughter, her Blessing, if a life, a land, had not been wrenched from beneath her feet. The girl loved her too. What choice did Cassie have but to take that weight against her heart and make it enough?

Rowan, Lydia, and Jack Dane

Port of London, 1691

To give up meant to die and, even among the most wretched, that kind of daring is rare. And so, instead, they braved a world of waves and misery, where time collapsed to light and dark, shades of white gray, of blue, and always the plunging. On the roughest days, waves swept across the decks, gushed down the stairs, drenched the passengers in their hammocks, and pried at the very timbers to which they had strapped their lives. But becalmed days were desperate too. The wind refused to blow, threatened to strand them, to leave them bobbing endlessly, like sea trash, like kelp or driftwood, or a fish with its fins cut away. For many onboard, it was not the first time they had been set adrift. Three generations before, their great-grandparents had been marooned on confiscated Gaelic lands.

Before the first calf dropped or the first oat was sewn, Ulster Plantation was seeded with hatred. How could it not be? One group of poor peasants—the surplus peons of English and Scottish "Undertakers," men grasping enough to claim the land of Northern Ireland but far from desperate enough to work it—was sent to supplant another. Ulster, the Catholic, Gaelic province would be "civilized" by Protestantism and English. Towns would be built. All the king's subjects would dwell in peace.

Evictions followed the arrival of the new settlers as the former residents were driven to poorer land. Soon, blood flowed as the interlopers were terrorized by woodkern, armed bands of displaced landowners and tenants. For generations, violence visited the plantation like lightning from a dry thunderstorm. Without warning, there were fast, deadly strikes—smoldering debris the only evidence of the lives and livelihoods that had been.

Eighty-one years later, in 1690, the descendants of those first Ulster plantation settlers, known as Scots-Irish, once again trod the road. To stay in Ulster meant to fight either for the Irish Catholic Jacobites or the English Protestant Williamites. Most of the colonists who left were not cowards. Simply, they did not have a dog in the fight. At war's end, no matter the victor, they would still be landless peasants.

With few regrets, they swore allegiance to the kin they could carry and walked away with their lives. And so, down in the hold of *The Venture*, huddled a microcosm of Great Britain's most miserable, a gathering of the failed and put upon. They had been scooped up from the wagons that brought them to cities; they were purged from hospitals and sold from debtors' prisons; they had been relinquished by overburdened parishes and lured from houses of coffee or ale; they were shanghaied on the doorsteps of inns with offers of free drinks and suspect friendship.

Some had been tempted with hiring pennies, money enough to buy a boy, his pregnant mother, and grown father more food than they had eaten in months, enough victuals to quiet an ear-ringing hunger so the father, Rowan Dane, could hear the promise of certain work for good wages—twenty pounds sterling a year—a small holding of his own, acres and headrights, careers for his children beyond that of beggar, pickpocket, and prostitute. His boy might be apprenticed, learn carpentry, masonry, or bottle-making. The need in the colonies was great, so much so that his family would be "transported gratis" to a land where "food would drop into their mouths!"

All the procurer required was that Rowan agree to twice the ordinary term of four years, which was fair, since the woman would not be able to work right away, and the babe within her was being transported for free. The children, of course, would be bound until they were of age, according to the custom of the country, and if that seemed unfair, Rowan must consider the great expense of transport. For him alone, ten pounds sterling and six weeks of provisions for

the crossing, his family left behind. Half a year's salary for a working man of some skill. Impossible to attain in the Old World for a
common laborer like Rowan. But the tobacco coast? Now there he
had a chance!

Even as the procurer spun an impossible tale of free land and livestock, Rowan watched his son tear at a sausage like a wolf set loose
on a carcass. At eight, Jack had known mostly fugitive years. Always
hungry. Always cold. Always wet and walking toward the promise
Rowan held out to his wife and son of a "place where things will be
better." Presently, Jack was so thin, Rowan swore he could hear the
boy's bones clack as they wandered from place to place. And with
the baby growing upon her like a tumor, Lydia was even worse off.

Roses had bloomed in her milk-fattened cheeks when Rowan
had claimed her from her father. Her blue eyes had held a distract-
ing sparkle. Now she looked dully upon their son as she pushed
more food toward him. Rowan read her thoughts: The man plying
them with meat and drink, all the while speaking rapidly and pushing a contract toward her husband, could not demand back what her
son had eaten. With the man's attention on Rowan, Lydia hid hunks
and slices in the pocket of her coat. Surreptitiously, she glanced at
Rowan. She watched him for the signal to run.

But they were not going to run. Even if rumors of unpaid wages,
of sickness and cruel masters were true, wouldn't it be cowardly,
base, to cheat his family of their one chance at betterment?

Rowan motioned for the contract. Lydia rose. One hand clawed
Jack's shoulder, pulling him up, the other grabbed for the plume.

"Rowan?" her voice arced in disbelief.

"Shall we remain here, Lydia, and die like rats?"

The procurer surveyed their gaunt faces. "Rats is better off
than you lot."

"Leave forever?" Lydia wailed.

"For the children," Rowan said.

It was at that moment the babe tumbled, revived by a meal of
more than watered porridge, all they had been able to beg or buy in
the many months since they'd fled from Ulster. And Jack drew his

knees to his chest and slumped, sated, in his seat. He would sleep the night through. He would not wake to mewl with pangs of hunger.

Lydia felt the baby settle, its weight prying at the bones of her pelvis. And as she would soon surrender to the dictates of labor, she capitulated to bartering the last thing of value they possessed—their lives.

"Sign," she said.

Rowan made his mark.

The very next day, he and his family boarded a ship bound for the British colonies on the Atlantic Coast of North America. *The Venture* had crawled from port to port, down and around the coastline of the kingdom, cajoling, conning, and corralling all who had arrived at their last choice: the New World, their only hope in hell.

• • •

The families were symmetrical: A father, a mother, a boy, but they differed in both the fine details and blunt strokes, in delicate shading and granular coarseness. Accidents of birth and the meanness of mankind had made one family a pitiful caricature of the other. They came momentarily face-to-face in the chaos of boarding.

Leading his family, the patrician young merchant wore a thickly lined satin coat in the cool May weather. A cravat as white as suds peeked from the collar. His breeches were of black velvet, the cuffs gathered just below his knee and trimmed in a border of ribbon. If his true hair color matched that of his periwig, then he was a blond with the glacial blue eyes so common to that coloring. Rowan Dane, a laborer, wore a full-sleeved smock tucked into his tow-cloth knee trousers. A shapeless, uncocked felt hat covered his brown hair. The sons were miniatures of their fathers. One boy dressed like a well-to-do undertaker, the other like an out-of-work ditch digger.

The mothers were similar in the most important way: Both women were with child. Lydia had unlaced the corset worn over her blouse to make room for the child, but out of modesty and utility, she wore a jacket and a checked apron to make her state less obvious. She'd coiled her lank yellow hair into a bun and covered the whole oily mess with a kerchief knotted beneath her chin. The merchant's wife was smaller and darker than both Lydia and the men. Of brown hair and eyes, she may have been Portuguese, yet the warm coloring did not thaw her demeanor. She was beautiful in her green travel-ing attire with a gathering of curls resting against her pale neck, but Jack could tell, before he could ever imagine why it mattered, that she was not the type of mother to pull a boy onto her shrinking lap though his legs dangled and his father warned, "That boy'll be squat-ting on you when he's thirty!" The merchant's wife was the type to be appreciated like a fine figurine, with only the eyes. Still, in a burst of gratitude, Lydia forgot herself. A fellow woman burgeoning with child, also embarking on this uncertain journey! She uttered a little cry and reached forward.

For the first time, Jack noticed his mother's hands. Hers were hands for scrubbing. The nails, torn to the quick, the crescents of dirt, the bloody and ragged skin of her cuticles. The calluses on her palms would catch on the woman's fine sleeve just as they snagged in Jack's hair.

The woman swatted Lydia's hand away. She clutched her hus-band's elbow and looked to him in distress. The woman shrank against her husband as if beset by an angry mob.

"I'll speak to the captain," her husband promised.

A flush of mortification leapt from Lydia's spurned hand to her cheeks. "I don't know why I—"

"Come along," Rowan said, pulling her quickly away, hoping the couple would not remember which woman among the crush of peasants had had cheek enough to touch her.

They hustled off, joining in the flow of ragged passengers. Lydia gripped Rowan's sleeve, and, fearful that she would lose her son in the crowd, she clutched Jack by the cheap material of his too-thin coat. He tried to wriggle out of her hold, ceasing his struggle only when Rowan's heavy hand landed on his shoulder.

At the hatch, the Dane family jostled this way and the other as the sailors shunted the steerage passengers belowdecks. The melee resembled nothing if not a flock of laden beasts prodded into a cote. As he glanced around to get his bearings, Jack's gaze chanced again upon the merchant's son. The boy stood fast between his parents, his hands encased in their smoothly gloved palms. The mother's face had eased into calm. The father looked assured and stern. A man in braided uniform escorted them away from the chaos, toward their cabin.

Jack had spent much of his life hungry, but this sudden stabbing yearning was different. He longed to be in the other boy's place. Jack chafed beneath his parents' rough and clawing grip. He looked up into their faces. Haggard. Frightened.

As he descended the hatch, Jack realized that though they were on the same ship, the families were embarking on wholly different journeys.

Andrew Cabarrus

Northampton County
Colony of Virginia, 1692

Half of his land on Virginia's Eastern Shore in exchange for one wife, two daughters, and three sons. Those were the terms. And each time Andrew Cabarrus canoed and walked the three-hour journey to visit his family on Othman Scarborough's plantation, he intended to strike the deal.

Certainly, Andrew did not love land more than his family. He did not begrudge them an inch of his two hundred acres, but he knew his neighbors well. Northampton County was not a province of benevolent men. The men in these parts were as pitiless as fever, as relentless as bloody flux. They grasped all they could, and some were not averse to slaughter. There was no man of any color whom they would not swindle or ill-use in return for acreage and influence.

Property, crops, and cash were the only protections against bondage. If Andrew gave up the land, he would be reduced to what he had been when Englishmen first dragged him to Virginia—powerless. What help would he be to his family then?

Andrew Cabarrus was among a small number of Negro planters trying to hold a stake in that world. They were householders, scattered on both the bay and ocean sides of Northampton, and dotting each of the creeks: the Pungoteague, the Mattawaman—King's Creek and Cherrystone Creek alike. Out of necessity, they bore the names of one or another enslaver—Cane, Cabarrus, Mongum, Rodriggus, Johnson—European men who had been, if not kind, less cruel than the rest. But their farms—Zaire, Benin, Angola—flaunted names of longing and pride.

But the names of enslavers or lands—whether lost, adopted, or longed for—did not matter. Africans like Andrew had no illusions of returning home. No path led to the men they might have become. They grabbed onto the only choice left to them—to root and rebuild in this land.

The days and weeks away from Phoebe and the children were spent accumulating resources against the time when he could offer Scarborough a sum not to be refused, or at least enough to buy the influence of a judge or member of the burgesses who could force Scarborough's hand. Andrew raised tobacco and corn, cows and hogs. He felled and sold the pine and oak from his land to ship-wrights. When rain kept him from the fields, he ferried passengers across the Pungoteague on his canoe. He traded with the Accomacks, buying their animal skins and selling them elsewhere.

But no matter how much Andrew offered Scarborough, the terms stood fast. He did not want sterling. He required soil. He would only sell Andrew his wife and children in return for prime acres of the land. Specifically, Scarborough demanded one hundred acres of the Negro's most fertile tobacco acreage and the inlet deep enough to land a shallop.

When Andrew bought the land, it was a few acres no English-man yet coveted in the bootheel of Pungoteague Creek. Since then, it had been recognized as one of the few places in Northampton with an inlet deep enough to land a sizable sailing craft. Andrew owned one of the few ways of shipping tobacco directly from the pier to the mainland without the expense of smaller, more danger-ous crafts to haul the product out to harbor.

It was a constant source of embarrassment and consternation for Scarborough that Andrew, one of his former bondsmen, recognized the value of that "swampy bit of marsh" and bought it before Scar-borough did. But many other things, besides Andrew's status and bit of wealth, had also changed in the twelve years since Andrew bought himself free and purchased his own farm. In that time *partus sequi-*

tur ventrem—"that which is brought forth follows the belly"—had become the law of the land. Phoebe, the woman Andrew had married, was known to be Scarborough's "Negro for life," and so went Andrew and Phoebe's children.

David was their firstborn. In the days after the boy's birth, Andrew and Phoebe had passed him back and forth, shaking their heads, marveling at what they, together, had made. They held in their hands newly born evidence of home. "Mouth shaped like *maame*," Phoebe said. Like her mother. "Moles like *agya*," Andrew replied. His papa. What they did not voice, "Part of me is on another shore. I will never be the full measure of myself again. But I look into the face of this child you made with me, and I think, 'Maybe for this. Maybe for what I did not choose but will not relinquish. Maybe for *him*, all else had to be stripped away.'"

On the night of David's birth, while Phoebe slept, Andrew had the baby to himself. He held the boy in his hands. The child looked at him with curiosity, completely untroubled, no concept of sorrow within him. He grasped his father's pinky in a hand that was tiny but strong, the lifelines dark and deeply etched.

And just like that, a great deal of Andrew's suffering eased. This was the reason the burning years had not reduced him to ash. The son in his arms was sufficient cause for everything that had happened and for anything Andrew might do. If he could provide land, a few cows and freedom, this boy, David Cabarrus, could do anything.

So, Andrew bided time. Not buying his family but building it. Not relinquishing his ground but extending it. Putting both at risk.

Cassie and Bless

Willow Oaks Plantation
Kecoughtan Settlement, Elizabeth City Shire
Colony of Virginia, 1692

"Cassie! Cassie!" the mistress called as she breezed over the well-trod footpath that connected the main house and the kitchen. "Cassie, little Miss Rebecca wants Bless."

Cassie bent over a pot of collards, pressing them down so she could fit the lid on. "Yes'm," she said. "I'll wash her face and hands and send her on."

Bless heard her name but pretended not to. She did not want to go to Miss Rebecca, who pinched and who let Bless watch her play but not touch the toys and who got Bless in trouble for splashing mud the last time they played, even though Rebecca pushed Bless into the puddle. Bless was perfectly happy where she sat, on the warm hearthstones, playing with the newest corn-husk doll her mother had made. It had no face, no blue, glass eyes like Miss Rebecca's doll, but it had enough corn silk hair to plait, and a dress and head rag made out of the scraps of Cassie's mending.

"You come back when you hear the girls bring in supper," her mother said to her. "Mistress don't need you underfoot."

"No, Cassie. You must fetch her things. Rebecca is going to keep Bless."

The cast-iron lid in Cassie's hand fell into the fire. Embers scattered, lighting on the dry silk-and-husk doll in Bless's hands. Bless beat out the sparks and clutched the doll to her chest.

"Miss?" her mother said. "Please, miss. She all I got."

The entreaty alarmed Bless more than the clanging lid and fly-ing fire. Her mama did not beg. "It don't do no good," she'd heard Cassie say. "Want in a black skin don't make no sense to them. They sooner puzzle out bird chirp." Bless scrambled to her feet.

The mistress looked around the kitchen. "Cassie, those herrings should be in brine by now."

"She my last, miss."

At the notching upward of Cassie's tone, the faint demand to be heard, the mistress stopped. "I thought you would be happy."

"Happy?"

"You would prefer that we send her to the fields? Bless is well past earning her keep."

"She helps me, miss—"

"Sitting here playing with dolls?" Her disparaging gaze scraped over the doll Bless clutched to her chest. "Nonsense. She has clung to your skirts long enough."

Cassie was prudent enough not to mention that Bless and Rebecca had been born in the same year. Dolls and wooden puzzles and spin-ning tops with string were scattered across the floor of the children's room in the main house. It was Bless's job to put them away in the evening, after Rebecca and her brother, Dalton, had been put to bed.

"He said I could keep her, miss."

"Why, the child is simply coming to live in the house!"

"If she could just come home nights, miss. I could bear it through the days."

"Nights are when Rebecca needs her most! That child calls to me just as I drift—"

"He took the others."

"Took?" the mistress repeated the word meticulously, sounding each letter so that the *K* sounded hard and sharp, like the stab of a sewing needle.

"My other young'uns. The master, he promised me this *one*." Cassie gestured toward Bless, her hands reaching and falling as though the empty weight was too much to carry.

"My husband makes no promises to other women. Gather her things and send—"

"Ain't you got a mother's heart?"

The words rang, taut and twanging, like a plucked string.

The mistress stopped lifting lids and peering into clay jars. "Your master will have you at the woodpile," the mistress said. She thrust out her hand to Bless. "Come."

Cassie stepped between her daughter and the woman who meant to claim her. "Bless," Cassie said, "you my child."

Outrage flooded Cassie at the breaking of this, the last promise she had believed. If they took this child, she may as well have died in the raid on her village or thrown herself overboard into that depthless ocean. She should have been smothered beneath the weight of the men who had raped her. The girl felt the upswell of her mother's fury. As if they were still cord-bound, Cassie's will flowed into Bless's small body. *Do not move. You better not move.*

Bless could not see beyond the height and breadth of her mother. She could no longer see the mistress standing behind Cassie, fuming, growing angrier and angrier at the impertinence of a slave. But this was a lesson Bless knew well: You don't have to see a thing to know its power to harm.

Dolls of husk or dolls of porcelain, hair of twine or hair of silk, there is no childhood for a slave. Bless knew what happened at the woodpile. When her master whipped one slave, all were summoned to see. "Put down the hoe, the eggs, that iron!" the overseer shouted. "Come get this lesson!"

Bless knew the sounds of whipping though Cassie never let her see the stretched body shackled to the whipping post or the lash spraying fresh blood. She pressed Bless's face into her shoulder when the girl was small enough to carry, into her skirt when the child grew too heavy to hold. Cassie never thought to plug her ears. By the age of four, Bless could tell the hiss of bullwhip from the slap of unbraided rope. She knew the full range of human screams.

"You *my* child," Cassie said again. She lay a restraining grip on

Bless. Bless looked into her mother's face, wet with sweat, wet with tears, anguished.

And love, like cord blood, flowed both ways. Bless would sacrifice anything, even her own small body, to protect her mother.

She pulled from her mother's grasp. "She our master," Bless mumbled.

As Bless shuffled around Cassie to thrust her hand into the hand of the mistress, she lost her grip on the doll. It cracked against the hearthstones. She squatted to pick it up, but the mistress jerked Bless to her feet.

"Leave it," the woman said. "The house is just now free of lice."

Andrew and David Cabarrus

Northampton County
Colony of Virginia, 1692

They set out at nightfall, when whatever had been silent all day began to buzz and clack and shake the grass, sound cover for the man and boy hurriedly passing through planted fields, farmsteads, and woods.

Andrew and David walked the miles in near silence, not because there was not much to say and see, even in the dark, but because Andrew did not have permission to take his son off of Scarborough's land. If anyone missed the boy, Phoebe would divert attention by claiming David was abed, afflicted with some short-lived, common purging of the stomach or bowels to which no one, not even the overseer, would want to get close.

The lie was necessary. If Andrew were caught, he would be charged with stealing another man's property. So, as they moved through the forbidden night, he used touch and gesture to show his son the moonlit world awakening around them. When they came upon a rangale of deer, Andrew halted David with a hand on his shoulder; father and son watched the small herd as they fed on low branches and frisked in and out of the cover of the trees. He cupped his ear and pointed to draw the boy's attention to the call of an owl; hearts beating hard, they watched as the predator launched, swooped, and pelted up from the grass with some broken creature in its talons.

The excitement of being alone with his father, of leaving the Scarborough plantation for the first time in his life kept David on his feet for nearly the whole three hours. He fought sleep until his father rowed the canoe he'd left at Pungoteague Creek to Cabarrus land.

That was fine with Andrew. He had much to tell and show the boy, and the visit would go better if David rested. Andrew rowed with quick and even strokes. He wanted to reach the farm in time for David to watch the sun rise over their land.

When David woke, Andrew fed him bacon, the meat cured, the rind tough, and biscuits that Phoebe would have laughed at because of how flat and overbaked they were. They ate their food as they walked. This was not the slave cabins where the overseer might eavesdrop below the window or burst through the door in hopes of catching someone out of place. On Cabarrus land, it was safe to meander, to speak aloud of dreams and plans.

"Do you know why I brung you here?" With his jaws full of bread, David shook his head.

"Swallow and say, 'No, sir,'" Andrew instructed.

David minded. "No, sir," he said.

Andrew smiled. "Come 'long."

There was both much and little to show David. The boy was impressed by the two-room house of wood and wattle, with a hard oxblood floor and a chimney. Unlike the slave cabins, drafty wall chinks were sealed so that not even light, let alone wind, slipped through, and the floors felt cool and dry. Outside, the rails of the ox and pig pens reached high and neatly notched into the posts. The plainness of the clapboard-covered tobacco barn belied the fact that it was the most important structure on the farm. Much of the farm's acreage was still timber and shrub, river birch angling out over the creek, the red oak and pine broken up by redbud, sweet bay magnolia, and bushes of white shadblow.

With his own hands and any he could hire—African, English, or Native—Andrew had felled the trees and muled-up the stumps. All day he worked the land and made it yield. Andrew, stolen from a people who knew both the hoe and the ax, knew to change the crops according to the needs of the soil. He plowed by moonlight and seeded at sunrise. He napped and rose and worked. And the fact that he had just traveled on foot through the night, even the momentous presence of his son, made no difference. The day would be spent in labor.

But first, Andrew needed to talk to his son. He took David to the most coveted spot on the farm. With his own hands, he brought the sweet creek water to the boy's lips to chase down the salty pork. Side by side, they stood on the pier where Andrew's next tobacco harvest would be loaded onto a shallop. The pier that white farmers would have to pay him to use.

Andrew and David watched the morning light pick through the birch trees until it found a spot on which to settle. They watched jewel-blue, early-riser, dragonflies pluck mosquitoes from the water and witnessed the ever-widening circles of that feeding. They settled beneath a canopy of oak and pine, among shadows of green and black, curved and deep.

"You just a boy," Andrew said to David, "but I have to talk to you like you a man. Understand?"

"Yes, sir." David answered, ready to be a man in his father's eyes.

Andrew knew David was old enough to comprehend the words. He hoped the weight of them would settle on him later.

"This going to be your land," Andrew said. "When you older, you and your brothers'll farm it. Y'all gone have to work hard and stay together to keep it."

"What about the girls?" David asked.

Andrew smiled. He liked this streak of fairness in his son. "They'll marry and go off to farm with their husbands. But if they come back, you make 'em welcome. Promise?"

David nodded but worry puckered his face. Andrew had expected questions but not the look of pensiveness, almost ridiculous on the face of child.

"What you thinking?"

"Will the girls be mad if they can't get married?"

"Why can't they get married?"

"We need 'em to farm here *and* Master Scarborough's."

Andrew gave a resolute shake of his head. "You won't be farming Scarborough's."

David knew it was risky to contradict his father. Often, parents saw no difference between "you wrong" and "you lying." Either could end with a boy nursing switch welts on his hiney. But his father had said they would talk like men.

"But Mama say—" He paused to see if Andrew had begun scanning for a fat switch.

"Mama say what?"

"Mama say we belong to Master Scarborough and we got to work for 'im. That's why we don't live with you. We slaves."

So, the boy had asked. Phoebe had not warned him. And now Andrew had no time to prepare for the next question, the one for which no answer existed. The mechanics of love or the mystery of death—almost anything else would be easier to explain. Andrew would rather try his luck at those.

"Why we slaves?" David asked.

Andrew cleared his throat. He coughed. He hawked and spat a thick wad of phlegm onto the browning pine needles. He would not swallow what ought to be the white folks' shame. "Because some people take what they want," he said, "and some earn it. It's writ in they law that it's okay for them to take."

"They law say I belong to him?"

"Yes. But that ain't God law."

"Who God say I belong to?"

Andrew wanted to say, *you belong to your mama and me*, but he was not a lying man. If the sheriff walked on his land and demanded David right now, Andrew's blood claim would not hold. On Scarborough's whim, the boy, any of the children, could be rented out or sold away from Phoebe.

Rather than lie, Andrew told the part of the truth that would hold David in good stead if his father succeeded in buying him free, but more importantly, if he did not.

"You the son of a *free* man. You belong to yourself. Them the two things you always got to remember. Hear me?"

"Yes, sir."

"I earned this land, an' I'm working on earning you all free."

"Yes, sir."

"You was meant to be free."

"Yes, sir."

"I brung you here so you know what freedom look like. What it feel like." Andrew smiled again. It was the most David had ever seen his father smile unless he was holding one of the babies. "It feel like tired feet an' sore back. Come 'long."

And they went off to collect the eggs and milk the cow, to gather acorns for the hog, to sharpen the ax and hitch the oxen to the plow, to clear and bust up a few more acres.

When the sun withdrew, and whatever had flown and clucked and gathered retreated for the night, Andrew and his son returned to the creek and climbed into the canoe. David perched in the bow, tired but eager to see what moved in the night water. He called his father's attention to a brisk shiver in the reeds, wondered aloud in the most grown-up expression he knew that did not cross the line into cursing, what in the "round world" it might be. Andrew gave David the laugh he knew the boy desired, but his chuckle was brief.

What in the round world, indeed? Andrew rowed upstream, laboring against the current, against nature, wondering what kind of father delivers his son back into the narrow straits of slavery.

Andrew and Phoebe Cabarrus

Othman Scarborough's Plantation
Northampton County
Colony of Virginia, 1692

If Andrew woke in his wife's cabin on a Sunday morning, he rose first. He hauled and heated the water for baths and coffee. He made cornmeal batter and fried it in the bacon fat Phoebe stored in a clay jar. In spring and summer, while the meal cooked, he sat on a chair by the open door and smoked. His household awoke, one by one, to join him on the stoop. One of the children always came first, until his lap filled, and one child leaned sleepily against each of his legs. Phoebe always came last, barefoot and looking rested, her hair still tied in a head rag. They sent the children in to eat, but Andrew and Phoebe remained on the porch. They took their first sip of coffee alone together.

After breakfast, Andrew organized the children into a line, David at the head, then Ruth, Peggy, and the boys, George-Lee and Will, according to age. Andrew fed each foot-dragging child a spoonful of vile castor oil to flush out worms and keep out cold. He kept a switch on the table near his left hand. "Swallow it," he would say in his commanding baritone as soon as their lips puckered. He hardly ever used the whip. Even Will, the three-year-old, obeyed. Phoebe had to chase and capture them one by one when she wanted to give them a dose, but the children never ran from Andrew.

Perhaps that was because he gave them more than medicine. Before his brief visits ended, Andrew would find a moment to take each girl or boy aside and gift the child with something found, sometimes made, something that, "Put me in mind of you." The brilliant blue-and-green carcass of a dragon fly. A rock of sunrise colors. A blueberry bush seedling, "You grow that an' Mama'll make us pie." He hid treats in his pockets, behind his ear, under his hat, and sometimes in his beard. The children climbed over him, prodded him. He nipped their searching fingers and poked into their armpits. The game always ended in squeals and a caution from Phoebe, "You gon' ruin them children."

With Will on his hip, Andrew rose to touch her. "Loving ain't ruined you, have it?"

Sometimes Phoebe would roll her eyes or swat his hand from her hip. Sometimes she went sad, her gaze darting between the child, happy in his father's arms, and Andrew's joyful face. "We'll see," she'd say, "might be the thing that ruin me yet."

If there was enough time, they would leave the children and go for a walk and talk through the plan—again. Each birth had changed the timetable. If time was running short, Andrew would send David inside to watch the other children while he stood on the steps with Phoebe's face in his hands. "Scarborough can't say no to cash forever," he promised, "I'm gon' get y'all free."

But a freeman married to an enslaved woman cannot stand idle making pledges for long. Andrew Cabarrus was not encouraged to linger, spreading his influence among the unfree. These visits were courtesies, dependent on the goodwill of Scarborough. So, before he left, Andrew gathered a week's worth of wood. He hunted up a string of croaker, a possum, a bushel of corn, or a mud turtle. He patched wall chinks that filled the house with cold or mosquitoes. He fried corncakes, put coffee on to boil for his wife, and fed his children castor oil. He crammed birthdays, remembrances, and milestones into the stingy hours between two sunrises. When he had done all the benevolence of white folks allowed, Andrew kissed his children and his wife and left them, for a fortnight or a month, or more, at the mercy of their master.

Jack Dane

Aboard The Venture, *1691*

As Jack Dane, his mother and father, and the other steerage passengers were prodded belowdecks, Jack saw porters hefting the trunks, furnishings, carpets—even a spinet—belonging to the gentry-class families, while his mother, clumsy and swollen with child, stooped to help his father heave the one trunk they were allowed. Jack himself struggled under the weight of the one bag they could keep with them. It contained their meager clothing and few necessities like pewter plates and cups.

While the gentlemen and merchants and their families were led in an orderly fashion to the few small cabins, the Danes, along with other "'tween decks" passengers, were crammed down a steep ladder that led to the narrow space between ballast and storage. Just the voyage before, the space had housed cattle, and it still bore the stains and scents. In preparation for the emigrants, the sailors had mucked but not scrubbed the area before laying planks for "family bunks." Straw and mucous and cow shit clung to the walls against which the travelers would rest their heads.

The emigrants had been relegated to the rightful place of useful things, the cargo hold. A space so low that grown men had to stoop as they moved from end to end. So far from the head, where seawater washed away human waste, that pails—which overturned and spilled their contents beneath the bunks—had been placed for community use.

These, the bartered class, would repay this miserable passage by giving years of their lives to those asleep in the cabins above, those who seemingly had a more pressing claim on dry bedding, sunlight, and sea air.

'Tween decks, they ate food so salty it burned the lips and drank sour water from leaky barrels. They slept, whole families, jammed in bunks, in the thick company of lice, with the crash of the sea always a little too loud, too close. And even when the sea did not cry out, the people did, for disease and death scuttled bunk to bunk with the ease of shipboard rats. Night and day, the space resounded with fervent prayers, passionate curses, and continuous weeping.

David and Phoebe Cabarrus

Othman Scarborough's Plantation
Northampton County
Colony of Virginia, 1692

Saturday morning, seven days since Andrew had come and gone, Phoebe stood near the end of the stumpy line at Master Scarborough's back door to collect her rations for the week. She knew what to expect: a peck of cornmeal, a half peck of flour, a piece of salt pork no bigger than the size of her hand, a small block of lard, and a smaller crock of molasses. The question was how to make it stretch to fill seven days and six bellies. Her boys, David and George-Lee were working more, running messages to all corners of the farm and doing some chopping in the field. They came in hungry. Ruth and Peggy ate almost as much. They were big enough to help scrub and pin up laundry, to plant and weed in the garden at the master's house. And all of them were growing like weeds.

Phoebe thought of what she had to trade; the few potatoes left in the shallow hole dug into the floor of the cabin might get her three salt-herring from one of the other women. She thought about what she could harvest from her garden—dandelion greens, onions, beets, and a few ears of corn—if the beetles and leaf borers hadn't got there before her. And there was a chance Andrew might come along with a couple of rabbits, squirrels, or muskrats, maybe even oysters, before the evening was out, but she couldn't depend on that. They both wished she could. His absences might be as long as six weeks. Children could not eat only "When Papa come." She alone had to fill the gaps and make up the shortfalls.

Phoebe and David took their turn on the porch. She said her greetings to the master and his wife, thanked them, and began to unpack, from the basket balanced on her head, the empty vessels into which Scarborough would measure her food. David had come along in case there was some kind of surplus. Perhaps saw beetles or moths got into the cornmeal or flour; stores too louse-ridden for the missus to put on her table but too good to throw away were handed off to the slaves. Or there might be a bumper crop in the garden—cucumbers, tomatoes, or peas—a plenty that the family had grown tired of eating. David would help Phoebe carry that back to the cabin.

"'Drew been 'round lately?" Master Scarborough asked, squinting into the morning sun, or perhaps narrow-eyed in search of the truth. Phoebe could not tell.

"Naw, sir," she answered quickly. If Scarborough thought Andrew filled her children's bellies on a weekly basis, he would cut her rations. He would give someone else her children's portion.

Without even a side glance in his direction, Phoebe squeezed David's hand, an urgent reminder of the rules for living with white folks: Obey them if you could; that was always easiest, and tell them nothing, ever. In almost every circumstance, safety lay in feigning yourself tame and dull. Therefore, it was not strange for David to see his mother transform from the brook-no-foolishness woman of their cabin to a faltering girl before their master.

"When you expect to see him again?" Scarborough asked.

Phoebe lowered her head in affected shame. "That nigger, sir? I don't when he be 'round."

"I heard tell he's here often enough."

Phoebe lifted her gaze. Who among the cabins was spying, reporting back to the master? "Where you hear that, sir?"

Scarborough cocked a brow at the direct question unrelated to his immediate needs—more coffee, sir? Another log on the fire, sir? Phoebe looked at the ground, and David felt again the clench of her hand. This tightening was reflex, his mother containing something she did not want the master to see.

When Phoebe looked up again, her face was composed, every feature in place, like that floor hole dug into the dirt of the cabin: three boards set in a tight, particular order, a rag rug pulled over the hollow to hide it from view. The few potatoes and coins, everything valuable they owned, kept out of sight. Just like Phoebe's feelings. Just like her thoughts.

"There's been a bear roaming since y'all cleared the Butler wood," Phoebe said. "I seen it lumbering not far from the coops, headed back toward the woods. That could be what the folks saw, a bear flushed out, turned to chicken hunting."

"You think so?"

"Might be so, sir."

"Heard tell this 'bear' had a cub 'long with it."

"This the time of year cubs be out, sir."

Scarborough paused in the dipping of meal and flour. He sized up Phoebe. No bonnet or mob cap; instead, hair wrapped the way West African women did. Skin dark as purple plums. Cheeks plump except where dimples slashed. A powerful body. A heavy ass. Already the mother of five and plenty of bearing years ahead of her. Andrew would come around soon.

Scarborough began to measure her short.

"Heard 'Drew bought him a new sow," he said. "Spent good money on that. He tell you I offered him a deal on you and the children?" A measure less of cornmeal.

"First I'm hearing of it, sir," Phoebe answered.

"A free nigger now. All that land he got. You'd think he'd want y'all with 'im."

Phoebe kept her mouth shut and her gaze on Scarborough's doling hand. Three-quarters the normal pour of molasses.

"Yet here you stand," Scarborough said, "in front of me with your hand out. If he do right by you, Phoebe, you won't need these little rations at all. Why, you'll be living like them free Johnson and Rodriggus Negresses."

Two fingers' worth of meat cut off her salt pork. Scarborough wrapped her ration in the greasy length of linen she brought back empty Saturday after Saturday. He held it out to Phoebe, but when she reached for it, Scarborough did not let go.

"Tell him that, Phoebe. Next time he come, tell him how you want to live."

Phoebe slackened her grip on the pork. The weight of her fingers remained but the strength for holding had gone. She should have lifted her hand away. The only dignified answer to Scarborough's demand was to walk away without his piddling mouthful of meat. But David, patient and respectful through the long morning wait, leaned into her, used his mother for balance as he scratched his left calf with the ragged nails of his right foot. The trusting weight of him caused Phoebe to think.

She assessed her circumstances: five young ones to feed; a husband who lived three hours away by foot and canoe; a white man who would decide whether or not her boy had fit shoes when the ground turned cold; and a promise that Andrew would somehow get her and the children free without relinquishing the very land he needed to *keep* them free.

"If I was you, I'd tell him," Scarborough said.

Phoebe closed her fingers around the fat and lean that she would cut thin and use sparingly until every rind and dripping had gone into the mouths of her children.

"Yes, Master," she said, and because he required gratitude for the less than she needed, the less than she deserved, the so much less than she had worked for, Phoebe said, "Thank you, Master."

She left with an empty-handed David by her side, the basket so light it swayed upon her head.

Down the path, away from the hearing of the master and any eavesdroppers, David tried to draw his mother out of her worry.

"Papa say he be to see us 'round Ruthie birthday. You say that's June. Just a month away."

The meat might last until Tuesday.

With a hard squeeze of the hand, Phoebe said, "Hush, child."

Cassie and Bless

Willow Oaks Plantation
Kecoughtan Settlement, Elizabeth City Shire
Colony of Virginia, 1692

Bless was used to being somebody's child. Come morning, she was used to being nudged out of the warm quilts and body heat of the bed she shared with Cassie. She was used to the feel of her mother's hand on her head, its weight on her shoulder. She was used to a slap on the thigh if she ventured out of a child's rightful place. She was used to a few raisins, a dollop of cream, or a new corn-husk doll when she did right. Bless was used to love.

The day she felt most loved, most cherished, was hair washing day. Not so frequent in the winter, when Cassie feared the child might catch cold, it was a ritual of warm Saturday afternoons.

Bless knelt at the tub while her mother poured warm water over her hair, telling her, "Turn your head this way," so Cassie could rinse the oak ash soap from the soft wedge of hair in front of Bless's ear. Bless caught glimpses of blue sky and green leaves, and her mother's face, set and serious the way it was when Cassie worked hard in the kitchen. Washing her daughter's hair mattered as much as kneading bread.

What came after her hair and scalp shone, scrubbed clean by Cassie's strong fingers, had always been Bless's favorite part.

When Bless was very small, Cassie would lay the child across her knees to comb through the girl's tightly packed hair. Bless dozed as Cassie pulled plaits into neat formation by braiding the tail of one into the kinked roots of another or tucking them behind her ears.

"Your hair just as feisty as you," she would mumble, and Bless felt as if unruly hair and feisty daughters were things to speak of with wonder and pride.

A year or so ago, Bless had outgrown her mother's lap. At nine, she was long in limb but light, so Cassie crossed her ankles and let the girl sit on them like a stool. Bless still fell asleep, snug between her mother's knees, her drool staining Cassie's skirts. But sometimes Bless awoke with her toes scraping the floor, head cradled on the soft meat of Cassie's thigh, having been dragged up and across her mother's lap. She felt Cassie tugging the small hairs at the back of her neck into tiny plaits.

Months after being taken from her mother's care—weeks of being awakened from the mat where she slept next to Miss Rebecca's bed by the girl's summons, weeks of taking her meals in a closet that stored dishes and serving pieces—the mistress finally stood close enough to Bless to notice the gray film in the parts of the girl's hair, to sniff the sour smell rising from her scalp.

"Wash it," she said.

"I don't know how, ma'am," Bless said. "Mama always do it."

The mistress shook her head. "Big girl like you don't know how to keep herself clean?" she said, forgetting that Bless hauled the water and stood on hand with soap and towels on Rebecca's bath night. "Go. Come straight back when it is done."

Bless dashed away, a "Yes'm" thrown over her shoulder like a pinch of salt. And the child did hope for good luck.

Bless ran the whole way, only slowing when she saw the cabin door pulled shut on a day brimming with sun. Disappointment struck her like a board in the face. There was no way to know when she would have another chance. She would go in and wait. Her mama had not known she was coming. She might be off visiting as was a Saturday afternoon privilege. If the mistress asked why Bless stayed gone so long, she would say she had to wait. She was afraid to come back with dirty hair.

She pushed open the door. It took her eyes a moment to adjust, to see Cassie there in the closed-up cabin, sitting by the unlit hearth.

"Mama?"

Cassie roused, "What you doing here?"

"Miss say for you to fix my hair."

• • •

Cassie moved slowly, first like a shadow peeling away from the wall, then like a sleepwalker. At the tub, she wet and soaped Bless's hair with the eagerness of scrubbing the kitchen floor—thorough but begrudging. Her fingers were strong enough to clutch and wring the neck off of a chicken, and she did not temper that force. Bless endured. Soon, she would sit between her mother's knees and rest the back of her head on Cassie's inner thigh while her mother combed and braided.

Hunkered by the tub, Bless waited with her eyes squeezed shut for the feel of Cassie blotting and gently tugging her hair with the soft flour sack they used for a towel. Instead, she felt the cloth pushed into her hands. Bless quickly scrubbed the sack over her face so she could see her mother, but Cassie had already turned away. "Sit in the chair," Cassie said.

Comb in hand, Cassie stood behind Bless. She parted, greased, and braided Bless's hair the way she tended the table when the mistress had special guests. Grim, silent, efficient. Cassie was as meticulous and stoic as when she served a meal on the plates sent from London. No questions about what it was like to live in the big house, if they were treating her kindly. Not a word of missing or apology.

Bless sat upright in the ladder-backed chair. She sat still and straight. She was not a bit sleepy.

• • •

Cassie was shocked by her own coldness toward Bless. Since her child had walked out of the kitchen hand in hand with Miss Olivia, Cassie had felt almost nothing but a stiffening fury. She knew no fault lay with Bless. The child had been afraid. She had fallen back on the one ploy that was supposed to turn away white wrath: obedience. And even if Bless had done the unthinkable and honored her mother's command over the mistress's, Cassie's pride in victory would have been short-lived. Punishment would have been immediate and irreparable. It would have fallen on mother *and* daughter. The price one slave paid to protect another was often collected in blood.

To lay blame where blame belonged was to invite the whip or worse for both her and Bless. White folks hurt slaves then brutalized them for showing their suffering.

So, Cassie heaped misdirected anger over seeds of bitterness against her own child. There was no other safe ground in which it could root. It was better to pretend that Bless went willingly with the mistress than it was to command, "Come to *me* if you walk through fire," for then they would have burned together. And the child knew it. The girl knew her mother had no power to protect either of them.

Until the moment Bless walked away and joined her hand with the mistress's, Cassie had thought she'd been some good at hiding—with treats, with tenderness, with corn-husk dolls—what she was, what they were. Turns out, her baby knew all along. That knowing was what Cassie had not yet been able to forgive.

Only nine, and the girl had more sense than her mama. For Cassie *had* believed. When he sold away her only son, two older daughters and each of their fathers, Master Benjamin Hampton held out one promise: "I'll let you keep the last one."

No, Cassie had not been fool enough to believe he did this out of some small sense of compassion. It was good business. A woman continued to work, continued to rise in the morning, if she believed there was something to live for. Master Benjamin called it "incentive." Each woman on the place was guaranteed one child to raise as her own. How much cotton would a woman pick, how many sheets would she scrub, how many pots would she stir to secure her one last child? Cassie had given everything and fought for nothing because she had taken the devil at his word. And nothing was exactly what these white folks would leave her with if she did not find a way to win back her daughter.

So, Cassie stood outside of the children's room as young Rebecca read to Dalton and Bless from *Pilgrim's Progress*. The tray she held trembled in her grasp. On it sat a little pitcher of small beer and two porcelain cups. Cassie had also brought a cup made of clay. She would treat Bless, too, and sit with her in a corner or out here on the steps while Rebecca and her brother had their "tea" party. Bless would know her mama was sorry, that she had meant no lasting harm, and though they lived apart, they still belonged to each other.

"So he had them into the slaughter-house, where was a butcher killing a sheep; and, behold, the sheep was quiet, and took her death patiently. Then said the Interpreter, 'You must learn of this sheep to suffer, and to put up with wrongs without murmurings and complaints. Behold how quietly she takes her death.'"

Cassie rolled her shoulders. She prepared to push open the door but paused when a mewling sound interrupted Miss Rebecca's reading.

"You must wait," Rebecca scolded. But the urging continued. Cassie feared she knew what it was. Those children had dragged some mangy animal in the house. Fleas would overrun the place, and the mistress would have a fit.

"Very well," Rebecca said. "Up. Beg. Beg," and there came the sound again, higher pitched, more urgent.

Cassie shouldered open the door. "You chil'ren know better—" But there was no one-eyed barn cat or scabby dog.

On the floor between the children's chairs, bouncing on her knees, with her hands bent like paws, was Bless. She ate shortbread from Rebecca's hand. She lolled out her tongue while Rebecca stroked her plaits as if they were fur.

The porcelain cups rattled. It took all the control Cassie possessed to cross the room and set the tray down instead of dashing it on the floor. Rebecca recognized fury in Cassie's face before the other two children. She pushed Bless away. With her gaze on Cassie, she slid from the chair and ran from the room. Dalton soon followed. Wails, first Rebecca's then Dalton's sailed backward.

"Come here," Cassie said to her daughter.

Bless remained on her knees, shuffling toward Cassie.

"We playing puppy," she whispered.

"Get up and come here," Cassie said.

Bless stumbled twice before gaining her feet.

Cassie snatched Bless up as soon as the child was within reach. She shook her, snapping and bobbing the child's head. "You ain't no dog, you hear? You ain't no dog!"

The mistress barreled through the door. Master Benjamin arrived on her heels, a belt looped around his hand, the thick leather tongue dangling.

"Did she put her hands on the children? Did she put her damned black hands on my children?" he shouted as he pushed in front of his wife.

Cassie did not let loose of Bless. She shoved the girl behind her. "I did not touch Miss 'Becca and Mister Dalton, sir."

"Then why are they crying? What is all of this fuss?"

All three of the children were crying, but now for different reasons. Bless had been afraid; she was now ashamed. Dalton cried because his sister did, but Rebecca's fright had turned to a kind of excitement.

"We were playing puppy," she cried.

"Makin' my child out to be a dog," Cassie said.

"And what of it?" the mistress said. "They were playing a game."

"My child ain't no dog."

The mistress turned on her husband. "I told you. She does not know her place. You refused to whip her the last time, now look what has come of it. Our children chastised by a Negro! You've been too lax with this one. Making her promises—"

"Hush!" Master Benjamin said. He cut the air with a whistling slash of the belt.

This dragging him into the nonsensical inner workings of domestic life would stop today. He was far from pleased to find himself in the middle of a nursery room dispute. Truth be told, he did not approve of the way his wife had commandeered Bless. He *had* promised Cassie that she could keep the child, and it was a promise he'd intended to keep. He saw Olivia's interference as a breach of the trust he'd cultivated with his Negroes and a challenge to his authority. Further, he did not think Rebecca needed any more pampering than she already got; the child was damn near ruined.

When he learned of the confrontation in the kitchen, he'd declined to have Cassie whipped. He did, however, warn the cook that another show of temper and impudence would be severely punished. Secretly, he had given Cassie a small bag of coins and enough calico to make herself a nice dress. He had considered the matter closed. Now this.

The gazes of the women and children were riveted on the belt. He raised it, pointed it first at Bless, then at each of them in turn.

"That child is whatever I say she is," he said. "As are you, Rebecca, Dalton. As are you, Cassie. As are you, wife."

He changed the angle of his stance as he called each name, making eye contact, pinching the belt in his fist until the thick leather doubled over.

"You are *all* dogs if I say you are dogs. Now, Cassie, tell me. Ain't you a dog?"

"Naw, sir."

He let out the length of the belt. Cassie flinched. Bless gripped her mother's skirt. Master Benjamin's children moved closer to their mother. But instead of striking, their father and master began to feed the belt into the loops of his pants. They watched with relief as he fastened the metal prong into a notch and pulled it tight. While his hands worked, Master Benjamin nodded, a careful up and down of his head.

"Know why I put that away, Cassie?"

"Naw, sir."

"'Cause it won't do no good with you. You ain't scared of a beating. I know what do scare you, though. Rebecca, Dalton, come here."

The children moved farther into the folds of their mother's skirt. She held them by the shoulders and said, "Benjamin, just make her apologize."

Without taking his eyes off of Cassie, Benjamin said to his wife, "Olivia, hand me those children. Cassie, you a dog," he said. "Say it."

But even Miss Olivia, who had summoned her husband, now

had reservations about the punishment he had in mind. "Benjamin, I want her to apologize. That is all."

Benjamin turned to his wife. "You *want* her to know who is master. Well, I am master, and I want *all* of you to know so you will cease to trouble me with your household squabbles. Come here!" he demanded of his children.

The mistress pushed them, once again crying earnest tears, toward their father. "He won't hurt you," she said, and hoped it was true.

Dalton and Rebecca stepped, sniffling, to their father. He pushed the children between himself and Cassie.

"Now, Cassie, you are going to kneel before these children, and you are going to say, 'I am a dog.'"

"Whip me, sir."

"Or I will sell Bless come morning."

Rebecca twisted around to look up at her father. "No, Papa! She is mine!"

"No!" he said. "She is *mine*. Every goddamn one of you is mine, and I will have you know it and cease pestering me! Cassie?"

Cassie reached behind her to tug Bless. "Go to the kitchen."

Eager to obey, to be away, Bless stepped from behind her mother. Master Benjamin's face turned a red that radiated heat. As Bless set to run, he snatched her into the line beside his own children.

"*You* have no command of this child," he said to Cassie. "She is yours only because I have said so," he told Rebecca. "This is a lesson all of you must learn. Cassie, I won't wait for a trader. At first light of day, I'll carry her to market myself."

"I beg your pardon, Miss Rebecca, Master Dal—"

"Is that what I told you to say?" He set his hand on Bless's shoulder. He gripped the small bones with less restraint than he fisted the reins of his quarter horse.

"Whip me, sir. Please don't make a animal outa me in front of her."

"Come tomorrow dawn, she won't be here to see what I make 'outa' you."

"I'll go to market, Mama," Bless whispered. She would do anything to spare her mama's dignity.

"Shush!" Cassie ordered.

Cassie looked around at this room for children. Miniature tea things, children's cots sturdier than the bed she, a grown working woman, slept in, doll baby clothes that cost more than the dress she wore, and the reddened white faces that believed, or were learning, that they had a right to every part of her, not just her hands but all the wonder that made them work. They wanted *that* at their disposal, to dispose of as they pleased. The parents were convinced. The children ceased to cry. In a very few years, they would pass her from hand to hand, from generation to generation, and they would handle her the same. "Well," she said. "Well, Lord."

"Behold how quietly." Cassie's skirt muffled the cracking sound of her knees, of something ineffable breaking beneath the weight of sacrifice.

Cassie knelt before six-year-old Dalton and ten-year-old Rebecca. Her own child, slightly off to the side, bore witness. "I am a dog," Cassie said.

When the sound of leather-clad steps receded, only Bless remained. Her mother did not rise. "Mama?" Bless pleaded. She reached out. She touched her mother's neck.

Cassie jerked. She struck her daughter's hand away.

Bless drew back, first her hand, then, like a leaf in autumn, the withering edges of her heart. For the hatred she saw in her mother's eyes was fleeting, but it was real.

Jack Dane

Aboard The Venture
Fourteen days on the Atlantic Ocean

"I'm William," the young boy from the day they boarded said. He wore suede breeches, polished shoes, and a linen shirt finer and whiter than any Jack had ever seen before. "What is your name?"

"Jack Dane," he said, his voice gravelly, adjusting to speech like his eyes adjusting to light when he crept up from the hold. This William had sought him out. Jack had not wandered. Except for specific times, many areas of the ship were off limits to steerage passengers. But as long they stayed near the hatch, as long as there were not too many of them congregating and they didn't create a ruckus, the sailors let them stay on deck beyond the designated times.

"You're quite ragged, aren't you, Jack?" the boy said, perusing Jack from his greasy cap and limp ringlets to his tight and patched britches.

Jack looked down at his feet. The rags his mother had stuffed into his shoes were bulging from the edges. He shoved his hands into the pockets of his breeches and pinched the skin of his naked thighs. Lately, his mother had been too sick for mending.

"Well, come along, then," William said.

Jack looked up, startled. "Where?"

"Best place on the ship," he promised.

Jack glanced around. His parents were down below, Rowan tending Lydia. This last month, the baby made it impossible for her to lie down and sleep. She had to sit up to find any comfort, and there was little enough of that to be had in the press and noise of the hold. When she was awake, she moaned with seasickness. His father sat with his arm around her. He left her only to push to the front of the galley line in hopes they might have something she could keep on her stomach. Jack's parents had no time for him just now. The other travelers loitering miserably about the hatch were strangers. They didn't care what he did.

"All right then," Jack said.

William would not tell Jack where they were going, only when to hide and where. Ducking low and freezing when a sailor approached, the boys dodged behind barrels, crouched beneath a staircase, and hid in the folds of a jib sail that awaited mending. Stealthily they made their way around the edges of the main deck, portside, toward the stern. When Jack realized where William meant to lead, he stopped.

"We can't go there," he whispered.

"Of course, we can," William said. "I've already been. The captain took my father and me there to watch the sunset. I thought you might like it too. You can see the whole world from there. But if you are afraid—"

Jack already felt ashamed before this boy. "I ain't afraid," he declared, and fell into step behind William.

The poop deck perched upon the roof of the captain's cabin in the stern of the ship. The highest deck on the ship, only the captain, high-ranking officers, or invited guests were allowed there. The small space was almost holy, at least Jack thought so. The intricately carved railing reminded him of the pews and beautifully carved altars he had glimpsed the few times he'd been able to poke his head within a church. The awe that entered him now felt more powerful than on those occasions. The whole world *was* visible, and it seemed like he stood at its center point of terror and reverence.

Jack turned about. He clutched the rail. But that was not enough. He whirled about. He squared his shoulders and threw back his head and screeched, and only then did the press of huts and hovels, burdens and holds leave him. On the other side of that deck railing lay a new world. Jack could see the whole horizon curve and bow beneath the weight of water. Multiplied and magnified by the waves, the sun scattered in every direction. Creatures—dolphins, William said—

leapt and glided alongside the ship, traversed beneath, appeared and disappeared like fantastic figures within a mirror. Jack grinned at William, and William grinned back.

"What are you doing here? You don't belong up here." A man in a velvet waistcoat and fine breeches snatched Jack at the shoulder and whirled him about. With only recent mastery of sea legs, Jack fell to the deck. "And, William, what have you to say for yourself?"

The boy barely hesitated. "He brought me here, Father."

Both the lie and the fall stunned Jack. On his rump, Jack could see no higher than the fine ribbon hem that gathered the man's breeches. Jack thought William's father would kick him. He began to crab backward, on the heels of his feet and hands. The horizon disappeared as he tumbled down the short flight of steps to the quarter deck. He landed with a bruising thump on the boards.

William's father stood at the top of the stairs looking down at Jack. "The captain will know about you wandering the ship," he said, then turned back to his son. He grabbed William by the ear with enough force to lift the boy onto his tiptoes. "You should know better than to go about with vermin."

"I didn't want to come, Father!"

Jack raised himself as quickly as his trembling hands and feet would allow. He ran over the slippery deck and through the curses of sailors. He threw himself down the hatch. Sliding on the filthy floor, he did not stop until he reached a familiar bank of planks in the hold. His parents huddled together, Rowan murmuring and bathing Lydia's face with a frayed rag.

"Are we vermin?" Jack demanded.

"Who said that?" his mother asked as she panted to ease the pain of labor. Lydia squeezed her eyes shut. She extended her hand toward Jack, but the boy shrank from her. Jack looked to the left, then to the right.

On each side there was suffering. Sick people, retching or moaning. A man held a woman by the shoulders and shook her. Though her head struck the timber, no one moved to intervene. Curses filled the air like ash. Jack's knowing gaze fell on his mother. His parents had brought him here, but worse somehow, they had destined him for such a life long before they ever boarded *The Venture*.

"Don't look at me like that!" Lydia said. She raised her hand to strike Jack, to turn away the accusation in his eyes, but she snatched it back as hurt took hold. She moaned her agony at Jack's question and the anguish of labor into Rowan's shoulder.

Rowan murmured to her. He stroked his wife's limp, sweaty hair as he, too, assessed the brutal scene. A long inhale coated his tongue with the stench of the hold. Women, men, and children huddled and slumped together on the airless deck. His young son standing before him, thin and ragged as an old beggar. His baby about to be born in a shithole.

"Yes, Jack," Rowan nodded. "We are vermin. Now help me tend your mother."

Andrew Cabarrus and Othman Scarborough

Othman Scarborough's Plantation
Northampton County
Colony of Virginia, 1692

"Phoebe say you cut the rations."

"What of it?"

"I 'preciate if you leave her and the children outa this. This between us two men."

"Got you here, didn't it?" Othman Scarborough asked.

"You ain't got to take food outa their mouths to get me here, sir," Andrew said. "I made you a cash offer."

"You know cash ain't what I want."

"If that don't serve, I can give you something off the rate I charge for using—"

"You think I'm angling for an allowance?"

"This my family, sir."

"Behave like it. Buy them."

"I don't want nothing more than to buy them, sir. If we can come to reasonable terms—"

"These the only terms you're going to get, Andrew. And I know you've been talking to other planters. Trying to get around me."

"I have a right to keep that land. I bought it."

"Don't matter you bought it. You bought it before we knew what it was. You think we gon' let you *keep* such a piece of land?"

"There's other land, sir, where a man ain't planted fields and fences and put up a house for his family."

"That might be the most valuable spot of land this side of the shore, Andrew. The men around here, they aren't ready for a n—" Scarborough hesitated. He found a word less insulting than the one that had come to mind and tongue. "You to get ahead of them. They ain't coming to beg nothing of you. You better get out of this the best way you can."

"And if I was an Englishman, even an Irishman, would you keep after me so?"

Scarborough shrugged. "You ain't."

"A man without land is—"

"Nothing."

"You telling me to go back to being 'nothing.'"

"I'm telling you what it costs to get Phoebe and them young ones under your own power."

Andrew looked away to give the sting of tears a chance to diminish. There were signs of a home-life here: the children's string and top underfoot on the porch, the chemises of Scarborough's wife and child-sized stockings hanging from the clothesline. And the house was not silent. Bickering, instruction, and laughter, the sounds of family, reached the men as they stood in the yard.

"What if it was your missus and your young'uns?"

Scarborough paled. He was a slaveowner and knew how filthy the business of slavery could be. Not the public rooms of the auction houses where slaves stood arrayed across a stage after they'd been fattened and dressed in pressed chambray. Not the orderly and airy counting offices in the downstairs quarters of brokers. No, Scarborough, an occasional importer of flesh, knew what befell the "goods" in the alleys and backrooms, in the cellars and closets of slavery. He knew the use of a slave—woman, child, or man—was only limited by the possessor's imagination and willingness to inflict pain. The suggestion of his own wife and children used in ways too cruel or humiliating for animals bolted him forward, hands fisted.

"They ain't niggers. You calling my family niggers?"

Andrew did not tense at Scarborough's breath in his face. He did not brace or step back or cock for a swing.

"Not calling no man nothing. 'Preciate if you do the same," Andrew said. "Asking what you do if somebody try to force you out of all you got to keep your missus and young'uns safe. I am offering you a fair price," Andrew said. He swallowed the bile that rose upon talking of his family, his children, as merchandise. "More'n what the market will give you for the young'uns."

Scarborough's fists unclenched as he listened to the steady tone of the man's voice, saw how he remained as still and solid as a fence post, and realized something: Andrew Cabarrus did not fear him.

How could he? Cabarrus had been snatched, subdued, and kidnapped, swallowed into mists at the end of the Ghanaian horizon. More than once, he'd been entombed with the dead and dying in the rancid hold of a slave ship. He did not die beneath the whips, privations, and diseases of "Sugar Island" seasoning. Instead, he'd been spit out on the Great Land, the English colony of Virginia, then shalloped and oared across twelve miles of bay in an open vessel, only to be delivered, again, into the hands of men who hogtied and hauled him.

His lot was a lifetime of men who were certain no will or wish mattered but their own—men like Othman Scarborough. Andrew had endured them, outwitted them, outworked them. For years he had toiled on Scarborough's land, and all Andrew had earned for his labor was Phoebe's admiration and love. Only by hiring himself out on Sundays, the slaves' one day of liberty, did Andrew manage to buy himself. He had become a free, landholding man.

And just as he had accepted that he would never in this life return to his homeland, likewise, the man before him would have to accept that Andrew meant to keep his land, all of it, his family, too, and remain free.

The man who stood before Andrew Cabarrus was equally immovable. Scarborough was all but royalty on the Eastern Shore. His name was spoken in the same breath and with the same reverence as names like Burdett and Littleton, planters who owned nearly half of the county.

These were men who did not think in terms of right or wrong;

rather, they thought of expedience. They made money on both sides of the law. Land could be accumulated through outright purchase or headrights, but they were not above speculation or swindle. They owned mills and coasting vessels and factories that made shoes and salt, but if a Magotha or Nuswattock had sufficient goods for trade, these landed gentry sold them weapons and the munitions that made the guns worth something.

But perhaps more than money, definitely more than love, they prized the deference, the obedience of all with whom they came into contact. Truckling, no matter how obvious or oily, was as coveted as tobacco and caske. Yet standing before Scarborough, on his own two feet, was his former bondsman who would not submit.

If Scarborough could not control his own people, free or bound, how could he demand respect from the planters? They would revile him. And if it deterred this kind of insolence and rebellion among their own people, the planters would band together and crush him. For self-preservation, as much as to curb defiance among the middling farmers and the poor, Scarborough would not let Andrew Cabarrus live in peace.

Because Scarborough knew how far he was willing to go, his words rang of threat and pity. "This ain't going to end the way you hope."

But Andrew knew how far he had come—oceans, years, hemispheres, languages. Few traces of the way back remained. His only hope for home lay there on a creek, at Phoebe's breast, in the unfettered futures of his children. He would die before he took one rearward step.

"It will," he said. "For my children, indeed it will."

Bless

Willow Oaks Plantation
Kecoughtan Settlement, Elizabeth City Shire
Colony of Virginia, 1692

Bless mixed starch and water into a paste. She began at her forehead and worked downward. She worked from hairline to neckline, secreting herself beneath a sticky white mask. She even slathered the brown back of each hand. Then she stood before the looking glass in Miss Rebecca's bedchamber. She turned this way and that. She touched her own cheek.

White skin. Each night, it summoned the mistress to the side of Rebecca's bed where she smoothed the girl's hair or fussed with her gown or cap or folded back the covers or pulled them high—whatever Rebecca asked. White skin never slept on the floor where it was stepped over or stubbed. White skin did not wake each morning on eye level with the piss pot. So, by the same childish alchemy that turns a doll into a real baby and a stick into a sword, Bless turned herself white.

Painted-on whiteness felt like a dress without patches—not fancy, just a dress that was clean and whole, good enough to wear anywhere. She whirled before the wavering glass and did not see the blotches and cracks in her gray mask.

Miss Olivia screamed. A pile of lace scattered around her feet. She staggered at the sight of a child-sized, chalk-faced ghost lingering before the looking glass.

Eagerly, Bless turned to where her mistress swayed in the doorway. "Am I pretty?" she asked.

"Bless? Bless, you scared the life out of me!" Mistress Olivia stepped farther into the room. Sheepishly, she began to smile at her own silliness. She drew closer.

"Why, ain't you a little haint," she said. She cocked her head and studied Bless as if she'd never considered prettiness to be the longing of a Negro girl. "You want to be pretty?"

"Like Rebecca."

The invocation of her daughter's name as the standard of pretty sparked in Olivia an uncharacteristic moment of tenderness. She ran a thumb lightly over Bless's cheek. "What is this?"

"Starch."

"Starch?"

"Yes'm."

She put her hands on Bless's arms as she trembled with laughter. "Well, I s'pose I ought to be glad you didn't get into the flour."

Bless did not know why her choice of starch was funny, but she was happy to have pleased, to have made the mistress touch her face the way she touched Rebecca's.

"Bless," she said. "Bless!" Mistress hugged her, then set her arm's length away. "Bless, you funny girl!" She cupped Bless's cheek. "You are a nigger, honey. Nothin's goin' to change that."

Mistress Olivia rubbed her hands together to shed the false dust of whiteness. She checked her reflection in the glass and corrected the wayward fall of curls around her own porcelain hairline.

"Pick up this mess and wash your face." She stepped lightly over the spilled lace. "On second thought, leave it on. I want Master Benjamin to see."

Bless snatched breaths to forestall the weeping, a common dodge of children, a way to keep tears at bay until a bully took off after someone else. This time, the trick did not work. Tears made tracks in the caked white starch, baring the weeping brown girl beneath.

Rowan Dane

Aboard The Venture
Seven weeks on the Atlantic Ocean

"The child is hearty?" the merchant asked.

"Seems so, sir," Rowan replied.

"Heartier than her mother? No signs of sickness?"

"None, sir."

"I cannot place another dying babe in my wife's arms," the merchant said.

Lydia's baby had not been the only birth on the night of the storm. Above deck, the surgeon had delivered the child of the merchant and his wife, but the child was born too early. She died within days.

The captain unrolled a sheet of parchment. Always informed of what came to pass on his ship, he'd heard there was a newborn in need of a dame, and he knew there was a well-placed dame grieving a child. He recognized an opportunity—for himself.

Now the deal would be sealed in his cabin. An exchange. Simple, clean, and binding—a baby was no less legal tender than tobacco, bullion, or rum. Rowan made his mark.

"What is her name?" the captain asked.

Rowan cleared the grief from his throat. "Jack calls her Lydia, after his mother."

"And you? What do you call her?" the merchant asked.

"I-I don't call her anything."

The merchant paused in taking his turn with the plume. His gaze flickered over Rowan, as did the captain's.

Rowan swallowed their disdain. He was used to the callousness of the well-heeled. What did a rich merchant and a man who possessed his own seagoing vessel know of a poor man's life? If they'd not discovered some use, some need to be served by his flesh and blood, his baby, they never would have known he and his family were aboard this ship. *Damn their contempt. Double damn them, the hypocrites.* He could imagine how well a merchant and a ship's captain knew their own nurslings. Because, however it seemed, the world had little tolerance for children.

The parentless—the ones who roamed and begged and stole—were punished just like adults. They could be sentenced, beaten, or transported to prison colonies. Some were executed. And if a poor child escaped punishment, he was sure to be caught by disease. There was measles, pox, cough, and cold on the stomach, the unending ache of a rotted tooth or the jaw-breaking cruelty of having it drawn. A scratch or an uncovered sore could mortify into the stink of a bad limb. Poor children died like flies, and the rich were only slightly better off. Still, in the house of the wealthy, children were boons not burdens. If they lived—and money always bought a better chance—they were signs of prosperity, a hedge against old age.

Rowan had reasoned that he could not afford to keep the child, so what use was attaching to her? Where they were going, no matter how grand, would amount to no more than a clearing in the wilderness. There would be no one to tend and nurse the child. He assumed no almshouse or orphanage existed in the Virginia Colony, nowhere, at least for his kind, to seek the help he would surely need. And what of the things she needed? Cradles and clouts, swaddling clothes, infant stays and shifts, pudding caps and lead strings? And what of milk? The world, after all, is made up of commodities, each thing measured by its worth. He had to look at his newborn daughter that way. Added value versus cost. Each article—be it bricks, a keg of nails, or a child—obliged to pay, in pounds sterling, the cost of existing.

All of Rowan's reasons were sound. His duty as a father was to see the child safely placed. He did not ponder the opinion of the dead woman who had carried the child for nine months. He did not ponder the feelings of the boy who had toted her for six weeks. And Rowan did not look too closely at what he felt each night as he watched his children sleep. He studied the baby—lumped like a tumor upon Jack's chest just as she had been in Lydia's belly.

Rowan hardly thought of her as his baby. She had not grown inside of him. He did not know the weight of her curled atop his bladder. Neither did he know the flutter of her hiccups or the wonder of her sudden flips. Rowan had not carried the baby within his body, like Lydia had, nor in his arms, like Jack did. He did not notice when she began to master the flailing of her own arms or when she first smiled. Jack did. Because it was Jack who, daily, roamed the hold until he found a woman willing to nurse his sister. The boy learned to make clouts, to tuck and tie them and to slosh the soiled cloths in a bucket of salt water. Of course, there was no cradle, so at night, he lay down with the baby upon him. In his fitful dozing, the baby's mewling and fidgeting took the place of their mother's croon and stroke. Beneath the baby's ear, Jack's quick heart replaced the nine-month constancy of her mother's.

Rowan did not think of this. The merchant did not even deign to imagine. And the difference between children and livestock was so slight that a bargain was easily struck.

The merchant inked his name onto the parchment. The captain scattered sand upon the document to sop the excess ink. Silently calculating his cut, he did not look in sad wonder at the man who had just sold his child or the man who had made the purchase. Instead, he lifted the parchment and shook away the sand. He watched the loose grains scatter. The three men counted bills. They clattered coins of silver. Then, they sent for Jack to surrender the baby.

Othman Scarborough

Northampton County
Colony of Virginia, 1692

The men who owned most of the Eastern Shore were not ease-ful patriarchs. Othman Scarborough carried a pistol out of the knowledge that he was feared, not liked. His clothes were well-made but simple because the need to work the dirt or fight a rival might arise at a moment's notice. One thing feuding landowners such as the Scarboroughs, Yeardleys, Robins, and Waters of the Eastern Shore could agree on, however, was a social order in which they occupied the top rung. Though they fought over land bound-aries, political influence, animals, and accounts come due, they worked in almost flawless concert to neutralize anyone who threat-ened their standing.

Combined effort might be just what Scarborough's problem required. From the Great Land, presently, had come fresh news of a stirring, a mixing and mingling among whites of few acres, their indentured brethren, and the Negroes. New unrest had begun to move through the colony like a wave of dysentery. Already, the slaves and indentureds thought nothing of running off together though the crime was neither committed nor punished without great delib-eration. To run away was to literally risk one's skin if caught. Thirty lashes on the bare back and shoulders. An *R* branded into the cheek. Shackles worn for one year. And yet, driven to it by the donkeywork of plantation life, the Negroes, Indians, and servants sided with one another and, often enough, fled together.

And their fellow feeling seemed to be growing. From within the near hopelessness of slavery and the failed promises of bonded servitude, they were making demands. The indentureds who sought freedom and those who had achieved it wanted the acres and opportunities promised in their contracts. But the press of their claims threatened the peaceful order. To meet their petitions, the colonial powers would have to wrest more land from the tribes or force the gentry toward more equitable distribution of their holdings. Neither of which was likely to be achieved without spending treasure and blood.

The sparks that flamed into Nathaniel Bacon's Rebellion in 1676 had not been extinguished, only banked. They were threatening, once again, to ignite. One only had to look up the shore to the province of Maryland. Just a few years before, in 1689, that *rank Baconist* John Coode had led a rebellion against the barons of Baltimore, wresting control from the hands of the Calvert family, ending their dynasty.

The problems brewing on the Great Land, only a boat ride away, had made landfall on the Eastern Shore.

Already, a few owners made mention of having to discipline servants—returned to their masters by patrollers—who left their tasks, or even the boundaries of the plantation, to meet in secluded places for clandestine discussions. As an anticipatory defense, Scarborough paid slaves to spy, which was how he knew Andrew Cabarrus had taken young David off of the plantation.

Scarborough took stock of the times in which he lived, of the fears and aspirations riding the air like smoke or spirit. He found a way as effective as murder—but cleaner—to rid himself of Cabarrus.

In the prevailing climate of disgruntlement and self-interest, Cabarrus's refusal to cede ground to one of his "betters" was all the proof Scarborough needed of what would come. Preemptive measures must be taken unless the planters wanted to be driven from their lands by torch-wielding commoners and Negroes.

Scarborough's case was not hard to make. No planter—gentry, middling, or poor—could tolerate the loss of hands, even those as small as David's, or abide an uprising. Workers were as valuable as seed, soil, and rain. Defiant servants—indentured, enslaved, or freed—were to be feared as much as drought or flood.

Jack Dane

J ack would not let go. He held the baby like the last floating spar after a shipwreck.

When the sailor fetched him to the captain, Jack was suddenly glad for the hours Rowan spent topside, staring into the swells that had swallowed Lydia's body. Jack would not have to explain why the commanding officer of the vessel had summoned him. The boy resolved to take whatever punishment would get him out of the captain's presence soonest. At best there would be a tongue lashing for his visit to the poop deck. At worst, a caning across his backside. He hitched his sister into his arms and followed the sailor to the captain's quarters.

The first face Jack saw was Rowan's. Did the captain mean to have Jack caned by his own father? Did he mean to beat them both? Were they being expelled from the ship, set adrift over one errant visit to a forbidden deck?

"Give her to me," the merchant repeated as it did not seem the boy heard him the first time.

Jack recognized him, that boy William's father, the man in the velvet waistcoat and fine breeches who'd meant to kick him. The man who called Jack "vermin." That man held his arms out impatiently for Jack's sister. "Has she any other garments?" he asked Rowan with a glance at the petticoat in which she was swaddled.

"No—I don't know." Then Rowan saw Jack's face. "A moment, please, to talk to the boy."

"Our business is settled." He nodded toward the bills and coins on the captain's table. "Talk when I am gone. Give her to me," the merchant ordered again.

"No!" Jack said. He turned to run, but the captain barred the door.

"Jack, give her—" Rowan began.

Jack wheeled around and faced his father. Physically, Rowan took up as much space in the tight quarters as did the merchant and the captain but, somehow, he seemed smaller. Perhaps it was his gaze, flitting from one face to another in search of something; perhaps it was his poor man's attire, a meager shield for all he lacked underneath. Jack grasped why he had been summoned.

"What you done?" he asked. "What you done, Da?"

"I found a home for her, Jack."

"Ma said—"

"I can't, Jack. Not both of you."

"I get what she needs—"

"Jack, this man is rich—"

Jack shook his head. "The lady wouldn't let Ma *touch* her, now you're after giving her Ma's baby? That boy, William. He lied. Was his idea to go to the poop deck! This man says we're vermin. They ain't decent people!"

"Guard your tongue," the merchant said and took a step toward Jack. Rowan raised a hand to forestall him.

"Will you correct the boy or shall I?" the merchant asked.

Rowan stepped away from the table on which lay the bill of sale and the cash. He squatted in front of Jack. The baby wriggled in her brother's arms, his hold tighter than the swaddling cloth.

Rowan looked into Jack's furious and frightened eyes—brown eyes, the same eyes, the same frantic fear Rowan saw each time he chanced upon a mirror.

"Where we are going—"

"You promised Ma."

"I did not promise. She died, and I did not promise," Rowan hissed. The baby startled. She frowned as if she were about to cry, but then her gaze found Jack. She waved the one arm she'd managed to free and cooed instead of screeching.

Rowan began again. "Jack, do you even know what vermin is?"

Jack shook his head. He'd not known the book meaning, hadn't needed to. The implication had been right there in the merchant's tone. "Something ugly," he said.

"Vermin is nits, Jack. Bedbugs. Them things that bite when you try to sleep. Remember, your Ma was always cursin' 'em, trying to beat 'em from our beds?"

Jack nodded.

"And vermin is what makes you scratch sores in your head. And vermin is flies and rats—"

The baby's coo turned, after all, to a cry. Jack bounced his sister. "We ain't—she ain't vermin," he said.

"She will be if she stays with you and me," Rowan said.

Jack stopped bouncing.

Rowan asked, "You don't want that for her, do you, Jack?"

"I want *her*."

"You that selfish?" Rowan questioned, pleaded. He peered at Jack as if he were unfamiliar with the boy who stood before him. Had he raised a son who would not do the best, hard thing?

"No—" the boy faltered.

Quickly, Jack tried to reason whether or not holding on to his sister would be selfish. He had been responsible—food, a dry bottom, a warm place to sleep—needs and comforts he'd filled through his own wits and the kindness of the others. But sometimes his young wit and the pity of shipmates had failed. He would, he suspected, fail again and baby Lydia would suffer because of it. Did that make him selfish?

"She will have warm clothes and a decent house," Rowan pressed.

Jack stared down at the baby. He drew her against his body as if he would tuck her inside his coat.

"Give her to him. Give her to him. You ain't a selfish boy."

"Enough of this coddling," the merchant said. "Hand her over, so we can be done with this."

Jack stepped backward. He bumped against the legs of the captain. Rowan shot the merchant a look.

"She will have food enough, Jack." Rowan said.

Jack knew his sister's hungry cry. It was high-pitched, and it trembled, and it ebbed and returned, ebbed and returned. He had done his best, but the women belowdecks did not always have enough milk to spare. He had even tried feeding her from his own mouth, like birds do, chewing the hardtack until it was soft, allowing her to suck on the fibrous wad. But when she did not strangle on the chomped mass, her belly hurt her, and the boy despaired over which pain caused her the most suffering.

"She won't be hungry?" Jack asked.

"She won't be hungry," Rowan promised. "What say you, Jack?"

Jack gave a slow nod. His gaze never left his sister.

Rowan stood. The captain relaxed his stance against the door. The merchant in his well-made shoes and velvet coat and fine breeches trimmed in ribbon stepped forward. Rowan held out his arms for the child, but Jack sidestepped their father.

Careful of Lydia's wayward, wobbly head, Jack approached the merchant and offered the baby like a gift.

The merchant seized her.

• • •

Belowdecks, Rowan knelt beside his son. He kissed Jack's head and wet cheeks and held his face in callused palms as he had not done since before the death of the boy's mother. For weeks now, the only grief Rowan had felt was his own.

But empathy arrived too late. "Look at me, Jack. It *is* best. It is best for her."

Jack looked. He saw tinges of concern and outlines of certainty in his father's eyes, but nothing a boy could trust. Rowan would never fool him again. Not in any way. Never again would Jack be cowed by the threat of his father's strong hands, hands well-made for welting a disobedient boy's bottom. He would not be shamed by Rowan's sternness or anger, nor swayed by his kindness or wisdom. For Jack had seen the avid darting of his father's gaze from the face of the merchant to that of the captain, to the pile of money. A wordless lesson, it taught Jack all he needed to know about whom to fear and what to respect.

Rowan took Jack's momentary lapse into quiet study as acceptance, as the boy bowing to fate. "You and me'll start over Jack," he promised. "In a few years, we'll have land of our own. You might well have your own horse. How would you like that?"

He searched the boy's face. Jack seemed to listen, to believe. In Rowan's mind the matter was settled, for most people believe children are easily pacified. If not appeased, the will of a child can be broken.

But sometimes, the opposite can come to pass. Scorned and ignored, a boy's frustrated fury lengthens and hardens right along with his bones. And Jack Dane proved to be a fast-growing boy.

Bless

Willow Oaks Plantation
Kecoughtan Settlement, Elizabeth City Shire
Colony of Virginia, 1696

The whims of white folks wear on the mind and tear down the body. Though Bless had been Miss Rebecca's personal servant for four years, the enslaved girl hardly knew what waking would bring—a pinch from Miss Rebecca was as likely as a morning kiss. What had been fine the day before became an infraction with the dawn.

A child set adrift or born with a thoughtful temperament—and Bless was both—could lose hours puzzling over what misstep had set her outside of a master or mistress's good graces. Water too hot or too cold? An ill-timed smile? An audible sigh? Perhaps a thing she had done too well? Mastering a stitch that eluded the young mistress? Being more apt than the young master with sums? Apology might work or simply waiting for a change in notion. But there were no remedies for some offenses.

The very woman who had demanded Bless as a body servant for her daughter came to despise Bless's body. No one could miss the lengthening legs, the widening hips and rounding buttocks, not with the way the girl "sported herself about," according to Miss Olivia, with her bodice too tight and the hem of her dress inching up her bare ankles as she outgrew the clothes just rationed or handed down the year before.

Mistress Olivia was not the only family member who had noticed the changes. Rebecca also considered the more developed body of her companion. Comparison sometimes caused her to dissolve into weeping. Once, she demanded Bless bare the buds of her breasts. Like camelias before bloom, they were small and hard knots beneath the taut brown skin. In a fit of jealousy, Rebecca grabbed on and twisted. Both girls were shocked when Bless knocked her hand away. Only begging and promises of an even more devoted level of servitude kept Rebecca from running to tell.

Yet it was not the jealousy of Rebecca but the trailing gaze of young Dalton, and on occasion the wandering eye of his father, that fired Olivia's dislike for thirteen-year-old Bless.

Standing or sitting, covered or crouching, fresh from the tub or dripping with sweat, Olivia hated the sight, the footfalls, the scent of Bless. Almost daily, she threatened to whip her. She promised to have Bless scrubbed with a wire brush if she continued to "walk around smelling like a whore in heat."

The day young Dalton found Bless in the schoolroom was no different than the hundred other times she had already been ordered by the mistress to "find something to do out of my sight." Bless wiped clean the books of horn and damp mopped the chalk dust that had floated into the corners of the room. She shelved the leather-bound books Rebecca and Dalton cast about as if they were hair ribbons or pocket squares. And she picked up the toys that they, by unfathomable turns, loved or discarded.

Bless dragged a blue-eyed Susie doll out from under the reading chair and cradled her. She smoothed the satin skirt that whispered instead of crackled like the skirts of Bless's old corn-husk dolls. She wound a lock of yellow hair around her index finger to freshen the curl. Not a strand snapped or crumbled. Knowing she was not allowed to play with the toys unless partaking in a game led by Rebecca, Bless soon put the doll on the shelf among wooden puzzles and spinning tops neglected so long they rested under a layer of dust. She resisted the urge for just a few minutes of undisturbed, solitary play. She picked up her dust rag and her pail of soapy water and continued to set the room right. When the shelves were ordered and the floor cleared, Bless turned her attention to the windows.

Though she stood on a stool, bucket hanging from her left arm, Bless still had to stretch upward to reach the topmost windowpanes. Last year's dress, tight at the bust and hips, too short at the hem, rode up her calves and bunched on her buttocks. The swells bounced and the muscles flexed as she shifted to reach the farthest corner. Miss Olivia would still find something had been neglected or done wrong, but Bless would not make it easy for her.

So intent was she on digging dust from the joints of stiles and muntins, that she did not hear an approach. Instead, she felt the hand suddenly beneath her skirts, seizing on her calf, scrabbling on her inner thigh.

Bless screamed and whirled. Gravity heaped the water inside the bucket, pushing it off balance. It struck the window and cracked the glass.

It would have been more good luck than a Negro was likely to have for Miss Rebecca not to walk in the door the moment her brother stuck his hand up Bless's dress. She made a quick assessment of the situation: a chance to strike the girl she envied and the little brother she detested in one powerful tattle. Rebecca took off running.

"Mama! Mama! Come quick! Bless and Dalton playing nasty and they broke the window!"

Bless jumped down from the stool. Dalton stared at her for a moment, as if waking to himself, then turned to run. Bless grabbed his sleeve. "What you do that for?" She shook him. "Miss Olivia will whip me!"

What to tell her? Something about the weight and rub of the bedclothes at night? That he was as mortified now by his dampened sheets as when he'd been a little boy who pissed the bed? That he had lately understood all sorts of goings-on on the farm: why the rooster chased the hens and pinned them beneath his talons, why the stallion persisted behind the bucking and kicking mare, the sows' swaying teats, and sounds he sometimes heard outside his parents' door. All of that tangled, somehow, with the changes he noticed in Bless and felt in himself and the sanction of knowing every hoof, every stalk, every foot that walked and grew on the place would one day be his to command.

He snatched his arm from Bless's grasp. He struck her hand when she tried to capture him again.

Olivia found them in this posture: Bless grabbing onto her son, Dalton crimson with outrage. In a day of annoyances, this was the latest. Olivia would make it the last. All day, household Negroes had bedeviled her with sulky looks and clumsy hands. She had taken refuge from their insolence behind the closed door of her room only to be called out for this.

"What happened here?" Olivia demanded.

"Bless broke the windowlight," Dalton said.

"Tell her how, tell her how I come to break the windowlight," Bless ordered.

"You are bold enough to think that matters? Bold enough to speak to your master that way? It only proves you do not know your place," Olivia said.

"They were playing nasty," Rebecca chimed in.

Olivia looked at water puddling on her waxed floor. A broken pane of glass. Her son blushing crimson, his fist balled like when he was a baby and her milk would not come fast enough and she'd turned him over to a slave to nurse. And now her boy, like his father, grandfather, and uncles, showed an early liking for *nigger women*. Maybe it started at the teat.

"How playing nasty?" She aimed her question at Bless.

"Ma'am?" Bless said. She did not know the word for what Dalton had just done, only that she felt guilty and embarrassed. "We wasn't playing ma'am. He—"

"He what, girl? Your boldness fails you?"

"Ma'am, he—he touched me."

Olivia delivered a slap that caused the inside of Bless's cheek to cut on her teeth.

"Liar," Olivia insisted.

Bless tasted salt and the iron of her own blood. "He touched me," she insisted so forcefully that her red spittle dotted Miss Olivia's pale cheeks. It beaded like seed pearls on the bodice of her dress.

Olivia snatched the small cowhide flail from her waistband. She struck bared skin—face, neck, wrists, shoulders, legs—as Bless cringed beneath the apron of the window.

As silently as he had entered, Dalton left the room.

Rowan Dane

Rowan Dane watched as a ribbon of smoke lofted on the night air, rising toward a mist floating inland from Broad Creek. His companion, an indentured African man named Shango, dug about his person for a small pouch of pipe tobacco. It was Shango's turn to fill the "little ladle" from his small supply. Unable to sleep, the men stood on the threshold of their shared cabin. Within, Jack slept soundly, as only a child can.

The cabin itself stood on a crooked finger of farmland adjacent to the creek and owned by their master, Thomas Crewe. The land had been carved by jagged tributaries that rallied in the Great Dismal Swamp and surrendered in the Atlantic Ocean. The pipe smoke joined a fog that gathered and rolled along the three branches of the Elizabeth River. Converging with the haze that rode the James and the Nansemond Rivers, it would float all the way to the Chesapeake Bay and out into the Atlantic, perhaps drifting all the way back to the lands these men had once called home.

It was said among the colonists that sucking the smoke of tobacco, that "golden weed," purged gross humors. Perhaps it did the same for melancholy and sorrow.

"Ah!" Shango exclaimed when he found the right pouch among his bundled talismans. He stuffed the pipe with tobacco. Rowan struck flint and leaned fire into the bowl. They passed the clay pipe between them.

"What roused you?" Rowan asked.

"Rats," Shango said. "Running over my chest. Raking and chewing the dead."

When the nightmares came, Shango awoke still trapped in a grave, the slats above close as a coffin lid. No crevice of light. A head butted his, another brushed his feet. Bodies straitened his arms. He was unable to sit, turn, or crawl away in retreat. So tightly were they packed, that only cries traveled among the captives. At first. Then came the rats. Shango, too, began to scream.

Fifteen years since he had been captured in a raid on the compound of the oba in whose military he had served. After capture, he had spent almost a year in transit, prodded across the Portuguese Gold Coast, bartered and sold from one agony to the next, until he reached Elmina Castle. Inured to shock and cruelty by the time he reached the dungeons, Shango was certain there was nothing left to fear. Then, his captors marched him to the Door of No Return. Shango fainted and never truly awakened. He still felt the rats and struggled to accept that he would never again see his home. Pipe glow lit the scimitar lines etched into his cheeks.

"And you?" Shango asked. "What awakened you?"

"Lydia, standing over me, seawater dripping from her hair."

For a moment, there was only the trembling of embers.

"Them rats have long perished," Rowan said.

"It was your own sweat that woke you," Shango said.

Rowan shook his head. "She's not forgiven me. Nor has Jack," he said. "He only had the *leanabh*, the babe, a few weeks after his mother died. I didn't imagine he would grieve the girl so." Rowan exhaled, the stream of smoke ghostly against his face.

"Taking signals from the storm, that wee one were. Dragging out my dear one's agony. Could hardly hear the wind over Lydia's screams."

Shango drew from the pipe. He blew the smoke upward and watched it vanish. "Is that why you did it?"

Rowan cast a pointed glance about them. "I should have brung her here?"

"After my village burned, I was wounded, growing weak. Had to decide how to use my strength. I saved myself, but I am still ashamed."

"The child is better off."

Shango nodded. "Then you have no reason to believe you are unforgiven." He offered the pipe.

Rowan refused. "Finish it," he said. He made his way back into the cabin. Just before he disappeared into the lightless cabin, Rowan said to his friend, "Survival is no cause for shame."

Shango made no reply. There was only the glow of the pipe, sparking and darkening.

Inside the cabin, Rowan paused over the dark outline of his son. Jack slept on the floor, preferring a pallet in the dirt to a cot shared with his father. Rowan stooped to lift him. He marveled at the weight hard work and hot meals had put on the boy. Placing Jack in bed, he pushed a hank of hair off the boy's damp forehead. Jack rolled away, even in sleep preferring the scratch and prick of the wattle wall to the gentle touch of his father.

Rowan reminded himself that he'd done only what was necessary for each of his children to survive. He had no cause to feel ashamed.

Andrew Cabarrus

Northampton County
Colony of Virginia, 1692

On the word of Othman Scarborough, Andrew Cabarrus was wrested from his fields on charges of trespassing, possession of another man's property, and suspicion of "creating a conspiracy" to incite Negroes and servants to run away.

The like-minded gentry of the Eastern Shore jailed Cabarrus knowing he had spent his ready cash hiring hands to help with the costly work of transplanting his tobacco from bed to furrow. He could not afford bail. They incarcerated him through the four choppings needed to save the seedlings from the choking grass. They shackled him through topping and the long June days when hornworms feasted on the leaves of his plants. They warned away any friends who might have done the work so Cabarrus would have something left upon his return.

Around the end of July, he was released from the jail in which he'd been the only months-long occupant. Said the magistrate, after a long, inconclusive investigation, "There could be no legal proof so as to convict him, yet such was the insolence of the Free Negro, it is thought best to expel him from the colony."

Andrew ran straight to his fields. Though nothing could be done to salvage his harvest, he searched the chaos of grass, the crumbling decay. Still stinking from the jail cell, he wrenched a hoe from the wall of the barn and began to chop weeds away from the stems of worm-eaten tobacco plants.

He chopped for hours, yet Andrew did not find one whole leaf. All had given over to rot, wither, or worm. And like Job, he had only begun mourning the first catastrophe when news of the next incalculable loss found him.

Cassie and Bless

Willow Oaks Plantation
Kecoughtan Settlement, Elizabeth City Shire
Colony of Virginia, 1696

Cassie had once known Bless's wet cry, her hungry cry, the fretting that meant she was sleepy. When had she forgotten those? For she understood the whimper of hurt like a murmuring of her native tongue. She opened the door before Bless laid a hand on the wood.

"What they done?"

Bless stood barefoot, braids askew. On her face and neck, bleeding welts.

Cassie guided Bless into the cabin.

"Beat me."

"What else?" Anxiously, she looked the girl up and down.

"Just beat me," Bless whispered, barely able to speak over the buzz of pain, the thin line of fire that zipped from welt to welt, then flashed into a conflagration.

"Where?"

"Everywhere."

"Can you set? Set here." She pulled out a chair, but Bless refused. Cassie's girl leaned against the door lintel, eyes closed, pulling breaths to keep from screaming.

Cassie whirled into action. She made a beeline for the back door.

"I'm goin' to draw you a bath. We got to soak out the swelling and poison."

To keep the soreness from setting in, she would have to put in a handful of salt. Cassie went to drag in the washtub and heat buckets of water—all the help she knew.

"It's gone hurt," Cassie said, mostly to herself. "You just have to bear it."

• • •

As a child, Bless fit neatly into Cassie's wooden tub, and she loved it so much that Cassie trained herself to dump it out and turn it over, less the girl mistake clothes-washing for bath time and drown herself. Much too big for the tub now, Bless sat with her knees drawn to her chest, forehead balanced on knobby bones.

Cassie dabbed Bless's bare shoulders with a rag soaked in chamomile. She picked apart her daughter's plaits and poured water over her scalp. Drops hung in the black hair like raindrops from a cedar bough.

"You want to tell me?" Cassie asked.

Bless wagged her head but did not look at her mother. Instead, she reached for Cassie's hand where it rested on her shoulder.

"Let's go away from here," Bless whispered. "You and me, and live somewhere off by ourself."

Cassie dipped the rag. She crushed it in her fist even after the water stopped trickling.

In the timbre of Bless's plea, Cassie recognized her own girl-self. Much of that girl had been devoured aboard a vessel of sickness and rot and rape. Portions pieced away with the stealing of each of her children. Some bits clawed out, scoured off, torn apart as Cassie passed from hand to hand. Always someone dragging or prodding her to the next patch of horrid ground until she hardly knew how to go, or where, or when, without a chain yanking her by the neck.

She pressed a kiss deep into her daughter's wooly hair, right on the crown where a defenseless soft spot once throbbed. "Woulda been kinder to'a drowned you in this tub when you was a tiny thing," Cassie said. She withdrew her hand from Bless's stiff fingers. Too late for kindness now.

Cassie stood. She grabbed a piece of rough sacking and held it out.

"Get outa there now. I need to put something on them cuts. You got to get back 'fore they come looking for you."

Bless stilled. It seemed the hip-high water had frozen around her. "I can't go back," she said. "Mama, please don't make me go back."

Harms Cassie's body knew well—a sweaty hand up the thigh, cruel, twisting fingers, the slimy trace of a grown man's gaze over a young girl's body, the daily hurt of hatred—roughened her daughter's voice.

"Please, Mama," Bless said. "Please, please."

Cassie dropped onto the bed. "What you want me to do? You don't know what we is by now? You was my last bit of courage, Bless, and they took that too."

Cassie shut her eyes and shook her head. She held out the dingy flour sacking like a flag of surrender.

"I got no strength left to fight 'em, and I can't watch 'em hunt you, so you got to go back. You—please. *Please.*" Cassie covered her face with the rag. She cried the way Bless wanted to. "Please, baby, you got to go back."

Though she would rather have curled at the bottom of that foot tub and let the water close over her, Bless braced her tattered hands on the uneven rim. The palm welts, softened to blisters, tore open as easily as flour dumplings. She climbed out of the tub.

"It's all right, Mama," she said. "It's all right."

Bless left wet footprints on the dirt floor. She tugged the sacking from Cassie's hand and began to wrap herself in it.

"Bless!"

"I said I'll go back, Mama. Don't cry."

But Cassie had seen the blood—too florid, too rapid for the seep of welts—staining the thirsty sacking.

"No, Bless! You got your womanhood," Cassie said.

Bless glanced down at the stains. She paused, then sought her tattered dress.

"Bless?" Cassie said.

Bless did not turn. She yanked the dress over her head. "Ma'am?"

"Won't you let me put something on them lashes for you?"

Bless did not face her mother until every button and fastener on her dress had been strained into place. She collected the soiled sacking. She threw it in the washtub as if it were a thing of no consequence—like an unwanted touch, like a whipping, like being shut out from her only refuge.

"No, ma'am," she said. "I'll see to myself when I get home."

David Cabarrus

Courthouse at the Hornes
Northampton County
Colony of Virginia, 1692

I f they had ever been brought back together, a whole, clear picture of their parting might have been formed. Each child carried a piece, an impression, from that day. Ruth would always remember a pot of white beans, seasoned with salt and bacon fat, boiling on the fire. Peggy remembered it was a hot, green and dappled July morning, the clouds blindingly white mounds in the blue sky. George-Lee remembered he was teaching Willie the game of clay marbles as they played near the porch steps. David remembered how silence walked like rain up to the door of their cabin, as the slaves—in the wake of Master Scarborough and his men—turned their faces toward Phoebe's cabin and fell quiet.

Phoebe dropped the pitcher of buttermilk she had carried out to the children. David had looked forward to the cool tang of the drink. He felt like crying when the pitcher shattered. But it was not the waste of a rare treat that made his mother shriek.

As the men approached, Phoebe called, "David! The children!" in the screech she used when Willie almost stumbled into the fire or Peggy climbed onto the ledge of the well.

David jumped into action. He clutched his brothers by their hands. He yelled for the girls. Phoebe herself leapt at the men, heedless of the shards of clay from the broken vessel. Blood from her bare feet mixed with silky yellow milk. Already, she was swinging.

. . .

The cell measured four feet by four feet. Phoebe paced it off, again and again, while the children slept. Splinters stabbed her fingertips as she pried at the baseboards of the earth-fast structure, searching for rotten wood she might claw through. The cell door was oak, its one opening positioned more than a foot above Phoebe's reach. Studded with three iron bars, it was too narrow for even the thinnest of her children to slip through.

There was no way out.

Feeling as heavy as a sack of wet cotton, Phoebe eased herself to the floor lest she fall. Awake now, the children huddled around her. Through the one barred window, a piss-colored sunrise signified yet another morning in the jail. She had lost count of how many days she and her children had been imprisoned. The guards seldom spoke. Like clockwork, they brought barely edible food but no answers to her simplest questions: How long we been here? What Scarborough goin' to do with us? Any news of Andrew?

Today, however, along with the sour light, came faint but unmistakable sounds. Phoebe and the children could hear laughter and the voices of milling men, the patter of an auctioneer, and the grunts of cows and sheep. Then began the tuning of a fiddle.

A public sale.

It was hard to make out her features in the dim light, but David heard the anguish in his mother's gasp. Through their long ordeal, he had tried to be a man, a helper, in his father's stead. Just like at home, David wrangled the younger children. He made up games and stories that calmed and comforted them. He even slung an arm around mean ol' Ruthie who was liable to stick him with a pin when they shared a pallet at home. But the sound that escaped Phoebe sent David scrambling to her. At almost eleven years old, David crawled beneath his mother's arm.

"What's goin' to happen to us?" he asked.

Your papa will come for us. God will take care of us. We will meet again in heaven. Phoebe could no longer tell what was faith and what was foolish. She gathered her children, pulled them against her breasts and onto her lap. She stretched her arms around them all.

"I don't know," she said. "I don't know."

A key sounded in the lock. The bolt plate rattled, and the door swung open, admitting light as dingy as wash water.

"Up with you," ordered the guard.

Phoebe and the children refused to stand, refused to let go. They clasped on to one another with legs and arms, with promises and pleas. Their sorrow swelled until even the youngest, Willie, more frightened than understanding, wept.

The guard, a poor man of little patience, fell on them like a badger raiding a nest. One by one, he wrenched David and his siblings from Phoebe's grasp.

● ● ●

On the courthouse steps, a Negro hired for the occasion played a fast fiddle. The children were prodded to run and jump and bare their teeth. Awaiting her turn beside the platform, Phoebe's legs would not support her. She sank to her knees. No one paid heed.

Andrew Cabarrus

Courthouse at the Hornes
Northampton County
Colony of Virginia, 1692

What to do when presented with a choice: Sell all you have left and leave the colony within sixty days, a free man, or remain and be degraded, again, to slavery?

Everything went at a loss. Andrew's land, the house, and all of the furnishings, the surviving animals, the tools of iron, leather, and wood, even clothes—Sunday breeches, shirts, and shoes—any meat not looted from the smoke house and whatever persisted in the garden. Sold.

But Andrew Cabarrus did not leave.

On the fifty-ninth day, he gathered up the bills, the coins, the IOUs—blood tender. He walked to the courthouse. He waited in the shadows of a stable across the street for the sale to begin.

After the animals, a few Negroes that Andrew did not know were sold. Then, Phoebe and the children were led, blinking, out of the darkness of the jail cell onto the block. As each member of his family came upon the block, Andrew bid. He bid on Phoebe, the girls, Ruth and Peggy, and the boys, David, George-Lee, and little Willie. He bid knowing that the money in his pockets would buy one, maybe two of them.

Six times, Andrew found himself outbid. Each time, he hurried to the buyer, hat gripped in his hands, and offered not just the proceeds from the property, but the money for food, for lodging, for travel out of this godforsaken place. Six times the buyer refused.

By agreement, silent and otherwise, Andrew Cabarrus was made a cautionary tale, an object lesson for those with like ambition: Do not dare.

Jack Dane

Thomas Crewe's Farm, Lower Norfolk
Colony of Virginia, 1693

Jack's hair hung in hanks like soiled handkerchiefs, but his eyes were brown like Rowan's. He wore, like his dead mother, the clear face of an angel. A year of regular meals and hard work had fast turned his slight boy's body into lean muscle and powerful bulges. Jack woke early and labored late beside Rowan and Shango. The boy grew hard thighs and callused hands as he tended seed beds in frigid February and in the wet of March. His back grew strong, and his shoulders widened as he hilled and chopped to keep the plants free of weeds.

Ready enough to instruct his new men on the work he wanted done, Thomas Crewe taught them the proper way to wield the tools and to count every seed, but Shango taught the newcomers how to survive.

Shango took them to the creek and taught them to fish. He taught them how to snare squirrels and rabbits, and the sweet but serious business of harvesting honey. He taught them to hunt with bow and arrow, to take the buck and not the doe. When, at long last, Rowan brought an animal down, Shango taught both father and son not only to butcher and roast the meat, but how to cure the skin and sew it into garments.

There was an urgency to the way Shango tutored the indentureds. Jack and Rowan had to learn to do these things themselves; Shango would not be with them much longer. Each night after he climbed into bed, the African turned on his side and made a mark on the wall.

He mumbled himself to sleep counting the marks. So he also taught them to bide their time. But they did not know how many marks were left to be made. One evening, as Jack dressed a rabbit taken in a trap he had laid himself, Rowan asked.

"Thirty days," Shango answered.

"Thirty days," Rowan said. "So soon?"

"Soon? You've no idea how many years of my sweat are poured into this man's ground."

Shango spoke with sober hopefulness. "My freedom dues 'mount to a year of grain, a hoe, an ax, and a suit of clothes. I shall trade the clothing for tools. I shall plant an acre of tobacco straight off from the seed Crewe owes me, and that shall supply some small capital for the next year."

At the head of the table, Jack slit the rabbit's skin at the spine. He pried carefully at the slick gap. Shango had promised to help him make a hat of the hide. At the other end of the table, Rowan gouged the rot from turnips with, perhaps, too much savagery as he listened to another man's dream.

"When your time is done, you and the boy should throw in with me, Rowan. By that time, I should have enough cash for land."

Rowan set down the butchered turnip.

"Do you think we could, Shango?" Rowan asked. "I've already got a bit of a stake. Money from"—with a glance, he assured himself that Jack remained absorbed with the skinning—"from the ship."

"Of course," Shango said. "You put in that cash for a share of the land. Shan't be long before it's you and me that is owed the headrights."

Rowan and Shango began to spin out a plan. Neither man noticed when Jack's hand, beneath the rabbit's soft and serviceable hide, became a fist.

Jack used all his strength to strip the hide. It parted from the rabbit's flesh with a sucking sound. A fresh kill, the moist skin glinted with the same wishing light that sparked in Rowan's eyes. "Where would they buy? Land might be cheaper farther south. The cost of land per acre? Bound to rise in the time they had to wait."

Jack twisted the head round. Land purchased at the cost of his mother's life. He broke the bones of each foot at the first joint. Acres financed by the sale of his sister.

How many men might they hire if clearing had to be done? Not more than two. They both were strong, and Jack would be even larger and handier by then.

Jack stabbed below the ribcage. He flipped the knife and yanked the gut hook through. There was a slow expanding as the creature's entrails erupted then spilled, gray and glistening, onto the table.

"After a simple shelter," Rowan said, "first thing is a barn."

Rowan and Shango debated, chuckling, lighting the pipe, sketching crude structures into the dirt floor, then with a sweep of a bare foot, improving the plan.

"No," Shango said, "after shelter, we dig the well."

With his hand in the rabbit's cavity, Jack felt the thin but tough membrane that walled breath and heartbeat from digestion and waste. Rowan and Shango shook on the deal. Jack punched through that tough, translucent casing.

He held the heart, a mostly hollow mechanism, still and cooling.

David Cabarrus

Crossing the Chesapeake Bay to Cape Henry on the Great Land
October 1692

From the Northampton County courthouse, David found himself headed south, then transported across the Chesapeake Bay aboard a shallop, a speedy vessel with two sails belonging to a merchant who ferried goods and people from the "Great Land," the Colony of Virginia, to the Eastern Shore. In addition to the cargo and people he was paid to deliver, the merchant considered himself something of a speculator. He bought goods and chattels of his own—anything might turn to profit in Princess Anne County—and packed it in among the paid freight. The merchant wedged David in among livestock, hogsheads of tobacco, and bushels of oysters and corn.

The calves and lambs purchased along with David at the courthouse auction lowed and bleated for the dams and ewes that birthed them. They chafed at the close quarters, the teetering deck, the tumultuous waves of the bay. David remained mute, his knees clasped to his chest, his eyes wide and dry as he watched the receding shore.

The boy's stoicism was not what the speculator expected. As he made his way from stern to bow, he halted briefly at the sight of David, small but healthy-looking, dark and silent, crouched among the distraught animals. "You're a good little nigger," he mused, satisfied that he could turn such a tractable Negro into financial gain.

And so, he whisked dumb animals and a boy, dumbstruck with

grief, across thirty-seven, liquid miles of the Chesapeake Bay and rid himself of the whole cargo as soon as he reached Cape Henry.

A day's work. A good haul. A destiny, a life, a heart dismantled.

• • •

While the merchant and a prospective buyer haggled, David kept his gaze trained on the watery distance. That way lay his home. To his wobbly legs, the dock felt blessedly steady. Still, he eased himself down to the planks as a hereditary sorrow, a grief tethered to the stones of Elmina Castle, gusted over him, engulfed him, swept the legs out from under him.

"Get up, now," Edwyn Hawley, David's brand-new owner, said.

David lay down. Sand embedded in his cheek as he turned his face to the horizon. He shoved his small fingers and toes into the spaces between the salt-washed boards. Above him, the men argued. David heard the verbal equivalent of a shrug, "It is not my fault that you are unable to command a child." Then came the metallic jangle of money in a pocket or purse, receding footsteps and a curse.

"I will tell you one more time." Edwyn Hawley spit his command down at the boy. "Stand on your feet!"

David clung to the pier. Hawley stomped away but soon returned. The sound came before the strike. For the first time in his young life, David felt the shocking pain of a whip, the toe of a boot in his ribs—abuse that Phoebe had kept off her children by using her body and wit. David gasped. He jerked his body into a ball. Hawley scooped up his purchase. He dumped David into the cart among bricks of sugar, cast-iron pots, pieces of furniture, and other tools and comforts that were wanting at Hawley's Lynnhaven River plantation. David's knees barely scraped the wagon bed before he scrambled up. Hawley subdued the boy with a backhanded blow—knuckles and power.

Hawley hoisted himself into the driver's seat. He released the brake and slapped the reins. His horse jerked the wagon forward.

• • •

Miles down the road, David came to. Dazed and unsteady, he pulled himself to his knees. Scrambling over obstacles to reach the tailgate of the wagon, he searched for the watery horizon.

The coastline was gone. The wagon road they traveled threaded through wetland tunnels of bald cypress. Their canopies reached, spread, and meshed, closing off what lay behind, hiding what loomed ahead. The eternal-wood trees gave up nothing, barely even space to pass. Without bearings, David could not tell the way back. It was only then that he began to weep.

• • •

Edwyn Hawley's Plantation, Lynnhaven River
Princess Anne County

"Hark! The blackbird said to the crow! Why do the farmer hate us so!"

The children ran around the newly seeded corn patch, singing and waving their arms each time birds came near. One girl in particular seemed to be the creator and leader of all the work songs. When, for the time being, they had shooed away the crows and ravens determined to eat up the garden of David's new master, the children chased off to play games or beg scraps from Cecil, the cook, healer, and surrogate father to all who needed him.

The girl sat in a shady corner of the garden, arranging and rearranging field stones to some mysterious pattern of her liking. David, separated from his family by less than two weeks, was still too heartsick to play or eat. He sought out the little singer. He sat glumly beside her. For a while, he just watched the way she piled the stones one way, then another. There was something calming about it.

"What's your name?" David asked softly. He didn't look at her, but kept his gaze on her small hands, picking up, placing, balancing the round or jagged stones one atop the other.

"Celeste," she answered.

"Celeste," David said. "*Celeste,*" he repeated, letting the name hiss and curl over his tongue. He had never heard a name so fancy on a Negro girl. "What kinda name that?"

The girl looked up at him, straight at him, for the first time. She smacked one stone on top of another. "It's the name my ma'am give me," she said, pert with indignation. "What's your name?"

"David Cabarrus."

"That ain't so special."

"It is."

"Is not. What's so special 'bout it? They's three, four *Davids* running 'round here."

"David *Cabarrus,*" he said. "My papa name."

Momentarily startled and impressed, Celeste took her hands off the stones and gave her full attention to David. "Your *papa* here with you?"

Very few of the people on Hawley's place lived as families. Hawley picked up singles wherever a good deal could be made. He grew his workforce with no concern for the ties he severed.

As if he had run at full speed into the side of a barn, David felt again the stunning loss of his family. Having a "papa" who returned to Scarborough's over and over, who saw to their needs, who planned to buy his children out of slavery, had made David's little family much envied in the quarters. On their worst days, Phoebe had reminded her children, "You got a *papa*, and I got a *husband*." But that point of pride had been stripped away. And like cold air scraping across a naked nerve, David realized he had been robbed not only of his present but of his future.

"We was sold off from him," he said.

Both affront and envy drained from Celeste's eyes. She shrugged. "Well, you a Hawley nigger now," she said, as wise as an old woman. "'Member it and act like it." She quoted words passed from the overseer—delivered on the tip of his whip—to the adults to the children. With both hands, Celeste pushed her collection of stones toward David. It was all the distraction, all the comfort, she had on hand. "Might not be so bad."

David felt in no way convinced that being one of "Hawley's niggers might not be so bad," but with the girl Celeste near and offering some little bit of herself, nothing more than pebbles she tended and touched, David absorbed a bit of her hope just as the stones had absorbed a bit of her warmth.

A pile of stones in exchange for a family and a name. David lifted one and weighed it in his hand. He had just begun to shift and slide them into some new configuration when a bellow came from the kitchen door. Cecil, a pot-bellied, black-skinned man gestured with a wooden spoon and shouted, "What I tell y'all 'bout letting them birds get at my garden!"

Sure enough, the ever-vigilant birds swooped low over the newly furrowed rows. Celeste jumped to her bare feet and ran off in a whir of arms and legs. "Hark! The blackbird said to the crow! Why do the farmer hate us so!"

David chased behind her.

• • •

That night, instead of bedding down to sleep in the first empty spot he came to, David sought out Celeste. He dragged his burlap bag full of leaves and moss and husks until he found her on the floor of the third cabin he tried. Stepping carefully over the sprawled legs and arms of the exhausted children and teenagers, David wedged himself in on the crowded floor. Celeste looked surprised to see him but scooched to make room.

"Night, David *Cabarrus*," she whispered.

He knew she was teasing him, but that did not diminish the comfort of her bushy hair prickling his nose or her breath warming his throat. With the other children pressed in around them, it almost felt like bedding down with his brothers and sisters, the little ones who slept so wild, it was nothing to wake with an arm or foot across his face.

Celeste's forehead butted David's chin. Her arm fell across his neck. He nearly swooned into oblivion. For the first time in weeks, he did not cry himself to sleep.

• • •

The children who were old enough to be of use spent their days in a variety of ways—chasing scavengers from the kitchen garden, caring for the babies, carrying water out to the field hands, or running and fetching for Mr. Cecil. David did whatever Celeste did. She was something of a favorite on the farm. She knew everything from the best place to find honeysuckle to how to charm Mr. Cecil out of scraps and drippings from the ham.

Celeste had been born on Hawley's. When her mother was sold, she was herded in with the rest of the "young'uns." She knew she carried her mother's name but knew nothing of her father. The other children liked and followed Celeste because she was quick to make up a song or invent a game to make the chores pass faster. Slavery had orphaned them all. Celeste did not seem diminished by the most unjust fact of their lives. She made the days bearable. David devoted himself to her.

Jack Dane

Thomas Crewe's Farm, Lower Norfolk
Colony of Virginia, 1693

Jack did not call it spying. Rather, he listened for the right moment to interrupt grown folks talking. He stood just outside of Master Crewe's door with an armload of wood for the hearth. As he waited, Jack heard the phrase that put such bright anticipation in Rowan's eyes hissed with contempt from Thomas Crewe's lips.

"Freedom dues?" Crewe said as he glanced up from the papers on his desk.

Jack peeked around the doorway. Turning his cap in his big hands, Shango stood near a seated Master Crewe but not so close that the field hand would seem to be looming.

"Yes, sir, my freedom dues. My time here's up shortly, and I want to know when I can start collecting and packing what's owed me."

Crewe looked up. "Leaving? What foolishness got hold of you?"

"My contract, sir, with Mr. Bazemore, man you bought this place off'a—"

"I damn well know who Bazemore is. What I don't know is a damn thing about a contract."

"Sir? I come here indentured, sir. My time were up two years ago, but one a' the oxen got into the snake weed on my watch. Poisoned. Mr. Bazemore charge it to me though I wasn't the only one out there. He say I can pay him with my dues or 'stend two more years. I took the two years 'cause without my dues I'd been left with nothing to stake myself with. That time up end of this month."

Crewe stood. "What Bazemore told you, I don't know. What

you all agreed to, I got nothing to do with. But I got no contract with you."

"Sir?"

"The deed say I bought every animal, tool, and asset on the place forever, 'an African fellow named Shango included.' I own you."

The indentured man stepped backward as if Crewe might rush to lay hands on him. "That ain't what I agreed to," Shango said.

"Got nothing to do with what you agreed to. It's what's in the contract that matters."

"Sir, I indentured myself to Bazemore for a extra two years to pay off what he claim I owe. When he sold out to you and went back 'cross the water, I were under the same bargain."

"Boy, I bought everything on this place in perpetuity. That mean forever. That mean you."

"Naw, sir. Me and Mister Bazemore made a deal. I never agreed to nothing different."

"Where is your proof?"

Shango stopped turning the hat. He stared at Crewe. "Mr. Bazemore give me his word what the paper said."

Thomas Crewe wagged his head, whether at the treachery or the gullibility, Jack could not tell.

"Shango, I ain't letting you go in thirty days nor three hundred nor three thousand." Crewe said. "You my Negro for life."

Negro for life.

Slave.

• • •

A Kalabari African, Shango knew slavery in both the Old World and the New. He had known men, women, and children of many colors who came to slavery by debt, by war, by birth, as gifts. And though every slave he'd known had a tale of humiliation, few lived as New World slaves did, with a chain around the neck, in abject despair, without the hope of freedom.

In his Old World, Shango knew of slaves who had become wise men and honored mothers among their captors, who had earned or counseled or warred or loved their way out of bondage. Where Shango came from, it was uncommon but possible for a servant to become a chief, because everyone, even the most arrogant masters, respected the one inviolable imperative of nature: Man was born for the utter and absolute service of God and God only.

Thomas Crewe's gestures said "sorry," but he exuded triumph. For the man who stood before Shango, nothing was inviolate. Thomas Crewe had not walked on water, but he had crossed many oceans, and when it came to Africans he believed himself to be as good as God. For, though Shango dressed much like an English yeoman—a long, once-white osnaburg blouse with the tail fluttering, dirty chambray knee britches, and coarse leather shoes— Thomas did not see a man his equal. Rather, it seemed to Thomas Crewe that someone had put clothes on a bull.

Besides the carapace of measured scars on his cheeks and his hulking build, Shango was the blackest creature Thomas had ever seen. The African rarely smiled. But when he did, it was like the white flashes of lightning that disturb sleep, that portend sudden and violent storms. Even Shango's hair caused alarm, clenched as it was in riled little fists upon his head. He wore a leather thong of cowries hanging at the notch of his collarbones. Thomas knew the shells' name and worth from his years at sea, yet, at first glance, the ivory-hued shells with their serrated edges never failed to put him in mind of a string of teeth. The African looked as savage as a wood's hog.

"I ain't a slave," Shango said.

"Shango—"

"Naw, sir. I ain't a slave. I ain't your slave. I don't know what Bazemore put on that paper, but I know what I agreed to. I paid what I owed, sir. In thirty days, I mean to leave here with what's owed me."

Bless

Willow Oaks Plantation
Kecoughtan Settlement, Elizabeth City Shire
Colony of Virginia, 1698

Music wound between the floorboards and joists of the cellar like tendrils of honeysuckle. A waltz. The candle stub brightened as it fed on the perfume of apples, of potatoes still clinging to clumps of soil, of the brine of pickled fish, and the sweetness of fruit jellies and wines. From above, the muffled scrape of heels.

"Look what I brought you," Jason said.

He was the tall, sandy-haired fiancé of Miss Rebecca. Over the months of his engagement to her young miss, he had taken note of Bless, but not in a way that made her want to shrink, like when the master's gaze fell on her or when young Master Dalton's gaze trailed her around the room. No, Mr. Jason shot her looks of playful exasperation as if they were sharing a joke about Miss Rebecca's histrionics as she decided between the local officiate or waiting for a Church of England minister or threw a tantrum over dress fabrics and menus.

"Here, take it," he urged.

At the many dances and dinner parties required by the betrothal, Jason always knew where to find Bless—secreted at the top of the stairs where she could hear the music and spy the lovely dresses with their imports of delicate lace, and the variety of new coifs. He always slipped away to bring her beignets de gelée or sweetmeats rolled in cinnamon and sugar.

Bless accepted the dessert. She inhaled the wine-like bouquet of fruit transmuted by time and sugar. She knew what it was and who had made it.

Jason had secreted a slice of friendship cake in a fine white kerchief embroidered with his initials. No plain poundcake, this was the centerpiece of the engagement party. Fussed over almost as much as the wedding cake, it was the cake of first promises. Made from the prized fruit of the winter stores—cherries, peaches, apples, and a rare pineapple from abroad—the cake took fourteen days to make. Bless had caught sight of Cassie, peeling, pitting, and dicing. Once a day for fourteen days, Cassie stirred the gallon crock of fruit and sugar—more attention than Bless had received from her mother in years.

Bless slipped the cake into the long pocket tied about her waist. "Thank you," she said.

In the dim candlelight, she saw his frown. Secure in the knowledge she could demand nothing from him, it gave Jason pleasure to watch her enjoy even the humblest gift.

"You don't like it?"

"I don't have a taste for it right this moment."

"Why?"

"Because—because the wedding is soon, and you won't be here much after."

"I suppose that's true. For visits. Perhaps a holiday. Rebecca and I shall live with my parents."

"I was thinking you might—"

"Might?"

"It is just that no one else is kind—like you. I don't want—"

Above their heads, the tempo of the music changed. He would have to get back soon or be missed.

"Tell me. I will help if I can."

"I don't want to stay here. Miss Rebecca says you have staff enough to tend her, but I would like to go with you. You are pleased, aren't you, with the way I curl her hair? And the lace over her bosom, it was my idea to sew it there. And I suggested the sprig of jasmine behind her ear—"

Jason chuckled. "I haven't much say in ladies' maids," he said. "But if I intervene, what will you give me?"

"What do you want?"

He laughed. "A dance," he said. "Finish this waltz with me."

In the cramped cellar, Jason held Bless close within the frame of his arms. They hushed giggles as they box-stepped into caskes, buckets, and bags sewn closed with twine. One two three. One two three. One two three. An embrace. A stroke. A kiss.

Jason lifted Bless atop the sacks of flour and rice. He stood between her splayed legs. Where her skirt hitched, the burlap bit her thighs and calves like a horde of mosquitoes.

"If Miss Rebecca wants a fancy maid, I could work in the kitchen," Bless said, and Jason worked to free her small breasts and push his hands up the front of her skirt.

"I have no say in the kitchens," he huffed, pushing her thighs apart, reaching for the placket of his trousers.

Bless held on to his shoulders to keep her precarious balance on the shifting sacks.

"Please! Ask her to bring me—"

"Shhh—" Jason said. He pushed Bless backward. With a bit of fumbling and one determined thrust, he began to saw away inside her.

Jason stoppered her scream with his tongue. Bless's disbelief became whimpers then gasps of pain. Her head jolted from the support of the sacks. She failed to find purchase on the floor. Bless dangled, pinned in place by Jason's pounding. Still, she raised herself. She brought her hands to his cheeks.

"I love you," she said.

Jason dragged his hand from Bless's breast. He groped over her neck and across her cheek. He silenced her with a manicured hand.

David Cabarrus and Celeste

Edwyn Hawley's Plantation, Lynnhaven River
Princess Anne County, 1695

They had seen the grown folks do it. On nights when they sat up late or stole away into the woods to talk of matters that were "not for white-folk ears," the grown-ups turned a cast-iron pot or kettle upside down to catch their words. David and Celeste were too afraid to steal one of Mr. Cecil's pots. They settled for a calabash, all they had for dipping their portion of supper from the pot.

They hid beneath the spread of a magnolia tree that Celeste favored because some of the roots rested aboveground and tangled and twisted like limbs that never meant to uncouple. The branches, strong enough to hold the weight of Mr. Cecil, brushed the ground. Sometimes Celeste would sit in the gentle curve of one branch while David rested against the bend of another. The leaves surrounded them, filtered the harsh light, and created a hushed, secret place. Straddling a branch that swayed her like a cradle, with the calabash snug against the sparse grass, Celeste said, "Tell me again."

The enslaved were allowed to keep only what their enslavers did not know they possessed. Valued and irreplaceable things had to be buried in the thick kinks of one's hair, concealed beneath the floorboards of a cabin, behind expressionless eyes, secreted in the flesh or memory. And so, David concealed his last token of home from everyone but Celeste.

It had been three years since he'd first told Celeste the story, still he always began, "I ain't a 'Hawley nigger.' I am a Cabarrus, and I'll tell you why." Then he told her the story of stealing away in the middle of the night to Andrew's land, the trip over land and by river.

"He took me to see it. We planted tobacco, and I helped him feed the animals. He say it gon' belong to me and my brothers one day, but we got to be sure to make the girls welcome. That's how I know who I am," he finished. "That's how I know he gon' come for me."

Once when he finished the story, Celeste grabbed David's hand. "Can I go with you when your papa come?"

She scooted close. Her fingers interlocked with his, and that was the first time David noticed the brown of her eyes, like warm molasses, and how the hair hugged her skull like a soft cap of moss, and tiny moles splashed over her cheeks. "Yes," David said. "Yes, you can come."

"All right," Celeste said.

Their fingers intertwined and held like the anchoring roots of their magnolia. She smiled, and the moles on her cheeks danced upward, and David knew he had just entered into some type of agreement, some pledge. He did not know exactly what. But if it made Celeste smile just that way, he meant to keep it.

• • •

The weather that July was hot and dry. Cecil had moved his kitchen outside where there was less danger of a spark alighting on the timber walls of the cramped cookhouse and where he could catch a breeze. Standing over a fire was still hot work, but the sting of the woodsmoke dissolved, leaving behind only the flavor of hickory.

As Cecil carefully stirred handfuls of spices into a pot of greens with hunks of ham, he saw the two young people emerge separately from the rows of his garden. He had no doubt they had been together, somewhere off in the woods. The boy looked bashful. The girl wore a soft smile. Too big now to keep the birds from his garden, David and Celeste had graduated to grown-up chores in Hawley's fields. The shirts that the children wore until they fell off in shreds had been replaced by the long pants and skirts of young adulthood.

The boy would be broad-shouldered and long-legged. Ropey muscle tensed and stretched as he walked. The girl had begun to fill out. She would be pretty, poor thing. Not that ugly would have saved her. But pretty would make her life harder still.

Cecil knew this firsthand. He'd had two wives. He did not intend to have another. He no longer courted. He turned his gaze from the sway and curves of the farm's young girls and women as they went about their chores. A third marriage, no doubt, would end like the first two.

Cecil stirred the pot. His mind circled through memories like the spoon swirled through the pot liquor. He wanted to alert Celeste, to call out to David, to tell them how it had been and how it would be. *They gon' put they hands on her, like they put they greedy hands on everything else. Might wait 'til she alone or might do it where you can see. Might come in where y'all sleep and tell her, "Come on out," and say to you, "Do something 'bout it, Nigger." An' her eyes will beg you don't, 'cause the chil'ren is right there sleeping. An' that white man—overseer Goss or Hawley hisself, or some man visiting from outa town who saw your woman walking 'cross the yard or serving at the table and took a liking to her—gon' put his hands on the butt of his gun an' look your woman over an' say, "A piece worth dying for, is she? We'll see." An' when you move, he draw on you an' she say, "Please, please!" But she ain't begging you. She begging him, 'cause she know who got the power. An' she don't look at you when she leave. An' you can't look at her when she come back.*

He watched David go one way and Celeste go off in another. But with their steps so pert that they were damn near dancing, no one who saw them was fooled. Cecil marveled at the confidence of youth: Of all children, slave children should know better. The first thing slavery severed was love. Hadn't these children cried themselves sick over mamas and papas and grand-folk they would never see again? Lands and languages had been stripped from them before they were born. These children had been robbed of pasts and futures they could not imagine, and here they were, slipping off together, thinking slavery would not take more, that it would grant them even one lasting happiness.

"Young fools," Cecil muttered, then fiercely, "innocent *fools*."

His stirring slowed. He let the bottom of the pot scorch enough to lend the dish a faintly bitter taste. He tossed in a bit more spice than what Master Hawley liked. It was all he could think to do.

• • •

Sometimes, one or the other forgot to bring a calabash. Still, they dreamed in eager whispers of what life would be like when Andrew Cabarrus came to carry them away.

"My brothers and me, we gon' farm the land together," David explained to Celeste. "The girls can come help if they want. That's the way my papa said it would be."

"And I will live there too?" Celeste asked, her tone slightly disbelieving.

"Yes," David answered. He toyed with fallen magnolia flowers, separating the flower-heads that had browned at the edges from those that were still immaculate.

"Who will I belong to?" Celeste asked.

Surprised, David looked up. In his hand, he cupped one pristine blossom. He held it out to Celeste. "You gon' belong to yourself," he said.

Confusion played over Celeste's face like the shadows of the leaves.

Of her mother, Celeste carried a first name and a few stories the enslaved women who had known "Big Celeste" told her. She did not know how her mother had been forced into slavery. Did Big Celeste carry a memory of freedom? If so, it had not been transmitted to her daughter through blood. The only world the girl Celeste knew was the world Edwyn Hawley fashioned. In that world, Negro freedom—a "self" moving and doing for *self*, belonging to *self*—was nothing but tale and myth. When Celeste envisioned going off with David and Andrew Cabarrus, she had imagined a change of masters.

David wagged his head at her with the arrogance of a teenage boy. In a footrace, he could outrun Celeste. He could carry two brimming buckets of well water at a time to her one. Already, he out-picked her in the fields. *Of course*, he understood what she did not.

"We don't *rightly* belong to *him*," David said.

A clacking of the magnolia leaves sounded in Celeste's moment of wordless disbelief. Just an ordinary sound in a profound instant, so the two did not look up until light pierced their dim hideaway.

"Tell me, who do you belong to then?"

David and Celeste sprang to their feet. Edwyn Hawley stood there. He was a bullish man, short in stature, lacking a neck, with broad shoulders that tapered into meaty fists. Suddenly, the secret space turned constricting rather than cozy.

"What y'all doing out here? Come out in the light." Hawley peered at them closely.

He owned enough slaves by now that only the older ones were very familiar. He spent enough time on his other properties, one in Norfolk and another in Nansemond County, to forget the faces of the people he held at this one. Hawley took the lack of recognition as a congenial sign of his growing wealth, similar to the way his wife sometimes forgot the existence of ribbons or fancy stockings she had not had occasion to wear for a while.

"What your name, gal?"

"Celeste Hawley, sir."

"You, boy?"

"David Cabarrus, sir." He said it without thinking. Beneath this tree, in the presence of Celeste, he was always just himself.

Cabarrus. That set Hawley on the back foot. He had been inclining toward amusement. He had been a fourteen-year-old boy and knew what a feat of charm it was to convince a like-age girl to sneak off with him. Still, the two would be punished and the overseer taken to task. He could not have his people shirking work for afternoon trysts. He had thought to go a bit easy on these two, however. But this was something different altogether.

His gaze narrowed. "David," he repeated softly. "David, ain't you meant to say Hawley? That you a Hawley nigger?"

Celeste eased close to David. She nudged his elbow with her

own. David understood her message: *Nod and say, yes, sir,* just as he had understood the faintest squeeze of his mother's hand. Still, Hawley might punish them with extra work, take away their rations, maybe lay on a few licks for sneaking out of the fields, but that would be the end of it.

"My name David Cabarrus, sir."

Perhaps it should have been easy for David to claim the name "Hawley" and save himself the trouble that would befall him. He did not, after all, even know where his papa had gotten the name "Cabarrus." Surely it came from some other ravening white man. But to David, it was as precious as the seeds hidden in the hair of the first African captives, as dear as the tales and tastes carried in their memories. The only proof of home, of self, he had.

And it should not have mattered to Edwyn Hawley what the "niggers" called themselves as long as the work got done and one or another of them arrived when summoned. He cared little that they kept secret names from their heathen lands and called themselves after days of the week and seasons, and figurations from the land under their feet. He wrote the names *he* wanted in his ledger. And there was the rub: The ledger showed in plain ink that they belonged to him. This boy's name was whatever Edwyn Hawley said it was. For the boy to openly call himself anything but what Hawley ordained was defiance.

Hawley studied the boy from the tight pearls of his hair to his ragged toenails. "Boy, don't you know whose nigger you is?"

David looked down at his feet.

The lowering of the gaze, like a tail tucked between the legs of a dog. That signal of surrender. Done showing off for his little strumpet, the boy sidled back into his place. But Hawley had to make sure. The boy's submission and the girl's understanding of that submission had to be complete.

"Answer me, boy," Hawley commanded.

"David—"

"Shut up, gal," Hawley ordered. "I ask *this boy* if he know whose nigger he is. Do he know who he 'rightly' belong to?"

The boy raised his gaze. Tears shimmered in his dark eyes. But it was Hawley who suppressed a fearful shiver. "My name David Cabarrus. I belong to Andrew and Phoebe Cabarrus."

David Cabarrus's tears fell. He knew the reward for defiance. But the boy stood willing to take that punishment. That was what scared Hawley the most. Before him stood a gangly boy. But farm labor would grow David into the big, hearty sort. A bruiser. What would that mean for Hawley, for any white person who sought to control such a will within that powerful body? He shuddered to think what kind of proud and insolent man the boy would become if he were not cowed now.

Hawley cocked his fist and struck. The boy reeled but did not fall. The girl begged and cried for Hawley to stop, but he would not. You must bend a tree while it is young.

• • •

The slave grapevine, the network of watchers, listeners, and whisperers that stretched from the master's bedroom and supper table, out to the quarters, warned that David's punishment would not end with the beating. Armed with this news, Celeste begged her way past Cecil's barricading bulk and finally into his cabin where he cared for David.

"My god, my god," Cecil said on the day of the beating when he first looked at David's condition. After the first blow, David remained on his feet. This seemed to infuriate Hawley. He bludgeoned harder and faster. David curled forward to protect his abdomen. He wrapped his arms around his face and head, but he would not fall. Celeste begged and cried for Hawley to stop, for David to fall. Neither of them listened. Celeste pushed herself between them and took a hard blow. Only then did Hawley pull the next punch. Only then did David stagger.

She had not been able to see David since she had turned him over to Mr. Cecil, babbling the story, repeating Hawley's warning, "Them down in the quarters better learn this boy something."

"He say he'll flog and pickle him the next time," Celeste told Cecil, though at the time she could not imagine how that barbaric punishment could outstrip this one. David's eyes were swollen to slits. His cheeks and lips had been split by hard and callused knuckles. Surely, his ribs were cracked. A teenage boy had taken a beating from a grown man.

"Why?" Cecil asked Celeste. "Why? Do Hawley want you for hisself?"

"No! No!" Distaste momentarily replaced the grief and fear on her face. "David wouldn't answer right. When Hawley ask who he belong to, David wouldn't say 'Hawley.' He said his own papa's name."

Cecil studied the battered young man who whimpered softly and bled into the ticking of Cecil's bed.

"Cabarrus," Celeste said. Her voice trembled, but amid the quivers were throbs of admiration. "He talked up to Hawley."

Cecil looked at the girl. Yes, foolish. "Leave him here to me."

That was some days ago. Celeste had come back every day, and every day Cecil turned her away. Plainly, he asked her, "Don't you know this the kinda nigga get you dead or leave you grievin'?" The girl came anyway.

Today, though, word of the awful way Hawley meant to make examples of Celeste and David had arrived before the girl.

"Please," Celeste begged Cecil as she tried to crane her neck around his bulk. "Please. I got to see him."

Because he ruled the kitchen where the house slaves took their meals, Cecil had been among the first to know Hawley's decision. He stepped aside. "No matter what next, he lucky. If'n he was my age," Cecil grumbled as he gathered up his cap, his pipe, and a bit of tobacco, "a beatin' like that woulda killed him."

Celeste dashed by him. At the sound of her voice, David had begun the struggle to sit up. Cecil stopped in the middle of the small room to caution both of the young people. "He setting up, moving around some, but he ain't half well." His gaze swung from Celeste to David, but they were only looking at each other. "You remember that," he said to David. "You ain't well." Cecil closed the cabin door as he left.

Celeste crouched beside the low bed.

Covering David's dark skin were darker expanses of purple bruises that began on his cheeks and reached into his hairline. Some yellowed around the edges where healing had begun. His eyes were still puffy. Broken vessels radiated from the irises, spotting the whites with blood. The skin on his cheekbones appeared so swollen it was taut, like it might break open with even the gentlest caress. Celeste began to cry.

"It ain't so bad as it looks," David said as he let the nearly flat pillow and the headboard, made of rough parallel posts like a fence, take his weight.

Celeste raised her arms to reach for him, to touch him, for David had not been within reach for several days. But she could not see a place to kiss him without causing pain. The bruises were everywhere. Some would leave permanent marks, making it impossible to forget that day. At last, she pressed her lips to the center of David's palm, then to his wrist.

"You could'a said it for me," she whispered.

"No." She touched her fingers to his swollen lips. David kissed them though puckering broke the scabbed skin and caused it to bleed. "I couldn't."

Celeste allowed her cheek to rest in David's palm. Her tears collected in his lifelines. "Did Mr. Cecil tell you?" she asked.

David stirred then, releasing her and grabbing for the thin sheet that covered him. "Yes. We got to run."

Celeste pushed him back against the headboard. She tugged the thin cover from his hands and tucked it over his lap. "You ain't in no shape, and Hawley still mad. He'll set the dogs on us. I don't want to die like that."

"What then?" David grimaced with the pain it took to push himself forward, to raise his voice.

"Give me something?" Celeste asked.

"Anything," David answered.

"Anything?"

"Anything," David said as he struggled to think of anything of value he owned. His extra shirt? His one pair of shoes. She could have it all.

With a quick glance toward the cabin door, she stood and swiftly unbuttoned her dress. She shoved off her underthings and slipped beneath the sheet with David.

"We'll go easy," she said. It was both question and reassurance. Before this moment, before a few furtive brushes of their lips, the two had barely kissed.

Stunned and injured, David was hesitant. Still, his body reacted with the readiness of adolescence. "You sure?"

"No," Celeste said. "But if we don't, I'll always wish we did."

If not for the circumstances, they would have been able to wait until they were older. They would have been able to plan a rendezvous beneath their tree, where sun dappled the cool magnolia leaves that had fallen to earth, and white petals and starbursts of yellow stamens would have clung to their skin. Instead, the bed where they lay together smelled of David's blood and the smokey sweat of an aged man.

Because of David's injuries and their combined innocence, they used an abundance of care. Neither wanted to cause the other even one more instant of pain. Their awkwardness, however, was soon swept aside by curiosity and pleasure and urgency. Cecil might come back at any moment. He might call out or knock, or not, and even this would be stolen from them.

Celeste explored the hair that covered David, wooly, wavy, springy depending on whether she touched with fingertips, lips, or cheek. She kissed the skin above David's bandaged ribs. She kissed the pulse beneath his jaw and the Adam's apple that bobbed nervously. She found and kissed all of his uninjured places. "In my whole life," she whispered as she hunted for places left unscathed by Hawley's fists, "nobody never told me to belong to myself."

A child of farm life, close quarters, and insufficient privacy, Celeste worked out what to do. She straddled him, and as she leaned down to kiss him, the screaming pain of David's injuries muffled against the softness of Celeste's breasts; it smothered in the heat between her legs. David gripped her thighs, helping as he could. Celeste filled herself with all of him that she could carry away.

Had the first time not also been the last time, they would have held hands, fingers entwined like the branches of their magnolia, afterward. They would have touched and nuzzled as they dressed. Before leaving the privacy of their tree, Celeste would have insisted that they honor the loving with a little cairn of stones.

As it was, she dressed quickly. Before Cecil shoved through the door, she just had time to draw David's hand to her belly. "I will call him by your name," she said. "I will tell him he belongs to David Cabarrus."

• • •

When morning came, Celeste was sent away on a wagon to be sold with other "surplus goods."

Jack Dane

Thomas Crewe's Farm, Lower Norfolk
Colony of Virginia, 1693

Which did the breeze bring first, their stench or the dull drub of their irons? Were they sent for? Or was it serendipity? They arrived less than a fortnight later, after Master Crewe and Shango had words.

As always at their approach, something tainted the day. Milk soured in the pail; green shoots browned and curled; an egg, delicately spotted, warm and unhatched, rolled from a nest to rot on the ground. Before the prisoners appeared, there had been only beauty in the wood: the purple spray of nodding onion, white shadblow dropping among the fallen needles of pitch pines, all of it raggedly knitted with pipevine. The shuffle and drag of their irons scarred the ground. Oak seedlings and leaves of grass were ripped up by the root.

At the sudden silence of the birds, the tinge of rot in the air, Thomas Crewe shouted, "Jack, put on the mush!"

Jack, with the energy only an eleven-year-old boy could have after a full workday, had come dashing ahead of his father and Shango. He hefted the yoke of buckets from brackets fastened to the barn and clanged his way to the well.

The captives came out of the woods single file over an Indian trail, five males and three females, bound hands, naked beneath the long shirts that brushed their knees and the irons that stripped their flesh. The man who drove them, John Jeffrey, sat erect in the saddle though he'd been on horseback since just after dawn. Now the daylight drained west and pooled like blood on the horizon. He held the reins in one hand, the fingers of the other hand on the trigger of the musket that lay across his lap. He marched his prisoners toward the tall, bunched palings of an open-air stockade.

Thomas Crewe held up a welcoming hand. He swung the gate wide. As the bondservants shuffled inside, the two men sounded greetings, but they did not embrace, did not spring from the saddle or loosen the grip on musket, truncheon, or whip until the padlock sounded on the free side of the slave pen.

Within the palings, the slaves—dull-eyed, lethargic, like any other hard-driven herd—crowded together. A woman pissed where she stood. Wet runnels blackened the filth on her legs and soaked the sandy dirt between her feet. She dropped to the spoiled earth. The others squatted and slumped around her.

Jack kept one eye toward the captives. He had never thought to see suffering worse than life belowdecks on the Atlantic crossing. But he had never seen a slave coffle. Thomas Crewe caught him staring.

"Tend the mush," Crewe ordered.

Jumping to, Jack began to stir up a mush, a coarse grind of corn-meal littered with husks and small pebbles, boiled in well water. No salt. By the time his father and Shango appeared, the mixture had begun to bubble. Jack stirred it with a club about as tall as himself and as weighty as a Brown Bess musket.

● ● ●

Animals, unlike men, are seldom disappointed. The care of the ox team was the last hard work of the day. Each night, before tending to his own supper and bruised flesh, Shango or Rowan was tasked with currying the animals, treating, if need be, any wounds, as well as mucking the animals' stall and laying in fresh straw, water, and feed. The men had fallen into the habit of doing work together. They sent Jack ahead to start the evening meal while the two loped up the rutted path trading tales of what their lives had been and hopes of what they might one day be.

Crewe called for Shango before the men reached the ox shed.

The stiff offense in Scot and African was the same. Rowan bristled at having to do the work of two. Shango took umbrage at being called to a task that was sure to delay his dinner and rest, all he desired after a day of uprooting trees and burning brush.

"Be back," he said. Rowan grunted and followed the oxen toward the shed.

As he lumbered across the yard, Shango recognized the stink before he understood the words. "He would do well in the rice fields or perhaps cane." The smell was of sweat and sick expelled but not expunged. It was of unclean mouths and poisoned gums, fetid wounds and unwashed hind parts. An easily recognizable stink. The nigger trader had come.

"Shango," Thomas Crewe said, "come let Mr. Jeffrey get a look at you."

Shango lurched to a halt. "I will not," he said.

"What you say?"

"I took you for a decent man."

"You black bastard," Crewe said as he strode toward Shango. They spoke over each other as Crewe closed the space between them.

"I ain't no slave—"

"I bought your black ass just like I bought everything else on the place—"

"No man got a right to sell me—"

"You as much mine as the goddamned ox that plows my field."

They met eye to eye.

"You ain't selling me."

Crewe met Shango's proclamation with a fist. The African hardly swayed. And though both men had known brute work, their hands equally toughened on ropes and sails, weapons, and plows, only one was in a battle for his life. Thomas Crewe could not knock Shango down.

The shock of master and servant brawling held everyone transfixed. In the pen, the captives stood crowded together, gripping the timbers. Jack stood near the cookpot, uselessly holding the stirring paddle while the mush boiled over. Rowan trotted out of the shed to see the source of the commotion. He loped to a hard stop at the sight of Shango and their master trading blows. John Jeffrey stood in grabbing distance of his cudgel, willing to allow a fair fight as long as the end seemed certain.

When Shango landed a blow that staggered Crewe, everyone sprang into motion. The captives rallied. They yelled and shook the poles of the enclosure. Rowan threw down the pitchfork and ran forward to break up the fight. John Jeffrey took the cudgel in his fist. Closest to the fight, he would blind every slave in that pen before he allowed them to see an Englishman brought low by an African. He split the wood broadside against Shango's back. The African arched and swayed but remained on his feet.

It was Jack, darting into the fight, who brought Shango down with the bucket full of scalding cornmeal mush.

Shango howled as the mash fell on him like a blazing net. He buckled as the blistering paste adhered to his face, his neck, his chest.

Swiping away the blood dripping into his eyes, Thomas Crewe looked in shock at the fierce black man writhing on the ground. He told Jack, "Get something to tie him up."

Andrew Cabarrus

Walking Westward, Frontier-bound
1692–1694

A ndrew began again. He gathered up what was left, the clothes and hat he wore, the boots on his feet, a rucksack, a coat, and the money no buyer would take in exchange for Phoebe or one of the children. He bought one-way passage on a sloop headed from Northampton County to the Great Land, the mainland of the Virginia Colony. From the port near Half Moone Fort in Norfolk, he began to walk westward.

And mumble. Andrew's words were not the insane ravings of a man who had lost everything. They were not prayers for his family, nor were they curses upon the ones who pirated them away. "Phoebe to John Morris. George-Lee to Samuel Ruffin. Peggy to Robert Freeman. Ruthie to Richard Jones. Willie to Custis Slade. David to Edwyn Hawley. Phoebe to John Morris. George-Lee to Samuel Ruffin. Peggy to Robert Freeman. Ruthie to Richard Jones. Willie to Custis Slade. David to Edwyn Hawley." Repeated and repeated and repeated as he walked. Repeated in his dreams. He woke from troubled sleep with lips puckered to shape one of the names. The few people who caught Andrew unaware heard the whispers, and so he left a legend in his wake—the "Mad Nigger" who traveled roads and woods murmuring the names of a family chained into slavery.

But Andrew was not "mad" the way they meant. He could confine the repetition to the silence of his mind when necessary, such as when he bought and bartered and sold the odds and ends carried within the belly of his rucksack.

Along the road, Andrew bargained for loaves of sugar, cakes of soap, sewing needles, bolts of sturdy cloth, small kegs of nails—things he could carry. And though he was not a fugitive, Andrew lived like one. He only spent money on things that could be turned into profit. He ate off of the land.

At night, Andrew crawled between the intertwined roots of white cedars. If the weather was cold, he stuffed the gaps with moss and leaves before he bedded down. If the weather was hot, the underground dens offered cool relief. So hidden, Andrew could secretly collect the news of the rare passersby. This way, he learned of their needs and decided if he had anything to sell them or if they possessed anything he might want to buy. Andrew charted and corrected his course with information gleaned as he huddled underground and tried to fathom how he had lost family and farm and wondered what in the world he could have done differently.

Two years of recitation and wandering led him away from the coastal plain—the Chesapeake Bay became a spill, a blue stain, a memory. Andrew traversed the central hills of the colony. He felt with his feet the lift of the land, a sensation of surmounting the boundaries of captivity. He crossed the fall line, dynamic terrain of one-hundred-foot drops, rushing water, boulders, and the rise of granite rock. A difficult journey, it could not be traversed by boat.

The people, like Andrew, who crossed from east to west were leaving behind the easily navigable rivers and flatland plantations. And so, the fall line signaled not just a change in geography but a shift in the nature of men. The native peoples had not yet been disrupted or displaced because there were few white settlers beyond that boundary. The colonists Andrew did encounter wanted what he wanted: to trade for what they needed, to be free to go on their way.

He came to a nameless place. A fold, a fault, in the undulating land of the piedmont. It was a place where people paused to get their bearings and supplies as they turned toward a farther frontier. For a few, like Andrew, it was far enough. He rooted; this time compelled not by the need to create a future but by desperation to rectify the past.

Among the arriving and departing wagons, a few mongers pushed handcarts and called wares of fruit and salted fish. There, Andrew untied his rucksack and made a place among them. People bought what Andrew sold, but after a few encounters with the "Mad Nigger," vendors and patrons stopped trying to converse with him, stopped even making eye contact, lest his sorrow mark them like an evil eye or reignite their own. He let the useful things he had collected— shoes, curatives, harnesses—speak for him. He conducted business even as he kept the tally in quiet breaths: "Phoebe to John Morris. George-Lee to Samuel Ruffin. Peggy to Robert Freeman. Ruthie to Richard Jones. Willie to Custis Slade. David to Edwyn Hawley."

His customers had problems of their own, and the goods Andrew sold were necessities of good quality at good prices: a fox skin to keep a baby warm, pemmican for when game was scarce or shot needed to be saved. Travelers up and down the trail advised one another to trade with the "Mad Nigger," or, if kinder, the "sad, mumbling Negro." In a few more years, Andrew bought a cart and an animal to draw it.

When Jozachar arrived at the crossroads, she did not know how many miles of walking lay ahead because she had not decided where she was going. She did know she would need sturdy shoes, shoes that would hold out until a place felt right.

The "mumbling Negro" she had been told to look for was easy to find. Andrew sat on the tailgate of his cart, slightly removed from the other costermongers.

Among his wares were deer skins, leggings, and moccasins she would need for the journey west. She examined the seams, the thickness of his offerings, watching him all the while from the corner of her eye, listening to his muttering.

"These," she said, holding out her selection. Andrew glanced at the moccasins and leggings she held and paused his recitation long enough to tell her the price. As she searched out money from various places on her person, Andrew picked up where he had left off: "Peggy to Robert Freeman. Ruthie to Richard Jones. Willie to Custis Slade. David to Edwyn Hawley" and began again as he waited for her to extract the rest of the coin, finally, from her purse. "Phoebe to John Morris. George-Lee to Samuel Ruffin. Peggy to—"

"I can write them down for you," Jozachar said.

Andrew stammered, "Peggy to—Peggy to—"

"You won't have to worry about forgetting."

She dug into the satchel tied across her body. She extracted a ragged book, the pages made of some kind of pressed pulp, dried and sewn together. She held it out to him. "I will give you the pages to keep."

Astonished by her offer, Andrew fell wonderfully, gratefully silent.

• • •

As the woman stored her precious grains of ink, Andrew held the list as reverently as he had held each of his newborns. He ran a finger carefully down the page. Besides a longing he could form into neither words nor tears, the names of his wife and children spelled out on paper was the only tangible proof of them that he possessed.

"Thank you, *thank you* Miss—?" He felt a gratitude nearly as inexpressible as the loss.

"Jozachar," she said. "Call me Jo." She tucked the moccasins and leggings into her sack. She turned toward the road, but Andrew called her back.

"Do you have a list, Miss Jo?"

Jo looked away so he would not see her sudden flush of emotions.

She looked at all the people buying and selling, arriving and leaving as fast as the legs of human or beast could carry them. They were many hues—whites and blacks and browns and various mixtures of the three. In the air, there were almost as many accents— Irish brogues, Tidewater drawls, and the airy vowels of the Eastern Algonquians—as there were scents. Jo would bet everything she had, the money in her purse, the clothes on her back, the worn shoes on her feet, that every person her gaze fell upon had a litany of loss.

She smiled, scrunching her cheeks high until tears receded to the farthest corners of her eyes.

"We all got a list," she said to Andrew. "Only difference is you trying to remember what the rest of us trying to forget."

Cassie and Bless

Willow Oaks Plantation
Kecoughtan Settlement, Elizabeth City Shire
Colony of Virginia, 1698

Cassie donned her only weapon, the mask of servility. She shuttered the violence in her eyes. She coaxed her shoulders into a hunch of humility. She rounded her spine in a posture of ingratiation and forced her fists to unclench. Only then did she light a single candle to guide her up the servants' stairs—narrow, unlit passages carved like ant trails behind the walls of the house—to Master Benjamin's private room.

She knocked. "Go away," her master said.

Cassie opened the door. She found Master Benjamin behind his desk with the fire and candles lit, ledgers open in front of him.

"I heard tell a nigger trader coming today," she said.

"What of it?"

"He ain't coming for my girl, is he?"

Benjamin sighed and raised his gaze to her. "Do you want to be whipped? Is that why you are standing there inquiring into my business?"

"You made me a promise, sir."

"Cassie, it is too early in the day for this."

"You made me a promise, sir."

The force of his fist on the desk caused the candlelight to waver. "That was before your daughter was discovered fucking my daughter's fiancé at their engagement party!"

The ugly word, the hammering fist, were meant to shatter Cassie's resolve, but she stepped closer to the desk. "You made me a promise. When I tried to claim it, you made me kneel in front of my child and call my own self a dog."

Carefully, amid the cracking of her joints, Cassie knelt on the left-hand side of Benjamin's desk, within reach of his fist or his foot. "This time, you ain't got to make me. I am a dog. Have mercy and don't kick me no more. Give me back my child."

"Get up, Cassie."

"I can't. All I got to depend on is your word."

Benjamin fancied himself a benevolent master, a caretaker to a rude and backward people. He provided blankets for all and shoes for the adults. He supplied a new set of clothes for each of his people every year, and cornmeal, pork, and molasses enough for everyone. He sold people on occasion, as with Cassie's boys, but that was for the benefit of all. He'd had to keep the place afloat. Still, though, he recalled Cassie's howls as the cart rolled down the drive with her son inside. The whip had not been enough to shut her up. He had used his fists. But the skin-on-skin clubbing of a woman had lessened him. He told her before the last birth she could keep the child.

That vow had caused him nothing but trouble, and it looked like it would go on doing so. Benjamin's wife would not tolerate a "promise" to a slave being elevated over her own whims and wishes. So, he had broken his word to Cassie and taken Bless to serve in the household. Now the same wife and daughter who had demanded a slave girl for a pet wanted her sold so their eyes would never fall on the wench again. And here was Cassie, the least of all women, down on her knees, begging him to stand on his honor, to prove his "superior" sense of right and wrong.

"Get up," he said. He opened the right-hand drawer and produced the skeleton key. "Goddamn you."

• • •

Cassie jerked open the cellar door. Bless slept on the stairs, one arm stretched toward the locked door. She startled and cringed at the sound, blinked at the red-daubed dawn rising over Cassie's shoulder.

"Come on," Cassie said.

• • •

When she was a little girl, Bless had known the name of every man, woman, and child in each cabin. She'd known the name of every dog under every porch. But on the day Cassie sent her back to the house, Bless crossed some border, some invisible line, that made her an alien in the quarters. From that day forward, she rarely visited Cassie, though the distance between the main house and the slaves' dwellings was only a footpath, a stand of trees, less than a quarter of a mile.

The men and women who encountered Bless on the bright Sunday morning when Cassie led her home bit back greetings and swallowed words of welcome. They caught bolting toddlers or steered them out of Bless's way. For they did not imagine the distaste in her eyes. She held her rumpled skirts tight in her fist, as if she scorned anything they touched, even the ground.

In truth, these people had made the best possible outcome from every particle and scrap they came across and out of all their collective loneliness. They built a village out of disparate backgrounds and what was at hand. They arranged their six cabins in a circle, like the compounds they remembered, open onto a center clearing. Behind the cabins were garden patches and cookpots and chicken coops built out of bramble and sticks. In the clearing, a communal table. Upon it, the women shared the best river rocks for pounding corn. Leaning against the trees were fishing poles whittled by the men and crab baskets woven by the women. Their cabin walls were local timber, the cracks filled with mud they dredged from the river and straw harvested by their hands. Their doors hung open, and the small children wandered from house to house where they were chastised or changed or comforted by whomever was at home. Still, enslaved life bore only an anemic likeness to the full village lives they'd known.

Like the stranger she had become, Bless stared around the compound as if the cabins were built of human bones. The people absorbed the offense, stored it for later, and greeted Cassie, and she them, as they did every morning. Pretending not to see her disgraced daughter trailing behind, they went back to washing, to tending their little green plots, their few chickens, to fetching and hauling all the wood they needed for the week, to whatever family living they could squeeze in between Saturday noon and Sunday nightfall. Some folks set off and some returned. All who saw Bless shook their heads or sucked their teeth and wondered: What kinda fool the white folks sent back to us?

Jack Dane

Thomas Crewe's Farm, Lower Norfolk
Colony of Virginia, 1693

Rowan and Jack sat across from each other at the table Shango built. Both knew it had been shaped from a hackberry felled by a hurricane, because Shango had told them the story of the storm. Jack gripped the rough-planed slats.

Rowan's mind worked with questions. Hadn't Shango taken Jack fishing? Hadn't he taught him how to build a crab pot out of reeds? Hadn't he shown Jack how to pry out the sweet, secret meat of clams? Had Shango not answered the boy's demands for tales of the Calabar River? Over and over, the stories of crocodiles and elephants and white-faced monkeys until Rowan could recite the words himself.

"Shango dug potatoes the other night and roasted them for the lot of us. Taught you how to sew that hat. And him up first to light the fire. Almost every morning when it was cold, him up first and the room near warm when we set foot on the floor. I know you ain't forgot."

"No."

"Then why?"

Jack stared mutinously down at his hands. "Master Crewe was set to sell him no matter what I done. He thanked me."

Rowan sat back as far as he could to take in the entirety of his son. "What kind of person have you become?"

It was not the first time Rowan had wondered. Back in their village on the Plantation of Ulster, there had been a woman named

Saoirse. When her husband lost their land to the Ulster settlement, he became a woodkern, an outlaw. When he died in a raid gone wrong, Saoirse was left to fend for herself and her child on poor acreage, within view of the farm that had once been her home. Out of necessity, she made peace with the enemy. When she saw Rowan Dane marching past her hovel on rations day, she was certain to soon pay a call at the Dane's door. Lydia Dane, as Saoirse knew she would, always welcomed her and the child in for supper.

As Saoirse and her boy ate and drank of the Dane family's sparse resources, Jack Dane could hardly eat his own diminished portion. He stared at the woman and her child. Saoirse blushed, but she continued to eat and feed her son.

Rowan had sat on the rail of Jack's bed one evening. "You weren't kind to Saoirse."

In the same way Jack kept doggedly about his play when Lydia told him to brush his hair or put on his shoes, he ignored the admonishment. He flopped onto his back and studied his father. "Why don't you hide it?"

"Hide what?"

"The sack of rations."

Rowan hesitated, then he reached for the boy. He took Jack by the shoulders and sat him upright so that they could see eye to eye. He pushed the hair out of Jack's eyes. "I'll not have that kind of selfishness in your heart, Jack. Hear me? I will not have it."

But Jack had gone to bed with his belly half full, with little else to feed on but resentment. "We never have enough to last until next rations day."

"She has no one, Jack. And nothing. Not even as much as we. She has a little one. She does the best she can on her own. I will not have you begrudge her such mouthfuls as we can spare. I'd not have you be that kind of man."

Jack had flipped onto his empty stomach. Sometimes the slight weight of his body smothered the gnawing hunger. He turned his face toward the wall.

"You are not angry with her, Jack. You are angry with me, and

I suppose you've a right to be." Rowan had implored the boy once more before leaving, "I'll do better, Jack."

Rowan now realized that he had failed to keep his word. Their hunger on the plantation had lasted years more. Only the coming of war forced Rowan to pack up and save what was left of their lives.

"Tell me the truth, Jack," Rowan said. "This has naught to do with Shango."

Jack looked up into his father's eyes, and Rowan knew he was right. He examined his son's face. There had never been much baby fat. Hunger had consumed any layer of softness in the boy, but, still, hadn't there been *something* of a child? Rowan could find no trace of innocence now. That was his own fault.

"Well," he said. He scraped back the chair. At the hearth, he took down Shango's pipe, the little cask of tobacco, a piece of flint.

Only when the door closed behind his father did grief rupture Jack's anger. He hurled himself onto Shango's bed. He touched the carefully wrought markings. There would be no freedom dues for Shango. No freedom.

There would be no partnership. No friendship. Rowan would remain alone, miserable—just as Jack would always be without the one person he needed to sister him through this world.

Cassie and Bless

Willow Oaks Plantation
Kecoughtan Settlement, Elizabeth City Shire
Colony of Virginia, 1698

The same dishes and utensils—gourds and clamshells—lined up where the table touched the wall. Herbs and dried peppers hung from strings above the hearth. On the mantel below, a comb and a jar of pomade, a pot of charcoal and a chewing stick for mouth cleaning. A dry, brittle corn-husk doll. On the bed of crooked rails and splintered slats, straw poked through the homemade mattress. Beneath the blanket, the linens were flour sacks Cassie sewed together. The few pieces of furniture stood on a clay floor cold enough to burn the soles in the winter, damp enough to sweat out the scents of buried things in the summer. A night slops bucket stood near the back door. Home.

"You used to your own bed now, I reckon. Too grown to sleep with me," Cassie said. "I'll ask Jeremiah to help us gather some things an' make you a pallet this afternoon."

Bless said nothing. She looked about the slave cabin, from corner to corner, alarm rippling over her face, lodging in her throat. Her voice emerged as a whisper.

"I'm not staying here. Not for long."

"You thinking of running? Listen here—Mr. Benjamin done sent for the trader on account of you. Do one more thing and—"

"I don't have to run. He's going to send for me."

"He say you ain't to go nowhere near that house. Nowhere Miss Rebecca or her mama might see you—"

"Not him," Bless said.

"Who then?"

"Mr. Jason. He's not going to leave me here."

Cassie opened her mouth. She shut it. "You hungry?" she finally asked.

Educated only in cooking and childbearing, flavor and pain were all that Cassie had learned. They were the only tools with which she could teach. She moved abruptly to the safe, the hole dug into the floor and covered with a few boards, where she kept potatoes, rutabagas, salted fish, a few pieces of money. Fumbling with the few yams, she mastered the impulse to slap Bless.

Cassie set the skillet on the grate in the hearth. She lit the kindling beneath it and moved to the table where she'd laid out her potatoes, fatback, and a good cutting knife she had "borrowed" from the kitchen. She sat and began to peel the yams.

"S'pose he do come get you. What your life be?"

"Better than this."

"Hmm. 'Pends on what you think is better," she said as the potato peels curled away from her thumb.

"If he send for you, it's so he can put you in some hole or hollow on that plantation a'his where nobody can't see how he come and go. And he will come and what happened in that cellar gon' happen again and again 'til *he* get tired of it. Every time, it'll end the same way: he'll fasten up his britches and leave like what he done weren't no more than a trip to the privy. He won't think of you no more than that neither, not 'til he get the urge to go again."

With the tip of her knife, Cassie carved an imaginary path from Bless to the slop bucket. "That's what you want to be? Some white man trip to the privy?"

There were too many folks out front, carrying water, coming, going, and calling to one another, so Bless fled by the back door.

Cassie finished peeling the potatoes. She sliced and sizzled the pork, then fried the sweet potatoes in the grease. She plated the meal, then sat at the table and waited for Bless to return as the food cooled and the lard congealed. All the while, she could not help thinking a slap might have been kinder.

Jack Crewe

Towne of Lower Norfolk County, 1695

The deep blue of the sky paled to white as it neared the horizon on the Portsmouth side of the Elizabeth River. Jack and Thomas Crewe left the main street and turned onto the wind-scoured planks of Campbell's Wharf. It was Jack's first journey away from Crewe's in the two years since he and Rowan arrived at the farm. Thomas Crewe, who had positioned himself not just as Jack's master but as his new father in the three months since Rowan's unexpected death, thought it would cheer the boy to see something of the world. He brought Jack along on his most pressing errand: to buy a slave to share the work left behind by Rowan and Shango. Just a few days ago, ships loaded with slaves from inland territories of the colony and up from Jamaica had docked at the wharf.

Slaves, shackled together or singly, their chains fastened to the pilings, lined the pier. Thomas walked from one group to the next, stopping to peer closer. Here or there he nudged with the toe of his boot then stepped back to watch the reaction. Twelve-year-old Jack trailed behind, making his own assessments.

Their garments, he realized, did not amount to much protection from the chilly weather. Yet with faces averted from onlookers or staring toward the fading horizon, huddled in pairs and threes or solitary, they seemed removed from the cold.

"They are afraid," Jack said.

Thomas paused to look back at the boy. He studied his young charge before he said, "They are not burdened with the same human feelings that we are." He continued to inspect the available chattel.

Jack followed and did not dare contradict his master, but hadn't similar things been said about him, about Rowan and Lydia, when—in their bedraggled state, speaking in their muddled accent—they'd been mistaken for Irish as they roamed the streets of London in search of food and shelter? As they were herded into the hold of a ship where they were expected to endure the indignities of filth and hunger and count themselves lucky? "Better than where they came from," the crew and topside passengers said with confidence. But they were wrong. The wretchedness of the passage to the New World surpassed anything Jack had experienced before.

Thomas paused before a group of men and boys. "What you see before you, Jack, is movable wealth. Treasure. Security for a mortgage. Collateral for acres of land." To get a better look, Jack stepped closer.

There *were* differences: broader noses and fuller lips, shades of skin from pitch to honey. But there was also something recognizable: Whether round or almond-shaped, hooded or bagged, the light hue of baked-bread or the color of dark cedar—the bewilderment, the mourning, in their gazes was much the same as that Jack had seen in the hold of *The Venture*. The eyes, at least, were the same.

Jack might have said so, but Thomas Crewe placed a detaining hand on the boy's shoulder. "Not too close. They are an unpredictable lot."

He drew Jack closer to his side. Jack's temple brushed against the sturdy broadcloth of his master's coat. Even through the stench of the unwashed bodies, Jack caught a whiff of quality tobacco—so much more fragrant and sweet-smelling that the brittle remnants Rowan and Shango had crumpled into their shared pipe. Similarly, the confident, restraining grip of Master Crewe's hand felt like a new and foreign luxury, for Rowan had known he could shield Jack from almost nothing; therefore, he seldom tried. Instead, he offered platitudes like, "Do unto others as you would have them do unto you." But the substance and certainty of Thomas Crewe offered protection in *this* world.

It was almost effortless to relinquish the ephemeral beliefs of one father for the solid, guiding hand of another. Thomas Crewe possessed what Rowan lacked, traits Jack had also seen in the merchant, in the captain: command, assurance. Jack's new parent did not look to a child for help or sacrifice. He did not look to other men for means or consent. In fact, as they progressed down the waterside, from Campbell's Wharf to Marsden's Wharf, men doffed their hats to Thomas Crewe. They waylaid him to ask *his* opinion on political matters of the day and the fairness of export prices for their crops.

Jack lifted his chin as he walked at his master's side. He rolled his shoulders, down and back, out of their perpetual hunch. He met gazes of the men who spoke to Crewe and preened as the admiration they displayed was generously extended to him. "Who is this fine boy?" they asked.

"My apprentice," Thomas Crewe said. "Speak to the man, Jack. Offer him your hand."

Thomas taught Jack to firm up his grip, to maintain eye contact, to distinctly speak, not mumble, his name. That was only the first of the day's lessons. Thomas Crewe was a wellspring of knowledge. He overflowed with wisdom. Childless, he had only lacked a lad to teach. Jack latched on, drank thirstily, swallowed all Crewe had to teach about being the kind of man who owned another: The raising of the red flag means the sale is about to begin. Arrive early. Tuck your nose into your shirt until you grow used to the smell. Captives are grouped by what they might be good for: farmhand, body slave, wet nurse.

The first to be sold are cheap because they are damaged, made dead-eyed by the journey. In a day or two, these will be in fattening houses where they will be crammed full of corn mush and bacon rind. Surgeons will sew their wounds. Middlemen will oil and dye and dress them in clean linens to disguise what cannot be treated, for no matter where they are sold—to harvest on rolling acres or pole across the James River in the brisk pine air—in their minds, these remain sealed in a hold, tasting the shitty blackness. No matter how small the initial outlay, there is no profit to be made off the suicidal or deranged.

Never buy flesh from a speculator. Look them in the eye. Pull down their eyelids. Look up their noses. Pry open their mouths. Press your thumb to their gums. Run your hands over their hocks and haunches.

The ones you want have a bit of fight in them. A bit of fury is a good sign and not to be feared. Seasoning will mellow their impulses; the fight will keep them alive.

Check for lameness.

Show no pity.

• • •

Crewe led two poor boys—Adam, black, paid for, bound by the hands, and Jack, white, adopted, foot-dragging—to a spot downwind of the barn so the horses would not be spooked by the smell of blood. Crewe stopped in the first sturdy stand of elm and oak. He unwound a length of rope from Adam's hands, enough to toss over a low, muscular branch. Heaving on the dangling end, Crewe hauled Adam into the air until the boy's arms stretched awkwardly above his head. Adam's shoulder blades and ribs stood out in tender relief against his dark skin. His toe tips brushed the grass. The boy grunted and struggled, but he did not yet beg. In solidarity or horror, the noisiest of the forest birds—jays, cardinals, and crows—held their peace as well.

"Two cuts of the lash for every mile he was off the farm," Crewe said. Jack stepped backward, a precursor to his own flight. "Come back here!" Crewe said. He held out the whip. "Make him feel it."

"Sir? I can't, sir—" What he'd done to Shango had been an impulse. This was different.

Crewe brought the whip down on Jack. It felt like the devil's own tail wrapped around his head. Jack swayed, cockeyed from the burn.

"Ten lashes. Not one more. Not one less. Make him feel it," Crewe said.

Jack's pain gave off a buzz like the air after lightning—it sizzled beneath his skin. Crewe tapped his thumbnail on the handle of the whip as he waited for the boy to decide. He flicked his wrist, positioning for another strike.

"You or him?" Crewe asked.

Jack reached for the whip.

"Like you seen me do," Crewe instructed.

Whip in hand, Jack reared back until he felt a stretch across his chest. The whip flattened, arrow straight. The popper bit open a stripe of skin on young Adam's unmarked back. It ripped from him a scream as jagged as the torn flesh.

Jack dropped the whip. He watched piss stream down Adam's bare legs and drip from his toes.

"Pick it up," Crewe said, "or I will."

Adam flailed and corkscrewed as he tried to loosen his wrists or plant his feet on the ground. Jack could not look away. He squatted. He blindly searched until he felt the stock.

"Again," Thomas Crewe said. The whip whistled and cracked. "Again!"

More gashes opened on Adam's back. Jack gained power and accuracy. He struck the same furrow twice. Blood spattered the tree bark. It splattered onto the fallen pecans and poisoned the sweet meat within.

Crewe harangued Adam as Jack laid on the stripes. "You got nowhere to go. Stop running. There ain't a thing in the world but this."

Adam's head drooped. With his arms painfully stretched above his head, his toes scraped the grass. His chin lolled on his chest. From his face dripped sweat and spit and tears. He muttered in a dialect of the Yoruba.

"Speak English," Thomas commanded, "not heathen."

Adam's slurred words grew louder. "O kì í ṣe ayé," he muttered. "Y'all ain't the world."

"Again!" Crewe shouted to Jack, and the whip boomed, cracking open the air as it traveled.

But afterward, in the blood-splattered silence, Adam's words still rang in the air, "Y'all ain't the world," as clear as any other declaration.

• • •

"It was a hard lesson," Thomas Crewe said to Jack, "but you had to learn it."

Jack hid his trembling hands in the folds of his blouse.

"Yes, sir," he said.

"You are my son now." Rowan had been dead of fever and failure for almost six months.

"Yes, sir."

"Give me that whip."

Jack extended the whip, the stock sticky, the popper clotted.

Thomas took the whip to the barn and returned with a long gun.

"Here," he said. "This gun is yours now. You earned it."

Jack reached for the musket but did not take it in his grasp. His gaze darted between the gleaming barrel and the blood caking beneath his fingernails. A few feet away, Adam lay on his belly in the grass. He groaned into the ground. Every few moments, he jerked.

Feeling the blaze of his solitary lash, Jack knew some small degree of the enslaved boy's pain. And Jack knew that Lydia, his poor, bonded mother, had died in childbirth. His sister had been sold for a few silver coins. Rowan had sweated and shitted out his life on this very land, and, with Jack's help, Shango had been cheated out of his. Jack knew where his sympathies should lie. And yet, *You are my son now. This gun is yours. You earned it.*

Thomas's praise—like the cool metal of the musket pressed against Jack's flaming cheek—felt like a balm, like all the mercy Jack would ever need.

Cassie, Bless, and Jeremiah

Willow Oaks Plantation
Kecoughtan Settlement, Elizabeth City Shire
Colony of Virginia, 1698

"What they saying?" Cassie asked.

She and Jeremiah stood in the only bit of midday shade behind her cabin. Jeremiah emptied a sack of white perch into the sink, a contraption of his own making, a log troughed out and made to stand waist-high on pieces of wood he'd sized into usefulness.

Jeremiah shrugged. Cassie had been trying to break him of the habit since he had first come to her, three years before. One day, Master Benjamin had gone to market. He returned atop his horse, leading a new colt and a young man by ropes gripped tightly in his fist. He turned the colt over to one of the Negro grooms. He turned the boy over to Cassie. Cassie and the groom were soon of the same mind: Their charges were brash and unbroken.

The colt kicked holes in stall after stall until finally the groom was forced to hobble and tie him outside. The boy, Jeremiah, was equally brazen with his intention.

Cassie sat her charge in the cook shed at the table where she cut the vegetables and plucked the chickens. She gave him coarse bread and a bowl of hot stew. He looked at the food with distrust. It seemed vital to him that she understand: Stew would not win him over.

"I run from every place I been," he said. "Got the marks on me to prove it. I ain't staying here." He held out thin, scarred arms for her inspection. Indeed, those marks were manmade.

Cassie nodded sagely. "I understand," she said. "Meat broth ain't no vow of friendship between us." She nudged the bowl toward him. "Eat."

Jeremiah dipped the seeded bread into the stew. He closed his eyes and suppressed a moan at the richly seasoned soup. But no sooner had he swallowed than the moment of savoring turned to anger.

Jeremiah looked around the outbuilding. It was smokey, but safe from the weather. It had a fire against the cold. Plenty of food. "If the cook go hungry," he'd heard his grandmother say, "she got nobody to blame but herself."

In places like this, where there was shelter and warmth and plenty, how could this woman understand what it was like for the rest of them, the ones who worked the fields and used their bodies like mules from sunup to sundown? The woman had even placed, here and there, a few pretty things, like wildflowers in clay jars. If the cook had been there of her own free will, he would have called the place *comfortable*. But he also noticed a kind of heaviness about her, something more than her rotund shape. She was, in fact, sodden with sadness.

He glanced toward the door to make sure no one listened. He leaned forward, crushing the bread in his hand. "There's a place we can go," he said, "if we just got the chance."

Jeremiah had heard the whispered stories the whole of his young life. He had been born in Isle of Wight, a shire situated at the confluence of the Nansemond, James, and Elizabeth Rivers. Messages and runaways traveled the waterways. Jeremiah's grandmother had an account straight from the mouth of a *cimmaron—a fugitive, a defiant one*—a woman who had emancipated herself but come back to steal away the child she had left behind: There was a place, *a refuge*, where they could live, not in ease but in peace.

There, they fended for themselves. They governed themselves. Some nights, that meant bedding down in a cocoon of mosquitoes. It meant living among panthers and arm-thick rattlesnakes. And still it was better than the world out here. There—among the heat and elements and creatures driven by satiable hunger—the runaways had a fair and fighting chance. According to Jeremiah's grandmother, Africans had been running away to the *Paquesen*, as the Indians called the swamp, almost since the day they arrived. The swamp was their only hope of freedom and refuge. The swamp did not, as the masters told it, swallow runaway Africans and Indians and indentureds. It shielded them. The swamp would not even give up their bones.

"What your grandma call that place?" Cassie asked.

"*Paquesen*."

"How you know it's real?" Cassie asked.

"My papa left when I was still in my mama's belly. My grandma sent him on to make a place for us. That's where he gone. That's where I'm going."

"What's to stop me from going in there right now telling Master Benjamin everything you just said?"

The boy's surliness had become eagerness as he tried to convince Cassie of the existence of a refuge. Now that fever turned to fright. Had he miscalculated, given over his plan to a self-serving telltale instead of the sorrowful, burdened ally Jeremiah thought he saw behind her gaze?

"You don't know me." Cassie said. "You don't know what trouble I am or what trouble I got. But *I* know what trouble you gon' bring if your talk 'bout *Paquesen* reach the wrong set a ears. If you gon' do something, do it. But don't talk that foolishness to nobody else, you hear?"

Jeremiah looked down at his bowl. He shrugged. "Yes, ma'am," he muttered.

Cassie reached out. She held his chin in the hard grip of thumb and forefinger and raised his head until he looked her in the eyes.

"Yes, ma'am," Jeremiah repeated.

Cassie felt the soft bulge of his last baby fat against the pads of her fingers. Here was another child, headstrong and with more courage than wit, come to break her heart. She let go. "And don't hunch your shoulders at me."

Three years of scolding him, and he still had no better sense than to shrug and look away when she was talking to him. "That's how you answer me?"

"Beg pardon," Jeremiah said, meeting her gaze though he hated to deliver bad news straight on. "They ain't saying nothing good."

Cassie lifted a fish. The gills strained, revealing an inner shading of rose. "What?" she asked.

The fish thrashed in her hand as it smothered right there in the bright, open world. Jeremiah's face cramped in sympathy. He raised his gaze. "She uppity. A white-folks' pet and—" Jeremiah looked down at the fish again.

"And?"

"Miss Cassie, you know what else on account of what she was doing when they found her."

"Everybody know?"

"Nothing like that don't stay secret round here."

"Well, ain't for nobody to judge."

"They wouldn't talk so bad if—"

"If what?"

"She didn't look at folks the way she do."

Cassie did not need to ask what he meant. "She ain't use to us, Jeremiah."

"'Cause she never come down here. Rather stay up there with them."

"She come here."

"When they send her."

"Before. She come before. You wasn't here yet."

"Been here three years now, Miss Cassie. Ain't seen her. She don't even come down for Christmas."

"She ain't bad, Jeremiah."

Again, Jeremiah shrugged. The fish jerked in Cassie's grasp, pulling her attention to the job at hand. She made short work of it. Three quick cuts. She separated the gills from the jaw and snatched loose the throbbing guts.

"Tell me," she said, "'bout your mama."

"Don't remember her much. Was eight, maybe, last time I seen her. Day I was took, she run 'long side the wagon 'til she couldn't keep up. Master come 'long behind her with the whip. That's the last I seen her, running after me, standing middle the road, under the whip."

"I reckon that's why Bless ain't been."

"Huh?"

Cassie sighed. "Your mama run after you, held on 'til they whipped her off you. I just let Bless go."

Cassie handed the emptied fish to Jeremiah. With a pewter spoon, he stripped it of the transparent scales, raked delicate armor from tender skin.

"All right, Miss Cassie," he sighed. "I'll look out for her if that's what you want me to do."

• • •

"Get up! You can't be late. Do what Rove say. Don't say nothing back. Be quick. Jeremiah gon' show you what to do. He meet you at the gate. I left some'a that cornbread. Take it wit' you." Cassie roused Bless then left to begin the day of cooking and serving.

Bless had been "put to ground," sent to work the fields. Short of selling her, it was the worst punishment anyone in the household could think of. After growing up in the labors of the household, she was not accustomed to toiling under the lash and in the weather.

At all times, field work was hunch-and-bend-over work, work of rigor and force. No falling behind. No slowing. No ceasing. The fastest worker set the pace. The slowest took the licks.

Bless pulled on her dress and shoes. She wiped her face with a rag and cold water. In minutes, she stood at the split-rail fence, the boundary between the cabins and the fields. There was no sign of the boy, Jeremiah.

In twos and threes, other field hands rushed by. She looked anxiously into each face for a sign of the young man Cassie described. They avoided looking back. No one folded her into their group or offered to show her what to do. They knew the kind of day she faced. Working beside her meant becoming a part of it. The kind ones inclined a nod toward "Cassie's girl," but no one stopped. Their side glances and headshakes of pity made Bless's heart kick. But even as anxiety spread through her like tobacco suckers, a curious thing also happened as she watched for Jeremiah. She took real notice of the field hands.

They were a mismatched, patched, and mended people. Dressed in what they had been allotted, what they could make, or what they could find, they wore clothes of coarse fabrics and bearskin and buckskin, and striped homespun that fastened on by rope, twine, and leather thong. Everything fashioned of what was cheap or free, clothes that scratched, chafed, or smothered the skin. Defiance, however, lay in the colors. What had been rationed to them in drab or dun, they dyed red or yellow or green.

Like their clothes, their bodies bore the marks of whole-body labor. Some walked awkwardly on tender feet, others limped to favor a crooked leg or bruised hip. As they approached the fields, they rubbed at shoulders with strains and tears beneath the skin; they stretched the tightness from old scars or wrapped rags around new ones.

Everyone came. No one was spared on account of age, infirmity, or sex. Every black body set to work. Children chased crows and kept the chickens out of newly sewn seed. They hauled water to men and animals. Men cleared new ground with axes and brawn while women and boys dug out the bushes and hauled away the brush. It surprised no one if Rove sent a few of the women to build a fence or dig a ditch. The old watched the babies or prepared the lunch.

To be awake meant to toil at some task—sew seed, grub weeds, hold on to good sense, resist destruction. The effort of not perishing was all over them. Patches. Calluses. Scars. Gaps. Tears. At sunrise, Bless noted, they already looked tired and grim. Even the children looked old.

Bless turned in each cardinal direction to look for Jeremiah. On the last turn, she found herself in the sights of a young woman who did spare her more than a glance, more than a look of pity. She stopped with two other young women and looked Bless over from the crown of her braided head to the tips of her shoes. Bless felt their gazes like pennyweights in her pocket. She was suddenly aware of her attire, a hand-me-down day dress from Miss Rebecca. Not even a dress Rebecca would ever wear for company, but still absurd in the fields. It was the dress Bless wore the night she went to the cellar with Master Jason. She also wore slippers with a satin shell. Already scuffed and frayed from wear by the time Bless received them, they would be finished off in a day of dirt clods and fieldstones.

"Don't look like she gon' be much good out here. Wonder what she is good for?" the ringleader asked.

"I reckon Master Jason can tell us," one of the friends offered. The women chuckled, but the sound of approaching hoofbeats cut their laughter short. They stepped lively.

The reason for their haste arrived on the barbed tip of a whip. A slash from shoulder to buttock spun Bless around. She felt like she'd been doused with fire.

From atop his horse, Rove looked down. "What in hell you standing round for? Get your ass in that field."

• • •

Rove had shoved a hoe in her hands and sent her out behind the rest. "Learn her," he hollered in the direction of the closest gang of field hands, but no one did. With pronouncements of, "I guess she done found out she ain't white," they hurried to leave Bless behind. Later, when Rove caught her lagging in the same row where he had left her, swiping uselessly around the stalk of a young tobacco plant, he brought the whip down again. That was all the teaching he took time for.

At midmorning, Jeremiah appeared out of nowhere. He sprang up like a mushroom beside Bless as she doggedly swung and missed, swung and missed, the grass thrusting up to choke the young tobacco.

Jeremiah grabbed her elbow. "Time to eat. You don't see everybody gone?"

Bless looked up dizzily to see that it was so. At eleven, the hands were allowed their first break of the day. As if by stealthy agreement, they had headed to the cabins or shade tree to eat bread and meat rinds or cold potatoes stuffed in their pockets.

Bless let go of the hoe. Her legs gave way. Fear of Rove's whip was all that had kept her standing.

Jeremiah looked down at her. "Nobody come fetch you?"

Bless shook her head.

Jeremiah squatted beside her. "Rove set me patching coops and pens this morning or I'da been here. I thought some of the others would take you in hand." His gaze raked over the bloodstains on the back of her dress then settled on the shade tree where the field hands talked and ate their lunch. "They ain't mean. Just, they don't know what to make'a you."

That being the case, there was no need to lead her over to the group. The others would find reason to wander away, and they would be mad at him for causing them to waste their precious few minutes of leisure. Jeremiah did not relish taking his break in the sun, but she looked so tired, he sat cross-legged on the ground beside her. He examined Bless for a moment, the sweat beading in the parts of her braided hair and racing down her temples. From around his waist, he untied a small bladder of water. He uncorked it and handed it to her. Bless drank just a few swallows though she wanted more. She handed the vessel back to him.

"You come out here like that?"

She thought he meant her ridiculous clothes. "It's all I got," she said.

"No. With your head bare."

"Sun was barely up when we came out here."

He looked at her with a mix of incredulity and pity. Perhaps she'd thought the sun held the same position all day. Jeremiah snatched a kerchief from the waistband of his britches and held it out to Bless. He didn't miss the way her nose wrinkled.

"Naw," Jeremiah said, "it ain't clean, and it don't smell good. But it'll keep the sun from burning out your brain." He waited until she draped it over her hair.

Despite the powerful smell that enveloped her face like a caul, Bless had to admit that the top of her sunbaked head already felt better. "Thank you," she said.

"Bring your own tomorrow," Jeremiah said. "It's the only extra I got."

As Bless secured the knot of the scarf at the nape of her neck, Jeremiah withdrew cornbread smeared with bacon fat from his pocket. He took a big bite as he grimaced at the row she had butchered. "You better eat," he said. "I got a lot to teach you and Rove won't 'low much time."

Bless glanced away. She had also forgotten to bring the cornbread. Jeremiah had shared his water. He had loaned her his extra kerchief. She did not want to ask for his food. Then she remembered. Bless searched the pocket still tied to her skirt. She found the slice of friendship cake still wrapped in Mr. Jason's linen handkerchief.

She peeled back the squashed folds with their neatly embroidered initials and almost swooned from the smell of sweetly fermented fruit. After so many days, the nuts were soft, the fruit rubbery, the cake crumbled like sand, yet the essentials, flavor and spice, survived.

Flour, sugar, yeast, and milk, mixed and set aside in a warm place. Cassie had returned to it every day to feed the dough. She'd nicked her fingers on the cracked shells of pecans and walnuts. She herself laid the fire. She cooled and heated, cooled and heated again until the temperature was just right. Only then, after fourteen days did Cassie drain fruit from sweet liquor and mix it with the snap of nuts and sour, flourishing dough. Even stale, it was the best cake Bless had ever eaten. It tasted like mothering.

With care, Bless folded the delicate cloth.

"Whose that?" Jeremiah asked, his gaze on the lettered stitching.

"Mr. Jason's," Bless said. She returned the token to her pocket.

Jeremiah studied her, his gaze as penetrating as the darts of sun on her scalp, as if he were trying to *see* the structures and blind alley-ways in her head, but he said nothing else.

A few moments more of pensive chewing and draining the canteen, then he motioned Bless up and sprang to his feet. While the other workers finished their lunch in the shade of the big cedar, he showed Bless how to properly wield the hoe, how to use her weight, taut wrists, and the sharp edge of the blade to chop the choking weeds.

"Like this," he said, or "Uh, uh." Mostly, Jeremiah remained thoughtful as he showed, corrected, and covered for Bless by going back for the weeds she had missed.

When he spoke again, he did not dally in the details. "What I can't understand," he said, his bafflement sincere, "is how in the world you can love them."

Bless equaled Jeremiah's bewilderment when she asked in return, "Who else was there for me to love?"

• • •

From the first sounding of the horn, field hands had thirty minutes to wake, dress, eat, and hurry down to the tool shed. Standard punishment for lateness or loafing was ten lashes because Rove rarely raised his hand to lay on less. Each morning, Bless fell in with the other field hands as they stumbled toward the darkest three quarters of the sky. At the shed, they shouldered their tools and took Rove's commands. They would eat again at eleven. In the meantime, there would only be work and water.

By morning break, Bless's head would swim from heat and hunger. Over a few weeks, she had learned to tolerate the burn of sweat in her eyes and the sticky thickness of her tongue lest Rove catch her taking too many breaks to drink and mop sweat. Even if the lash did not fall, Bless's shoulders and back ached long before the dinner break. Her legs would go numb from standing, kneeling, or squatting, whichever position the day required. It was, therefore, beyond her power to help or hide the hope that reared in her the day she saw Mr. Jason riding across the field.

The heat in which the slaves labored had caused him to abandon his outer coat and wig. He wore knee britches and a waistcoat. He had brushed his longish, sandy hair from his face and tied it with a ribbon. Dressed so casually and leaning forward in the saddle of his cantering horse, he seemed to have come in a hurry, in search of something.

While the people around her remained bent to the task—the presence of a white man other than Rove being no concern of theirs and best ignored—Bless stopped chopping and stood. She swayed in some instinctive movement that would have set her whole body in motion if not for Master Benjamin riding up behind Jason, his arm and voice raised as he called out, "Rove!" And then she spied the overseer not far behind her—obscured by the tobacco leaves and causing no more disturbance than the evening breeze—sneaking up in her row. He made himself visible and shouted back.

The sidelong glance Rove spared as he hustled by slid over Bless like a razor. Then she knew. Everyone had seen. Around her, the field hands' surprised expressions curdled like milk left in the sun. Whispers rose like a wave of cicada song.

One woman stared at Bless longer than the others. Her look was one of undiluted hatred. Then, there was Jeremiah. Sorrowful, as if his disappointment went too deep for anger.

Bless looked away. She attacked bluegrass, cheatgrass, and field sandburs. She severed and uprooted with an aim and ferocity that had eluded her before.

• • •

They were allowed to leave the field when there was more darkness than light, when even a practiced hand could not be sure if the blade glanced weed or tobacco leaf. At the calls of others leaving the field, Jeremiah shouldered his hoe. A few rows over, Bless still chopped.

"Come on," he called. "Enough."

When she kept at it as if she had not heard, Jeremiah walked closer. He had to dodge her upward swing, fierce enough to take his head off, as she labored in a kind of haze. "Hey, now! Hey!"

He took the hoe from her. The wooden handle pulled skin and serum from her blistered palms. Years of household calluses were easily broken by hours of hard-swinging the hoe. Though she would not look at him, Jeremiah put his hand on Bless's elbow and turned her toward the toolshed. She would have to face the talk and stares sooner or later. May as well get it over with.

But the shed was quiet when they arrived. There should have been twenty field hands gossiping and yawning, sitting or leaning on whatever would hold their weight as they scraped clay off their blades and passed around files. Instead, the tools lay in a pile outside the door and Jeremiah saw folks scuttling down the path to the cabins. The woman who had looked at Bless with such hatred in her eyes, was the last of them. She was the same woman who'd asked what Bless might be "good for." She dropped her tool on the pile.

"Reckon this ain't the night you had planned," she said as she walked past Bless.

The woman's scorn pulled Bless from her trance. "What's her name?" she said hoarsely.

"Esther," Jeremiah said as he looked around for some indication of what in the world was going on. "Don't pay her no mind."

Rove stepped out of the shed. "Leave it," he said, nodding to Jeremiah's hoe. "She gone do it."

The tremor that moved through Bless traveled into Jeremiah. He stepped in front of her. "Beg pardon, sir, but she don't know how. Please, sir, can't I do it?"

Rove looked surprised. "Jer'miah, I must not gived you enough work today."

"Plenty, sir. A plenty. But it slow us down in the morning if them hoes ain't right. She don't know nothing 'bout it, sir."

In the waning light, Rove appraised Bless through his pinched eyes. He scratched at the hairline that began just over his ears. His wry grin revealed the pellets of yellow teeth usually hidden behind a bottom lip that collapsed into a chin and one long flap of neck skin.

"Nothing good come'a raising niggers in the house," he said.

"We 'gree on that, sir," Jeremiah said spritely.

The sudden accord drew a sharp look from Rove. He wasn't sure if the boy meant to mock him, but he felt the sting of a taunt.

"Learn her if you can," he said, "but know I'm'a lay a lash on you and her both for every nick I find."

Rove left them with the pile of dull and dirty grubbing hoes. He untied his horse from a nearby post and swung into the saddle. Pulling the horse around, Rove gave it a kick that made the animal neigh and jump into a tilting run. Jeremiah smiled. The overseer was furious. He never treated animals like Negroes.

The smile withered as he looked at two more hours of work dumped at his feet. "Go on up to Miss Cassie," he said without even turning to look at Bless. "I'll see 'bout these."

She walked away, but only the few steps it took her to reach a stump. "Teach me."

"Your hands need tending, and you 'bout to snuff out right there on that log."

"And tomorrow? He's not through punishing me. You'll stay out here and do this every night? What if he sends you back to the fences? Teach me."

Jeremiah shrugged. He went into the shed and returned with two files. He dragged the first of the tools over to the stump. He sat on the ground with a hoe on his lap, blade up.

"First you got to smooth out the nicks."

Bless angled the blade to the degree that Jeremiah instructed her to angle it. She rasped the file against the cutting edge just like he told her to rasp it.

"You know," he said, "all my life they treated me like one'a these old grubbing or hilling hoes. But they done you worse."

Bless kept her gaze on her work.

"You believed that man come to save you. Truth be told, he just as soon trample you under that horse. Turn that file a little more. That's right.

"One thing for sure," Jeremiah said as his gaze traveled to the dim shine of reed candles flickering alight in the cabins, "you can't live among us and keep loving them."

Bless gripped the file. New blisters snagged and tore on the iron and wood.

Her wounds did the weeping she could not do.

• • •

"Keep 'em in 'til the stinging stop." Cassie pressed Bless's wrists down until the hot salt-water lapped over the basin. Bless fought the urge to snatch her hands not just from the burn, but from Cassie's touch. "Got to draw out that poison," Cassie said.

Though they sat together at the table, Bless concentrated on her hands, raw in some places, still blistered in others. Cassie looked at the dark hearth, into the basin, at the gourd bowls shoved against the wall, down at the floor.

When the water grew cool, Bless raised her hands from the basin, palms up, fingers curved, slightly trembling, revealing milky, scourged skin. "You got a rag?" she asked.

Cassie hesitated before lifting the tail of her apron to dab Bless's skin dry.

She examined her daughter's hands. The right one bore freckles diagonally across the back, from pinky to thumb. Another of her children had the same markings on his her hand. That was all she remembered of that girl. Bless had the squarish hands and slender fingers of the man who fathered her. Probing an unbroken blister, Cassie traced the *X* at the joining of ring finger and palm. One of her other babies used to suck that finger along with the middle one.

"They say you begged Master Benjamin not to sell me," Bless said quietly. Almost no one spoke directly to her, but she had overhead.

"What of it?"

"Why?"

Cassie looked puzzled. "What you mean why?" She scraped back her chair and went to the hearth shelf where she kept little clay pots of pungent ointments and salves. Beside them slumped the old corn-husk doll.

"And that doll, that ugly old doll? Why did you keep it?"

"You left it," Cassie mumbled absently as she uncorked and sniffed until she found the right pot. Across the room, from the nail where she kept her extra dress, Cassie took down a shift. She ripped strips from the bottom until she had enough to bind Bless's hands.

"They won't give you another until next allotment," Bless said.

"They ain't give me this one. I'll make another when I come cross something to make it out'a." She scooted her chair closer to Bless's.

"Gimme your hand." At Bless's hesitation, she said, "Rove won't have a bit more pity tomorrow than he did today."

Bless offered her left hand. Cassie dipped two fingers into a cloudy unguent that was thick as lard and smelled of it too. With her palm cupped around Bless's hand, she smoothed the balm into the wounds. They did not speak. Proximity had not restored their closeness. Cassie began to wrap and tie the makeshift bandages.

"He was kind to me," Bless whispered.

"Rove?"

"Jason. Mr. Jason," she said as her mother tugged and tucked the ragged cloth strips. "He was kind to me all the time. Every time I saw him, he was the same. Kind. Not like—everybody else. I thought that meant he loved me."

Cassie looked up, astonished. "That's all the understanding you got'a love?" she asked.

"Yes, ma'am," Bless answered.

Cassie sighed. "Uh," she said, a sound like the one she made in the morning after soreness had all night to settle in her feet.

She set Bless's hand on the table. She picked up the pot of salve and plugged in the stopper.

While Cassie replaced the medicine among the other clay vessels and smalls casks above the hearth, Bless pretended to examine her bandaged hands, flexing and turning them as if figuring how she might grasp the hoe come morning. Really, she waited for this fresh wave of shame to pass over.

"This," Cassie said, suddenly beside her, "this *here* is *love*."

In her hands, she held the brittle doll. A desiccated beauty, it flaked husk and shed silk as she placed it in Bless's bandaged hands.

"Handle it gently," Cassie cautioned.

• • •

One unspoiled evening. A week's worth of bliss. A month of gladness. How much happiness is enough to live on?

Every day, the people of slave quarters squirreled away and toted up the smallest bits of joy. They stockpiled it for absent hours, for down-river journeys, for foot-sore, shackled treks from which no one returned home. They performed herculean tasks of memorization: Birthmarks and gestures, expressions and recipes and songs. They breathed deeply at the sour neck of a beloved, hoping to store the scent. They collected scraps of cloth and tufts of baby hair and tiny teeth.

On a Saturday evening, Cassie sat at her table with Jeremiah and Bless. Sunday, the day of liberty, still ahead. Simple food. Company of their own choosing. Time to enjoy both. Pleasures so seldom felt, they had become the stuff of longing.

Thin white fishbones and cornbread crumbs littered their plates. The dank cabin air honeyed from the smell of sweet potatoes baked in hot coals.

They lingered, picking their teeth, not saying much, just savoring, storing up against the coming seasons of need.

• • •

The grown folks remembered their true homes, the taste of the rivers and the taste of the clay, the bluer sky and the closer moon. There, they would have danced in animal skins, in shirts of woven grass, in nothing but cowrie shells at the neck, wrists, and ankles. In the colony of Virginia, they made do. On top of Negro cloth, they wore oyster and clam shells, the bones of rabbits and raccoons. They strung those bits and pieces on twine, on loops of dried grapevine, and tied them to ankle and knee, neck and hair. They turned all manner of clanging, whistling, noise-making rubbish into treasure.

The people pooled their harvest rations with things nicked and pocketed while setting up a separate celebration for the white folks. There was some meat, goose and ham, a bit of liquor, nuts and yams. But more necessary than food was music.

Two men squatted on birthing stools, their knees spread wide to accommodate the drums, while the others gathered. Sincere, a slave who often played at the white folks' fancy occasions, stepped from his cabin bearing his new fiddle like a scepter, though it was made of hollowed gourd and deer hide, with one string and a horsehair bow. To his wild plucking, there would be added a chorus of women, ululating to urge him on, and to that, the drums. The palm beats would gallop from head to heart, head to heart, until everyone had been cajoled into joy.

Some wore masks, others danced barefaced. Sweat—clean as the waters of the *Sassandra*, the *Anum*, the *Pendjari*—washed away the false faces they wore all the daylight hours of the year. They kicked off hard, bulky shoes. They stood as if their backs never had been made crooked by the endless swinging of a hoe, never bowed by bundles and barrels of tobacco hefted upon their heads. They transformed. They hopped and jumped and abandoned the daily effort to remain unseen. They erupted. An arched back. A whirling one-legged turn. Each body once again decided the bearing and intensity with which it needed to move.

When Cassie handed Bless her cup of dandelion wine to hold and spun into the clearing of firelight and drumbeat, and there, shut her eyes, Bless took one step forward, but in amazement, she faltered.

Odofoley! Odofoley! the other grown folks whooped. They clapped as Cassie dipped her torso and rippled her back. Her hip shakes were celebration, prayer, and summons. She wanted and took more than joy from the dance. *Odofoley* danced things that only they, fellow marooned souls, could decipher and echo and answer with their throats and thighs and feet.

The captive-born children, like Bless, like Jeremiah, like Esther and all the others, could mimic the steps but could never follow them, not really, not back to the *feeling* where they began. And when the grown folks all died, as surely they must, this drum-to-body talk and everything it told or aimed to tell would die too. For the grown folks carried what their bondage-born children did not—a living memory of an unalterable self.

Whatever they pretended to be—field hand, cook, wash woman—they were always sensible of a true self. A self born to harvest millet and gather the kola nut and trade palm oil in a bazaar, a self born to shape hot iron not just into the rings of a drum but into weapons. A basket-making self. A cloth-weaving self. A self that shepherded the cows of a grandfather who lay buried in the village grove. A self that lived close to the surface. A *self* wrestled down at every rising. A self that beat the drum and blazed footprints across the stubbled ground—a Ghanaian or Nigerian or Bantu self who gyrated until she obliterated 358 days of unholy masquerade.

Bless could not tell whether the drumbeat had hold of her mother or if her mother had hold of the drummer. Both were beyond her reach. Even if she stretched on tiptoes, they were up above her, somehow, beating free and leaning into the currents of a differently destined life.

With just a glimpse of who her mother might have been, the magnitude of that theft staggered Bless. She would have fallen if Jeremiah had not placed his hand on the small of her back.

"Too much wine?" he asked cutting his eyes at the cup.

"No, no," Bless said. She pushed the cup at him. "Fill it up."

Andrew Cabarrus

Cabarrus & Co., Crossroads
Frontier of the Colony of Virginia, 1694

Some of Andrew's neighbors were people who had been chased off their ancestral lands and kept off with specious treaties and loaded muskets. Some of his neighbors were people who had come by ship because the unknown, with its wilds and dangers, was more promising than the "civilizations" they knew. Some of his neighbors were people who had come by ship because they could not slip their chains or escape their captors long enough to jump overboard.

None of these people would have batted an eye, nor muttered a word of blame, had Andrew given up on Phoebe and the children and started again—new business, new woman, perhaps new children. All of these people found themselves stranded in the present with nothing to do but survive it. That meant accepting the loss of all the inhabitants of their pasts and all the lives they might have lived had things turned out differently. They pitied Andrew for trying to hold on.

Jo, however, marveled. She kept written records for Andrew as he built the cart into a store and turned his roadside customers into a clientele. Traders returned to him when they passed through. They spread word of him along the trails, telling anyone who might head in Andrew's direction of his wares and fair prices. So the cart became a store and Jo became a kind of secretary and clerk. She worked the counter when Andrew went to scout for merchandise. She wrote letters to the men on Andrew's list, the men who had bought his family, inquiring about the whereabouts, the health of Andrew's wife and children.

Occasionally, a response arrived. Most often, nothing. Still, Andrew had her write and post the letters. Through all the years of no discernible progress, he gathered and built, ignoring his solitary present, turning stubborn-heartedly toward an abundant future. "Willie," Andrew might say, "always been good with numbers," and he stood there and imagined aloud what it would be like to have the boy there, standing on a stool beside Andrew, counting aloud as Andrew meted out change.

The garden was the most tangible proof of Andrew's belief that he would reunite his family. He bought and begged seeds from travelers. He returned from trading expeditions with seedlings wrapped in wet burlap and cradled in his cap. "I reckon Phoebe never seen this color," he said to Jo as he went off to plant an azalea the color of flame. "When I seen how the dragonflies lighted on this, I knowed the girls would want it." He held up an arrowhead plant, the thin white filaments trailing, unbroken, past his wrist. He had taken care with its uprooting. And so it went with berry bushes and all kinds of flowers. When Andrew regained his family, they would find thriving evidence of his devotion. He never planned a future without them.

What Andrew wanted most, Jo most feared. Perhaps she was the one the neighbors would judge. For Jo had not been dispossessed. Neither had she been abducted. Simply, she slipped out of the life she did not want and into the life she craved.

She had not planned to leave. She had been staring into the hills—wondering how far they rolled—while the supper scorched, and the baby bawled in a sopping diaper. Jo shut her eyes against a longing that rose up within her. She turned and stalked away to compose herself—just a few paces, and a few paces more.

Each time she paused to go back she remembered: She had never wanted that man she married. She had never warmed to the children he gave her. They only existed because Jo grew up in a place that was inured to the weeping of women. A few years before, when Jo asked for schooling, wanting to further explore all of the things her brother had taught her on a dare, both she and her brother were beaten. But Jo's punishment extended beyond the rod, for the family ignored her, refused to speak to her, pretended to look through her, until she agreed to their terms of fellowship, their definition of a "good" woman.

There were nights when Jo awoke in panic, fighting off dream hands that had come to drag her back. Once or twice a year, those terrors coincided with nights when Andrew awoke, chest heaving, and crawled from bed to escape the nightmare in which he was stretched on a rack—head, arms, legs—pulled in separate, but equally painful, directions.

On those nights, Andrew went to Jo's door. For a few hours, they were each other's haven and ease.

The rest of the time, Jo was herself, and Andrew was a man determined to get his wife and children back.

Jack Crewe

Towne of Lower Norfolk County, 1695

Jack sat across from the girl in the offices of the slave market in Norfolk. He thought her his age, perhaps a little younger. Thirteen at the most. Someone had cropped her hair close to the scalp. She was very dark with an angular face and plump lips. Pretty. She wore a skirt, but nothing on her feet and no blouse. Her breasts were small and tight as peony buds. Jack sneaked glances at them, but felt ashamed, so he looked down at his own shoes.

Jack waited for his master to come out of the office where Thomas Crewe had disappeared with the slave trader and two other men. Jack did not know why the girl was waiting there inside instead of in the "jail" or pen where the rest of the slaves were kept. Her cuffed hands rested on her lap, but the toes of her shackled ankle stroked the leg of the chair nervously. She caught Jack looking at her breasts.

"Is you like them?" she asked.

Jack angled his ear toward the lilt of uncertainty in her voice. There remained some doubt? Had what he'd done to Shango, the whippings he had laid on Adam, left no outward, irreversible marks?

"Is you like them?" In the slight modulation of the Negro girl's voice, "Is you like them," Jack heard an opening. A breach. A gap between the rock and the hard place that he might just fit through. *Could* he be otherwise? Did he *want* to be?

The men Thomas Crewe associated with were powerful, influential. Over supper, they spoke of loans, land grants, and mortgages. They were anxious for nothing, arriving in well-made clothes on animals with coats sleek as fur. These men left food on their plates and wine in their glasses. The butts of their fragrant cigars might smolder on a windowsill, forgotten. Master Crewe and his lot were not men who made compromises or requests. They made boisterous deals over glasses of whiskey, and when Jack secretly lapped the dregs from their cups, his admiration for them only grew. These men swallowed fire. He *wanted* to be like them, yes.

"Is you?" she demanded.

Jack looked into her eyes and found himself startled anew. From her size, the baby fat that clung to the bones of her face, even the pitch of her voice, he was sure she was a child like him. But her eyes held a grown woman's look of fearful weariness. The girl did not know what might be next for her, but she had no expectation that it would be good.

He opened his mouth to answer her just as the trader's fortified office door swung open.

The men, Crewe included, came out shaking hands and grinning. An agreement had been reached. Jack jumped to his feet, ready to follow Crewe to their next appointment. Jack could escape the girl's question. His master waved him down.

The girl began to cry even before the trader came close enough to grab the chain between her wrists and steer her not back to the pen but toward yet another heavily fortified door. Though they were inside the business offices, all the doors were heavily armored. Not even sounds escaped.

"The bailiff has offered a private viewing. Go back to the inn. Wait for me there," Crewe said to Jack.

Jack grabbed his cap but paused. What was left to view? The girl sat there with her breasts bared. Jack had never seen a woman exposed like that. Even aboard the cramped ship, there had been skirts and shirts strung up when women needed a private corner. The girl begged now. Jack shuffled uneasily. "She is just a girl, sir," he said quietly.

The jailer and the other man hesitated. Thomas Crewe blushed.

The girl turned toward Jack. "Please! Please don't leave! Please," she begged.

She squatted low on her haunches to make it harder for the jailer to move her. "Please," she begged. "*Please.*"

"Crewe?" The jailer and the other man looked at him with disbelief. Had a *boy* just reprimanded him?

Crewe's blush burned to his hairline then quickly receded as a cold and brittle paleness overtook him.

"What you say to me?" Crewe demanded softly.

"Sir, I—" Jack said. "Sir, she—"

"What did you say?"

The girl squatted on the floor. She dug in her heels as the jailer tried to drag her. She begged, by turns, the jailer and Jack. "Don't let them! Please, don't!"

Jack's gaze ricocheted between the girl and his new father.

"Will you be a nigger as well as a *nit*, Jack?" Crewe asked, his tone softened by concern. The wave of shame that rose within Jack was harder to withstand than the bite of Crewe's whip.

Before they had been exported to Ulster, the Danes had been English serfs, peasants, shackled to whatever piece of land their lord set them upon. Not quite free, not quite slave, the Danes lived rooted to the land like any other thing that cropped up, be it blossom or blight. And like any other rooted thing, they could be plucked from that soil. Their sole hope for constancy was to make the land yield. Security lay in usefulness. So generations of Danes, for the better part of any day, for the better part of their lives, did what the master's land required: plowed fields, dug ditches, and built roads. Pay was the privilege to work—the right to be somewhere, not cast off, not wandering.

But even abject deference was not a guarantee of place. Every two or three generations the Danes were thrust upon the road—on the way to anywhere else that would take them—by crop failure or sheep scab, by plague or famine. In due time, the progenitors of Rowan, Lydia, and their young son found themselves among those "loaned," not unlike a seed spreader, to the plantation of Ulster. They were meant to be a kind of human barrier—like a swamp, a desert, or an icefield—a buffer between the civilized Episcopalians and the "backward" Catholics.

Their arrival in the Gaelic province was described as an "infestation," their names interchangeable with those of vermin. They were called *miol leapa*. "Nits." As a group, the immigrants were branded "lazy beggars" and "cattle rustlers," people who "wallowed in vice" and "indulged in filthy practices."

Jack—born from the bloodlines of these maligned and thrown-away people, with a strong predisposition toward shame and a long history of being at someone else's mercy—looked down at his feet. He shook his head. "No, sir."

"Get yourself to that inn," Crewe ordered.

Jack placed his cap on his head. He dragged himself through the doorway, onto the dirt of the wagon road. His steps were dogged by the pleas of the girl, the lewd laughter of the men. "Get up gal!" the jailer said. "You got yourself an appointment with a couple of one-eyed men!"

Jack walked away, and the small gap—the faintest chance of escape—closed for the girl and for him as well. They both had the answer to her question.

Bless, Jeremiah, and Esther

Willow Oaks Plantation
Kecoughtan Settlement, Elizabeth City Shire
Colony of Virginia, 1699

If they did not take too long, and if Rove was in a fair mood, female field hands were allowed to go to the tree line to do their personal business. If Rove was not in a fair mood, he might bark at them to do it where they stood. If he was in a perverse mood, he might lean on the pommel of his saddle to watch. On those days, the women held it or peed themselves within the privacy of their skirts.

Esther found Bless in the bushes, in a high, awkward squat, feet spread and skirts rucked up to avoid splatters.

Esther positioned herself directly opposite so that Bless had to make a point of *not* seeing her. Esther dropped low and let out a stream as strong as a horse. She kept her feet and skirts dry without trying. "You even piss like one'a them," she taunted Bless.

Bless stood and arranged her skirts.

"You low with us now. Act like it."

Bless turned back toward the field. By Rove time surely she had been gone too long. Her back had almost healed. She did not want it gashed open again because of this foolish girl. She had walked just a few steps before Esther yanked her around by the shoulder.

Bless knocked the hand away. The young women stood close enough to count the beads of sweat on each other's forehead.

"Don't you ever—"

"'Don't you ever,'" Esther mimicked. "Lissen at you! We

see if you still talking like Miss Rebecca after Rove take you in them woods."

"I'm not going anywhere with Rove."

"You going," Esther said. "You no better'n the rest of us. You going."

Bless flashed upon an image of herself spread on burlap, Jason thrusting like a blunt dagger between her legs. "I'll fight," she said.

"Well, why didn't none'a us think of that?" Esther mocked. "Better for him if he got to chase or fight you."

"I won't just stand there."

"You sure won't! You gon' be on your knees. He gon' make you say you like it." Esther looked Bless up and down, her gaze contemptuous. "*You* just might."

Esther made it back to the field before Bless. "Careful," Jeremiah said. He had ducked over to work Bless's row. As long as the grass was flying, it might take Rove a bit of time to notice who was making it fly. "You was gone a long time."

"Esther," Bless said.

Jeremiah looked around until he saw Esther. She was laughing with two of her favorite gossips while glancing in Bless and Jeremiah's direction. "What she do?"

Bless took her hoe from him. She turned away and pretended to examine all the chopping Jeremiah had done in the few minutes she'd been gone.

Already, he had asked her how she could love *them*. He had witnessed her reaction to Mr. Jason. Despite his loyalty to Cassie, Jeremiah probably didn't think any better of Bless than did Esther. What if he believed she would go "into the woods" with Rove like she had gone into that cellar with Jason?

Bless attacked the weeds. "Foolish talk from a foolish girl," she said. "Go back to your place before Rove notice you're gone."

• • •

"She lord it over all us," Esther said. "She don't let none'a us forget she were raised in the house."

Rove kept digging at a posthole. He did not tell Esther to *Get!* Neither did he put his hands on her, so she knew he listened.

"You seen her," Esther continued, "clutching them raggedy skirts like they silk. Dabbing her mouth after she drink from the ladle. And the way she talk down to the niggers. You think Miss 'Becca herself down here 'mong us!" Rove glanced up. "Nothing 'gainst Miss 'Becca," Esther said quickly. "That's just how Bless put on. She make everybody feel low. 'Specially Jeremiah."

Rove grew impatient. He rammed the posthole digger into the ground. He spread his legs and leaned against it. "Why you telling me this?"

"Jeremiah a good boy. She changing him. Got him puttin' on airs to suit her."

Esther waited, but Rove just studied her. A different kind of interest kindled in his gaze. He might punish her for wasting his time.

Esther hurried to her point. "She ain't 'mong *them* now. She 'mong *us*. She need to know it. She making people miserable, acting high like she do. I come to ask—not tell you your business. Maybe you got to let her act like she do 'cause she raised 'long side Miss 'Becca—but after what she done? Look like they sent her here for a reason. What I mean to say is, she don't know her place."

As she spoke, Esther's voice rose steadily, ending on a wail that surprised them both. And both Esther and Rove were more surprised still when tears brimmed onto her cheeks. She had not meant to cry, though she felt glad, for it seemed to impress Rove. Esther never cried, not even when Rove himself abused her.

Rove felt a stirring behind the buttons of his britches. But as he examined Esther from her head wrap to her bare and dirty feet, the feeling began to pass. He wanted someone else, someone who had a bit of dignity.

"You told me," he said gruffly. "Now gon' 'bout your work 'fore I give you what you looking for."

• • •

It was hardly ever about desire. Rove had a wife at home who knew her conjugal duty. No, it most often followed on the heels of disdain or insult from Master Benjamin and his ilk. Humiliation would have brought Rove around to Bless eventually.

The gentry held more contempt for overseers than for their own slaves. In this vast New World, they reasoned, if an Englishman lived only slightly better than a Negro, whose fault could it be but his own? No, men such as Rove made a choice. They wanted no better. Men of Master Benjamin's class spoke, not always in whispers, of their overseers' "disreputable employment," "degrading function," of the "meanness of spirit" and "contemptible character" one must possess to embrace such a career.

Yet Rove knew himself to be their single line of defense, the gate-keeper against all he saw brewing in Negro eyes—all they would dare to say, all they would dare to do—against the "masters" who claimed ownership of their mothers, their children.

To keep them "corralled," Rove all but lived among them. His only sanctioned day away from the plantation was Sunday, and then—if he went anywhere at all—he returned by nightfall. Each morning, Rove blew the horn to rouse the slaves of the field and the house. Rove, not sunrise, not Master Benjamin—not God—set the order and rhythm of their days.

He walked the quarters and into their homes, unannounced and uninvited, to make sure they were where he obliged them to be. He made certain none of his people wandered off and no stray Negroes wandered in. He settled quarrels and broke up fights when he happened upon them. To Rove's mind, he whipped them much less often than they gave him cause to. And it was not unheard of that he tended their sickness. He stood by, whip uncoiled, while they grudgingly swallowed whatever tincture he judged might best purge their complaint. Sometimes, Rove himself fetched the doctor. And in return for such stewardship, he earned the hatred they were not always able to conceal. They kept their mouths clamped shut, but he sometimes spied the fists balled in their pockets or wrapped in the folds of their skirts. Their gazes were not downcast out of respect, but to hide loathing.

With violent imagination and brute strength, Rove had made most of the Negroes fear him. Those who were not afraid, who still had enough man or woman left in them to stand up to him, thought about the consequences for the others. What would Rove do to the timid and the weak? The source of his control lay in that dreadful conjecturing.

Rove lived vised between two interests, despised and needed in equal portions. The Negroes could not always hide their contempt; the planters did not always try. No matter. Rove knew the truth. *He* owned *them*. All of them, planter and Negro alike. He kept "wild niggers" in check so rich whites would not be murdered in their feather beds. *Overseer.* An honorable profession. And time had come to get on his job.

● ● ●

Jeremiah did not know how in the world to court. Instead of sweets folded in linen, he'd gifted Bless a rag that reeked of his sweat. He'd taught her how to weed tobacco and sharpen a hoe well enough to keep the lash off of her back. His wooing culminated in a visit to a graveyard dotted with juneberry shrubs.

There were no Christian symbols to announce the graves of dead Africans. Ankhs, not crosses were scratched into their markers. The baptized did not sleep in those graves; they died not in Christ, but in exile. Smuggled into their coffins were the things they had clung to on the slave ships: native seeds and secret symbols of ancestral magic and waist beads they might offer to other gods.

Just as no gate or stone foretold the burial ground, there was no prelude to the kiss. It seemed as inevitable as the death and ripening that surrounded them. Jeremiah handed Bless a clay bowl and began thumbing berries off the bush. After a while, he held one, then another, to her lips as if he fed her every day. He ate too. When their lips and tongues were sweetly stained, Jeremiah kissed her.

The bowl tilted in Bless's hands. Jeremiah pulled his mouth free as he righted the vessel. He rested his forehead against Bless's.

"Please don't pour them berries on the ground," he murmured.

She laughed. They remained with their foreheads pressed together, eyes closed. Their breath came fast. They clutched the bowl between them.

"Where I come from," Jeremiah said, "they talk'a maroons out in the swamp. Say if you make it there, you never be found. Say the marsh water rush to fill a man's tracks. Say two, three steps on, you look back and the vines growed over your path. Build a fire in the morning and come afternoon it been smothered by cypress and reeds. That's where you go to be free, where the dirt, the birds, an' everything in between on a Negro man side."

"Why're you telling me this?"

"'Cause I ain't gon' be nobody's nigger forever. When I go, I want to take you with me."

Andrew and Phoebe Cabarrus

Cabarrus & Co., Crossroads
Frontier of the Colony of Virginia, 1701

Phoebe climbed down from the wagon on her own though the white man offered her a hand. The substance of her had not changed, though her stature had. Phoebe had been put to hard use. All that had been curved and voluptuous about her had been carved lean. Her hair, which she had always worn thickly braided beneath her headwrap, had been razored short and severe. Nothing moved in her eyes, not the light of curiosity, not the play of fear. She looked around, but her gaze was lusterless, resigned.

Andrew stepped from beneath the sign, *Cabarrus & Co.* that Jo had insisted upon.

"Phoebe?" and again, "Phoebe," as her gaze swung toward him. "Phoebe, you know me. You know me, don't you, Phoebe?"

Andrew held his hands in front of him. He approached his wife as he would an animal that might strike or a man with a gun.

"Andrew?"

"Yes. Andrew. Your husband, Andrew," and from there, the reunion came to pass just as Andrew had imagined it from the moment he saw Phoebe parted from her children.

She threw herself onto him, a fury of fists, feet, and nails. Phoebe ripped his clothes and snatched out Andrew's hair, and he raised his hands only to keep Jo and the hired white man from interfering. Andrew crossed his forearms over his face and head. Otherwise, he did not resist. Phoebe had grown thinner, but her strength remained. The blows hurt. She brought Andrew to the ground, and only then did her knuckled blows become the grasping and kneading of his chest and arms as if to ascertain that he was real. Only then did Phoebe's growls become sobs of grief that had been held at bay as fury overwhelmed her.

"My children!" Phoebe howled. "My children!"

Andrew wrapped and rocked her in his arms. "I will find them, each and every one," he swore.

Phoebe still struggled. In erratic turns, she tore at him, then caressed him, then struck him again. And right there on the street in front of the store that trumpeted his name, in front of Jo and Bill, the white man Andrew hired to find this woman, and every passerby, Andrew accepted this battering, this anguished reunion, as a small part of his due.

• • •

"Jo, will you take my wife inside and help her freshen up? Get her a new piece of soap and fresh toweling off the—"

"I know where everything is," Jo answered.

Andrew stood first, then helped Phoebe to her feet. "Go 'head with Jo. I be there in just a minute."

Jo approached slowly and held out a hand to Phoebe, "Hello, Mrs. Cabarrus." She hesitated, allowing Phoebe a moment to look her over.

"I am Jozachar. You can call me Jo. There is hot water on the stove and some fresh things for you to put on." Jo watched as Phoebe's uncertainty dissolved before the lure of such an offer. She did not resist when Jo linked their arms and led her away.

While Jo took Phoebe around the back of the building to where the living quarters stood, Andrew led Bill, his factor, into the store to settle the outstanding fee and hear what other news the man brought. Though it was soon after finding Phoebe, there might be something. Bill was very good at his job.

Before coming west, Bill had been a hunter of runaways. He could find anyone who had a bounty on him. In the first years of his occupation, his quarry had mostly been indentured servants who had tired of abuse and grown impatient for the promise of freedom. He'd had few qualms about tracking those people and dragging them back to honor their commitments. But as time went on and laws hardened, more and more of the runaways became Africans fleeing perpetual slavery. As Bill's commissions changed, so did his feelings.

He tried, at first, not to think too much about it—a fee is a fee. But "slave catching" required that a man get every part of himself— even his soul—dirty. It was not possible to do the job without a clear understanding of the part he played in the lifelong imprisonment of people who had been given no choice. Bill's parents had taught him that a thief was the worst thing a man could be. What was slavery if not life-stealing?

He switched sides when he hunted and found a runaway Negro woman he could not return. Though he had sent back the earnest money he had taken when he agreed to hunt her, Bill knew there was still an outstanding bounty on his wife. He would kill any man who thought to collect it.

Coin clattered and spun on polished wood. Andrew squinted through his rapidly swelling right eye as he counted through the cash box for the remainder of Bill's fee. The polite thing for Bill to do was stand silently and say nothing of the altercation he had just witnessed, but he had known Andrew for a while now. He rested his forearms on the counter and said in mock earnestness, "Horses is still hitched. I can take her back where I found 'er if you want me to."

Andrew began to laugh, a loud guffaw and a spreading smile that pulled at the bloody split in his bottom lip.

"Ow!" Andrew pressed a finger to the torn flesh. The men grinned at each other across the counter. Just as suddenly though, the mirth shining in Andrew's eyes condensed into tears. He bent his head and sobbed.

Bill gripped the lacquered wood of the counter. "Well," he said, "she safe now. She safe and you brung her home as soon as you could."

Andrew searched his friend's gaze for a hint that Bill was excusing him or discounting all the ways Phoebe may have been harmed in the years it took Andrew to find her and buy her free. But Bill was stating the facts. Here was where they stood. From here, they would have to begin again.

Andrew nodded and cleared his throat. He finished counting then spread the money on the counter. He raised a brow. "Expenses?"

Bill looked Andrew over: beads of blood where a tuft of beard had been, swelling eye, ripped clothes. "I got a lead on one of your boys," he said. "Though I don't know how many more of these 'reunions' you can stand."

Their laughter rumbled through the room.

• • •

Just as the store shelves were stocked with simple, useful supplies, so the living space at the back of the store held what was strictly needed: a washstand with its bowl and pitcher of plain whiteware, a mirror for shaving, a wooden bedframe crisscrossed at its base with sturdy ropes to hold the mattress someone had dragged outside, a dresser, a small table, two chairs with seats of woven grass, and a small fireplace for warmth and cooking. A window that channeled the colored light of sunset was the room's only adornment.

Phoebe turned about in the small space, looking for something but unsure what she expected to find—something familiar to tell her that Andrew was still the man she had known or some clue to the man he had become.

Meanwhile, Jo dragged in a wooden bathtub from the shed out back. Bustling about in a way that betrayed familiarity, Jo unerringly found the drawer that held a pad of rags with which to handle the hot kettle. She emptied in hot water from the kettle hanging in the fireplace and cooled it with a bucket of water she fetched from the well. She placed soap and cloths for bathing and drying on one of the chairs and dragged it beside the tub—all as if she had prepared baths there a hundred times.

Instead of eagerly shedding her worn and dirty clothes, the first step to washing away her old life, Phoebe studied Jo, who calmly withstood the assessment.

She gestured to the bath. "I can heat more water if you like," Jo said to Phoebe. "I'll be outside. Just call."

"What is you to him, to my—to Andrew?"

Jo did not pretend confusion or embarrassment. She appreciated that Phoebe voiced her suspicions instead of silently stewing in resentful imaginings. Any woman would have wondered the same. Few would have asked.

"I clerk in his store."

"And?" Phoebe's gaze settled on the double bed.

"You see any signs of a woman in here?" Jo asked gently. "Any needlepoint or a mislaid head scarf, a jug of flowers?"

"Y'all knowed I was coming. Maybe you took it out."

"Come with me," Jo said. She stepped through the open door and into the yard. With a gentle gesture, she motioned for Phoebe to follow. "Come on."

Bless, Jeremiah, and Esther

Willow Oaks Plantation
Kecoughtan Settlement, Elizabeth City Shire
Colony of Virginia, 1699

The couples in the quarters were recent joinings, husbands and wives separated from the partners and children of their youth. They were make-do pairings, middle-aged or old women and men who had grown that way before they joined together. They were couples who spent more time reminiscing over the past than imagining the future. They did not make promises like "keeping only unto" or "until death do us part." Thus, unencumbered by illusions of happily ever after, Jeremiah and Bless got down to the brave business of love.

In the tobacco barn, Bless traced the puckered skin of Jeremiah's scars. "All of these from running away?" she asked.

"Pick one," he said.

"What?"

"Lay your finger on any one of 'em."

Bless drew her finger over Jeremiah's left shoulder blade to the small of his back, then a three finger walk to his right buttock. The scar she landed upon was newer than the rest. The tough skin still had a hard, knotty core. It had not yet melted back into the substance of what made Jeremiah.

"That's Bennett's Creek in Isle of Wight. Gather enough duck eggs there to last you three days."

Down the back of his thigh. The next scar was thin and long, healed to a tight shine. "That's a path the wild hogs made, down in

Warwick. Leads to grove'a elms. One got the heart burned out in a lightning strike. Good place to hide hardtack and water. Too high for the pigs to reach.

On his side were permanent welts where a cat-o'-nine-tails tried to carve out his ribs in Fluvanna. Jeremiah closed his eyes as Bless's fingers moved over each welt. "Pine logs to walk 'cross Cunningham Creek when tide low," he said.

Each scar represented a landmark, a trail, a patch of moss for medicine, mushrooms safe to eat, a secret cistern where a hard-run man could drink. Puzzled together, Jeremiah's scars were a path to freedom.

"You think you'll ever make it?"

"I know we will."

Bless sat up. She rifled through their shabby pile of clothing until she found the small bag where Jeremiah kept a few coins, a seed carried from Africa to Virginia by his mother, and a small knife. She handed it to him.

"Mark it on me."

"What?"

"The map to find you. In case— Mark it on me."

Jeremiah sat up. "Bless—"

He stared at her for a long time before running his hand over the smooth skin of her thigh.

She shivered at the first cut.

Jeremiah carved Bless from hipbone to ankle. He kissed the cuts. He recited the way with blood on his lips.

• • •

Not the small pink filaments that wriggled from the soil after a hard rain. Not the bitter maggots that ruined the first bite of a windfall pear. No, Goliath worms lived up to their name. They were as long and fat as an index finger. Eyeless but horned, they hunched and pulsed as they wandered the leaves, eating the green, fibrous flesh, leeching the color. An unpracticed eye might overlook a worm, a jagged hole the only evidence of its presence. Worse, though, were the worms that lay plainly visible, covered in the wriggling white eggs of wasps.

Field hands had to pluck the worms and grind them beneath their bare heels: all day, the pulse of worms beneath their fingertips and the slick green leak of worms coating their feet. A few would almost rather take lashes. Each time Bless came across a worm, she shuddered. Gritting her teeth, she held the curling, wriggling caterpillar between thumb and forefinger. She flicked it into the dirt and stomped once before moving on to the next tobacco plant.

Esther withstood Bless's pulled face, the dainty picking, the high-pitched sounds of disgust, the glance of the foot over the insect instead of a hard, killing stomp, for as long as she could.

"Why don't you just invite them Goliaths for tea?" Esther said. She marched over. "I ain't interested in being out here all day. I ain't interested in taking a whipping on your 'count neither. Rove say he better not find one worm." She plucked three more insects from the plant Bless had just "finished" and pulped them with her bare toes. "That's exactly why can't nobody stand you," Esther said.

"I thought it was because of how I pee," Bless said dryly. "Now you tell me it's because I'm scared of worms."

By now, the knowledge of Esther's dislike did not trouble Bless. When their paths crossed, she expected a sneering look or a contemptuous laugh aimed in her direction. In that particular moment, Bless expected a scowl or an insult. She would not have been altogether shocked if she and Esther came to blows.

What she did not expect was the hatred that convulsed the slave woman's face, a passion as powerful as the fits that threw folks to the ground and caused them to foam at the mouth.

Bless stumbled back.

"It's everything about you," Esther said. "I hate *everything* about you."

Esther could not have even explained to herself why. She reckoned it had something to do with the fact that Bless had not suffered like the rest of them. Esther would bet a month's supply of rations that Bless carried no memory of jostling for a morning meal at a trough set aside for picaninnies. Raised in the "big house," Bless hadn't been able to hide her disdain for the few boards or bricks of difference that separated the slaves' shacks from the pens and sheds of the livestock. And instead of going barefoot like the rest of them, their feet grown hard as the hooves of pigs, Bless still wore the frayed slippers she arrived in.

But mostly, Esther hated her because Bless had not been cornered by the white man who had possessed Esther. Bless had not been set upon or hounded or dragged. She had walked into that cellar on her own two feet. When Mr. Jason kissed, Bless kissed back. She had been a fool, but a willing fool.

Esther, on the other hand, had trained herself to bend, to kneel, to lie down and shut up, to move, to hold still when a white man, like Rove, required. She had learned to set her feelings outside of herself until her body again became a fit dwelling place.

They were women. They were slaves. That was their lot.

What was the use of railing against it? Yes, they were owned. They went where white people said to go and came back when they called. They said "Yes, ma'am" and "No, sir," but they didn't have to mean a word of it. They ate after white folks, but they were still eating. They got up before the sun, but they were still rising. They were field hands. Their lot was worse than that of the plow horses. Yet they found ways to bear their lives.

But Bless came and, for Esther at least, what was scarcely tolerable became untenable. Esther discovered that it was only possible to live enslaved if she did not feel deserving of more.

She stepped forward into the space Bless stumbled away from, just as Rove appeared out of the bushes.

"Esther, go up front. Help prime," he said.

The women stared at each other.

"You heard me?" Rove barked.

"Yes, sir." She began to gather her things. Bless began to collect her things too—hoe, sweat rag, pail, water gourd.

"You ain't Esther," Rove said.

"No, sir, but I can't work a field alone." She spoke without think-ing and Rove slapped without warning, hard enough to dizzy Bless.

"Don't tell me what you can't do," he said. "Esther, you need help to move 'long faster?"

"No, sir," Esther said. She gathered everything in her arms. She left what fell.

"Esther," Bless called. "Esther!" She darted forward, but Rove grabbed her hair in his fist.

"Get along, Esther!" Rove ordered.

Esther did "get along." She did not want to be in earshot.

How many times over the years had she run from sounds coming from behind the smokehouse or from within a stand of trees? More than once, she had heard the scramble of footsteps or seen the flash of feet when Rove had her pinned, his arm on her throat, pressing pig-slaughter noises back into her.

As Esther fled, she tried to justify her own part in the attack. Bless was uppity. Sweet-acting. She needed to learn she wasn't better than anybody else walking the quarters. And Rove wouldn't kill her. He knew better than that. She would be all right. Esther would wager there wasn't a woman in the quarters hadn't been through it and even some of the men. Really, the girl ought to count herself lucky that Rove hadn't come for her early in the morning when she would have to go all day wearing his stink and slime. If it had to be, it was best in the evening when time would not be long before Bless could wash, before she could pick the twigs and burrs out of her hair, when she could soak the bruises and calm herself enough to whisper to Jeremiah and Cassie, "I fell."

Esther did not realize she was tear-blind until she tripped over a fieldstone. She scrambled up, empty-handed, her things left where they fell. She tore through the woods as if a black bear were chasing her.

She began to shout for Jeremiah before she cleared the trees. He came running. Through a throat clogged with snot and regret, Esther tried to tell him, but Jeremiah already knew.

All the men knew what Rove did to their mothers, to their sisters, to their wives and daughters. Rove was careful not to do it in front of them. The women were careful to hide their wounds. The men were careful not to let on that they knew. There were, of course, small vengeances—tools broken, crops destroyed, Rove's favorite dog secretly poisoned—but the satisfaction was equally small. Yet and still, they all went on. Rove not punished, the women not protected, not pitied, the men pretending that living was more important than how they lived.

Muffled assaults. Feigned blindness. What was done in the dark could not be let into the light. Because the women, the men, and Rove all knew that sometimes the only way to calm a killing rage is to kill.

Jeremiah, with a sharp-edged hoe still gripped in his hand, bolted back the way Esther had come.

Phoebe and Andrew Cabarrus

Cabarrus & Co., Crossroads
Frontier of the Colony of Virginia, 1701

Past the lean-to that housed Andrew's horse, the old costermonger cart, tools, and odds and ends like the bathtub Jo had fetched for Phoebe, a gate stood. Though nothing more than a swing gate made of pickets and hinged to two deeply buried posts, still it marked a boundary. It separated worlds. Beyond that gate, Andrew expended all the love and attention he could not give his scattered family.

The garden was the opposite of the store, the opposite of the room in which Andrew spent his mornings and nights.

Some of the things that grew in the garden—collards, corn, potatoes—were necessary. Most were not. The garden was lush with any growing thing Phoebe had ever expressed a liking for. The azalea bushes Andrew planted not long after buying the property had shed their blossoms back in April, but a few of the dry pink blooms still littered the ground. Now in June, the daylilies—some like stars, some like trumpets, some like lace—showed forth in colors flamboyant enough to make a harlot blush. In one sun-soaked patch where beans would have thrived or where prime tobacco might have taken root, Andrew had planted grapevines.

Phoebe recognized the variety instantly. Scuppernongs. The skin tough and sour, the seeds bitter, but, oh, the flesh so sweet! Even after they were married, Andrew courted Phoebe with scuppernongs, small baskets of golden-green treasure if the yield was small, wine if the vines sagged under sweet, luscious weight. On Andrew's visits, while the children slept, they'd nursed those bottles, sipping summer the whole winter long.

"For me?" Phoebe asked.

"For you all. Over there is arrowhead and sage for drawing dragonflies. He say—"

"The girls love dragonflies," Phoebe finished for her.

"Um hmm. And your boys love blueberries. A few bushes is mixed in."

Phoebe studied the garden. Yellow-winged butterflies, emerald-bodied dragonflies, and fuzz-striped bumblebees darted among the joe-pye weed and black-eyed Susan. She wanted to believe.

"But you know his house, his room," she said. "You know it too well."

"I know his heart better," Jo said. "It is hard to love a man who always got some other woman's name on his lips. 'Phoebe like this. Phoebe say that.' I clerk in his store. I am his friend. I have knowed Andrew for eight years now. Whole time, in any way that matter, he ain't been nobody's man but *yours*."

Phoebe opened her mouth in surprise. She closed it. Her face contorted around a humiliating confession. "They wouldn't let me stay his wife," she said quietly.

Jo had seen that Phoebe was a fighting woman, so she approached carefully. With a gentle hand, she raised Phoebe's chin so they looked at each other eye to eye. "I expect he know that."

"Leave me alone for a while," Phoebe said.

Jo nodded and withdrew her hand. She left through the gate, though it would have been just as easy to walk around it. As ever, she respected Andrew's invisible boundary.

• • •

Phoebe picked a path through borage and coneflowers to reach the tangle of scuppernong vines. She sifted through the leaves, each shaped like a serrated heart, to pluck a ripe fruit.

The honeyed flesh spurted into her mouth as she bit through

the tough, tart skin. A sour tang dimmed but did not obliterate the sweet. Phoebe spit out the husk. She closed her eyes to better taste what was left.

• • •

Andrew set bowls of venison stew on the table and sat across from Phoebe.

She peered into the bowls with raised brows. Bright orange cubes of yam and translucent leaves of onion dotted the thick brown broth.

"I learned how to make something 'sides chicory coffee and corn-cakes," he said.

Phoebe smiled. "You always could cook," she said. "You put on like you couldn't when you come to see me and the children, but you didn't never lose no weight when you was away from us." Her smile receded as other emotions scudded across her face. A shadow settled. Her gaze traveled the simple, sound room. "You do all right by yourself."

Andrew leaned into the light of the oil lamp so she could see him and believe him. "Nothing been right without you and the children, Phoebe. Since the day I lost y'all, I been working to get you back. Ask anybody 'round here. I work. I put all the money I make into getting y'all back."

"You ought never'a let us go," she softly charged.

"Scarborough had me 'tween a rock and a hard place, Phoebe. You see that, don't you? I suppose I thought I had time to make him see me as a man, to make him deal with me as a man. I'd done come so far. I never counted on going back. I never counted on him taking *everything*."

"I never thought he would do anything *but* take everything."

They had just been reintroduced after being apart for eight years, and there were things they would have to learn anew, but Andrew looked at Phoebe as though he did not recognize her at all.

"You never said nothing. You never pushed," he said.

"I shoulda," Phoebe said. "I mighta—I mighta if I hadn't been scared 'bout the choice you'd make."

Andrew fell back into his chair. He looked down at the bowl of stew. His stomach clenched. Even a mouthful would be rejected. But it was not the meal, the chunks of deer meat, yams, and onions that made him feel sick: Phoebe knew him, had always known him, as well as he knew himself.

His earnest gaze sprang to hers. "I told myself, when it come down to it, I would do the right thing." Again, he looked away. "But—I kept waiting. I mighta been scared of my choice too."

Phoebe also looked away. She found her gaze drawn, again, to the bed. It was neatly made, the mattress aired and in place, pillows in starched cases, rough but fresh linens tucked, and a quilt folded at the foot.

"I don't know if I can be a wife to you," Phoebe said quietly. "I don't know if I *want* to. Things happened to me while we been apart."

Their self-loathing thickened the air.

But then, from the corner of her eye, a beckoning. Phoebe swiveled toward the westward window. Andrew sighed.

The sunset blazed with several colors. There, the gilding of the scuppernong and the orange flesh of the yam, the violet blush of crushed blueberries and the emerald flash of the dragonflies their children used to chase. It was just enough.

Just enough reprieve from their confessions. Just enough beauty, just enough blessing, just enough grace to signal a greater forgiveness—for self, for others—than they on their own might be capable of. They watched until the last glint flashed and faded.

Phoebe and Andrew glanced at each other. Their gazes met. Questioned. Could Phoebe move past Andrew's selfishness? Could Andrew wait out her shame?

Hoping more than expecting, Andrew placed his hands on the table. He turned his palms upward and slid them toward Phoebe. Phoebe glanced at the bed, the window drained of beauty, Andrew's open, beseeching hands. She took a deep breath and placed her palms on the table. Her fingers clawed the wood.

"What if we can't? What if we can't get the children back?" she asked. "What if we can't get *none of it* back?"

But Andrew had learned the costs of restraint and hesitation. He would not, this time, allow either of them to retreat into fear. He reached across the table and grabbed Phoebe's hands.

Like the heartiest of vines, their fingers entwined.

Bless and Jeremiah

Willow Oaks Plantation
Kecoughtan Settlement, Elizabeth City Shire
Colony of Virginia, 1699

Rove's big bay mare had been tied in the shade where she should have been comfortable. But though no predator was in sight, the horse's eyes rolled, and her nostrils flared. She pulled against the reins, pawing, then backing until the small bush that held her ties scraped the ground. All else seemed still.

Jeremiah walked forward. Impressions of the women's feet still marked the rows. The tobacco blooms Bless and Esther had broken off withered where they had been cut and cast. A breeze blew. The agitated horse swished the long, rough hairs of her tail. The animal's ears stood forward and stiff, listening. At last, Jeremiah heard it too. Coming from ahead, from within the copse of trees, one human sound.

Nearer the grove, Jeremiah saw the broken tobacco plants, the gouged ground, the drag marks through the uprooted grass and the leaves stripped from nearby plants and bushes as someone had tried to hold on. The grating breaths grew louder. Running now, Jeremiah burst through the trees.

Rove lay face down—pants shucked to the raw skin of his thighs, the loose skin of his hips sliding forward from his flaccid buttocks—his skull broken open like a thick-hulled melon.

Bless stood over him, bloody foam on her cheeks, the hoe still locked in her hands. The pulp of Rove's brain clung to the whetted blade. She made the grating sound again.

Jeremiah's legs went out from under him. "Bless—" was all he could manage.

"He turned his back to piss," she said. "When he was done—he turned his back to piss."

As if waiting for him to rise and renew the attack, Bless did not take her gaze from Rove's corpse. She held her killing stance, feet widely planted and shoulders pressed down in the chopping motion Jeremiah himself had taught her. Her hair stood on end like a clutch of pine needles. Her blouse hung ragged from neck to waist, baring her breasts. Her skirt rode wrong—rucked up and twisted—the map-scarred thigh exposed.

"He told me to go back upfront, to go help you all chop."

Jeremiah forced himself to stand. He approached Bless cautiously, speaking softly, as if sidling up to a mare known to kick.

"I've got to hide him," he said. He eased his hand over hers. He pried her fingers off the handle. "Let me hide him."

Taking her carefully by the shoulders, Jeremiah turned Bless away from Rove's splayed body. He nudged her in the direction of the creek. "Wash the blood off. Don't come back 'til I call."

When she was gone, Jeremiah stood over Rove's body. He tried to summon some pity, at least as much as he felt for the gasping fish gutted in Miss Cassie's basin. Nothing. Rather, he saw Bless as he had found her. And he recalled how it felt to be pinned, neck staked to the ground, an iron bit tearing his mouth, and something he'd rather die than accept being forced upon him.

Jeremiah hacked a shallow hole with Bless's bloody hoe. With a kick of his foot, he thrust Rove in. He didn't even shut the bastard's eyes.

• • •

Esther hesitated at the cookhouse door. Cassie sat inside, in reach of the fire, close enough to stir the pots without having to rise. Within the hearth, the fire crackled like twigs breaking underfoot. The pots bubbled enough to gently clatter the lids, and the steam seasoned the air with the smells of pork and rosemary.

Sweat beaded on Cassie's temples and dampened the edges of her headwrap. She held a bowl of summer peas on her lap, the pods lay discarded on the floor. Later, one of the kitchen girls would sweep up the pile and scatter the crisp green sleeves for the chickens. But now, no one fussed about. Cassie worked methodically: thumbnail down the delicate seam of the pod; index finger to swipe the peas into the bowl, the soft, round fall. Esther wished life were kind enough to allow Cassie the enjoyment of such a simple task.

"Miss Cassie—Bless," she said. "You ought to come."

The bowl surged upward. "What happened?"

"Rove," Esther said.

Cassie did not have to be told the story. She had endured it. And she had known since the day Bless was born, a girl and black, that she would too.

Peas squashed beneath her bare soles, slowing her, gumming her steps as she heaved toward Esther. "Where she? Take me to her."

• • •

Jeremiah waded into the creek. Bless stood in the water, arms akimbo, staring back the way she had come.

Jeremiah stooped. He cupped the water and rose to let it fall over Bless until she dripped from braids to feet. But when he reached to touch her, to rub away the sticky blood and dirt, she shied. The hysteria, so slightly contained, brimmed.

"Shh, shh," he said, releasing her, holding up his hands so she could see he would not touch her if she did not want to be touched. "I know."

Not idle words. Bless trusted the inflection of his voice and her own fingertip memory of his scars.

She allowed Jeremiah to wash her.

Instead of sinking under the surface, she gave him her hand.

She let him lead her from the water.

• • •

Jeremiah met Cassie and Esther coming from the direction of the big house, hurrying toward the cabin. "They gon' come looking for you?" Jeremiah asked Cassie even as he felt the relief of not having to go fetch her.

"Sent a girl to tell 'em I took sick. Dinner 'bout done. They don't need me. Where she?" Cassie asked.

"In the cabin."

"Where Rove?" Cassie asked.

"Back in the grove," Jeremiah answered.

Cassie looked him over quickly. No bruises. None but the regular harms. "Hurt or dead?"

She did not know which to hope for.

"Buried," he said. "Esther, go get some of them men. You know which ones. Tell 'em hide that horse."

"You know they not gon' want to—" Esther began.

"I just need a few hours," Jeremiah said.

Esther nodded. She looked from Jeremiah to Miss Cassie. "Way she carried herself, I believed she thought she was better'n us—"

"We ain't got time for this, Esther," Jeremiah said. "Mend what you can by getting me a head start."

Esther hesitated as she turned to go. "Please," she said, "please don't let 'em catch you."

More than freedom or unjust punishment were at stake. Slaves who killed whites did not die easy. They all knew of the Negro woman burned at the stake; the man roasted alive with bellows; a newly arrived African dragged behind a horse until anything human was scourged away. Punishments served as warnings.

Jeremiah smiled grimly. "All them other times I run was just practice."

• • •

Bless was prodded from the safety of her stupor by the wet itch of her clothes, a crawling on her skin as Rove's dampened blood dripped and dried again, and the voices of Jeremiah and Cassie hashing a plan as they hastily filled an oilskin sack with food from the safe.

"Say I got jealous over Bless and Rove. Say I killed him and beat her. That's how come she all hurt up. They got a nigger who run, Bless's reputation, and a dead white man. That's all the proof they need." A bleak joke. Cassie gave him a killing look.

"This ain't funny, Jeremiah. If they catch you—"

"My whole life been coming to this," Jeremiah said. "Since they took me from my mama, I knowed I was gon' end up just like this. What I'm supposed to do but laugh?"

"We could tell the truth," Bless said.

Kneeling by the safe in the floor, they both stopped to look up at her. Miss Cassie began to struggle up from her knees, but Jeremiah stayed her. He went instead.

He knelt in front of Bless, his smile gentle and sad with a familiar bewilderment. "I ain't taught you nothing? Hm? Don't tell me you the same kinda fool you was when you come here."

"I can tell them what Rove did—"

"They know what Rove do! Listen to me. They gon' want to kill for this. A white man dead. Don't matter that he was low and mean. Don't matter to nobody but us what he done."

"Not much time, Jeremiah. We don't know how long they can keep that horse hid, and once it show up without Rove, they gon' start lookin' for him," Cassie said softly.

Jeremiah ran a careful hand over Bless's hair, down her cheek and jaw, then he began to rise. She grabbed him by the forearms. "You said I could go with you."

He shook his head. "Not like this. Ain't but one way for both of us to come out of this alive, Bless." Jeremiah tried again to rise, to pull free from her grasp, but Bless held on.

In her hands he felt the force that had opened Rove's head like a shucked oyster. He knew if he led guilt and punishment away from her, Bless had the strength to live beyond this.

"Recite me the way," he said. A moment of bafflement passed over Bless's face. He nodded toward her thigh. "Recite me the way."

She did. Every cairn. Every hillock. Every crossing to be made on foot, flatboat, or by canoe. Every hole where she might find a bit of hardtack or a palmful of water. Every path that led to refuge in the Great Dismal Swamp.

Her hands loosened then tightened again. "Swear I'll find you there," she said. "Swear."

So it happened: the parting more solemn than the marriage vow, just as sorrow is more faithful than joy.

"I swear," Jeremiah pledged.

"Jeremiah!" Miss Cassie urged as she yanked closed the strings on the bag of potatoes and dried fish and took the blanket from her bed.

Bless let go. Jeremiah stood. At the back door, Cassie pushed the supplies into his hands.

"Go on now," she said, pushing him out the door. "Keep your promise. Be somewhere she can find you." Jeremiah held Cassie's hands. He leaned in to peck her cheek.

"I am grateful, Miss Cassie," Jeremiah said.

He stopped once at the sink where they had scaled the fish. He looked back and smiled.

Then he was gone.

• • •

Jeremiah had been rightly named. His words were prophetic. The story fit all the white folks believed of Negroes. Bless's punishment: twenty lashes, well laid on, for the crime of being a "strumpet" and a "temptress." Since Rove was not available, Master Benjamin executed the sentence himself; likewise, he came in person to deliver the killing blow.

Still dressed in bloodied shirtsleeves, he entered Cassie's cabin without knocking. She sat by the hearth, the farthest point away from the brutality on the other side of her door. She studied her owner from the chair Jeremiah had built for her. Pegged and lashed together though it was, the chair was oversized and as elaborately carved as a throne.

"I ordered everyone out to the whipping," Master Benjamin said.

Cassie drew herself straight. With that motion, something between them reversed or righted itself. The "savage" became the observer, the one seeking a clue to some barbarian tongue. Cassie angled forward as if seeing Master Benjamin better would help her understand. Surely, he had not believed she would stand witness to the flogging of her child.

Her incredulity seemed to unnerve him. His gaze slid from hers to dart around the humble room. "I will not punish you," he said when he returned to her scrutiny. "I've found little fault in you up 'til now. But you'll not make a habit of disobeying."

Cassie laughed. Could she have stopped the sound, she would have used the same power to stop her breath, thwart her heartbeat. "You think that's a kindness?"

Benjamin took two steps toward her. "Mind your tongue. You mind your tongue, you old bitch, or I'll make you cry mercy."

"That's all I been doing." Cassie stood. Humility fell away. She met him eye to eye. "Ain't none in you."

The anticipated blow—a backhand across the face, a fist to the head—did not come as she expected.

Master Benjamin said, "I am selling her out of the district. Never to set foot in it again. The men will bring her to you. Make her fit to travel."

"What I got to do?"

"Begging on your knees won't save her this time."

"No. What I got to do to make you see *me*—what I got to do?"

The question caught him by surprise.

He did peer closer then, first at her scarred hands. Though held up helplessly, they were still nimble and clever. Her skin, no longer youthful but fine like smoothly grained wood. The long frown lines carved into either side of her mouth made her face almost manly in suffering.

But then Benjamin's attention shifted to the grease-stained head rag. From there, he sniffed her perpetual smell of bacon, coffee, and smoke. Kitchen smells. And so, he pictured Cassie with a plate of biscuits in her hands and her large breasts brushing the table as she set his meal before him, and she was what she had been.

It lasted barely a moment, but Cassie saw the cloudy cataract of distortion, the lens through which her master viewed her, clear. He looked *right* at her. And then she saw it darken again.

Master Benjamin stepped back.

"Make her fit for travel," he repeated.

He left Cassie there, the door wide open, the house emptied. She dropped into the homemade chair. As it absorbed such a weight, the humble seat shuddered, but it did not give way.

David

Edwyn Hawley's Plantation, Lynnhaven River
Princess Anne County, 1695

David ran as fast as his injuries would allow, but by the time he made it from Cecil's cabin in the quarters to the long path in front of Hawley's house, slaves who had known Celeste all her life were wiping away tears and lumbering back to their chores. The wagon, with its goods and the sunshine that was Celeste, was gone.

David was gutted. In that moment, he knew with certainty that Andrew Cabarrus was dead. Perhaps Phoebe too. No one could survive this anguish several times over. David himself might not survive it once.

He returned to Cecil's door more broken than he'd been the day Hawley beat him.

Cecil poured the boy half a finger of rum. He filled his own little cup to the brim. He drained it and filled it again.

"Sip it," he told David, but the boy tossed it back. Even as he choked down the burning liquor, David held out his cup for more.

"She might have a baby," David said.

"I figured. You will wonder about 'em 'til you die."

David looked into the sad eyes of the old man. He looked around the cabin. He saw his future. One set of clothes hanging from the peg. A pot only big enough to hold victuals for one. One pair of shoes by the door. No signs of women or children or joy.

David asked, "If it's always gon' to be like this, why go on?"

Cecil needed to think about his answer, so he took his time pouring more rum into the old gourd cups. This was no idle question but a decision in the making.

"What if it ain't?" Cecil asked.

"Huh?"

"What if it ain't always gon' be like this? What if you live long enough to get back one thing they took from you? One thing. Ain't that worth holding out for?"

"Is that what you doing? Holding out to get one thing back?"

Cecil sipped his drink and nodded. "Indeed I am. And sometime, a friend like yourself come 'long, and the wait ain't so lonesome."

· · ·

But David decided, no matter how desolate his life, there would be no second gutting for him. After Celeste and the question of their child, he kept most people at arm's length. He lived on the fringes of friendships, and families and love affairs that he yearned to belong to. He shut up his heart. David almost never revealed the bulk, the accumulation, the weight of his stored-up and thwarted love. Girls he kissed spoke of his smothering embrace and the tears that shone in his eyes after a caress, and strangest of all, the way he pulled out or pushed away and finished himself against the soft meat of their thighs or the warmth of their bellies but never inside them where a great aching loss lived.

When their whispers made their way back to David, he stopped "courting" all together. He waited, instead, for the cover of darkness, for the infrequent times when he was all alone, and serviced his own needs.

When Hawley sold David to a man more brutal than himself, David withstood both the beatings and the yearning for a woman's touch. He refused to let anyone get too close.

Three years later, when he was sold, a solitary man-of-all-work to Jack Crewe, the lonesomeness of Crewe's was almost a relief. There, David, just like Cecil, began the long, aching wait for one thing that might return to him—even if it was only a friend.

Cassie and Bless

Willow Oaks Plantation
Kecoughtan Settlement, Elizabeth City Shire
Colony of Virginia, 1699

The woods and paths and lanes that had been loud with the shriek of the whip and Bless's shouts of pain, with the barking of men and the baying of dogs, with the whispers of all that had come to pass, quieted as the search for Jeremiah spread outward and elsewhere. The cabins were all but silent. Anyone could be swept up in the aftermath of Rove's killing. It was best for Black bodies to huddle inside, away from the speculation, suspicion, and anger of the men who hunted Jeremiah.

Though her back and torso were wrapped in bandages and pain felt like fire in the furrows of her skin, Bless had risen from the bed. She knelt with her head on Cassie's lap. Her mother stroked her face and the soft wool of her hair.

"I'll come back," Bless promised.

"Don't never come back," Cassie said.

"We'll go to him. I've got the map marked on me."

Cassie lifted Bless's chin so her meaning would not be mistaken. "If you get the chance, you go to Jeremiah, but don't never come back here. Won't be nothing left of me you can carry 'way with you."

Bless's face began to crumple. "Stop that," Cassie ordered. "We gon' let them see how hurt we is?"

"No, ma'am," Bless said. "No, Mama."

Cassie sighed the kind of relief that escaped when she set her feet in a pan of warm water at the end of a grueling day.

"I'll tell you something," Cassie said.

"What?" Bless murmured.

"All them years, I had to hate you just a little bit."

"Why?" Bless asked softly.

"Only way to survive it."

Bless studied her, memorized her.

"You understand I'm sorry?"

"Yes, Mama."

"All right then." Cassie allowed Bless to rest her head again.

They remained that way as they waited for Master Benjamin and the slave trader.

Like breath and blood, fear and courage flowed between mother and daughter as if the womb cord had never been severed, as if it never would be.

• • •

It was not their ancestral land, nor their promised land, but they could live unchained. That made every hummock and scarp dear. They lived among the thin places, where the ground protruded high enough to create dry space, where white cypress left room for the people to spread. In that sequestered space, they worshipped, gossiped, governed, and disciplined. They rebuilt whole lives—constructed communities—out of the counsel and potsherds and broken arrowheads of the Nansemond who peopled the land before them, alongside them. They wasted nothing. They found a use for everything that came to hand, a place for everyone who came in peace.

And so, they welcomed Jeremiah, celebrated his arrival, not only because, hallelujah, he made it to freedom, but because they had loved, lost, birthed, and buried sons just like him. Jeremiah lived among them, the maroons, learning to build, to hunt, to hide. To become the stuff of rumor and shifting shadow at the sounding of a whistle or the landing of a footfall that did not belong.

Jeremiah lived. But all the while, he searched the face of every newcomer. Sometimes he knew straight off—the skin too light, the stance pigeon-toed. But sometimes he was fooled by the angle of a chin, the filtering of light, the faithfulness of love.

• • •

The breeze that reached the quarters smelled like a whole week of Christmas: sweet potato pie and spiced pudding, sweetness and sorrow whipped and simmered together until just about everybody on the place was crying with hunger.

Cassie dressed the dining room table herself, placed every dish with her own hands. She artfully fanned slices of ham around bowls of peanut soup. She arranged nut cake and bourbon balls on a crystal dish. She poured wassail punch into goblets then set them, like jewels among greenery, on the sideboard.

She filled the table, laid it out like a feast, then tainted every morsel by hanging herself from the beam that ran right above her master's table.

She used her own apron as the noose. It was, folks said, the most vengeful surrender anyone had ever seen. Cassie blighted every mouthful. She denied her masters, for all the days they lived, the relish of a good meal. Every whiff of what they craved, every bite and every sip, would serve them the bile that had been her daily bread. Forever and ever, amen.

The slaves refused to cut her down. Threats of whipping could not make them. When Master Benjamin tried to force them across the threshold, they held up the charms they wore on strings around their necks and backed away. He cursed them and searched for two days until he found whites poor enough to do it. For two days, Cassie hung there, death-smoking the porcelain dishes and bone china cups, the pretty clay pots, the plaster walls, and the oxblood floors.

The gentry were so astonished at the "impudence of that nigger wench," that they mostly left the Negroes to their woe. Except, out of meanness, they denied them the body. Cassie was not laid to rest in the small burial ground that lay among the juneberries. No one in the quarters knew where they took her—a ditch? A dung heap somewhere, most likely.

No matter. The slaves did not need a body, not Cassie's nor their own, to mourn. Anyhow, they reckoned a human form too fragile a thing for pure sorrow. It could not moan low enough; it could not keen high enough. *Sassandra*, *Anum*, *Pendjari*. Flesh is too shallow a vessel for a river's worth of tears.

Instead, they used Sincere's fiddle.

The music started somewhere deep, like their misery, then twined and took a turn on those strings and lifted up to something like joy, but not joy because it came at too high a cost.

Still, there was something jubilant in that sound.

PART
TWO

David, Jack Crewe, and Bless

David worked alongside his master, Jack Crewe. Bare shoulder to bare shoulder, the two men dripped sweat as they worked to split rails for fencing. The sun shone on them equally as each man worked the turning and hefting of an iron-forged ax so it bit precisely into wood positioned on the block. The sun shone on Jack's back, draped like a burning cloak over his shoulder and folding into the creases of muscle and skin at his waist. The sprinkling of moles Jack had inherited from his milk-pale mother pinkened, then browned and almost disappeared into his darkening skin.

Equally, the sun spilled over David's skin, the brilliance emphasizing the ridges of his scars, pulling Jack's gaze to the puckered places, to the various shades created by the cutting and gouging of whips. Jack put scars like that on Adam. As his gaze swept over David's mangled back, Jack reassured himself that whippings were a duty, a responsibility, of his station.

Jack had only dared to question the necessity of whipping once while Thomas Crewe lived, a question to which Crewe had responded, "How do *you* propose we bring them to heel, Jack?"

As he had waited for Jack's response, Crewe studied the boy. Jack felt himself being turned and measured the same way Crewe considered merchandise in the stalls and pens of the Norfolk market. Thomas Crewe assessed Jack's potential for yield and whether or not the boy was worth the investment.

"I spoke out of turn, sir. Out of ignorance," Jack had said, swallowing his objections like a gritty wad of spit.

"Indeed," Crewe said, nodding. "Sometimes I forget your inferior blood, Jack. The best thing your father did for you was to die and leave your raising to me. I don't know if it is possible to overcome both the blood and the twelve years of ill-raising, but I intend to try. You should be grateful you've fallen into my hands."

Jack felt his face redden like a sunburn. He looked down. He saw the good shoes on his feet. All leather. No rag-stuffed holes. Room to grow.

"Yes, sir," Jack mumbled. With the evidence before his eyes, what could he do but agree?

Still, a kind of sympathetic pain stirred in Jack as he watched scars ripple and stretch with every movement of David's shoulders and back. Jack grew certain of the plan he was about to propose.

"You have landed well here with me, David," Jack said. "You could have done a lot worse." He tipped his head to indicate the geography of scars on David's back. "You have done."

"I suppose, sir," David said. He reached for another piece of wood, positioned it on the block, and swung the ax. Usually when he worked with Jack, they were silent, sharing only words and gestures necessary to complete the job. David preferred that.

"What I mean to say is you are an uncommon Negro. Them that owned you before didn't see that."

David grunted to show that he listened. He reached for another piece of wood. Though he appeared unconcerned, he listened not just to the words but for the raising and lowering of pitch, the hardening or softening of intonation. Any inflection could be a clue. David was unsure where this line of talk would lead. He knew, however, that it would cost him something. Only, he could not imagine what he had left for anyone to take.

"I have given you every opportunity since you came to this farm," Jack said. "You've been beside me when I shaped every brick and dug every posthole since my father died. I got you trained as a blacksmith, and now the traders don't leave without carrying off your ironwork.

I am as good to you as I know how to be, and I don't punish you no more than I have to make you do right. Ain't that so?"

The sinews of David's abdomen tautened and rippled as he brought the ax overhead. Deeper within, the very tissue of his guts clenched. What could Jack want that required such a pitch? What did David still have within his power that he could deny Jack? He tried to keep his voice as steady as his swing. "I reckon so, sir."

"What I am asking in return, Cuddy and Archie"—Jack referred to his matched pair of oxen—"would give for a bucket of oats."

David stopped. He rested the head of the heavy ax on the ground between his feet and allowed the upturned handle to bear his body-weight. The pose looked like casual interest. In fact, David needed that tool for support.

"What you asking me to 'give,' sir?"

"Issue," Jack said.

Jack had been conceiving this plan for a while now, even before the death of his adoptive father. In fact, Thomas Crewe himself had unknowingly started the transition by collecting his fees in sterling *and* barter. When a coffle passed their way, Thomas offered corn mush and a safe place to pass the night on the dangerous road for the slavedrivers and their charges in return for the labor to clear more land for crops that sometimes flourished but too often failed. When his luck held, a planting left Thomas no worse off than he had been before. But sometimes there was debt.

Before the old man died, Thomas had to sell off each of the handful of slaves he had managed to acquire, never hanging on to any of them for long. As he watched his adoptive father's struggle, Jack realized that—for men of a certain luck—the profit in crops was thin and hard won. There were too many variables: rot and drought, horn and bud worms, crickets and mice, plagues that withered or drowned the roots, carried off the seed, or sucked the sap. In the years since Thomas and Mary Crewe had died, leaving their land to Jack, and even before, what kept the farm in roof and meat was not the crops they grew but the slaves they jailed, fed, and watered.

Jack had slowly seen the sense in turning the farm into a way station. For even as their own crops failed, Jack knew that men with better land and better luck would always need slaves. The western frontier of Virginia opened as hunting grounds were pried and swindled from the Choktaw, the Chickasaw, and the Cherokee. At the same time, slavery had become more than a convenience, no longer an emerging or temporary solution to the demand for cheap labor. In the minds and hearts of many white men, it became the only solution. One by one, they blocked any existing paths—conversion to Christianity, common-law birthright, manumission—to freedom. But as the circumstances hardened, so it seemed, did the will of would-be slaves.

Nothing brought a determined African to heel. Terrified as they were, they would not come along quietly. In the coastal dungeons along the Bight of Benin, they raised insurrections. Aboard ships they staged mutinies. Slavers found that murdering a few was not an always reliable control over the many. Some captives ran toward the onslaught of bullets, sacrificing themselves for others. Among the survivors were those as stalwart, in their way, as the warriors. They died by leaps into the sea, by swallows of gunpowder, by starvation.

In the New World, some colonies sidestepped the contradictions and dangers of trans-Atlantic slavery by ending the importation of Africans. Virginia levied a penalty of one thousand pounds for every illegally imported slave. More than guilt guided the votes of the Virginia Assembly: In Charles Town, Kongo-born captives, fleeing to Spanish Florida, raised a blood-red *Liberty* banner and killed thirty plantation owners and shopkeepers on their brazen march. On Manhattan Island, African slaves pitched hot coals into the governor's house, into cow stables and barns, warehouses and even churches. From New Hampshire to South Carolina, white men decried the importation of "rebellious Africans."

Jack Dane Crewe was as astute as his adoptive father: In a time when opportunity and fear filled the air, he realized the slaves white men needed would have to come from within the country.

Presently, Crewe's Way Station catered to anyone buying, selling, or transporting slaves overland. The way station provided beds for the traders, pens for their merchandise, and hot meals of some kind for all. By the time Thomas died, he and Jack had one slave pen in regular use, and they had begun digging post holes for a second. The traders' cabin boasted rail beds and hard floors and could sleep six. More would have fit, but Jack prided himself on not "packing working men in like niggers."

As the business grew—providing not just a place for slave traders to sleep but everything from Negro cloth to shackles—so did Jack's vision. Without his father around to shoulder half the work, Jack bought David—a generation removed from old Kalabaris like Shango and Adam. David had been born into slavery; within him, there was no memory of freedom. The Negro learned fast, took instruction well, and followed orders. On the day Jack caught himself desiring three or four Davids in his service, the idea was born. He supplied everything else, why not the perfect Negro, not just bred strong but raised right? Negroes cured from the outset of the notion that God had made them to work out their own destinies. With David as the rootstock, Jack would rear Negroes to serve, a people who knew their place in this New World, who were groomed to dwell in that place with the same ease Jack had come to dwell in his own.

"I want to make something of you, David," Jack said, "I want to make something of your children."

David knew very well what had been made of him, what Jack wanted to make of David's children: commodities, movable goods, animated tools that could take instruction and punishment.

"How many times you been sold, David?"

"A few, sir."

"What if I promise you no more? You can get to be an old man here. Together, we will create something new. Your children will not suffer the way you have suffered, because from the beginning we will raise them right, teach them their place.

"I never told you about Adam, the first Negro I ever whipped. He was my friend, and I sure did not want to do it, but Daddy Thomas made me. You got no idea how hard it was for me to raise that whip, and afterward me and Adam wasn't friends no more. After 'while I come to realize that we never was. Adam didn't know his place, and I didn't know mine. Well, he kept running off, and I kept whipping. Daddy Thomas sold Adam eventually. He probably perished down South in the indigo fields. Point is, all that suffering, his and mine, could have been avoided if Adam had been trained to his place.

"You're a damn-near perfect Negro, David. You do your work. You don't cause no more trouble than what's to be expected from your kind. And there is still something of a man in you.

"I am offering you the best deal you will ever get. I am offering to find you a wife, somebody your equal, and settle y'all here. Y'all work and build a family, all the young ones you can get on her. Raise them right from the beginning so they will suffer less in this world."

Jack talked on, but it had been some moments since David could hear. The faint breeze circling in the grass and brushing over his back had stopped his ears. David glanced at the sky, the trees in the distance, down at the earth beneath his feet. He squeezed the wooden handle in his grip just to feel, to test: Did the world still make sense?

David spoke slowly to better control the strange words forming on his tongue. "You want to *breed* me, sir?"

Jack startled.

His expectations of Negro intelligence had been dulled by years of listening to Thomas Crewe talk of Negro inferiority, by the cruel and careless power that forced men like David to wear the dumb mask of assent. But how precisely, how astutely, David summed up the plan.

Jack cleared his throat. "That is one way to look at it, David. A better way is to say I want to establish this place as a supplier of some of the best Negro servants in the colony. You will be my rootstock, David. You will be my cornerstone. For a man in your position, don't you think that ought to be enough to satisfy?"

David thought of how far he had been driven from anything approaching satisfaction. When was the last time he had been deeply satisfied? As far back as when he lived in a ramshackle cabin and slept wedged in between little brothers and sisters, a sleep swaddled in the murmur of Phoebe and Andrew's voices? Or was it in more recent years when he sat secreted beneath the spreading branches of a magnolia with Celeste? Would he ever feel peace like that again?

David shifted the ax. He raised it high and slammed it into the stump. It bit dead center, heartwood.

He wanted what Phoebe and Andrew wanted for their children—for him. A sound roof above and a solid floor beneath. Work hard enough to foster pride. Enough decent food in his children's bellies that they could romp hard all day and sleep soundly through the night. David wanted to live peaceably on his father's land, among his own people and anyone else who wanted to be welcomed and decent.

Unobtained by his mother and father in the New World, David's desire was already a generation deferred. Indeed, it was ancient: He wanted loved ones within reach. He wanted a family to keep.

But as David stood there, he toted up what he had to show for all his parents' striving: a scattered family, perhaps a child somewhere out there in the world, a scarred back, a name he could not use.

Jack's heinous offer looked to be the closest to *satisfaction* that David would ever get.

"Ain't it?" Jack prompted, jarring David from his thoughts. "Ain't that enough?"

"I suppose it will have to be, won't it, sir?" David reached for another piece of wood, positioned it on the block, and split it precisely in two.

Jack marveled at the indifference. He had expected what? Excitement? Gratitude? But Negroes, he had learned, could be a gloomy lot.

Jack went back to splitting rails, making the chips fly as he planned his future, each drop of sweat a coin in the purse. He hardly noticed when David fetched his shirt and shrugged it on: All the young man could do to cover his shame.

• • •

David moved among the nearly naked shackled slaves without meeting their dulled gazes. He balanced gourds of water corded from a beam on his shoulders. He handed them porridge on corn husks. Through tight lips, he sipped air rather than breathe in the stench that hung about them like a cloud of gnats. Some of the captives wore shirts and trousers. Some wore blouses and skirts with petticoats. But others were shirtless or wore no pants, grown men and women wearing long shirts, like children, with little underneath. Almost all were shoeless, their feet swollen to blunt clubs. Road filth and worse caked their legs. Their uncombed hair spiked like cockleburs. Crusts of sores dotted their arms and faces. Though he was fully clothed and wore only the grime of that day upon him, David felt their shame.

Jack and the slave trader talked nearby as David handed out the grub. The white men stood with their hands on their hips and legs braced. They pointed, nodded, and gestured, mulling and assessing the humans enclosed behind the bars.

"What do you think of that one?" the trader asked.

Jack tried for nonchalance. He had already noticed the girl, but to let on interest was to cause an immediate increase in her price. She was just what he was looking for. Aged somewhere between sixteen and twenty. A body as straight and sturdy as a loblolly pine. Unlike the rest of the gang, she wore shoes and what had once been decent clothes. Through her blouse, he could see the work-broadened shoulders and muscled back of a field hand, but her manners—even the way she lipped cornmeal mush off a husk—were refined compared to the "stock" around her. The trader confirmed the difference in her, not because he wanted to but because it was obvious. "Only one mark against her: she can read," he said.

"Is that so?"

"Brought up in the main house, and you know how some people ruin their niggers."

"Why was she sold?"

"Stirred up some trouble among the men."

"Cross the water in Kecoughtan? Caused that overseer to get killed?" Jack asked. The story had escaped just like that enslaved young man.

The trader sighed. Apparently, gossip traveled faster than horses. "That's her."

"They ever find that buck?"

"Not yet. Advertising him. Dead or alive."

Quite the opposite from hiking the asking price, the trader now knew he had to lower it. He was furious with himself for mentioning the girl's past to the one potential buyer who had not yet figured out her identity. Everywhere else he'd been, even the vast farmlands of Nansemond Shire, something had told on the girl, her speech or gestures, the clothes she wore. And though the story had reached this small corner of Princess Anne County before the slave stringer, John Jeffrey, and his gang, Jack had not yet put two and two together. Jeffrey should have kept his mouth shut. Trying to sell a slave tied up with a killing was like trying to sell a dead horse. Still, he'd noticed Jack Crewe had not taken his eyes off the girl.

Thomas Crewe had trained his son well. Jack recognized quality when he saw it. But now that he knew who she was, he had reservations. He wanted a breed of intelligent, strong Negroes, but he wanted their fierceness to be manageable. Still, the girl herself had not done the killing, and her association with violence against a white man surely meant a discount.

"I'll have a closer look," Jack said coolly.

He examined her there in the open, a few steps away from the other captives. The men made one concession to modesty: they allowed her to shield the apex of her thighs with her skirts. All else was on display. The trader stood nearby to ensure his merchandise would not be damaged, to point out selling points Jack might not see, to explain away any flaws.

The girl stood 5'3" and solid. Did Jack see the muscle cutting from calf and knee, ending in the hams that were her thighs? The scars on her leg? Some African witchery. Nothing that mattered here. Look at the width of those hips and the spread of her buttocks. Sure to be an excellent breeder. Look at the dugs on her! She could nurse a tribe of picaninnies! The scars on her back? Surely, Jack didn't expect she got off scot-free after the commotion she'd caused?

Beyond the salesman's patter and the sturdiness of the girl's limbs, as important as the vigorous muscles that played beneath the skin of her arms and shoulders, it was the glint in her eyes—like the shine off a blade or gun barrel—that convinced him. "The ones you want have fight in them." It was the abhorrence, the speckle of loathing, that would keep her alive.

The girl snatched on her clothes as Jack and John walked away from the slave pen. Their talk was lively with the gestures and intonations of negotiation. Four hundred pounds. Four fifty! Four twenty-five. She stared straight ahead as she buttoned and tied, refusing to look down though she had just been inspected like horseflesh.

Each time, it was like this. Each time, she refused to show her shame. She had passed through the hands of three traders. She stood on blocks of stone, on stools and small hills, bared, prodded, and cuffed, ordered to turn, to jump, to squat, while an auctioneer's patter called her "very lusty" and signified her "comely face" to drive up the price.

The price: front hall chairs, pier glass and table silver, barrels of herring, nets, quilted petticoats and night caps, horse collars and andirons, fire shovels and tongs, brass pans and bedsteads, two pails and brewing vessels, chests of linens, malt and a malt mill, kegs of beer and kegs of rum, looking glasses and a spice press, pounds of lead, pestles, trenchers, earthenware bowls, feather beds, leather, lumber, pease, bees, scales and weights, tea. Broad hoes and hilling hoes, dibbles, baskets and butcher knives, hemp, flax, straw hats, vests, a whetstone, a bastard file, rakes, a shovel plow, flax breaks and pitsaws: everything bartered and bought with Bless's body and soul.

David walked over to the bars of the pen. "Th-There's more mush," he said offering a small balm to distract her from the shame she must feel.

She lacerated him with enough anger to flay his hide off the bone. "You go to hell," she answered.

• • •

Before the coffle of slaves shuffled off the next morning, the deal was struck. Jack called David over. In a perversion of romance, Jack requested of John Jeffrey, "Let him do it."

"Do what?"

"Unlatch her."

Jeffrey shook his head in surprise, but it was far from the most eccentric request ever made by a buyer. Checking first for his pistol, the stringer handed David the key to the shackles that bound Bless.

"There you go," Jack said. "David, this is Bless, your wife."

•   •   •

The bride and groom stood nervously. Bless's gaze darted about, looking in the direction from which her coffle had come, forward toward the distance into which they had marched. Her gaze flickered over the main house, the outbuildings and corral, and settled on the lone slave cabin. She looked frightened, as any woman discarded in the hands of two strange men should be. She looked trapped. David knew she would run if she could only fathom a safe direction.

"Over there," Jack directed them to the lee of a scraggle of bushes. He had fetched a few things, ribbons and baubles that had belonged to Miss Mary before her death, and flung them over the bushes for decoration. Jack's idea of festive. It looked to Bless like a scattering of a magpie's shabby, stolen treasures. Unwillingly, Bless recalled the cloth delivered for Miss Rebecca and Mr. Jason's wedding. Colorful, silky yards to be tied into bows and intricate flowers, festooning for the pews and altar.

"One more thing," Jack said, and the colors in her mind faded. He went off toward the barn.

David shut his eyes and pretended to be standing with Celeste beneath the branches of their magnolia. No need to decorate. White blossoms with their yellow-seeded centers bloomed round about. Sunshine glinted off the glossy green leaves and warmed the petals so they surrendered the slightest hint of lemon. Celeste wore one blossom tucked behind her ear. Yellow pollen scattered over her cheeks.

"All right. That will do it," Jack said when he'd returned with a broom and arranged all to his liking.

The broom handle smacked, heavy and staccato, against the hardpacked dirt. Like being awakened by a slap, David opened startled eyes onto Bless. In her widened pupils, he saw despair. On her skin and in the rips and tatters of her clothing, she wore all that she had suffered. Celeste, wherever she stood, suffered the same. Likely, she had been forced to marry. Certainly, she had been forced to mate. David felt the heat of hatred burning him up. He wondered if Bless felt it wafting off his skin. She absolutely saw it in his eyes. She took a step away.

"Stand here," Jack said.

David positioned himself shoulder to shoulder with Bless on one side of the broom. Jack stood across from them.

Jack spoke first of the favor he conferred upon them. Neither David nor Bless would suffer the trials of an "abroad" marriage where, to see each other, they would have to walk miles between farms on Saturday afternoon and return by Sunday nightfall, and then only if each master granted permission. Phoebe and Andrew had shared such a marriage. David imagined the love that had kept his father coming back.

On the Saturday afternoons when Andrew had promised to return, Phoebe would scan the tobacco rows and fields emptied of workers for the sight of one man. Even when she seemed absorbed in the washing or the children, she looked up at each rustle or snap as she listened for footfalls. Somehow though, Andrew always seemed to catch her unaware, wrapping her in his arms from behind, once singing her name from high in a tree. And when she caught sight of him! Phoebe seemed to grow straighter and unburdened—the way she did when she lifted a bucket of water or a load of laundry from its careful perch upon her head. David, too, would walk miles, crawl them, to give Celeste that feeling.

Discomfort simmered beneath the heavy, hot folds of Bless's filthy clothes. She wore the dress she had walked miles in, slept in, the dress she hitched high when she had a chance to squat and do her business. The dress that clung to her wet legs when she had to do her business walking. The soil of the road and the soil of all the hands that handled her in the last days and weeks remained on her skin. *My tail is itching!* she thought. Hilarity bubbled up in her. This was her wedding day! Her wedding day, and all she could think of was her stinking, itchy tail!

David glanced at her. Her face creased in laughter. "You all right?"

Bless tried to force herself back to the stoic control that had protected her from one degradation after another in the last few weeks. "We gon' let them see how hurt we is?" She focused on the mildewed doilies scattered on the bushes. She bit her lips hoping the pain would keep her crazy laugh from spewing forth.

"Hold on," David said, raising a palm to Jack. "You want me to get you anything?" David asked. She shook her head quickly, as much in warning as refusal, but it was too late. One small show of concern, and her stifled hysteria spurted forth as tears.

As David watched her lose the fight for control, his own anger dimmed. He grabbed her hands. He understood. In the sense that they had just met, they were strangers. In the grief and shame of enslavement, they were not. *Hold on* said the clutch of his hands. They would survive this together.

"She's happy," Jack said. "You've never seen a woman cry on her wedding day?"

On the day she wed Jeremiah, Bless had not shed a single tear. How could she do this? How could she become a wife to this man when she did not know whether Jeremiah was alive or dead? How could she do this when she wore the promises of *their* marriage etched into her body? That marriage, while not sanctioned by a minister or written down in any book but memory, had been real. This was mockery. No different from when children played "minister" and wed together their dolls or the dog and cat.

"This is a new life for y'all," Jack said. He motioned to the broom he used for dragging down cobwebs, for cleaning stalls and gathering up scraps of hay. "Sweeping away the old. Today, by jumping this broom, you, David, and you, Bless, agree to take care of each other, to be fruitful and multiply as the heavenly Father has commanded you, and in all other things to be obedient to your earthly master. I pronounce y'all married."

That was it. Slightly more formality than turning a stallion loose in a mare's pasture. "Kiss her," Jack directed.

Bless knew how she smelled. So did David. They allowed their cheeks to hover closely without meeting. But they did not let go of each other's hands.

Jack, the only one smiling, the only one happy about this joining, gestured to the barn broom as if it were a flower-strewn threshold. "Jump that broom!"

"Remember," he cautioned as they tensed for the jump, "don't touch it!" Jack vaguely recalled that caution from the village broomstick marriages of his childhood. For either of the pair to touch the broom was bad luck, and Jack wanted nothing to interfere with the fruitfulness of this joining.

But theirs was a sluggish, flat-footed jump. The girl did not even gather her skirts to keep them from catching on the besom's straw. When she turned, the broom, tangled in her trailing petticoats, flailed behind her.

All three looked down at the dirty, unadorned broom, clinging to Bless by ragged twigs, and felt the sordidness of the moment.

Jack kicked the implement free. "Show her where y'all live," he ordered David.

• • •

Jack scowled at the backs of his servants as David and Bless stiffly moved away. He looked at the kerchiefs and ribbons scattered on the bushes and felt foolish. David had barely glanced at the trinkets, though maybe that was to be expected of a male, but the girl seemed to find them ridiculous. Did she know some masters would have just sent her and David directly into the cabin to act out their nature? But Jack had reckoned that any woman would long for some kind of sanction. A Negro woman, more than any, must crave it.

He picked up the broom. Daddy Thomas would mock him as a fool, but Jack believed in some kind of benevolence, some measure of right and proper. The image of that long-ago Negro girl from the jail threatened to surface. He forced her back to the edge of his mind. Angrily, he stalked toward the barn. A broom in the dirt was not much of a license, but wasn't it better than nothing at all?

• • •

The great pity of the place, as Bless saw it, was that someone had tried to make a home out of what was never meant to be a home. Woven grass mats and rugs made out of rags covered the dirt floor. A table and chairs cobbled out of lightning-strike wood. On each piece, the maker had carved some small flourish, a feather, a petal, a burst of sun. And the cabin was as clean as a house made of dirt and straw could be. Every possession had been patched or painstakingly repaired. Someone had even pieced the shards of a clay vessel. It sat on the table holding a branch of drooping yellow flowers. The mended vase was nothing less than an attempt to dignify, with beauty, a walled and roofed stall.

David followed Bless's gaze to the old water pitcher that sat in a basin he wiped clean after each use. He had filled the pitcher early morning. By now, the water would feel as warm as the air around them. The silt and stray bits of straw would have settled. It would pour clean. The young woman wiped at her face and knocked a bit of trash from her hair. Weeks, at least, had passed since her last real bath. She motioned, a little gesture of head and right shoulder.

"I'd like to wash," she said.

David pointed her to the door. "Trough 'round back."

When he heard her struggling with the stiff handle of the pump, David allowed himself to breathe deeply. It did not help. His lungs felt like a pair of bellows, filled to bursting with feeling and tension. He should have dragged in a wash tub. He should have heated water to fill it. But David needed the young woman to get away from him and to stay away. As it was, he could still feel her palm clinging to his.

The coming of shackled slaves always pitched him right up against what Jack meant for him to be: brawn and meat to make stock. Now, Jack had finally found the one he wanted David to breed with. *Your wife*. Crewe meant to work her all day, making the farm pay in vegetables, in meals, in soap, in clean linens. David was meant to work her at night, making the farm pay in grade A-1 niggers. He was sick at the thought.

Sometimes when Crewe left David to himself in the smithy or sent him off to work some corner of the farm while Crewe tended other business, David imagined himself as just any other man tending his farm. He imagined the family he would return to at the end of the day. Phoebe and Andrew, older now, grousing or gossiping in the back room of the house. The wives of David's brothers would be busy preparing supper as children of all sizes did chores or played about the yard. Celeste would come to the edge of the field to meet him. They would walk back to the house together, into the noise and news and commotion that made a family. They would stand on David's own patch of earth, surrounded by his own people. That was the kind of life David wanted to bring a wife into. Which was why, in the cabin, he had wanted to take Bless's hand and say, *Lord, girl, I am sorry.*

Instead, he'd said, "Trough 'round back."

He and the girl had one thing in common—meanness was all the protection they had from Jack and each other.

• • •

Ask any trader or jailer. Slaves fight in their sleep. They weep. They scream. If they were any other animal, it would be a mercy to shoot them and halt such pain. David's sobs were as raw and grating as a bowsaw.

Bless rose from her pallet. She stood in the strange dark—cold from the floor seeping into her—as she decided whether or not to touch him. But the sound of David's weeping threatened to loose her own tears.

She touched his arm. "David?" He jerked but did not quiet. Bless sat on the rail of his bed. She grabbed him by the shoulders. "David? David?"

He opened his eyes. He smiled though he still wept. He mumbled. A name? Names? He grasped Bless beneath the armpits and began to pull her into an embrace. His heart had awoken before his mind.

Bless stiffened. Two months since she had been sold. Many hands had grabbed her. None had been tender. But this was a different touch. Palms of gratitude swept her back. Fingers of disbelief probed her cheeks. As she teetered between pressing closer and yanking away, a cloud shifted. Moonlight arced into the room.

David awakened. This was not the sister his heart had taken her for.

The hard rail of the bed dug into Bless's hip as David shoved her away.

Bless had missed her chance.

• • •

It wasn't her belongings that overfilled the cabin so that David had to go outside to draw a full breath. She didn't have much, just the dress she wore, and a few things tied in a bundle. It was her sadness. Everywhere Bless went—the hearth, the table, the privy—there came a drift of sadness as grave and cold as January. David trembled in the sunny patch where she'd knelt to dig potatoes. He shivered crossing from one end of the room to the other.

He spent most of his time trying to stay out of her way. That wasn't hard. Crewe worked them from first light until full dark, later if there was moon enough to see by. That was what started David thinking. One evening with enough respite to watch the moon rise—not quite full, thumbed into shape, brightening from tarnished to gleaming—he realized that after more than a month of living with Bless, he had seen no signs. She had not done any of the things women have to do, gather grass or moss, collect cotton lint or old rags. Not even a stain on her skirt.

She was young and there were no other women around. David wondered if she even suspected. Her ignorance softened him. He began to look after her more. It seemed to him that every time he came upon Bless, she was hauling wood or water for the wash or cooking. Always, the load was too heavy.

One day, as he came in early from the fields to shore up a worn trace on the ox pair, he found Bless trudging from the well, full buckets hanging from the yoke on her shoulders. David tied the team then trotted over to her. He hefted the yoke from her shoulders.

"Keep on like this, and that babe gon' fall outa you," he said. David saw her surprise, her disbelief.

If she had thought about it at all, Bless would have reckoned that her body had lately been through too much grief and shock to retain any life but her own.

Her gaze cut across the yard, to where Jack Crewe sharpened ax blades, working the foot pedal of the grindstone. She whispered even though he could not have heard her over the buck of the stone and the screech of metal. "You think he knows?"

"*You* didn't even know." David shook his head. "He don't live with you."

"Don't tell him."

"Why not?"

"This is my business. Woman's business."

" 'Woman's business,' " David said, then again, slower, " 'Woman's business'? You know well as I do why he bought you."

"And yet," she said, "you haven't touched me."

David was not the only one who suffered nightmares. Unlike her, he kept to his bed. He listened as Bless fought her own pale phantoms. Come morning, he pretended he'd not heard just as he pretended he had not dreamed.

"I ain't one to take what somebody don't want to give. I figure you had 'nough of that."

Water in the buckets churned and sloshed as David stepped closer to her. He did not want Jack to even see what they were saying. "I ain't got to touch you now. Neither of us got to do something we don't want to do."

David had once worked a farm with a plow horse named Samson. When liquid waves of heat wafted between the rows and each step felt like wading through fire, the slaves toiled on, but Samson folded down on all fours. No matter how the driver cursed or bribed or flayed him, Samson did not rise until someone unhooked the plow. David had admired that determination, wished for it—until he saw it in the young woman before him. Bless squared and straightened and seemed to dig in and rise up at the same time. She looked, quite suddenly, older.

The water spilled, slapping drops as dark as blood into the sandy loam. "What you gon' do?"

The screech and heavy bucking of the grindstone stopped just as Bless began to answer.

"What y'all standing 'round for?" Jack hollered.

David spun so quickly that Bless had to jump out of the way of the buckets. "Jus' offering a hand, sir!"

"Don't tell him," Bless commanded. Before David could protest, she hurried away. She left him standing there, her burden on his shoulders.

. . .

A week passed, almost two. Daily, David shot the girl questioning looks that she pretended not to see. She made no mention of the pregnancy. She kept up the strenuous work, hauling water, dragging heavy pots, and toting weighty baskets of wet laundry until David cornered her at the washpot. He threatened to tell Crewe if she did not take more care.

To keep him from drawing Crewe's attention, Bless let David heft the heavy basket over to the clothesline. Instead of the thanks he expected, she snatched up a shirt and wrung it like it was his neck. He would have to take a different approach.

That night, despite her protests, David took the pallet and gave Bless his bed. He doused the lamp. Corn husks cracked as she tossed on the mattress.

"Know who the daddy?" David asked.

Bless did not answer. Perhaps she had only been turning in her sleep.

"I know who I hope it is," Bless finally said.

"Where he?"

"I don't know."

"Living?"

She drew a breath and slowly released it. "I don't know."

"You chose him?"

"Yes."

"You love him?"

"Yes."

For David, that was enough to settle the matter. "I'll see what's round to make a cradle outa." He pushed onto one elbow and tried to peer around the dark room. "I'll see what we can't move to make a little room."

"Don't set your heart on this."

"Too late."

"Those names you call in your sleep, Peggy, Will, Ruth—are they your children?"

"No."

Bless waited. David did not offer more, so she said, "My mama told me it would have been kinder for her to drown me when I was a tiny thing."

"That's just talk."

"She was right."

David turned to face her in the dark. "I ain't never met a woman didn't want her child. Nor a daddy neither for that matter."

"I didn't say she didn't want me. I said she was right. It would have been kinder."

"We oughta go to sleep. Morning come soon 'round here," David said to lead her away from that train of thought. She tossed, the husks in the mattress cracking. Then she settled.

David had almost drifted off when he heard Bless's whisper. "I'm not my mama. I'll swallow this baby whole before I give it up to slavery."

. . .

When David cautioned Bless to stop braiding her hair lest the umbilical cord tangle around the baby's neck, she did. And when he began to bring in scraps of wood for the cradle he planned to build, she stacked them neatly in a corner. She said nothing else worrisome about the pregnancy. After those few dangerous words whispered fiercely in the dark, Bless seemed to accept the state of things. There would be a child.

David allowed himself to look forward. As if it were a gift, an ornament, something too precious to be used every day, David took the memory of Celeste, wrapped it carefully in his heart and laid it by. On that memory, that "might have been," he silently swore he would do for Bless's child all he could not do for his own. After all, every Negro he had ever met, including his mama and daddy, missed someone, longed for someone. What choice did any of them have but to pour that love into the person at hand and hope it all balanced, that they all somehow got a full cup of love in the end? If he had a child out there, David hoped some other man was being a good father in his stead. And he would do the same for Bless's man, if she let him.

They had not long put out the candle when David asked, "You hope it's a boy or you hope it's a girl?" He heard the bed creak as Bless settled, but there was no answer. "Don't matter much to me neither," David said, "though, I reckon it do matter when it come to names."

Nothing.

"You thought'a any yet?"

Bless breathed quietly.

"Celeste, she was my—" David stopped. "I don't know if she was bearing when we was parted, but she promised—she said if she was, she would give him my name." He waited. He lifted onto one elbow and tried to see Bless through the dark. Now he could not even hear her breathing. "I think you ought to give the baby your man's name—"

"I am tired, David."

"'Course, we don't know what it's gon' be. How 'bout we call it 'Bean' 'til it's born? My daddy called all us 'Bean' 'til we was born. That's how I always knowed a new brother or sister was coming. Mama and Papa start talking 'bout beans." David sat up in the silence. "You ain't 'sleep, Bless."

"Call it whatever you want, David. Bean is as good as anything else. Just—I am tired, all right?"

"All right," he said, satisfied with this small win. Naming, even a silly name, made a thing real. "All right, you and Bean take your rest."

David lay back and smiled as he shut his eyes. They had a *Bean* on the way.

• • •

From across the yard, David saw Bless stooping low to lift the yoke of buckets onto her shoulders. He secured the brake. "I'll be on back," David called to Crewe as he trotted over to Bless.

"Come out from under that," he said as he reached her.

Fiercely, Bless pushed to her feet before David could take the yoke from her. She slanted her gaze quickly to Jack then back to David. "Get away from here. You want him to guess?"

David reached for the yoke, but Bless took a step back.

David kept his voice quiet, but his smile resounded. "He think I'm courting you. He don't know nothing 'bout Bean."

Bean. David said the baby's pet name, and Bless felt a flutter, a faint winging in her womb that shocked her to a halt. She felt it again, a puff of tumult in her belly. She rested her hands upon the yoke that rode her shoulders and awaited the next ripple.

With his face creased in concern, David watched the curious turns in Bless's expression. Her annoyance at him shifted to blankness then amazement.

"What is it?" he asked urgently.

"It moved," Bless whispered. She looked up at him with wide eyes. "It *moved*."

David smiled, surprised by her reaction, but Bless no longer saw him. All of her attention turned inside. The baby took the shape of a person, not a misfortune or an awful circumstance. She tumbled into wonder. She easily imagined the plump nubs of her baby's toes, the fat hams of her thighs and sweet folds of her neck. Bless felt the soft strength and curiosity of the baby's hand patting over her own cheek.

But she could not imagine her child's face. Would it have the warm molasses skin of her mother, of Cassie or Jeremiah? Or would her skin be ashen like the paste Bless once caked on herself, like the skin of Rove? Would the baby have beryl eyes and bone-deep kindness or gray eyes and marrow-deep meanness? Whose baby did she carry? And did either color, either father, make her baby less a slave or more deserving of the miserable fortune ahead?

No. To be a good mother, Bless had to act while what she felt was not love, not bitterness, just wonder and pity, pity for a baby—her baby—already bound up in the body of a slave.

"Bless? Bless?" David said. He reached again.

"No," Bless commanded as she dodged his hand and righted herself beneath the swinging, shifting yoke. "It'll draw Crewe's attention. I'm not ready for him to know."

"He might go easier on you. Less strain. Better food. You gotta do what's good for the Bean."

Bless hitched her burden more securely upon her shoulders. "I know I do."

• • •

David was steps away from Jack and the ox cart when Cuddy, one of the bulky, horned plowing oxen, began to toss his head and heave.

"Whoa, Cuddy. Whoa," David crooned as he approached. He slowed his pace and held his hands out as he tried to see what was pestering the animal. Jack sprinted around the cart to grab the bridle of the ox, but it was too late. Cuddy shook the cart, strained against the harness. His eyes rolled. He mooed, a low-pitched warning that seemed to escape the housing of his great shoulder hump. In a clatter of iron, a splintering of wood, and rending of leather, he bolted.

In the upheaval of the cart, Jack was knocked to the ground. In the path of the maddened ox, David threw himself aside. He landed hard, rolled, and found himself on his hands and knees.

"Move!" he yelled to Bless who stood in the open space between the well and the kitchen. "Move!"

But Bless did not even sway. She planted herself beneath the weight of wood and rope and water. She stood as if she were a fence post driven into the ground or a rooted tree, something that could not go or change course of its own volition. And when Cuddy veered toward her, Bless looked relieved.

Stand. Her last conscious thought before the impact of the charging ox. Bless had worried over the question for days and weeks. How to save her baby? When the time came, she only had to make one decision. *Stand.*

The animal, its hump reaching the height of a man, glanced Bless with its tremendous bulk, not trampling or goring, but enough to send her soaring and a landing hard enough to jar loose the delicate webbing within her womb. Only then did she let loose of the weight on her shoulders.

• • •

White folks say Negroes and animals are the same. No souls. Niggers, they say, turn to dust.

Slaves believed their spirits walk the waters back to Africa.

Bless stood at the shore, washed in the spray. Clear water bathed her toes. Her heels sank into the cupping sand. Eddies raced in and out, in and out, pulling her along, and she was going, arching for a headlong plunge. Then, a hook of pain snatched her back.

It was Jeremiah. Calling, sounding so troubled, sounding so lonesome, in the land she left. Bless opened her eyes.

And she was neither dust nor wave.

• • •

"Stillborn." The midwife's word sounded strangely serene. Not *dead*, rather, *stillborn*, a quiet and ongoing occurrence. Patience Basnight—the Negro woman Jack raced to fetch when David lifted Bless from the ground and confessed, "We need the midwife"— severed the cord and handed the warm but lifeless baby to David.

Patience returned her full attention to the young mother. Quiet now, and quietly weeping, Bless sat with her legs spread and hips canted forward on the expanse of two chairs. Her feet had braced against Miss Patience's thighs when the woman squatted to check the progress of the birth, against her shoulders when she crouched low and urged Bless to push. As David stood over her shoulder, bewildered by the small, still creature in his hands, Patience kneaded and pressed Bless's belly to force the afterbirth free.

• • •

"Why you just sending for me?" was the first question Patience directed at David when the cabin door slammed on the back of an angry Jack. Most women—free or enslaved, Negro or white—sent for Miss Patience, the granny midwife, as soon as they had strong grounds to suspect a child was on the way.

Women sent messages by word of mouth if they had nothing to fear, if the baby was a happy occurrence. They employed other, quieter, ways if the baby's existence had to leave no more trace than a whisper. In a busy field, an enslaved woman might hum up a chorus of a particular song, knowing some little bird would catch the meaning and sing it all the way back to the ear of Miss Patience. Another woman might make a mark on a tree, tie a string on a bush, or arrange a pattern of stones on a road Miss Patience was known to travel. Women found ways to signify. As long as the need existed, they would find ways to help one another.

Sometimes Patience came openly, in broad daylight up the path, astride her horse or comfortably in the back of a wagon sent for her. Sometimes she met a woman at dusk or full dark on the edge of a pine woods or dead center of a camouflaging field.

Patience asked the "daylight" women about their familial lines, as much as they could tell her, and about the ailments of their mothers. Had their grandmothers birthed with ease? She stayed two days to assess the homelife. What demands on the mother? Other children? Heavy work? What was lacking in the house, and how might it be supplied? Patience bargained with husbands and masters, winning small comforts and reprieves for her mothers. She visited as much as she could and always returned at least once before the onset of labor to help ready the house, to make sure everything that would be needed had been put into place.

The "dusk" women required one visit only. There would be no reason to return; they only needed a remedy. For their children had been planted by force, or the woman had tried every trick she knew to prevent it, or the woman could barely provide for the two or three she already had. Another would kill her, then where would her other children be? Imagining what they had risked getting to her, knowing how excruciating was the decision to seek her, Miss Patience asked only what she needed to know to determine which mix of herbs or tinctures would serve best. How long since your last blood? Have you given birth before? Have you ever before had an untimely birth? These women were mothers too, full of the same tenderness other women used to nurse and tend their children, for this, too, was necessity and love.

"She didn't want him to know," David said.

Patience held his gaze. Then she looked at Bless, the bruises blooming, the abrasions on her skin. That she would do herself so, all to release this baby from her body, told Patience all she needed to know.

• • •

The baby was curled into herself, tight as a tulip bud, little fists pressed beneath her chin. Bless had delivered her with a cry like the uprooting of a tree. Blood-splotched and covered in the fine hairs and defensive cream of the womb, she slid free from her mother. A tiny girl. Syrup brown beneath the residue.

She was beautiful, this unblossomed baby, her face hinting at the oval shape of Jeremiah's, Bless's full lips, and Cassie's wide nose. Bless rubbed the fuzzed brow and kissed the closed eyes. No eyelashes yet. Bless counted the tiny creature's seized fingers. She uncurled each tiny digit, each miniature toe.

David drew close. He sat an arm's length away, hunched on the rail of the bed he'd vacated for Bless's sake, and watched a long time as she handled the dead child.

He didn't realize he had spoken his thoughts, but he could not call them back. "She would have brought joy into our lives."

Bless had already made that calculation. She turned the baby in her hands. She drew her finger down the child's back, over the little hills of the buttocks. Bless wanted to remember every detail.

"Our little bit of happiness up against her whole life of suffering, David?"

"You ain't sorry at all?" he asked.

Bless did not look up from the tiny head, still warm in her hands. She traced the hint of a hairline. "I'll never be sorry this baby is not a slave."

• • •

When Bless slipped into a deathlike sleep, David lifted the child from her arms. He wrapped the baby in a clean shirt, his only spare, knowing full well it would be winter before Jack Crewe issued him another. As David swaddled her, he wished for something warm for the months she would lay in the frozen ground, something pretty for a girl. But there was only his sweat-stained osnaburg shirt. He tied its long arms and lifted her. She felt lighter than the last brown rabbit he had caught for supper.

David had forgotten almost everything he ever knew about babies. She was nearly the first child he'd held since he himself was a child, helping his mother corral George-Lee and Ruth and the rest of them. He did recall one thing, though. David leaned in to brush his lips against her head, to gather that sweet smell babies bring from the realm of grace, but the coolness gathering in her skin stopped him.

. . .

The next time Bless woke, David was gone, and her arms were empty. All that remained was a dimly burning tallow light and the midwife. Miss Patience sat close enough to lean forward and touch Bless's forehead. When she saw Bless's eyes open, Patience went to the kettle and filled a cup. She returned to the bed and pressed the drink to Bless's lips.

Bless took one swallow, then closed her lips and turned her head away from the bitter brew. Miss Patience followed with the cup. When Bless refused to drink, she pinched the young woman's nose until she opened her mouth. Patience poured in the drink until only a dark spattering of leaves remained in the bottom of the cup. Tears pooled in Bless's eyes.

"You are punishing me," Bless croaked.

Miss Patience studied her with a kind of quizzical tenderness. "No, child. Fighting off childbed fever."

. . .

Jack came as David descended the cabin steps.

"David," he said.

"Yes, sir?"

"The traces broke. Cuddy got loose 'cause the traces broke. Ain't it your job to keep the traces in good repair?"

David recalled the day he'd brought the team in to mend the traces. The discovery of Bless's pregnancy had distracted him—the pregnancy Bless had allowed to be stampeded out of her because of the man who stood before him, because of all the men like him.

"I have right many jobs to keep up round here, sir," David said, and neither he nor Jack could deny the defiance that hardened his voice.

"I'm going to show you which one is important."

David nodded to the bundle in his arms. "Let me see to the burial first."

The newborn made such a small armful that Jack had mistaken the baby for a wad of rags. His voice turned strange. "The child? What is it?"

"A baby girl."

Jack surprised them both when he said, "Let me see."

David hesitated. His grasp tightened around the bundle.

"Show me," Jack ordered.

David took one step toward his master. With two fingers, Jack nudged open the placket of David's shirt, revealing the tiny face. Miniature perfection. Tiny wisps of hair. Eyelids and nostrils almost translucent. Much as he recalled his sister. In the changing, uncertain light, she could be anybody's baby; everything about her was frozen in an indeterminate state. A grief he had dammed off for years filled him, heart and lungs. He snatched his hand away.

"Bury her," he said to David. "Decent. Then bring your ass right back here."

• • •

"Do you think hard of me?" Bless asked Patience the question she would not dare ask David. She studied the midwife's face in the dawning light, sure that no matter what words the woman said, her face, her eyes, would answer truthfully. Patience had a face sculpted from ebony, a face of angles with a long line of dark brows. Her lips hardly ever curved up or downward. Except for the deep wrinkles settled on each side of her mouth, the rest of her face was ageless, indecipherable.

The midwife was slow to answer. Bless turned her face away. She worried the taste of bitter tea from the dry cracks in her lips as Patience said, "On the boat after they stole me from my home was two girls. Both big with chile. I delivered both of them babies within a few days'a one 'nother. I delivered both of them babies into all that mis'ry. An' both them mamas smiled through they tears an' they pain when they seen dem babies. An' they kiss on 'em an' smell 'em and count they toes."

Patience sighed. She massaged her throat as if to coax free the words lodged there. "An one'a them mamas ask me to teach her how to nurse her baby, you know, 'courage him to latch on. An' the other mama look 'round an' watch how they done us, an' she ask if I can't help her get to the side'a the boat.

"An' I say 'yes' to the one want to feed her baby and see him strong. An' I say 'yes' to the one took her baby 'gainst her heart and jump into the sea."

Patience patted Bless's hand and rose to fetch more tea.

• • •

Grave dirt still caked David's hands as he walked over to the hitching post. He stood at the place where oxen, mules, and horses were tied. He gripped the rail.

Salty spit filled David's mouth as Jack tied his hands. He hardly listened as Jack laid on blame and claimed the right to beat him. David salivated with the desire to strike. His arms and legs contained the strength and will of wild horses. He bridled each one. He did not allow his hands to choke, his fists to batter, his feet to stomp. He closed his eyes to dim the blaze of truth. For all of Jack's ropes and whips and speeches, he could not do anything that David did not allow.

Jack saw the fury in David's eyes. "The ones you want have a bit of fight in them. A bit of fury is a good sign and not to be feared. Show no pity."

And look what this Negro's slothfulness had cost Jack. An injured animal, a dead picaninny, and Jack had no idea what damage might have been done to the mother. And all because of David's negligence. Even a "good Negro" could only be trusted so far. The world was ordered as it should be. That he owned David was proof enough that he *should* own David. Jack had seen the Negro lift a keg of nails straight over his head. He knew the man could move a kilderkin of beer on his own, yet here he stood, strong and dumb as a mule while Jack tied him. Even David knew the right side of things.

Jack left David tied to the hitching post. In the barn, he took down Thomas Crewe's whip from where it hung among an assortment of tools. Jack bounced it in his hand to reacquaint himself with the weight. The lash had been skillfully, awfully, made. Thomas had loaded shot into the buck-antler handle for balance with every twitch of the wrist. Replacing the natural velvet, he had wrapped the cool bone in the same leather as the two-bellied thong and finished it all with a cow-hitched cracker.

Jack closed his hand around the handle and felt the shape of Thomas Crewe's grasp. The marks of the dead man's grip spread wider and deeper than his own reach. It would take time to reshape the handle, just as it had taken time for Jack to learn to use the whip with neither fear nor pleasure but, simply, with effectiveness.

"You want the bit?" he asked David.

The bound man shook his head. He huffed, blowing air like a horse to prepare himself for the pain. David did not, could not, hide the hatred this time, and the look chilled Jack's guts. But he did not hold the look against David. Punishment was unsavory business.

"You brought this on yourself," Crewe said. Drawing the whip back to his shoulder, he felt the shot in the handle shift like scales, weighing David's crime, weighing his own intentions.

This whipping was *not* salve for his own anger. Jack had made up his mind to punish David as soon as he found the break in the traces, as soon as he saw the bloody patch rubbed into the ox's shoulder by the serrated leather. Simple chastisement.

Or so Jack told himself.

The first blow moved completely through David. It forced a tremendous grunt. Sweat popped from his flesh. His skin tensed, tightened, and crawled. His legs shook. The ground between his feet darkened.

But Jack was not done. The power of the whip's strike returned to his shoulder doubled, trebled. He began to lay David open. The whipping was the reprimand not the lesson. The lesson came in the healing. The painful crusting and wrenching of every scar would forever remind David of his disobedience.

If there was a moment much later—after he had washed David's blood from his hands, when he cleaned the tear in Cuddy's hide and covered it with a poultice—that Jack suffered for the ox's open flesh and thought of David, he would dash the sympathy away. Animals and men are not the same. Animals cannot help themselves.

• • •

Patience jumped from her seat when the cabin door banged open. Crewe must have kicked it. His left arm was wrapped around the Negro man's back. One of David's arms rested on the white man's shoulders. Crewe held tightly to the wrist of that arm to keep David from sliding to the ground.

"He drunk?" Patience exclaimed.

"No," Crewe answered.

"What happened—" Then she saw the blood.

Crewe dragged David to the table. He tried to push him into the remaining seat, but the battered man refused to sit. David jerked away from Crewe. He braced himself against the tabletop, smearing the blood running from the backs of his arms to his fingertips. Now Patience saw the long suppurating stripes on his back and the blood on Crewe's cuffs and shirt.

"You whipped him?" Patience asked.

Crewe's voice echoed the sound of her own disbelief. "You think I can afford to have oxen injured, a servant run down, and a valuable piece of my property killed?"

"Prop— The baby." Patience stepped away from Crewe.

"Worth twenty-five pounds in the first year of its life." Not since his sister was sold had Jack forgotten the cash worth of a child.

Stained in blood, Jack stood aloof, businesslike. David wobbled but held himself upright.

"Tend him," Crewe ordered.

The moment the door closed behind Crewe, David thumped to his knees. His head banged the table as he caught himself with his forearms braced against the wood. He had not yet fallen to the floor where his open wounds would press against the damp dirt, but he was sliding.

"The chair!" Patience said. "Not the floor! You'll take fever. Don't fall. Let me get the chair." David trembled and blew with the effort it took to obey. Water ran from his eyes, nose, and mouth.

Patience turned backward the chair David had refused so it propped against the sturdiness of the table. She squatted, angled herself beneath David's arm to help him rise, all the while commanding, "Don't you fall out! I can't lift you." He looked at her, seemed to acknowledge that he was trying to obey, trying to help her carry his weight. It occurred to Patience that the whipping must have happened out by the barn, well within hearing distance, but she had heard no screams or cries.

David's eyes shone with tears. "That's right," Patience said. "Keep your eyes on me. Listen to my voice."

David passed out just as Patience got him straddled on the chair. The heavy table rocked from his weight, but it held him. His head thumped forward. His arms dangled at his sides. Patience had a clear view of his plowed back. The rind of brown, the furrows of blood-rich pink. She stood for a moment, frozen between the fevered young woman lying in the bed and the beaten young man bleeding on the chair. She did not know who to help first. She felt much as she had on that ship all those years ago, moving to help one mother then the other.

"God knows," she sighed, "I can't tell who was right." Then she opened her satchel and set to work.

• • •

Patience slid the packet of herbs across the table. Bless looked down at it, then back up into the midwife's unreadable face.

"You already gave me his medicine," Bless said, meaning the willow bark she was to boil for David's pain and fever, as well as the herbs and honey she would mash into a dressing for his back.

As David slept fitfully in the bed from which Bless had only lately risen, the women sat at the table and sipped a brew of herbs Patience had gathered on her few rambles from the cabin. It would "keep off cold," Patience said, and "fortify the blood." Though they sweetened it with wild honey, Bless would not call it tasty. Still, it was better than anything else Patience had poured down her throat. She tried not to frown as she peered into the dregs of the cup.

"This for *you*," the midwife said.

Startled, Bless met her steady gaze. "You said everything look fine. That I'll heal up good as new."

Patience nodded. "That's true. No reason you can't bear a string'a healthy young'uns." She dipped her head in a meaningful gesture. "If that what you want." She sipped from her cup. Her face was still and clear.

Clumsily, Bless set her cup on the table. Its clatter disturbed David. The women watched him. He moaned and twitched in his sleep. Bless waited until he settled before she lifted the packet. Parchment paper folded into an envelope. Lightweight. When she tilted it this way or that, the herbs inside shifted and whispered like sand. But she understood, suddenly, that each grain held the value of gold dust.

Bless said, "This is—"

"Protection from runaway oxes," Patience finished.

Because a woman would find a way. Not only would she stand before a charging ox, but she would throw herself from a galloping horse or down a flight of stairs or beat her belly with a rolling pin. Fear of death, let alone injury, could not stop a woman determined that there would be no more children to share the hunger of the rest, no defenseless bundle in her belly or her arms to make the next flight from fists and boot heels impossible—no innocent child to surrender into the rapacious hands of a white man.

Patience listened for the snuffling of David's quiet snore. When the sound filled the quiet, she said, "They's things you don't tell a man. Not even a good man."

Tears rose faster than Bless could swallow them. Patience stood before even one drop could fall. "Boil it. Drink it hot," she said. Then she set about packing her things.

• • •

Jack placed a few coins in Patience's palm. She did not glance down at the money.

"I treated the young man too," she said.

Patience exercised her right to demand more. Just like the Negro milliner, wigmaker, or wheelwright, she could do well what most people could not do. In all but the rarest of instances, she kept both mother and child alive and healthy. Both Patience and her master took it as a matter of honor that the pay for her services reflect her value. And if Patience used the freedom of thought and movement that came along with her rare skill to help a woman like Bless or smuggle messages or supplies for an occasional fugitive, she saw her quiet resistance as no more than deserved by the system that ensnared them. In fact, the smallness of her acts of sabotage pained her. Patience wanted to gallop across the countryside setting fire to everything.

So she did not lower her gaze or glance aside as Jack attempted to stare her down. Patience looked him in the face. She would wait as long as it took. She enjoyed watching men like Jack come to this moment of irreversible understanding, that she, a woman, black-skinned, illiterate, a slave, thought he was nothing more than a case of piles or flux—a hardship to be endured. Her clear, steady gaze said all that was forbidden to her lips. *Without a whip, without a gun, you nothing.* It shook them.

The day Patience learned their secret was the last day she shrank or showed fear. She learned to school her features. The skill had come at a terrible cost. Now, most of the time, she could not weep or bring herself to touch, or be touched, even when she most wanted to. Still, she would pay the price a thousand times over to deny them what they wanted: the thrill of her pain, the disdain of her sorrow. Patience gave them nothing. She smothered every outcry. She hid each wince behind an expression of irritated indifference. What harm could the white man in front of her inflict that one had not acted out on her flesh years before?

"Done yet?" she inquired of Jack. How long did he plan to stand there scowling before handing over the rest of her fee? She'd asked the same question of the last man who tried to rape her. At her icy annoyance, he'd gone soft against her thigh.

Jack flushed red to the roots of his hair as Patience's gaze seemed to riffle through him, turning over this and that, then withdrawing. Clearly, she found nothing she did not anticipate. Nothing to covet. Nothing to respect or fear. No low thing he did would surprise her. To cheat her as he was inclined, to slap her as he desired, would only prove what she suspected.

He was not sure why he cared what an old Negro woman thought of him. But he did. Jack had not felt so small since his life before Thomas Crewe. For, reflected in the midwife's gaze, Jack saw the boy he once was: landless, powerless, hungry; the son of a man desperate enough to sell his own child.

He reached into his purse and dug out twice as much coin. He did not do it because he felt he owed her. He did it so she would look away.

Patience weighed the money in her palm. At last, she closed her fingers around it.

She nodded decisively. "That cover the medicine too. I left both of 'em what they need."

Jack led the way to the barn. He saddled the midwife's old horse, walked it to the block, and held the head steady while the woman mounted. He was not humbled by Patience. Not exactly. But he was glad to see her go.

• • •

"It's time," Bless said. She turned away from David's scowl and began to arrange the pots of ointment and honey, the bandages, and the cloths she needed to tend his wounds.

"No concern of yours," he said.

"It is. You can't tend your own back. Miss Patience said change the dressing every two days. She's been gone three." And for each of those days, every inhale brought the raw smell of David's wounds. Each time he hissed in pain, Bless remembered that she had caused his misery.

"I rather not have your hands on me."

Bless had not expected him to speak so directly. In the days since Patience left, he'd hemmed and hawed each time Bless mentioned his dressings. It hurt to hear his anger, but that was the least of her hurts.

She arched a brow and crossed her arms. "Who's going to do it then? Master Jack?"

She waited. He did not meet her gaze, but, gingerly, David walked to the table and straddled the chair. He bared himself in silence, out of necessity. Bless had lived with David for months; in close quarters, and despite modesty, they had glimpsed each other in various stages of undress, but never had their quarters seemed so small, nowhere to retreat, no private space to lay hurt bare.

David looked straight ahead. He seemed to ignore, or endure, the touch of her hands. And as she peeled the bandages away, Bless saw reason enough for his reluctance. His back was ugly with old maiming and crosscuts from the fresh lashing. Though she stood behind him, Bless was grateful there were no mirrors, not even the dull bowl of a pewter spoon, to reflect the shock she felt. In some places, the flesh had been dug away like the eyes of an old potato. In others, it had healed in puckers and thick, ropy keloids. Bless let her hand rest on David's raised flesh, knotty with the blood or skin hardened within. So much brutality, she had to touch it to believe.

She collected herself. She wrung out the rag steeping in a basin of boiled water. She tended the scarred skin of David's back as if it were the soft, unblemished skin of her newborn.

"My husband, Jeremiah, his scars came from running away. Every time they caught him, they beat him. He used the scars to remember the way to water or a safe sleeping place along the way, things that would help him the next time he ran. He says you never forget how you come by a scar."

"He right."

"You remember every whipping?"

"I remember every lash."

She paused. She watched the steam rise off the basin. It made sense that he could remember every cut and rip of his skin. Bless carried an undimmed memory of Rove's brutality. "How then?" she asked.

"How what?"

"How could you expect me to—how could you want her so much?"

David turned his head just enough that Bless could see the rebellious light in his eyes. "Some grab what little joy come our way. Everybody ain't so willing to sacrifice as you."

Bless's exhale cut the rising steam to ribbons. She took her hands from him long enough for the pain to judder through her. Then she laid them on again. Cleanse. Smear the honey. Bandage.

As soon as she knotted the last dressing in place, David grabbed his shirt and left.

With a sweep of her hand, Bless knocked the basin of dirty water to the floor.

Neither had raised a voice or a hand, but both felt the violence. Their accusations were as naked and ugly as David's back.

• • •

"Bless!" Jack called. "Bless, come out here!" and with that, the peace of the morning shattered. Bless tightened her grip on a piece of pork belly she'd been slicing into bacon.

Outside of the kitchen, the other business of the farm had also begun. The bucket splashed down into the well. David was pulling water to fill the troughs. Animals began their early morning squawking or lowing for feed. Birds whistled or chirped. Bless heard the rattle of harnesses and the thud of the yoke on the hump of each ox. Orders and questions flew from Crewe, the center of the fray.

"Bless!" He shouted again, "Bless!"

Bless finished up her slicing even as her master kept calling. She wiped her greasy hands on her apron and searched her pocket for the cap that would protect her plaits from the dust kicked up in the yard. Then, with seeming hurry, she went to discover why Crewe wanted her so urgently.

Just over the threshold, she lurched to a stop. Bless's white cap dropped from her hand. It landed by her feet like a flag of surrender.

They were not crying. The demented music of the rattling, dragging, swaying chains was the only sound they made. Their silence was worse than screams. Boney, hunched in their dark and haggard skin, they looked as if all the miseries of the world had been sized to their thin, young shoulders.

Ten of them came in single file—boys the colors of red clay, wet loam, and dry dust. All were in different stages of boyhood: knobbed knees and jutting elbows, collar bones in sharp relief, Adam's apples lodged like plums in the throat. They bordered on naked, wearing tattered breeches or long linen shirts; only the oldest wore both. They trailed from tallest to shortest, each boy wearing a neck cuff linked by chain to the boy in front of him. Only the smallest child—a runt or very young—had been spared the iron. He wore a slack noose, looped around his spindle of a neck, knotted to the chain of the boy in front of him.

A white man on horseback led them. A boy with the same boxy build and light coloring as the man on horseback harried them from behind. The tallest captive kept the pace with long-legged strides.

Those shorter and younger trotted. The last small one was run out. He stumbled at the tail end of the gang, yanked along more than keeping up.

Jack greeted the man climbing down from the horse. "John Jeffrey! Good to see you!" He shouted orders as he shook hands with the stringer. "Bless, run up there and open the pen, then put on mush! David, fetch water!"

Grim-faced, David obeyed. Bless stood unmoving, fixed in place like the day with the ox.

"Have you gone deaf?" Jack yelled as she stood watching the line of boys trudge by.

She had not gone deaf. Bless understood each word separately, but together, they made no sense. "Bless, open the pen." She heard, instead, what Crewe meant. *Pen these little boys.* And a line of Negro children shackled together was enough to stun the heart of even one who had worn shackles and marched in a coffle herself. Not one enslaved adult trudged among them. No one to console or encourage them. No one who would gather them in the dark to reassure them they had done nothing to deserve such a life.

Bless couldn't have been a whit more shocked if this stranger had strolled up with a coffle of elderly folks or if he had come dragging a line of the infirm. He had shackled those who did not possess the one strength—wisdom—that fuels the fight.

Even as she finally obeyed, as she wrestled and wrangled the lock and hasp, it did not make sense. Bless's hand, the same hand she had joined to Miss Rebeccas's, once again an instrument of heartache.

• • •

"Not one of them older than sixteen," Bless said as she helped David haul water.

"They backs mostly clean," he said. "Ain't been whipped much—yet."

They doled out water and cornmeal mush seasoned with bacon fat. Bless and David watched as the boys licked and snuffled the mush off dried corn husks. The only sounds were chewing and swallowing and hopeful requests for more. "More is coming," Bless promised the boys ringing the inside of the pen. Their hands clasped the sturdy pine poles as they watched and waited for the mush boiled in an ash-blackened pot.

The very eldest of the boys had not yet grown his first whiskers. The youngest had not been given his first long pants. Bless turned away from them as if the pot needed her attention. David followed.

There were things for which Bless was sorry. Every morning she rose and left the cabin before David stirred. His wounds and scars tightened overnight, and mornings were painful for him. No matter how he tried to muffle his sounds of suffering, Bless was attuned to his every wince and gasp. To help him heal faster, at every meal she heaped extra servings onto David's plate, but she had not yet apologized for her decision that earned him the whipping. When Bless looked at those boys, she was no longer sure that she would apologize. Because even his broken skin and her bruised limbs did not seem like too high a price to pay to save her child, any child from a life under the yoke and the lash.

In silence, she and David stood watching as bubbles of mush formed and burst. "I know what I should say," Bless said. "I know what I ought to feel." She inclined her head toward the pen. "But that one there, he could be my brother. And him over there, he could be my son. I-I wish I had done it a *different way* so you wouldn't be blamed. Can that be enough?"

Bless did not seek David's gaze until her apology was done. He, too, studied the pen full of black and brown boys. David also saw lost brothers. He saw the sons Jack wanted him to produce. He saw the sons he wanted shrinking themselves to fit the pen, hunching, bending, making themselves accustomed to the weight of shackles.

David slipped his hand into Bless's hand. His grip was tight. "I'll show you where I buried her," he said. "It's a pretty place."

Bless nodded. She rested her temple against David's arm, and what forgiveness and thankfulness there could be flowed between them.

• • •

There was always work in the smithy when a coffle came through. David fed wood into the forge. Sure enough, Jack brought an order as soon as the pen was locked and the slave stringer and his son were settled in their cabin.

"Make a neck iron," Jack said. "Shackles too. Smaller than woman's size. Jeffrey say the ropes on that littlest one keep working loose. Lose time when he has to stop and check him. He's scared the boy might run off in the woods."

"Neck iron for that little chile?" David asked, his voice horrified.

Jack turned to go, but David's tone gave him pause.

Jack had given no thought to whether or not it was appropriate to clap a small boy in irons. He had seen it as a necessary precaution to save work and time—no different from shoeing a horse or belling a cow. Now, as he considered what it meant—a boy yoked to a chain—Jack leaned into the quickest relief.

"Do you think that man got time to go chasing a picaninny through the woods?" he demanded of his blacksmith.

David looked down. "No, sir."

"Ain't nothing in here to fit the boy, is there?"

"No, sir."

"Then make it," Jack said.

The matter was settled. David was set firmly in his place. Still, Jack felt unreasonably angry as he walked away.

• • •

The boy was dark, not a dapple of light, and small. The joints of his wrist and ankles made knobs against his skin. His lashes were as thick as a bristle brush of pine straw. Outside of the pen, while the other boys looked on, David unraveled the rope that hung from his neck and stood the boy in front of him.

"What's your name?" David asked.

"'Lijah." The boy's voice was husky as if he had not spoken in a long while. "What's yourn?"

"David." He had to squat in order to work Elijah free of the rope, and it seemed to him a long way down. From Elijah's vantage point, David's shoulders blocked the slave pen. His head blocked the sun.

"Can you take me home?" the boy whispered.

David's fingers convulsed once. He kept unknotting, unlooping. "Where home?"

Confusion cramped Elijah's small face. He looked over his shoulder. On tiptoes, he peered behind David as if searching for a path, a landmark.

"We been walking a long time," he finally said.

David could not prevent himself. "Who there? At your home?"

He put his hands around Elijah's neck to measure for the collar. Beneath his heavy hands, David felt the delicate jawbone and measured the length of neck muscle and the span of the collar bones that were barely hardened bone at all. The boy seemed pliable, breakable. What weight and thickness of iron would be best? What could a child this small carry without being overburdened and rubbed raw?

David turned the boy to face him once more. Elijah, a dogged child, broke David's reverie by repeating his first question. "Can you take me back?"

"Wish I could."

Elijah studied David, taking in the height and power of him. "How come you can't?"

"They took me off too," David said. "When I weren't no bigger than you."

"Oh," Elijah answered.

David could not withstand the sadness of that one syllable. He knelt on the ground. He could see himself, miniaturized, in Elijah's pupils. When Edwyn Hawley claimed him, David had lain face down on a pier filthy with gull droppings and coarse with sand. He'd refused to get up—not for a cut of the whip, not for a kick meant to jar him loose. Still, Hawley snatched him up and knocked him out. When David awakened, he found himself lost.

"My ma, she at home. She fought the man who took me," Elijah said. "He hit her, and she fell down. Didn't move. You think my mama dead?"

David looked into Elijah's eyes. There remained an innocence as vast as the bay that separated David from his family.

"You ain't gone see her again, son," David said. "That's just the same as dead."

· · ·

Bless forced herself to walk inside the gate. She brought a pot of molasses, the whole month's ration. Once eaten, she and David would go weeks without a taste of sweetness.

"Dip your finger," Bless said as each boy approached. None could resist.

Bless asked their names as they came and tried to remember a scar, a widow's peak, *something*, about each—James and Matthew and Butler and Arthur—just as she had tried to learn by heart the face of her own lost child.

· · ·

David was not expected to speak until spoken to. Like the forge, the anvil, and the vise, he was a sight on the tour, proof that the shop stood ready and was well-equipped. And so, he stood wordlessly at the anvil, beating molten iron with a ball-peen hammer, turning and squeezing it with tongs until it would fit the neck of a small boy.

Crewe spoke to John Jeffrey of "sound materials," "craftsman-ship," and the "firsthand quality" of David's wares. He showed the man an array of tools and a long table spread with nails, hinges, horseshoes, and shackles—the mundane utensils of plantation life.

"You'll agree we've come a long way since the days under Daddy Thomas's direction?" Crewe asked.

"I do!" Jeffrey said. Before the tour of the blacksmith's shop, he had spent a comfortable night in the cabin. He had seen the new slave pens, the neatly planted fields, and strong split rail fences. Jeffrey's belly was full of coffee and molasses-soaked corncakes.

"I hope you'll spread the word about us," Crewe said.

He and Jeffrey stood to David's left, removed from the flying sparks that singed the slave's leather apron, but close enough to watch him work. David stood in reach of the flaming forge. His face and arms were streaked with the ash and black that scattered with each strike.

"Certainly, I will," the stringer mused as he watched David, "but I wonder if he can make something more complicated than horse-shoes and shackles?" He motioned for Crewe to step to the table with him. From his coat, he removed a leather-bound book. David's wares clattered as the man pushed them out of the way. He flipped through the book until he found the drawing he wanted. "There. Can he make that?"

"What in hell is it?" Crewe asked.

"A mask. When I was last in Charlestown, a slaver came in with a rogue Negro. The bastard had tried to start a rebellion on his ship. Marched the fellow off in irons and wearing this. I asked to copy it. I could make great use of a thing like this for my hard cases. Boy, come here."

David waited for Jack's nod before setting down his tools. At the table, he stood between the white men, a head taller, the evidence of power bulging in his shoulders, but the drawing took his strength.

"This for slaves?" David asked in a whisper.

"Who the hell else would it be for?" Jeffrey replied.

David could only liken it to a headstall and bridle. But it was crueler than that. Crafted to fit a human head. Made for the function of malice. In the drawing, four metal bands fit over the head like a helmet. The eyes, ears, and back of the head were open, but a curved plate, a cusp of metal fit over the nose and mouth. Small triangular openings and a few holes allowed for the passage of air. From a small hinge hung a metal protrusion to be fit inside the mouth. Not like a horse bit meant to signal speed and direction, or perhaps just like it—it was a weight to restrain the human tongue.

David answered Jeffrey's question. "A animal, sir."

"Well," Jeffrey let his gaze slide to Crewe, "perhaps *you*, too, could find good use for a mask. Can your man make it or not?"

David did not say another word, but his eyes begged Jack Crewe for the mercy he had not sought on the night of the whipping. Shackles and cuffs were enough. He did not want to turn his hand to such an instrument of torture.

Crewe also found the mask shocking, but surely it would be used as a tool of last resort, only on the most defiant of slaves.

"If my plans are successful," Crewe said as he studied the drawing, "there will come a time when such tools will not be needed. I plan to raise a servant without a mulish will." He spoke as if offering a vow in which the enslaved man could somehow find comfort. David looked away.

Crewe set the book on the table and smiled confidently at his guest. "But while we await that day, David will make whatever tools you require."

Interest livened Jeffrey's pale eyes. "Slave stringing is lucrative but not many places on the road with the comforts you got here. Traveling, vigilance, robbers—all hard on a man. I wouldn't like to do it for too many more years. I am always on the lookout for investments, ways to diversify my holdings. Tell me," he said, "what you got planned for this place."

They left David with the drawing and instructions to craft the mask with haste. They went off haggling a fair price for such a contrivance. Jeffrey promised, "And I will not be the only buyer. Many a man needs to break a defiant servant."

David turned to the forge, the anvil, the unfinished neck cuff. With tongs, he lifted the cuff and rammed it into the fire. He could work or he could weep. He took a hammer in his fist and beat the iron until the muscles of his shoulder quaked.

• • •

Crewe walked Jeffrey over the acreage, showed him the animals, the outbuildings, storage capacity and proximity to Broad Creek. Jeffrey grew even more impressed with the farm's potential. At Jack's table, with the noise of David's hammering shuddering the air, they got down to business.

"I have capital to invest," Jeffrey said. "'Tis vertical expansion I'm after. Slavery is the framework of these colonies. Everything else will be built upon it. I mean to have a hand in it all—from molasses to rum to cloth to Africans and, when that door closes, the domestic trade. If there's ever a time when a man of common blood could build an empire, that time is now. I like what I see here, Jack."

"I am flattered to hear that."

"No flattery intended. This is business pure and simple. I think we can make this place flourish. I have access to many good breeders. I can think of a man right now—past his peak in field work but a magnificent sire! I have sold two of his boys recently at sizable profit."

"What would you want in return?"

"Profit!"

"No say so?"

"Negligible."

"'Negligible'?"

Jeffrey laughed. "A bit of counsel here and there," he conceded. "But really, Jack, I pass through once, perhaps twice a year? I'll not interfere with how you run the place. I'll put in cash for expansion and improvements. You will steward the place as Thomas wished, and we'll both make money."

"Daddy Thomas never indicated anything but that he wanted to own his land free and clear."

"Which is why it grew hardly a whit in his lifetime. Listen to me, Jack." Jeffrey leaned across the table, and Jack had a sudden, hazy recollection of meat and bread, sausage in fact, the best-tasting sausage he had ever eaten in his short lifetime. With the taste came a buzzing in his memory, persuasive, persistent, the patter of another "procurer."

"You may not know it, but you have hit upon a timely notion. Because of the Quakers—damn their hides—our time for importing Africans will end. Perhaps not today nor tomorrow, but that is what they are agitating for with their *abolition societies*." Jeffrey sneered. "They've begun to put their demands in writing! As if Pennsylvania Quakers have a right to command the rest of us with their 'Act for the Gradual Abolition of Slavery'! Mind you, though, things like that tend to spread, and there are bleeding hearts all through these colonies. Even here in Virginia. An idea like that will slither its way South. If you and I work together, we'll be well positioned in the domestic market when shipping from the Slave Coast is no longer possible. What say you?"

"You must have an answer now?"

"I pass by my solicitor's on my journey to the province of South Carolina. I should like to have him draw up an agreement and have your signature on my return trip."

"I need time to think."

"Of what? It is a simple transaction. I will advance you cash. You may use it in whatever way will best improve the farm. We'll agree upon an interest rate. The return on my investment will be paid first, then your payments will apply to the principal. You'll expand your holdings and power in this industry. My idle funds will be at work for me even when I retire to my hearth.

"Do not take my offer lightly. I do not make it to every yeoman kind enough to give me and my cargo shelter for the night."

"Why me?" Jack asked.

"Because you are like your father. Thomas, I mean. Not your sire. And you are like me. Many of the men who crossed the ocean as we did may just as well have spared themselves a miserable trip. In this land rife with opportunity, they will come to little more than they would have if they'd stayed where all the doors were closed. But you and I and Thomas! We have mettle! I saw it in you when you took that nigger down with a pot of mush—"

Jack raised his hand. He did not like to be reminded of what he'd done to Shango.

"You saw an opportunity and you seized it. That day, you turned yourself from servant to heir purely by instinct! Now go the rest of the way. You are solidly established, but you are still but one modest way station on one modest piece of land. I am a stringer with ties stretching from one end of these colonies to the other. With my capital and your foresight, we can make this place the center of Virginia's domestic slave trade! Perhaps we could dominate the entire Chesapeake region." He shrugged. He sat back. "I can carry my capital elsewhere if you've not the stomach for greatness."

Greatness. In fact, Jack did *not* have a stomach for greatness. He did not know that any of his parents had possessed it either. Rowan and Lydia had simply come upon their last chance. They could board *The Venture* or perish with their children on the London streets. Thomas Crewe, Jack was certain, would find the idea of partnership repugnant. To Thomas's mind, a man made his way with his own brawn, coin, and wits. Then he made himself satisfied with what the three brought. No less, no more.

Except—everything Jack had was gone. Thomas and Mary Crewe were dead. Rowan and Lydia Dane were dead. Everything brought with him on the voyage from London was gone. There was not even a grave where he could visit his mother. He had neglected Rowan's grave for so many years, Jack doubted he could find it now. His sister was mostly gone from memory too. Most strongly, he recalled that she looked at him through their mother's blue eyes.

And so, greatness? A way to mark his passage in this land, so as not to be another refugee swallowed by an ocean or an unmarked grave? A hedge against the hunger that had set Jack's family on the road, out to sea, and adrift in the first place? A declaration to the rich—like the sea captain, the merchant and his wife, a woman who would not abide Lydia's touch but took her child—that his flesh was no longer available for barter.

Greatness seemed like fitting return for all he had lost.

And yet, the prudence taught to him by Thomas Crewe demanded satisfaction. "What if I am unable to repay you?"

John Jeffrey looked at him with such befuddlement that the possibility of a bad season or a downturn in the slave market seemed, in that moment, ludicrous even to Jack.

"Do you plan to fail?" Jeffrey asked, closing the question with an incredulous lilt.

"No, sir."

"Do you think I throw money into every enterprise I pass by?"

"No, sir."

"Listen, Jack, there are penalties, of course. Additional interest if a loan payment is late. Compound interest, in fact. Recourse if a man don't pay me at all. You understand I have to protect myself? That's just business."

Jack nodded.

"But you are not any man. You are the son of my *friend*—a man I respected! I will treat you as such. If you fall behind," Jeffrey said with a shrug, "I'll allow you grace. Now, if you don't trust my word, I can have my solicitor amend the standard contract. That'll take more time and delay us getting underway, but—"

When Jack rose to his feet, he surprised himself. Up until that very moment, he had believed the sage practicality of Thomas Crewe was more than enough to restrain him, to hold him back from impulse, from risks. But an inherited desperation—the desire that it all be *worth something*, that Jack himself should be *worth something*—held sway. John Jeffrey had endowed him with the selfsame faith he'd placed in Thomas Crewe. Jack Crewe, still and always the boy, the *vermin*, from the hold of *The Venture*, could not resist such an anointing.

And so, the concern was swept aside.

"Your word is enough," Jack said. He held out his large work-roughened hand.

Jeffrey, the pitiless slave stringer and cunning negotiator, stood also. He enclosed Jack's hand within both of his own.

• • •

Crewe knelt beside the hobbled ox. He had already pried stones from the animal's hooves. Now, he checked the tears in his hide. He rubbed salve in wounds caused by a bolt through the brambles. The ointment stank almost as much as the creature's own dung, but it was certain to keep out the maggots. Crewe spoke softly to the creature, urging him to hold still, reprimanding him for this latest escape.

"What's his name?" asked the slave stringer's son. His question was as surprising as his sudden appearance. Besides saying hello and thanking Crewe for meals, he'd said nothing Crewe could recall. A farm-bred boy with a healthy respect for bovines, he stood near the ox's head where the animal could keep track of him. He peered into its gentle face with interest.

"Cuddy," Crewe said. Then, a stilted, "What's your name?" He'd not talked to a child since he'd been one.

"Ethan." Someone had tried to crop the curls from Ethan's hair with a knife. The hair jutted and asserted itself in odd patches like hair grown back after a bout of sickness. Formed of a boxy build, the boy tended to hunch, as if he walked about expecting a blow. "Did you beat him?" Ethan asked.

The boy examined Cuddy's shoulder wounds. Crewe kept his hands busy with the ox, but he, in turn, studied the boy. Dark blond hair that would lighten with washing. Ears, neck, and throat ruddy from the sun. Stocky. Not one to be quick on his feet. Tight lips as though, at only eleven or twelve, there were words he must withhold. Squinting gray eyes. A boy like this would take a long time looking at the world. High on Ethan's cheek, a livid gash.

"He found himself a berry patch," Crewe said. "Went charging in." He jerked a thumb at the boy's cut. "You took a gallop through my berry patch?"

"No, sir." The boy shook his head vehemently.

"Here." Crewe held out the pot of ointment.

The boy frowned. "It stinks," he said.

Crewe twitched a smile. "The healing is in the stink." He dragged his fingers through the ointment, and before either of them knew what he was about, he reached out and dabbed at the angry trench on Ethan's cheek until it glistened with ointment. The boy was stiff as saddle leather, but he softened under the care.

Something happened to Crewe too. Just a flash, but as bright and sudden as heat lightning, he recalled Rowan's red, callused hands, scratchy but gentle, as he turned his son's face toward the light, exclaiming, "Ah, Jack! And what have you snarled yourself in now, my boy?"

Abruptly, Crewe turned his attention back to the ox. "You fell?"

"No," Ethan said.

"One of them boys give that to you?"

"No. No—ahh—" Ethan realized the fix created by his denials, but Crewe had already changed tactics.

"You like stringing with your pa?" he asked.

Silence. Then Ethan spoke as if he were reading by rote from a hornbook. "We shall be the richest nigger traders from Rhode Island to Georgia."

"Not a thing in the world wrong with that if that's what a man wants to be."

Ethan stroked Cuddy's warm, velvety nose. He scratched the animal's whiskers. "I ain't a man," he said.

Crewe glanced at the boy. Neither had he been a man at that age when he scalded Shango with cornmeal mush and chained his friend to slavery. What Jack meant for payback against Rowan, Thomas Crewe took to be an act of loyalty, a sign of ambition. That action set Jack on a path of snares and pitfalls. Once he had gone so far as to wield a whip against the flesh of another boy, another friend, he saw no point in turning back. There was nothing to turn back to. The boy who had been Jack Dane was gone.

"No, you are not a man," Crewe said to Ethan.

Some of the salve had melted. It slid, globby and shiny like a tear, down Ethan's face. Crewe asked, "What do you see when you look at them?"

"Boys. Why what do you see?"

Crewe saw just one boy: Adam.

In the mornings, Mary had handed Adam his breakfast at the back door. The African boy ate outside while Jack ate at the table with Thomas and Mary. Unless there was rain, Adam was expected to wait near the steps, patient as a hunting dog, until Jack came outside. It was, Jack's adoptive mother said, "Adam's place." But the sight of the boy waiting, sweating or hunched against the weather, always made Jack recall his time 'tween decks, waiting in the woebegone line for food that was often too salty or worm-ridden to swallow. The passengers above ate in a dining room with the captain or privately in their own cabins.

At the farm table, Jack ate heartily, pretending to be absorbed in his breakfast, but as Thomas and Mary talked over the needs of the day, he palmed or pocketed a wad of sweetbread or a rind of bacon—whatever Adam smelled but was not allowed to eat. No sooner than Jack was out the door, he slipped the tasty bit to Adam. Jack chattered and Adam chewed as the boys crossed the yard or field or forest, off to whatever task Thomas Crewe set them to.

One morning, not long after that first whipping, the boys crossed the field in silence.

"Here," Jack said. From the deep pocket of his breeches, he offered Adam half of a baked yam. Adam held out a trembling, receiving hand to meet Jack's unsteady, bestowing hand. But somehow, in the transfer, the yam fell. Or Adam knocked it away. In any case, neither boy bent, and something scarce and sweet was left to rot on the ground. Adam and Jack were no longer friends. Moreover, they were no longer boys.

Men understood things that boys did not: Being the "richest nigger traders," or even a middling slave jailer, had to cost somebody something. *Greatness* had to cost somebody something. Ethan, like Jack, would have to learn to be grateful that prosperity came at the expense of those Negro boys and not his own.

Jack shut his eyes hard. When he opened them, the first thing he saw was Thomas Crewe's whip hanging on the wall. "I see brutes," he said to Ethan.

"But they cry," the boy said, his voice sagging like Cuddy's dewlap. "Not in the day. At night. They want to go home. I want to go home too. What we do, it's wrong."

Ethan spoke with the same conviction Crewe had felt, years ago, in the moment Rowan made him hand over baby Lydia, and again when Thomas made him raise a whip to Adam. *This is wrong.*

A fresh upwelling of hurt tightened Crewe's throat and flooded his ears, his eyes, his mind. The sensation threatened to drown all other certainties.

Crewe cleared his throat. "We make fruitful use of them," he said, repeating Thomas Crewe's words. "We train them in the way they should go. We do them a service. In their own homes, they are savages," Jack said. "Without us, they would be nothing more than—than vermin."

Ethan's hand slowed on the ox's velvet muzzle. He realized his error. He had taken an act of kindness for kindness itself. But Crewe was no different from Ethan's father. Jeffrey beat him and Crewe put medicine on the wound, but their discipline was the same.

Ethan ducked his face into Cuddy's warm hide to hide his tears. He squeezed his eyes shut until the red behind the lids turned black. Ethan hated his father because of the man Jeffrey demanded he become. He hated Crewe just as much for making him believe, even for a moment, that there was another kind of man he could be.

● ● ●

No one—not slave, not master, not child—rested well that night. Long into the evening, David battered the quiet as he beat molten metal into terrible shapes. The sound drove chickens to the high branches of the trees and the oxen to the farthest corner of the corral. It crazed the chirping crickets until they fell into befuddled silence.

The pounding drove Bless from the kitchen. She fled farther—from the cabin to the barn, beyond, to the pack house, and, finally, down to the creek. And still, it seemed, she could hear that clanging, ceaseless, doleful echoing—striking the sun down, down, down, declaring darkness upon them all.

● ● ●

"Move out!" Jeffrey commanded. Ethan and the coffle of boys sprang to obey. Jeffrey plodded off, high atop his mottled, buckskin draft horse. The boys marched close behind the animal's shifting haunches and swinging tail. Ethan brought up the rear of the unspooling line, right behind Elijah, newly chained to the coffle.

Directly behind the boy, Ethan hunched beneath his hat, dragged along by an invisible chain that ended—just like the real one—in his father's fist. The chain David had made unfurled and grew taut, yanking Elijah forward, almost pitching him to the ground when the slack was spent. In half-hearted acquiescence to his father's wishes, Ethan poked Elijah between the shoulder blades with the butt of his whip. That earned him a cutting look from the child. Had Jeffrey seen, the little boy would have suffered a backhand or the toe of Jeffrey's boot. Ethan pretended not to see. A painful lot-to-learn lay ahead for both white boy and slave. Because in the face of unrestrained trade, a system where everything—spices, oils, ore, animals, cloth, and people—could be supplied if demanded, doubt and indignation did not matter.

Crewe did not mean to stand on the strip of fluttering grass between the cart ruts and watch until the string of boys disappeared. He certainly did not mean to take three strides after them, Ethan's name a wad in his throat.

If he stopped him, what would he say? That, coming to this coast in the rancid belly of a ship, Crewe himself had been a kind of merchandise? That he had fallen under the fragile power of his newborn sister and gaped in awe at the big African, Shango, only to consent to the sale of both? That, Rowan and Thomas, each in his turn, taught Crewe to take whatever opportunities fate and law bestowed on a man such as him and to hell with the rest of it?

Crewe believed morality to be a luxury beyond his reach. More importantly, he had never met a rich man who preached the concept or aspired to it. Years ago, Jack had been converted by the testimony of the balance sheet: It made little sense to hire, train, and support a man who would leave in a few years' time when, for seven or eight pounds more, a common man like himself could own a slave for life. There was no complex moral calculation: The law said yes; the pounds were sterling; the weaker men, by chance, were black.

And yet: "What we do, it's wrong." Ethan's certainty stirred ashes within Jack, fragments that survived the immolation of Rowan's betrayal and Jack's own.

So, Jack stood on that strip of grass, Ethan's conviction a bone shard in his throat.

• • •

"What he standing there for?" David wondered at Crewe pausing in the road as if he would call the group back or run after them. David handed Bless a pitchfork. For a few moments, they, too, watched the boys march.

Elijah wore a neck cuff and doll-size wrist shackles. That ghastly mask weighed down one side of John Jeffrey's saddlebags. He had not packed it away but wanted it close in case he had cause to use it. All of the bellies in the procession were full of victuals Bless had cooked at dawn. Biscuits and strips of dried meat were somewhere in bags tied behind Jeffrey's saddle. Thusly provisioned, those boys disappeared into slavery.

In time, the noise of their shackles faded, but their smell of unbathed flesh, sunbaked urine, and secreted sorrow remained.

Bless and David did not wait for the order; they began mucking out the slave pen. Together, they cleared the ground of footprints, handprints, dents left by knobby knees, and tracks of scrawny backsides, of straw and hair and nails, the leavings of boy bodies. David and Bless worked in grim determination as if they could sweep over, rub away, or dig out the truth.

Amid the raking, shoveling, and pitching, Bless paused. "What if we refuse?" she asked.

David glanced at her. "Refuse what?"

"To cook the food. To make the shackles."

David, of course, had already thought of this. "Then they whip us. They sell us to somewhere worse, some place farther from home. They buy somebody else and put 'em in our place."

"We are a part of it," Bless said.

"We part of it."

"So you understand now—what I did?"

"I wasn't never confused, Bless. But dead is dead. There ain't *no hope* in the grave. And I *hope*. I hope there's some way some of us, some of our children, can live and be free."

They finished the work in silence. Bless and David cleared the pen of all remains and fragments left by the coffle. Each carried away whole the memory of boys in chains.

• • •

David walked to and fro near the edge of the tall meadow grass. Hands on his hips, he studied the hues of green and tangles of bushes and weeds in the manner of a man who had undertaken an important job. Finally, he called, "Here jimson!" He bent over a low-growing, flowering bush. The blooms were white trumpets, the throats rubied as though each flower had once brimmed with wine.

He and Bless were on a hunt to replenish the dried herbs Miss Patience had left for their fevers, aches, and pains. Bless carried samples of dried blooms and stems in the long pocket tied around her waist. Cautiously, they matched what they could. What they could not find, David supplemented with plants remembered from his youth.

"What is it for?" Bless asked.

"All kind of things. My ma used to dry it. She'd twine it up and hang it in the sun. Us bigger ones helped her gather it. Come cold weather, she set fire to a bundle and pass the smoke before us. You better not hold your breath! Now our Pa, he never hit. Ma? She give you a smack! So all us breathe in the smoke. Such coughing you never heard! Children going off like canon shot! Nobody sleep that night. But come morning, everything quiet. The cold gone out'n us."

"You never mention your family." *Except in your sleep*, Bless could have added. But who knew what secrets escaped her nightmares? She did not want the worst of her dreams trotted out into the light of day, so Bless did not mention the names David still called out at night.

He twisted the supple vine, then worked it back and forth to create a break. He shrugged. "What to say 'cept 'gone'?"

Bless could not say why she pushed. She knew as well as anyone that the losses of slaves could not be expressed with words or toted in numbers, but David had contradictions that she wanted to understand. "Were there many of you?"

"Right many."

"And you were all together for a while?"

"A good many years."

He did not elaborate. Bless tried to find the way into his loss. "Cassie, my mama, she had other children," Bless said. "All gone by the time I was born."

David paused. "You didn't know any of 'em?"

"I don't even know how many there were. All I know is, I was her last child. Her master promised she could keep me." She held out her hands as if to say *here I am*. "Nothing more to be said about their promises."

"Was you lonesome without brothers and sisters?"

Bless considered. "I don't think so. I was always with her. Tucked up beside her in bed or playing on the hearthstone while she cooked. Then—"

"Then what?"

"The mistress claimed me, and Cassie stopped."

"Stopped what?"

"Stopped everything. Then I was lonesome. I was lonesome for all the years until Jeremiah."

David studied her. He jolted as if lightly plucked by some epiphany. "You don't know what it's like then."

"What?"

"What? To be surrounded by love. To steep in it. Be full up with it."

Bless shook her head. "No," she said. "I suppose I don't."

David stared. "What?" Bless asked again.

He gave his head a quick wag as if to clear it of a memory or to shake away a revelation. "I was wondering—"

"What?" she prodded.

"Wondering which one'a us is lucky."

Bless composed herself by looking down at her samples of dried plants, then up across the meadow. She pointed in the general direction of tall, yellow weeds. "I think that's bitter button," she said and tromped away.

David allowed her the privacy of some distance before he followed. "What's it good for?" he called.

"Flushes worms out of you. Good, too, if you've got a sore ache."

As he followed Bless across the field, David grunted in agreement. "We got plenty of need for that."

• • •

Farming only allowed a certain degree of separation. There were days when Bless, David, and Crewe worked shoulder to shoulder, hand in hand, to get it all done. Always, there was planting, harvesting, milking, grooming, gathering, fencing, and sharpening to be done.

The best hand was the free hand, so there were times when David or Crewe rolled up his sleeves to labor beside Bless at "woman's work," and days when she worked like a man in the fields. Livestock did not care if the hand that fed them was male or female, Negro or white, only that the oats were poured, the hay spread, the troughs filled with water. Garden weeds choked the corn and beans of master and slave alike. The distinct line between master and slave was sometimes overshadowed by the authority of who best knew the task. For soapmaking or sugar boiling, Bless gave the orders. At hog killing, Crewe and David traded ideas about the best way to cull a wily hog and how best to land a single killing blow between the eyes. Bless, Crewe, and David took an interest in canning; done incorrectly, there would be nothing bright or sweet to carry them through the bleak winter.

And so, for hours, sometimes days at a time, Bless, Crewe, and David lived as three people with a common purpose. Faced with the next task, savoring the salt of fresh-fried crackling, or shutting the door on a smokehouse full enough to carry them through to spring, it was possible to set just out of mind that one, more than the others, reaped the benefits of their combined labor.

Together, Crewe and David completed a new slave enclosure and brought it into use. It filled and emptied of women and children, young men and old ones, slaves who carried West Africa undiluted in their veins and some so nearly white, it seemed a curious trick had been played. No matter the differences, each group dragged grief along like an unburied carcass. It was that wretchedness that Bless and David tried to eradicate from the pens by scraping, digging, and scouring each time a chain of captives left.

As they set about their work, Crewe waved the slave drivers on to a safe journey, wished them a lucrative time at market, and climbed the steps to his house, where, undisturbed by the clatter, the raking, and used to the lingering smell, he counted his coin.

• • •

For that Saturday, David had plowed, sharpened, fed, and mucked all that was assigned to him. He could have rested. Instead, he joined in Bless's work. Out in the yard, David hauled wood and fed the fire while Bless dipped hot water from keeler to tun. He raked the oat mash.

All afternoon, they made beer, David wrestling the heavy tun and straining the mash, Bless measuring green hops and stirring thick, dark molasses into the sweet wort. They worked from cool mid-morning well into the heat of the day. By three, they had the strong ale and table brew barreled. They were tired but joked as they began the last task of the day, the small beer.

Their laughter reached Jack Crewe as he balanced the ledgers. A breeze that traveled between the raised window and the open door should have made sitting at his desk, while slaves labored for his comfort, a pleasant task. With eye-reddening smoke and burning steam, the slaves had the harder task, but it was Jack who grimaced over spilled ink and unbalanced numbers, while in the yard Bless and David batted gaiety between them like a shuttlecock.

"A man riding along in a place where he was unacquainted," Bless said, "came upon a young woman carrying a pig in her arms. Hearing it scream, he addressed her thus: 'Why, my dear, your young child screams amazingly!'

"The young woman turned and looked him in the face. With a smile, she said, 'I know it! He always does when he sees his father!'"

Their laughter roused Jack from his seat. Concealed in the shadow of the doorway, he watched David and Bless become smooth and lit and shining as they laughed. The fierce lines, the frowns, the chronic scowls were all gone. He went out, thinking he might ask to hear the joke.

Relaxed over the tun, stirring slowly, David first noticed the master's approach. In some wordless way, he signaled Bless. She glanced over her shoulder. Her smile withered. Their laughter evaporated.

The offense Jack felt was jarring. As surely as if he'd stubbed his toe on a stone or tripped over a root, he jolted into knowledge. Bless and David would not share their jokes or laughter with him. Worse, their holding back had nothing to do with fear or respect as Thomas Crewe had taught him to assume. No. Simply, it was what they *could* keep from him. He had no way to compel them to share this part of themselves. So they would not. Their rigid shoulders, their grave faces, signified a privacy he would never gain access to. Yes, he could enslave them. Law and violence granted him that. But he would forever be locked out of the cage in which he contained them.

Jack felt too embarrassed to turn and walk back to the house. So his anger—at them and at himself, at everyone—compounded with every step. This was where Rowan's fathering had failed him. This was what Thomas had tried to beat out of him, this craving for the friendship of Negroes. He had learned it from watching Da and Shango. He had sought it, for a time, with Adam. This misplaced empathy might have cost him Thomas's affections that long ago day at the jail. "Is you like them?" the girl had asked, and he'd been on the verge of sacrificing everything until Thomas's counter question: "Will you be a nigger as well as a nit, Jack?"

Who *did* he want to be? Certainly not one of them. Of course, Negroes can laugh. They have no understanding of how hard it is to build a life from nothing. They reap rewards without worry of failure.

Jack fended off failure every day. He set his feet on the floor before first light. He inhaled the dust from the plow along with morning mist. He woke his animals with a bucket clatter of kernels and husks. In winter, he cracked ice in the trough to free their water. In summer, he hunkered under his hat and remained in the field when the heat shimmered and rippled. All seasons, he kept track of every seed and every dram that existed on the place and made those measures multiply. Because if Jack failed, he would be no better off than the beggar he'd been when Rowan landed them here.

So, of course, slaves could hoot and snicker. The burden of growth was not upon them. If it were, they could not cast it off so easily. They suffered no lasting cares nor worries because he shouldered them all. He told them when to rise. He directed their days. He chose and bought their victuals and meted them out. Jack measured out the cloth with which they covered their bodies. How dare they keep anything from him, even their pleasure. As their caretaker, as their master, he deserved their labor, obedience, *and* good cheer.

He had fallen into the same trap as that boy Ethan. Jack had grown too close to them. He had forgotten his own place. Like Ethan, he had begun to treat them as something they were not. This open merrymaking was proof.

It was time for all of them to be about his business.

. . .

"Something you need sir?" David asked. He stepped from behind the tun, placed himself between Bless and Crewe.

"Look like y'all getting along," Crewe said.

Bless turned around to face him.

"Yes, sir," David answered.

"How she doing?"

Bless opened her mouth, but again David answered for her. "She coming along, sir."

"Then there ought to be good news soon," Crewe said.

"Sir?" David asked.

Crewe took a wide-legged stance. He held them both at full attention. "Grass grown up over that little grave," he said. His gaze slashed between them. "I can't feed a hound won't hunt nor a heifer don't milk. You hear me?"

Crewe waited for their stiff nods.

"You know what I got y'all here for," Crewe said. He waited. Realization darkened their faces.

Satisfied that he had chased away the joy in which he had no share, Crewe turned to go, then seemed to think better of it. "A taste of the strong ale," he said.

Bless's hands barely trembled when she tapped the keg and passed Crewe a tin cup full of beer.

He tasted the still-warm brew as he contemplated his slaves over the rim of his cup. Not so much light in their faces now. Not even so much as a guttering candle burned to its last bit of wick.

"Sour," he said and dashed the work of their day onto the ground.

● ● ●

Crewe was right. Nearly a year of grass had grown over the baby girl's grave. Daffodils bloomed there too, and in place of a headstone, some months back, Bless had planted a bush that blossomed yellow flowers in tiny clutches like crowns.

The very day David brought Bless to the grave, she began to tend it. She kept the little plot no less neat than the braids she would have plaited into her daughter's hair or the hems she would have stitched into her smocks. Even as Bless and David sat on each side of the little mound, she raked her fingers through the grass, gathering stray leaves and pebbles that had pushed up from the ground.

David answered Bless's question before she had time enough to ask. "He ain't gon' let this go. It was his plan before he bought you. It's why he bought you."

Bless cast away a palmful of rubbish. She raked her fingers again and again through the vivid green grass before she looked up at him. "If we don't?"

David looked off toward the tree line. "You heard him just like I did. He gonna put us in his pocket."

Bless's flesh crawled at the memory of what it was like to be sold, to be used and passed from hand to hand like a soft-worn banknote, yet she said, "I rather be sold a hundred times than have a child of mine sold once."

David sighed. He closed his eyes.

Perhaps because he was not looking at her, Bless could speak her heart. "Now, this little girl? I would have made her corn-husk dolls," she said. "I would have held her on my lap and taught her to make them, like my mama taught me."

David watched Bless from the other side of that grave. "You had dreams for her?"

"Of course."

"Mine, I woulda raised on a plot of land like what my daddy meant for me. I woulda built a house on it and had one child for every brother and sister took from me." Tears glimmered in David's eyes. "Celeste mighta been carrying our child when she was sold from me."

They sat with the immensity of never knowing. Then, David said, "It's a chance."

Bless looked up at him, away from picking through the grass. "You can't be thinking—"

"He say he won't sell us if we do."

"White men *never* lie."

"We can grow old here."

"And the children? Where would they be?"

"What he planning, it's like a pedigree—"

"You mean like a hunting *dog*? Like a blooded *horse*?"

"*I mean* they won't be like the little boys passed through here"—he forced little Elijah's baffled face from his mind's eye—"on they way to God knows where. Not like me and you neither. They'll know where they come from. They'll know the way back."

David shocked himself, lobbying for the merchandizing of his own offspring, for the heartbreak it would bring. But before that, there would be time. Precious time. He pictured children climbing on and off Bless's lap, learning to make corn-husk dolls. Out of pure longing, he conjured up the handful of years when they would be small, when they could sleep, knees tucked, upon his chest, and their feet would be tiny enough to fit in his mouth. When they would walk and learn to speak. Years in which he would carry them, then they would follow behind and finally run out ahead of him. Maybe ten years. Maybe twelve or fifteen before Crewe sold the children. No time at all. But immeasurable when held up against the prospect of nothing.

He nodded at the baby's grave. "How many times you think you can do *this*, Bless? If he split us, somebody, somewhere gonna force you. Once he sell you away from here, don't you see you ain't gonna be able to help it?"

He was right. Bless knew it. Still, she shook her head in refusal.

"I know this ain't like you and Jeremiah," David said. "It ain't like me and Celeste neither."

In the wake of those words, he did pause to consider what he was asking of this young woman, little more than a girl really, and him not too much older. But he was tired, so tired, and not just from the boonless labor in another man's fields. He was tired of wanting and not having. Weary from the strain of trying to recall faces, sounds, and smells of the people he had loved. Hungry from the ever-thinning milk of memory. Disheartened enough to accept that a small part of what he wanted was better than nothing at all.

"I don't want to be parted from woman after woman, leaving young'uns behind. And I know you don't want to do this again," he said.

The desperation in David's voice rang as clearly as his hammer on the anvil. Crewe wanted this, yes, but Bless realized that David did too. Not only wanted, but had permission, a mandate, from the only person whose consent mattered.

"Would you force me?" Bless asked.

David looked at her in a kind of puzzled disbelief. Then, just as he had on the night Crewe tied and whipped him, he freely offered his hands.

"I carried her here," he said. "I dug that hole. I laid your girl in the ground *with these hands*. You reckon I would use 'em against you?"

She did not.

She called to mind how careful David was each time he lifted the yoke of buckets from her shoulders. And she saw, almost through the veil of a dream, how gently he had lifted her baby and cradled the stillborn in his hands. He had wrapped her in white, she seemed to recall. A shirt? And she imagined David laid her daughter in the ground in the same gentle way he'd lifted Bless from the hard turf where she landed. She remembered how carefully he'd tilted the head of the boy, Elijah, as he fitted him for the collar, and how David's callused hands cupped light and loose, so as not to crush or bruise, around the buds and herbs they had gathered.

No. She did not believe he would force her. From the very beginning, Crewe had marked Bless down for use as a farm tool for breeding and given David the right to use her so. Never once had she been afraid that he might.

"I don't—" she started to say. But she had taken too long sorting through it all.

David had already gone.

• • •

Bless had no timepiece except the moon, no way to tell how many hours had passed since David had entered the darkened cabin. She had not even heard him come in. Though she tried to wait up, Bless had slept. Now, she had no idea how many hours had passed since he'd left her alone beside the baby's grave or how many more would pass until sunrise. She awakened partially when she heard David tossing restlessly. She awoke fully when he rose and left the cabin.

Bless sat up. She was sure he'd waited until he thought her asleep before coming into the cabin. And she guessed he would rise and leave early to avoid her in the morning. That meant he would go another entire day thinking Bless believed he would force himself on her.

Bless tossed back the quilt. She stuffed her feet into her shoes and used the bedcover as a shawl.

• • •

On either side of the path, grass crackled with mice, possums, or racoons nosing about for lost seeds, chewing and scratching bark or roots, searching for a meal or trying not to become one. The moon was partial and white, as thin and brittle as the ice crust that rimmed the water troughs.

Up ahead, David's white shirt billowed softly. Where was he going? She would have called out, but the thought of waking Crewe and having to explain why his two enslaved servants were running about at night kept her silent. She followed the white shirt.

David followed the path through a thicket of trees and pushed through the frosted grass to the other side. Bless could have called to him then. A whisper would have carried, and he would have turned, and they would have talked.

She said nothing. David pursued something here that he could not seek in daylight or in her company. Bless wanted to know what it was.

David stopped at the edge of a recently cleared field. Bless hid in a blind of trees. He stood partially turned from her, hands clenched at his sides, staring down at newly tilled ground that would be seeded with corn as soon as the days grew warm enough. Moonlight revealed his tears. Bless was about to rush to him, to step from the cover of the thicket, when she noticed the hurried movements of his hands.

Almost angrily, David pried at the button of his breeches. He shucked the pants to his hips and took himself into his own callused palm. He turned his face skyward. Unable to retreat, Bless watched. She watched him swell. She watched him rise and lengthen.

David worked himself rapidly, roughly. Mouth open, jaw working, he gulped in the moonlight, and indeed, when he groaned and began to shudder, threads of silver erupted.

His head drooped. The tears in his eyes dripped, along with his seed, into the ground.

David buttoned up. He dragged his foot over the earth.

● ● ●

Bless pretended to be asleep. The straw in David's mattress popped and cracked as he settled. Soon, she heard the soft rhythm of his snores. She opened her eyes and tried to see him through the blackness. But the man who slept across the room was barely more decipherable than the dark shapes and shades of the cabin.

How many nights had he done that, slipped from the room to ease himself while the woman designated for the task slept unbothered?

David had hidden his desires well, concealed them behind concern for her unborn child, couched them in sensible-sounding talk about the upsides of Crewe's despicable plan. The truth, however, was that David desired a woman. He craved the children coupling would bring. Yet he left Bless sleeping. He buried his seed in the ground rather than become a brute that Jack could turn to profit.

Bless settled against the lumpy straw of her mattress. She released a long, wondering breath. They were not so different, she and David. Outwardly, they endured—the days, the decrees, the damage.

Inwardly, their hearts thundered with insurrection.

● ● ●

David shut the door, but he did not cross into the room.

The beds were pushed together, the space between them closed, their meagre coverings combined.

Through contrivance and the demands of the farm, David had been able to avoid being alone with Bless since their conversation by the baby's grave. For two days, he had risen early and worked late, seeing Bless only when she passed him meals, able to avoid the plea in her eyes by looking or hurrying away. Now she had done this.

Bless waited beneath the quilt. A tallow candle burned low, lighting the white of her nightgown, leaving her shoulders and face in shadow.

Before she could explain, David said, "You don't owe me nothing. You don't have to prove nothing."

"I know that."

He inclined his head pointedly at the beds. "Then why?"

The gown shifted up then down over Bless's bosom as she shrugged. "'Cause you care more about me than you do about yourself. I realized that. I want to give that back to you."

David's gaze slid from the material resting on Bless's breasts to her face. He shook his head. "No, you don't want to—"

"I *do* want to make you happy. I *do* want to stay with you. I do want us to be happy for as long as we can."

Bless rose to her knees. The quilt fell away, and the light shone through the thin cotton of her gown, revealing the curves of her silhouette. She held out her hands.

David moved across the room slowly, shambling, giving Bless time to change her mind.

But she did not change her mind. David pulled Bless into his arms. He lifted her. He wrapped himself around her and held on. They came to rest at last on the bed with Bless straddling David's lap. With his head against her collarbone, he savored the feeling of Bless's hands stroking his head, his neck, and shoulders. David looked up at her. "I will do right by you," he swore.

He kissed her and trembled at the reward of her hands sliding beneath his shirt. His breath hitched as Bless explored the ridges of his stomach, the dusting of hair on his chest, and the smooth skin of his sides before her hands slid to the rough topography of his back. David gasped as her fingertips brushed the sensitive territory of his newest scars. He clutched Bless's thighs, kneading the skin to contain his desire. Where her gown had ridden up, he discovered that she bore scars of her own.

He raised his gaze to hers. "How did you—"

"Never mind," Bless said.

David felt the moist suction of her lips against his neck, and how she got those scars, their orderliness and precision, who put them there, and for what purpose no longer seemed important.

He and Bless were going to be happy.

● ● ●

Bless sat with her hands wrapped around a steaming cup, waiting for the herbs to steep. Heat burned through the thin wall of the gourd into the pads of her fingers.

The only light in the cabin shone beneath the kettle. Embers popped and shadows stretched. From the bed came David's snoring. He rolled to face her.

The flame of the bedside tallow candle had drowned in its own wax as Bless and David made love, but even in the dim light from the hearth, Bless could see a hint of a smile on his lips. He would have no bad dreams tonight. He would not cry out for his family. He would not leave the cabin to seek lonesome relief in a barren field.

Of all the evils, Bless was choosing the lesser, the least, the lie that would make David happy while keeping another child from being born into this merciless mess of a world.

She lifted the cup and sipped as David awoke. "Bless?" he murmured. "What you doing up?"

"Go back to sleep," she said. "I'm just having a cup of tea."

● ● ●

Except for Bless, everyone was happier with the lie. Crewe gave David approving looks as the exchanges between his slaves became openly affectionate. He told Bless to "speak up" when lighter duties became necessary.

As if she were a full and willing partner in his scheme, Crewe told Bless time and time again, "We will make something out of your children." Bless always turned away, never sure what response he expected of her.

"This place," Crewe told her, "will be known far and wide for quality Negroes. How do you feel about that?"

One day, Bless asked him, "How do you think I should feel, sir?"

Crewe hesitated. "Well," he said, "proud, I reckon."

Then, Bless did an extraordinary thing. She looked straight at him, considered him in a way no one enslaved was supposed to consider a master, and asked, "Would you be *proud*, sir, to have your flesh and blood sold?"

Taken aback, Crewe, in turn, took in the whole of the woman he held in bondage, something he had not done since the day he bought her.

Beneath his gaze, Bless materialized. For just a moment, Crewe saw *her*. Where only a useful shape or shadow of her stood before, she unified, the separate parts of her—the laundry-scrubbing and biscuit-making hands, the water-toting shoulders, the vacant, fertile womb, the quick mind, and vulnerable heart—all came together, momentarily, in the shape of a person.

His expression changed. For the space of a pain-filled flash, a different man, Jack—astonished, embarrassed—looked back at her.

But he looked away. He snuffed the glint of recognition as quickly as it flared.

Crewe's tone was gruff when he said, "Negroes have no lasting emotions. It would not be the same."

Rather than give the only answer she had, one that would surely bring down the whip, Bless seized her tongue between her teeth. She walked away.

But pain, even the memory of it, can make its own rebuttal. Within Crewe, there was a dim remnant, a quiet but insistent voice, a younger, wiser self who whispered, *But what if it is?*

• • •

No sooner had David set down the ball-peen hammer, than he heard a whinny. He squinted through smoke and falling sparks at the horse, then the stranger. The animal shifted restlessly, and David had the feeling that man and horse had been standing there awhile, watching as he worked.

"Help you, sir?" David asked.

The man's gaze traveled over David, sweeping down then squinting up again. "My horse throwed a shoe," he said.

As if by signal, the horse shifted, trying to find balance, trying to redistribute his weight among the three shod hooves.

"I can get that fixed right up for you, sir," David said. He scrubbed his hands down the front of his leather apron and stepped from behind the anvil.

"What's your price?"

"Usually charge two bits, sir. But you have to get the price straight from Master Crewe." David jerked his head. "He up near the barn."

"What's your name?" the man asked.

David tensed. Most white men were not interested in a Negro man's name, only what service he could render. If this was one who tried to be polite, David would spare him the trouble. He picked up the hammer again. "You find Master Crewe up at the barn or near the house."

"I asked your name."

David lowered the hammer once again, but he did not let go of the handle. "David," he said.

The man huffed with impatience. "David what?"

David corrected himself. "David, *sir*."

The stranger shook his head. "No. What's your last name?"

Wiser now, David would not fall for the same trick in one life-time. "My master name Jack Crewe."

"You called 'David Crewe'?"

Ready to end whatever game the stranger played at, David said, "Don't make me no difference what you call me, *sir.*"

The man studied David anew.

Beside the stranger, the horse whinnied, but the man did not seem to be in a hurry to find Master Crewe. He stepped farther into the smithy. Leaning a shoulder against one of the posts that framed the bellows, he rested one booted foot on the swage block. He took cigarette makings from a pouch worn around his neck and placed them on his thigh. He spread out a paper, shook a line of dried tobacco into it, then rolled and twisted the thing together. He pressed the end of his cigarette to an ember in the glowing forge.

He took a long pull and blew out. Swirls of smoke camouflaged his words. "You put me in mind of a somebody I used to know up on the Eastern Shore. Nigger by the name of Cabarrus."

"That so, sir?" David asked.

"Indeed."

Pointedly, David turned away. He rummaged among the shelves for the tools he would need to shoe the horse.

"Shame what happened to 'im," the man continued. "Had him a nice setup there. Good piece of land. Prime waterfront. Bet he wish he never laid eyes on it." He leaned against the wall as if to settle for a long chat. "It got 'im too big for his britches. Tried to hold out against one of them barons that wanted it."

David kept his back turned. He could not say what he would do if the man took pleasure in the telling.

"Wasn't long 'for they relieved him 'a everything he accumulated— not just the land and house, but his woman and young'uns too. Scattered 'em far and wide is what I heard."

He chuckled. "Hell, you might be one'a them Cabarrus Negroes! You sure put me in mind of 'im."

David turned. Only soot and sweat marked his face. Only the tension in the hand that held the hammer betrayed him. Had the wood not been so tough, David's grip would have cracked it. "You want to buy something," David repeated, "you talk to Master Crewe. He up by the barn."

The man shrugged. He pinched the ember of the cigarette between his thumb and forefinger and tucked the nub in his pocket. He sauntered away in the direction of the barn.

David and the horse watched as the man crossed the yard. The animal gave an uneasy snort.

David shoved the hammer into a pocket of his apron. His hands trembled with anger streaking from shoulder to forearms to fingertips. He rolled his shoulders and waited so as not to touch the animal with angry hands.

Only when the anger ebbed did David kneel to drag steady hands over the animal's hock and canon, down to the fetlock. Soothing and muttering as he went, David lifted the animal's leg and examined the shoeless hoof.

The shoe had not been off for long. Not much dirt. No bloody or tender nailbed to make the horse shy. No jagged edges caused by a break to be filed. In fact, the horse had not thrown the shoe at all. Rather, with patience and care, someone had loosened the shoeing nails and carefully pried the iron away.

David released the heavy hoof and turned toward the barn. The two white men stood talking, Crewe with his back to David, the other man standing a head taller, listening, nodding, glancing over Crewe's head every so often to meet David's eyes.

• • •

Bill was not averse to lying. Before a job, he dyed his silver hair black, slicked it back, and did not trim it again until the job ended. He grew out an uneven and wiry beard. He went days without bathing. He hardened into the skin of an itinerant slave buyer.

He was appalled at the ease with which he became a flesh peddler. Insults, cruel jokes, threats streaked from his lips. On the handle of a whip, his grip held sure, his aim true. Ruthlessly, he suppressed the memories of his wife, herself a runaway, and their two daughters, waiting back home for him. Bill had a debt to pay to people like Andrew and Phoebe. The irony that he could only repay it by becoming the worst version of himself was not lost on him. So he cheated, he stole, he lied to pay what he owed. For practical reasons, however, he stuck as close to the truth as possible.

When Crewe noticed his glances at David, he said, "I'm scouting skilled Negroes for a man out on the frontier. That type ain't so common out there."

Crewe glanced over his shoulder to where David shoed the horse with a minimum of clatter and fuss. "That one ain't for sale."

The entrenched frown lines framing Bill's lips flickered into a grim smile. "How you know? You ain't heard my offer yet."

Crewe shook his head. "Don't need to. Him and his woman, they're my cornerstone."

"They got little ones?"

Children running about were usually easy to spot. Bill hadn't noticed any in the time it had taken him to scout the farm and locate the slave cabin. Knowing how Andrew felt about his own children, Bill was sure he would want any grandchildren factored into the calculations. Bill was not sure about the woman. Children sold cheap. But a woman in her childbearing years would significantly deplete the funds set aside for buying the rest of Andrew and Phoebe's scattered children.

"Not yet," Crewe said. "Got them working on it."

Bill clamped down on the shudder that threatened to rise and ripple over him at Crewe's weasel words for breeding, no different really from saying, *I pastured them together. Waiting to see what comes of it.* Certainly, it was not the first time Bill heard a slave owner tell how he arranged or dismantled the most intimate aspects of Negroes' lives for profit, spite, or whim. Bill's last night as a slave catcher was spent with men as heedless as Crewe, albeit bloodier.

Bill became a runaway taker when he was young, single, and constantly seeking money that came from anything other than an ox and plow. This was back in the days when only white men had to have passes to exit the colony, before slaves had to carry tickets. Bill brought back plenty of indentured servants who took their freedom rather than waiting to see if they survived the deprivation and labor, as well as men who skipped out on debts. Bill was good at the job.

Before long, he picked up the occasional work of hunting down a runaway slave. As slavery hardened into a nearly impenetrable line, Bill chose a side not because of ideology but because the colony's legislature pledged one thousand pounds of tobacco for every runaway fetched back to his master. Before they reduced the amount to two hundred pounds a year later, "if the runaway be found within ten miles from his master's house," Bill had accumulated a small fortune. Mostly he worked alone and preferred it that way, but on occasion, if the quarry was multiple—say, a group of white servants and slaves, and the other slave takers promised a fair portion of the pay along with provisions and fresh horses—Bill worked with a posse.

On the eve of such a hunt, Bill sat around a campfire with a gang of seasoned slave takers. Two had hunted slaves in Jamaica and Barbados. They entertained the rest with tales of Cuban-bred "nigger dogs," conditioned from pups to hate black skin. A slave was compelled to kick and badger the dogs, to starve and whip them. To make them mean. To make them hate the sight of black skin. Perhaps it was their own fear of the whip, or perhaps it was a way to slough off some of their own misery: "But them niggers trained the most vicious dogs you ever seed! Take a run'way by the throat, the nape, the nuts, or titty and don't heel 'til they brought to ground," one man had said.

By turns, the old-timers were matter of fact about the maiming or gleeful when they told of a wily fugitive who had been particularly hard to catch. They crowed over dreadful deaths. They talked while chewing. The swirl of meat and bread, spit and tongue, mimicked the viscera of their tales. Bill's stomach had twisted.

He'd thought he had few illusions about the nature of slave catching. Though it was not his way, he knew that rape and abuse were often baked into the task, but Bill did not trouble himself with the methods of other men. He did not judge himself better or worse. Bill had lashed black flesh. He had turned a deaf ear to pitiful pleas and cries. He had run black bodies to ground, tied or chained them, and dragged them back to whomever laid claim. When a fugitive cursed him, spat on him, he might go so far as to deliver a stunning backhand or land a quelling fist. Standing over the dazed fugitive, Bill advised that they were lucky: he did not enjoy, like some others, like these men with whom he broke bread, inflicting pain.

That night Bill had set aside his half-eaten rations. "What good is a mauled or dead slave?" he asked.

"Tell you what good!" an old-timer said. "One mangled nigger save three or four from running off!" Firelight revealed a bright spark of meanness in his eyes. Around the campfire, other men agreed.

Bill glanced from face to face; he saw in each the same flinty, depthless cold. When had these men turned away from the chance he had then, the chance not to become the worst man he could ever be?

Later, as Bill crept past the makeshift dog pens, the animals moaned and huffed in canine sleep. It was the growl-like snores of the men, already dreaming of the hunt, that sent Bill fleeing into the trackless night.

* * *

To hide his disgust, Bill made a long project of scuffing the dirt with the toe of his boot before he looked Crewe in the face again.

"Name your price," Bill said. He counted on a lack of imagination, the poverty of mind that slavery engendered to keep the price in a reasonable range. In fact, Andrew had put much of three years' profits at Bill's disposal. What wouldn't a man pay to regain a son?

Bill was not disappointed. As if on a whim, Crewe named a sum slightly higher than the market price for a healthy young buck. Andrew would gladly meet it.

"Done," Bill said, enjoying the widening of his adversary's eyes.

Instantly, Jack regretted his rash flirtation with selling. "David ain't one I'm trying to be rid of," he said. "Money or not, he's mostly been a good boy, and he's took to that girl. I won't sell him off if he don't want to go."

Surprised, Bill sized up his opponent anew. Perhaps within Jack lay a man like himself, a man who might still be salvaged. He tested the notion.

"How much," Bill asked, "for his wants not to enter into it?"

Crewe's eyes widened. Darted. How much could he profit in the long term by briefly postponing his plans? He would need to look at the ledger. He also had to consider that after months of trying, David and the girl had not gotten with child again. Would it be a mistake *not* to offload him onto an eager buyer and use the funds to buy another stud? In a few months' time, if the fault proved to be the girl's, it would not be hard to find another wench to replace her.

Crewe hedged, "Dark soon. Ain't safe to be on the road. You ought to stay the night. I got a place you can sleep. My girl, Bless, will bring you some supper."

"No need," Bill said. "My man pitched camp not far from here. He ought to have supper going by now. I only doubled back to see about the horse."

Crewe nodded. He examined the quality of the man's clothes—travel-stained but not mended. Shoe leather tough enough to withstand blade and fire. And even at a distance Crewe could recognize the quality of the horse—well-muscled with a long neck, sun glinting off the hide, the gait long, with only a slight unevenness from the thrown shoe. Whoever this man represented could afford to outfit his factor well.

"I'll have a number for you in the morning," Crewe said. "Got to feed the animals now."

Crewe walked away, his excitement concealed behind those abrupt and dismissive words, but Bill was almost certain the sale would happen. He felt a burst of gladness for Andrew. The man would have his son.

But behind that elation came a gust of sadness. David's wants, after all, did not enter into the deliberations about his life.

• • •

"You do good work," Bill said.

He had watched as David heated and bent the iron, then hammered it into the tough keratin of the horse's hoof. Sweat still beaded at the young man's temples. David's fingers were blackened with soot, and his arms bore the pockmarks of hot iron filings, yet the coins Bill paid for the young man's exertion and skill would end up in Crewe's purse. *A goddamn shame,* Bill thought as David handed him the reins to the horse. The animal stood relaxed from brushing and the handful of oats David fed him for being patient.

Bill had one foot in the stirrup when David finally asked. "You know what happened to any of them?"

Bill eased his foot out of the loop. He released his hold on the saddle horn and turned. "Them Cabarrus Negroes?"

"Yes," David answered.

"I might. You really want to know?"

"Yes, sir. I do."

Bill exhaled, a sound of unburdening and relief. He had wondered what kind of man Andrew's son had become. "Then come find out for yourself."

• • •

David knew why he kept the secret from Crewe. He did not know why he kept it from Bless. They ate dinner in near silence and undressed for bed. Bless did not seem to notice anything amiss. Their quiet was nothing new. It was one of the things that made it easy to be together.

David blew out the candle stub and slipped beneath the quilt alongside Bless. She reached out to touch him, exploring his skin from jawline to chest. She had come to enjoy lovemaking with David. She savored the way he moved his hands over her body. His touch was gentle and stirring. She knew that to be a rare combination.

Bless nuzzled the lobe of his ear and blew gently into the opening. David shivered, but he halted the progress of her hand, lifted it to his lips, then matched their fingers one against the other: pinky to pinky, ring finger, middle, pointer, and thumb. He folded his fingers between hers.

"You know I love you?" David asked.

Yes. She knew from David's actions that he loved her. She had never needed an exchange of the words. Bless probed his gaze. The night, densely dark without the flicker of candle, hid whatever burned in his eyes. She knew he worried about his ability to get her pregnant.

She kissed the knuckles of their joined hands. "I love you too."

If the darkness had parted, curtain-like, for just a moment, Bless would have seen David's face stripped down to two emotions: humility and fear.

He peeled away her gown.

He loved her differently that night, turning her, positioning, and opening Bless to reach her in ways even Jeremiah had not. David challenged and exhausted her and himself more than once. Only at the third trembling, when Bless begged, "Please, no more," did he allow her to curl at his side.

Feeling her body soften, tracing the circle where the skin of her breast became the gingerbread-brown flesh of her nipple, David fought hard to win against his own sleepy ease. He waited until Bless became heavy and boneless against him.

David dressed without lighting the candle. Bless did not stir—not a twitch, not a change in her rhythmic, full breaths—not when he slipped from her arms nor out of the cabin, in search of Andrew Cabarrus.

● ● ●

David prepared himself for a fight. He expected an ambush, a blow aimed at his head, a small gang of bandits leaping from the trees or scrambling from a ditch to steal him away. Yet this was a risk he had to take. Braced and listening, he stopped, doubled back, and walked a long and convoluted route, but when he reached the baby's grave, the place where he had told the white man he would meet, he found only one man waiting there, an older black man standing in the light of a three-quarters moon.

His profile, the height and movement of him, were familiar to David in the way of a dim memory suddenly, sharply recalled. The man turned. Then David knew exactly what his own face would look like in twenty years.

The man hunted over the young man's height—the broad shoulders, the farm-built torso, and long legs—for something of the knock-kneed boy with the big, believing eyes. He found echoes of his child in the mouth shaped like Phoebe's, in the structure of his own face grafted onto this younger, sturdier sapling.

Father and son grabbed on. They held each other by the face, with hands cupped and caressing the forehead, the chin, the back of the head. It was the strangest thing, seeing that your baby had become a man; it was the strangest thing, seeing the man you would become. The same thinly curved mustache, one black, one gray, the squarish face with the high cheekbones, the same beautiful, black-winged, arching brows, the elemental umber brown of their eyes, differentiated only by the pockets of worry riding the fleshy cheeks of one man, the other's eyes set above firm cheeks and not yet clouded by the strain of looking backward.

David knocked aside Andrew's cap. The black hair, once dense as moss, had thinned, some silvered, soft and sparse like filaments of wool. When had his father begun to grow old? And Andrew wondered when the thin slope of David's shoulders had gone, which year among so many lost years, had the boy grown so tall?

They stood forehead against forehead. "Son," Andrew said. "Son."

"Daddy."

"I come to take you home."

David lowered his arms, but he held on to his father's hand. David shook his head. "I-I— Tell me," he said finally. "Tell me everything that's happened since—"

Andrew recited the mantra of names, the buyers of his wife and children, and how he had gone from man to man trying to buy his family back, how over and over he had been refused, told that he must leave town, and how, finally, he had done so, all but empty-handed. He told him about traveling to the frontier, the store, the pinching and saving and resolve that had brought them to this moment.

"I found your mama," Andrew said. "Now you."

"Mama? You found Mama?" David looked around as if Phoebe might step out from behind a bush.

Andrew shook his head. "She at home. At the store. She waiting on you."

David let go of Andrew's hand. He sat on the crude bench he had erected beside the baby's grave. A promise kept. Bless liked to sit there sometime. She had planted a bush that bloomed a joyful yellow. Andrew sat beside him. He took in the small marker, just a pile of stones, the blossoms, and the bush.

"Yours?" Andrew asked.

"No. This girl belong to Bless and her man from before she come here."

"Bless? Bill told me there was a woman."

David nodded. He was slow to speak. His words fell one by one, like leaves. "I hoped for you for a long time," he said. "All those plans— Remember when you showed me the farm? I thought it would be just like you said."

"I believed it too. So much. I held on to the wrong thing."

David inclined his head toward the baby's grave. "The next one, the next baby," he said, "will be mine."

"She pregnant?"

"We been working at it."

"But she ain't—"

"She might be."

"I would buy her if I could."

"I ain't asking you to. I wouldn't ask you to sacrifice one of the others. I'm just saying, I can't go with you. I thought I would feel different. I thought if you ever came—but somewhere along the way, I stopped waiting. I made promises, and it's too late."

"Son, you don't even know if she pregnant."

David pointed at the grave. "This little one ain't here by no accident, Daddy. Bless don't want babies. I convinced her. She trying to make me happy. No telling what will come of the child if I walk away now. I can't put my freedom above my child—"

"Like I did? Like I put what I wanted ahead of all y'all?"

David stood. He wished for a brighter moon so his father could see he bore no hard feelings. Simply, it was too late. "I ain't judging. I just— I can't leave my child behind."

Andrew stood. He matched his gaze to David's. "Neither can I."

"Daddy—"

"You got used to the cage. That's my fault. But I ain't gonna make that mistake again. I ain't gonna let you make it neither."

"You ain't hearing me."

"I'm hearing and *listening* too. *You don't want to be like me.* But staying in this cage, staying in slavery, ain't gonna make you a better man than me. All it's gonna make you is a slave. Please, please, let me free you."

"I can't leave," David said.

"You love this girl that much?"

"Yes."

"She love you the same?"

David thought of the day he had walked into the cabin and found the beds pushed together. How Bless reached for him now. "Yes."

"Then ask her. Ask her if this what she want for you."

"Put her in the place to decide 'tween her own happiness and my freedom?"

"I'm familiar with that place."

David exhaled. He looked up. The moon tracked steadily toward the west. The stars would fade soon. He said, "I got to head back."

As he turned to go, Andrew grabbed onto his son. He held on with the same firm grip that had kept David from harm when he was a little boy, brimming with more speed and will than good sense.

"David, I can't stay long. Scarborough's reach is far. The wrong person see me, I'll be back in chains."

"But you free."

"For now. But they closing all the roads to freedom, David. Passed 'em a law say a freed slave got to leave the colony within six months. He don't, and he run the risk'a chains again. Who know what they'll come up with next, son? I got to get you out *now*."

"Daddy, I told you I can't—"

"Ask her. See what she say. See if it really is love."

David strained to see his father's face in the shifting moonlight. He memorized the scattering of moles that fanned across Andrew's cheeks.

"I can get Bill to stretch out the dealing for another day," Andrew said, "act like he got to think over Crewe's asking price."

David seized on that. "He features me in his plans for this place. He may ask a lot."

Andrew cupped his palms around David's face. "It won't be too much," he said.

He let David go. Andrew watched his son disappear into the darkest part of the night before he himself walked away.

. . .

"Where have you been?" The sun had not risen, but Bless had. She sat at their table drinking that awful brew she liked so much. When she rose and turned, David could see the worry, taut in the skin of her face, clenched in her shoulders and fists. It gave him courage.

"I went to meet a man."

"What man?"

"I didn't tell you yesterday, but a man come to the smithy to get his horse shoed. Only, losing that shoe wasn't no accident. He come to talk to me—"

"What about?"

David took Bless's hand. "Hush, now. Don't look so worried. I'll tell you." He pulled out the second chair and set it in front of her so that they were knee to knee. "He brung news."

"A man? A white man?" David nodded and Bless continued. "A white man pretended his horse needed a shoe so he could bring you, a prime Negro blacksmith *news,* and you went out in the dead of night, without a word or a pass, to meet him? That right?"

"If you listen, I'm trying to tell you."

Bless crossed one ankle over the other. She leaned back in the chair and crossed her arms over her breasts.

"He knowed things, Bless."

"Um hmm."

"All about my daddy, Bless, where he come from and how he lost the land. I ain't have to believe him, he said. He said I could ask the man his self, so I did, Bless. The man I met with tonight is my daddy. Bless, I met up with Andrew Cabarrus."

Bless sat up straight against the ladder back of the chair. She uncrossed her arms and planted her feet on the floor. Still, she felt as though she might fall.

"You never told me his name."

David shrugged.

Bless said, "No, not much point, I reckon."

"I ain't said it out loud in years."

"Not even to whisper it?" she asked.

David shook his head. He could not help remembering: the first beating he earned was the last time he uttered his father's name. He licked his lips.

"Say it again," Bless urged.

David took a breath. "My daddy name Andrew Cabarrus."

"And that make you?" She smiled a trace of a smile as she teased the name out of him.

"David Cabarrus."

Bless said, "Pleasure to meet you, Mr. Cabarrus."

David's smile began but faltered. "That's who I was supposed to be. A free man, like him."

"Your daddy was free?"

David nodded. "He was going to buy us all free."

"What happened?"

What indeed? "Too big for his britches. Relieved him'a everything he accumulated. Scattered 'em far and wide." Knowing the stranger worked for Andrew did not diminish the ring of truth. *A man who wanted too much could end up with nothing at all.*

"A powerful man wanted his land, so he ruined my daddy. Took it. Scattered us like dandelion seed."

Bless reached across the space where their knees touched. She took David's hands in her own. She toyed with his fingers.

"I saw it once," he said.

"What?"

David kept his gaze on their joined fingers. "The place he had for us. It was beautiful. Set on a little finger of land that fed right into the river." David told Bless the story of how Andrew had taken him overland by moonlight and canoe up the river to the homestead where he intended to settle his family.

"He built a log house on it," David said. "He meant for all of us, brothers, sisters, husbands, wives to live on that land, farm it together. Like the village he come from in Africa." His breath fell on their joined fingers. "That's all the life I ever wanted."

In the moment before she asked the question, they were both aware: Bless already knew the answer.

"What is he doing here now?"

David cleared his throat of whatever emotion beat there. "He here to buy me. He come to take me home."

"Oh," Bless said, a sound like a fist to the gut.

David looked up.

"Yesterday," she said. "That man came to you yesterday?"

"Yes."

"You finished your day of work. You came back here. You pumped the water and put it over the fire while I got our supper. We washed up. Ate. Put on our nightclothes and we—you had to be thinking about it."

"I wasn't sure, Bless, if it was real."

She nodded, considering. "Sure enough to climb out of our bed and walk through the dark, risk getting caught by Crewe or the night patrol. Sure enough for that."

"I-I don't know what you want me to say."

Her face creased in thought. "You had to be excited. You had to be scared. But you didn't let on."

David pulled his long fingers from his wife's grasp. He slumped. "I didn't let on—I didn't tell you because I-I ain't going."

"What?"

"Me and you got a promise, Bless, a plan, to be together and raise our children for as long as we can." His gaze darted to the bed. "You could be carrying my child right now."

Bless followed his gaze. She put it all together. Yesterday, in that bed, on the first day they spoke of love, the loving had been different.

"You were trying to put a baby in me so you won't have to break your promise?"

"Last night was just—even before, you might'a already been— We don't know."

Bless's gaze swept to the teacup. She opened her mouth. On her tongue, she tasted both the truth and the bitter brew. Grabbing the cup, she rose and dashed the dregs of the bitter herbs into the hearth.

"We better get what sleep we can," Bless said. "Morning comes soon."

David followed her to the bed. They adjusted themselves as if everything remained the same: arms and legs entangled, her head against his chest. Close enough to feel each other's heartbeat and the soothing brush of breath.

Both were exhausted, yet neither slept.

Each lay awake dreaming of the life David Cabarrus was supposed to lead.

• • •

The solution was simple: Say nothing. Hush. David said he wanted to stay with her. All she had to do was believe him. And yet, she watched all morning for her chance. Bless went about her chores as usual, keeping an eye and ear turned to wherever Crewe sent David. She would follow him out to the fields or the far fences if she had to.

Finally, late into the morning, Crewe saddled up his horse to go "talk business" with a man "camped up the road." He was only specific about the work he expected to see completed upon his return. It was, Crewe made sure, enough to keep his slaves "out of mischief" for hours. He never mentioned that settling on a price at which he would part with David was the sole purpose of his errand.

Bless waited until the earth kicked up by the hooves of Crewe's horse settled, before she went to find David. Crewe had left him occupied with cleaning and sorting tools in the smithy. David balked when she asked him to take a walk with her. "Crewe left us a lot to do, Bless. Hell to pay if it ain't done when he get back."

She stood in the doorway with her hands planted firmly on her hips. "We got time."

"For what?"

"What you think 'for what'? We haven't really talked about this, David. It is not decided."

She walked away.

A curse. A long sigh. David wiped some of the soot and oil from his hands, threw off his heavy leather apron, and followed.

• • •

Bless reached the baby's grave a few steps before David. He had not tried to catch up with her. They both needed the silence and movement of the walk to compose their arguments, to think of rebuttals.

As Bless stood looking at the blooming bush of flowers that she had used for months to keep her womb barren, she felt herself stepping into a hole of loneliness, about as deep, about as wide as the one she had dug to plant the bush; she imagined how long the days would feel without the quiet company, the humble sweetness, of David.

"Like I told my daddy, Bless," David said as soon as he reached her, "it ain't your decision." She turned to him, her look questioning. David relented. "He told me to ask you."

"But you didn't."

"Because there ain't nothing to ask. The decision ain't yours. It ain't even mine really." David looked pointedly at her belly. From there, he let his gaze roam the small burial place where they were standing. "You think I could stand another child lost to me?"

Bless could leave it at that. She could nod and be grateful. She had found not just Jeremiah, but another man true to his word, willing to forgo his freedom—his life—for her. David had made his own decision. Bless could rest on his resolve and believe life was not calling on her to sacrifice her little bit of happiness *again*, as it had called on her to do over and over, ever since she was a little girl in Cassie's kitchen.

Her knees felt weak, so Bless hobbled two steps to the bench David had pegged and lashed together out of stumps and fallen limbs. "Sit with me."

"I know what you gonna say."

Bless held out her hand. At first, David ignored it. He watched her with his face and fists balled tightly. Then, almost angrily, he grabbed her fingers and pressed her knuckles to his lips.

Bless almost lost her will. Her mind raced to words, phrases, angles, that would make the way she had deceived him sound better. She could say that her woman's body—in that mysterious way no man could decipher or dispute—had sent her monthly blood just this morning. A concrete sign that there was no baby. No reason for David to remain enslaved. She looked into his eyes.

Conflict. Will. Compassion. Bless saw these and more as David fought himself. In the tenderness of his brown eyes, Bless could see that *she* had won. She could keep him, and she would have, if she believed in any kind of slavery at all.

She had to tell the truth, stark and straight, so that David could freely leave her.

But first, Bless pulled David down to the bench beside her. She kissed his mouth, found his lips plump, and soft, and clinging. Then, she kissed David's hands. Each in its turn, calluses and scars on the fingers that so often lifted the heavy water yoke from her shoulders, the hands that had laid her baby to rest.

She held his palm against her face. "There is not going to be a baby, David. Not from last night. Not from any of the nights before."

"How can you know that— Did Miss Patience tell you something? Was there—damage?" David watched her with love and worry. In moments, Bless knew that look, those feelings, would be gone. She was not sure what would fill his gaze once he knew the truth, but she was sure she could not sit so near to him as to witness the moment of change. Bless let go of his hand. She cleared her throat. She stood and walked to the bush she had planted at the head of the grave. She broke off a branch of blossoming yellow flowers and held it out to him.

"Miss Patience told me how to protect myself. She told me how to grow this bush, how to harvest the buds, how to dry them and grind them, and brew them into a tea. She told me to drink that tea after every coupling so that your child would not take root inside me."

The confusion came first. Then the betrayal. Because he was David, the anger came last. "You told me it was for healing. You drank it right in front of me. I-I should have known."

"Maybe you did know," she said. "Do you think maybe you did know, just a little bit? You are not the kind of man to do awful things, David. And what Crewe is telling us to do is the most awful thing I ever heard tell of. And no matter what you said to win me to it, I know that you know it's not right."

With her hand extended, Bless took a step toward David. He drew back from her. Good. Bless had to make him withdraw all the way.

"Don't forget," she said. "I know a thing about you that you don't know about yourself. I hear you cry in your sleep. David, if you weren't so scared of having nothing, you would never go along with such a thing."

"You been lying to me. Each day, every night, I thought *I* was failing. I was so scared Crewe would put somebody in my place who would hurt you."

"I asked you not to blame yourself."

"'Cause you knowed I wasn't to blame! You said, 'these things take time,' but there wasn't never gonna be a 'time'! What was you hoping? That Crewe wouldn't think I was barren? That he would change his mind?"

Bless shook her head. "I knew I would run out of time."

"Then what?"

"Then he would sell me, or he would sell you, and our happy little while would be done."

"Happy? You was *happy* lying to me?"

Bless let go of the proffered branch. It struck the ground between them. "Don't talk foolishness to me," she snapped, relieved when anger stabbed through the sadness that thickened, descended, and rose up from the ground to encase her. "I was happy making *you* happy, David. Tell me you weren't happy."

David stepped on the fallen branch of flowers. He crushed the petals beneath the hard, filthy toe of his boot. The thin twig snapped. He did not look up at Bless.

"You can't, can you?"

David turned away from her. He looked in the direction from which they had come. That way lay the cabin where he had thought himself happy, living with the woman he had come to love.

In the corner of the cabin, an empty cradle waited for the children he would make with that woman.

But the cabin, the woman, the would-be children, even the cradle David made with his own hands, belonged on land, in a life, over which another man claimed ownership.

"Tell me you are not glad that I lied."

Bless grabbed the back of his arm to yank him around but stopped. Beneath the chambray of his sleeve, she felt ridges—raised scars. Her hand and voice gentled.

"You are *not* a man to do awful things, David. So if you tell me you are not glad that I lied, that you are not glad I prevented a child, I will throw out the tea Miss Patience left. I will uproot this bush and let it wither. I will give you and Crewe what you want from me. Tell me."

Beneath her palm, Bless felt a cascade of tremors. She did not give in to her own shaking. She waited as David calmed, as his fear broke like a fever.

"I was wrong to ask you to go along with it," David said.

Bless's arms encircled him. With her head resting against David's back, she nodded.

"Looked like it was all we could have," David said.

"Now, you can have everything," Bless said.

David turned and pulled her into the tight circle of his arms. "What's gonna come of you?" he asked.

It was barely a twitch of the lips, but Bless did smile. "The same thing that was always going to come of me." Bless pressed her cheek against his heart. "Loving Jeremiah didn't stop it. Loving you won't stop it. Having babies won't stop it. All that just makes it worse."

She felt David nod. He let his chin rest heavily on the crown of her head. She gripped his shirt in her fists. As the road dust began to rise in the distance, they stood together beside the grave of the only baby they would ever share.

• • •

While Bill completed the deal, Andrew sat on the tailgate of the wagon. He wore his hat low so the brim cast a shadow on his face. He did not speak. He and Bill had agreed it was best if Crewe did not notice any resemblance between the Negro men. They wanted to hand over the money, take the bill of sale and David. They wanted to put this place behind them and never look back.

"I hate to see you go, boy," Crewe said to David. They stood in front of the barn, within reach of the fence to which he'd tied David and whipped him bloody. "I guess she ain't happy neither." Crewe's gaze flickered toward the cabin. The door remained shut. The oiled hides that hung from the windows had not been pinned back to allow in light and fresh air. Bless should have been bustling around by now, fetching water and wood for cooking, but the only sign of life had been David, leaving the cabin with a burlap sack of belongings over his shoulder.

Crewe knew that slaves tended to get "mulish" when one or another was sold. He was not without feeling. He would indulge Bless's sulking for as long as it took to get this business squared away.

He finished counting the money Bill handed to him. The paper pounds were crisp with possibility. The agreed-upon amount was there. Crewe turned his attention back to David.

"You wasn't getting the job done," he said by way of explanation, or apology, to the man he had just sold. "So, I suppose this is best."

David barely registered Jack Crewe's justification. The words were little more than mosquito-whine in his ear. David's goodbye nod was more of a jerk, a spasm, a reflex. Being bought and sold did not engender sentimental farewells. David climbed past Andrew into the bed of the wagon. He knelt behind the driver's seat where the view of the tiny cabin was unobstructed by the well.

At Crewe's careless dismissal of all the years of David's labor, it was Andrew, rather, who slid nimbly from the tailgate and stepped toward Bill and Crewe.

Bill knew enough to quickly move between the two men, his hand thrust out as if it had been his intention all along to seal this deal with a handshake. Crewe, busy tucking away the cash and extracting the bill of sale from his pocket, barely noticed anything amiss. Bill, however, understood his friend's intention.

He had watched Andrew's gaze rake over the seeded fields and the well-kept animals. The buildings stood in good repair. The fences were sturdy, their rails cut precisely. No one man could keep a farm in such good order. Andrew's son had done much of that work. How much of David's sweat, vigor, and blood had been plowed into Jack Crewe's fields, a harvest for this man's future? And yet, David was leaving with empty pockets while Bill forked over Andrew's hard-earned money. Andrew's brown eyes darkened to the burning black of tar.

Bill plucked the bill of sale from Jack Crewe's hands and pressed it against Andrew's chest. "Put this in my saddlebag," he said sternly.

Andrew brought himself up short. He heard Bill's actual command, the unspoken one, *We are so close! Don't foul this up!* Andrew opened his fist and closed it around the parchment. David's bill of sale. His son's freedom.

Before he could follow Bill's command to stow away the precious proof of ownership, the wagon's springs creaked loudly under

David's shifting weight. With his bag still on his shoulder, David scrambled back toward the tailgate. Andrew's gaze arrested David just as he tensed to jump to the ground.

David would have climbed down. He would have insisted that he could not, after all, leave Bless, if not for the look on his papa's face—a mix of boy and old man, of joy and grief—as he gripped the paper. David would break his own heart, and Bless's heart, rather than Andrew's. He set down the burlap bag. He reached out a hand to his father.

As Andrew grasped David's palm and heaved himself onto the wagon bed, Bill let go of his pent-up breath.

"It is," Bill said when he turned back to Crewe.

Crewe arched a brow. In the commotion of movement, he had lost the thread of the conversation.

"You said, 'I suppose this is best.' It *is*. It's the best we can hope for in a world such as this."

Bill didn't stay to enjoy the perplexed frown on Crewe's face. He strode toward the front of the wagon, jumped onto the bench. He slapped the reins against the horse's flank. The animal set off at a trot.

• • •

Length after length, Jack Crewe's way station became smaller and smaller in the distance. Yet even when it was safe, the men did not whoop for joy or even speak. All of them, David, Andrew, and Bill, were thinking of who was left behind.

Aware that he had no right—because of the skin he wore, because of the epithets and actions that came so easily to him, because he differed from Jack Crewe only in the constitution of his heart—still, Bill dared to issue one order to Andrew and David.

"Don't look back," he said. "Neither one'a you. Don't look back."

• • •

When David rode away with Andrew and Bill, the insects, the animals, the air, the leaves on the trees stilled. It seemed to Bless that everything lowing or clucking, everything buzzing or breathing followed David.

She barricaded herself in the cabin. She lit no fire, no candle to see by. The loneliest night of her life fell around her and lingered, dreamlike. She ignored Crewe's shouts, his orders that she come out and see to her duties. On the third day of pounding, cursing, and demanding, after he had tried and failed to shoulder open the door, Crewe threatened to burn the cabin down around her.

A blaze of light replaced the dull glaze in her eyes. Bless straightened from her slump. The flame of self-hatred that flickered and ignited within her surpassed Crewe's anger at being disobeyed, at being left to cook his own meals and empty his own night slops. Fire would work, yes, but after three days of reliving and ruminating, she had just hit upon a better way to punish herself, a better way to embrace the shame she felt for being born a woman and a slave. Bless left her chair by the cold hearth. She unlatched the door.

Red-faced, Crewe stood on the other side with his fist raised to strike the wood. The gust of his demand, "Open this door now, damn you!" hit Bless in the face. She did not give him time to berate her further. Bless grabbed Crewe by his hair, yanked him down to her, and ground her mouth—three days unclean—against his.

At first, Crewe tried to free himself by pulling at her wrists, but Bless would not relent. She held on with hands and nails, mouth and arms and legs. She bit and fastened to Crewe like the vermin he was so afraid of becoming, and she did not let go until his own blood betrayed him. Bless knocked the hat from his head, but it was Crewe who tugged the shirttail from his breeches and yanked loose the metal buttons.

Bless dropped the dress she wore. She disregarded the disgust she felt at the smell of her own unbathed body and, worse, at the sight of Crewe's pallid thighs and the reality of his penis, a swollen, mottled stiffness, as threatening to her as a club.

They grappled. Bless tried to hurt Crewe by embedding her nails in his flesh, by biting and striking when she could. He tried to overpower her, to turn and arrange her to his liking. At first, neither kept the upper hand. But when they fell to the floor, Bless kept falling, back into that cellar with Jason, where the burlap bit her back like a horde of mosquitoes; she smothered beneath the bulk and bashing of Rove; she shrank in the corner of a slave dealer's stall, cringing from the groping hands of prospective buyers. And now, as Crewe's pelvis struck her like a blunt sword, Bless reckoned herself where she deserved to be—in the dirt, beneath him. It must be that she deserved the pitiless fucking of white men. That was why she had been taken from Cassie and parted from Jeremiah. That was why David had to leave without her.

Bless dug her heels into the floor. She turned her face from Crewe's heaving and the gusts of his breath. She sent her mind into a dark corner beneath the bed. What she had told David was true: This was always what was going to become of her. This was *all* that was going to become of her.

Still, she wished she had chosen fire.

• • •

The door of the cabin stood open like the gate of a stall. Crewe had gone. Bless pressed up from the earthen floor. She wrapped herself within the tangles of her dirty dress. She took down the last of the dried asafetida left by Miss Patience.

While water for the concoction warmed on the hearth, Bless stepped out back to wash herself in cold water from the trough. She dressed in her only other clean garment. She wrapped her hair beneath a length of cloth. She would deal with its tangles and matted plaits later. She sat down at the table to watch as the brew colored the water and darkened. She watched the steam rise like an apparition and disappear the same way.

The cup grew cold. She did not bring it to her lips. The drink turned cloudy, and still she could not remember how it felt to love or fear anything enough to kill it. With her left hand, Bless raised the gourd. She held it aloft. She tilted it until it began to pour in a steady stream that splashed her bare feet and stained the floor.

She rose, left the cabin, and returned to her duties.

• • •

Andrew and David made camp—putting down bedrolls, arranging stones, and gathering wood for the cookfire—near the banks of the River Anna. Bill would return soon. In the three days they had been on the road, he had taken up the habit of leaving father and son alone while he went to "reconnoiter" their surroundings before they camped for the night.

They had seen little evidence of human company, a few fading tracks and charred animal bones scattered near a long-cold fire. As they followed the river home, Bill himself had come back with a rabbit from the hickory and oak forests, a string of bluegill that David and Andrew helped clean and roast over a small fire. They did not really need the food. They were decently provisioned from the stock of Andrew's store—he'd even remembered to supply a proper set of clothes and moccasins for David. But each night, Bill saw to the horse and then wandered off with a sling shot, fishing line, or gun, to give Andrew and his son time to get to know each other.

Left alone, the two men were mostly silent. The past was, as yet, a too painful thing to touch. They preferred to watch and learn each other as they were now.

David came up from the riverbank with a pot of water. He set it on the tripod while Andrew built a fire beneath. They settled down to wait as flames from the kindling licked at the seasoned wood. Above the crackles and pops of the growing fire, unseen birds whistled and trilled. A breeze ruffled the pines, sending a soft shower of spent needles twirling to the ground. The green of late summer was just beginning to drain from the oaks and hickories. Yellows and reds, soft signs of change, dotted the landscape.

"I know it's soon, son," Andrew said, turning his attention to David, "but I got to ask, you put any thought to what you want to do?"

Taken aback, David stared at his father.

"Now, I'd like to have you at the store 'side me. And I'm sure your mama won't want you to go—"

Andrew noticed the distress on David's face, that frowning moment before a child cries. Hastily, he backtracked. "You don't *have* to work at the store. We can look into getting you a little piece of land—son?"

David shut his eyes tightly and shook his head.

What could he do in a wide world where he'd had but two narrow choices: Obey and survive, or disobey and be destroyed. He wanted so little: to decide on his own when to rise up and when to sit down. He wanted so much: to learn to read and write. To work beside his parents in their store. To raise crops for himself. To open a blacksmith's shop. To earn money of his very own that he could keep. To give everything he had to help buy back his sisters and brothers. To know if *he* had a child.

"Ain't no rush—" Andrew soothed.

David opened his eyes and cleared his throat. "Nobody never asked me that before."

"Well," Andrew said.

He took a moment to swallow his own tears. Instead of weeping, he would, he decided, savor the freedom to ask. He would relish his son's freedom to answer. "What do you want to do, David Cabarrus?"

David's gaze darted, scudded: the rolling foothills, the tumbling river, his father's expectant face, the winding wagon path, the sky that dipped and climbed as it traced the treetops, the line of the horizon that reached everywhere.

"All of it, Papa. I wanna do all of it."

As the giddiness of possibility overtook them, Andrew's and David's smiles grew, curving and spreading into grins.

Then they laughed.

• • •

David found his mother in the garden behind Cabarrus & Co., among a tangle of grape vines—scuppernong he would guess, though the fruit had been plucked away. She snapped off dead leaves and pruned the excess wood. With that kind of care, the harvest would grow each year.

"Mama?" he called. Phoebe turned.

They stared at each other: a broad-shouldered young man over-laid the boy David had been; a gaunt older woman carved from the softer, rounder figure of his mother.

"Who you?" Phoebe asked.

She knew Andrew and Bill had gone off in search of one of her children. But she also knew the lives of slaves were taken lightly, held in low esteem. She had not dared believe the men would return with more than a story, a tale of what had befallen her child. She would make herself content with that. It was more than what she had now.

"David," he said.

She shook her head. "You ain't."

Andrew came through the garden gate. Over the young man's shoulder, she looked to her husband.

Andrew nodded.

"Yes, ma'am. I am David," the young man said.

"*My* David?"

"Yes, Mama. Your David."

Phoebe did not move. She let the clippers fall from her grasp and held out her hands, fingers opening and closing like a child learning to wave. It was all she could manage.

David, who had lost enough to understand why his mother could not step toward hope, remembered that he could.

• • •

Andrew moved by rote through the darkness. He did not want to wake Phoebe, whose joy had exhausted her. David was asleep as well, across the room on a pallet in the corner. The store secure, Bill and Jo gone home, Andrew sat on his own cot. He smiled to himself. They would have to build. As he brought more of the children home, they would need more room.

"Andrew?" Phoebe whispered.

"Sorry I woke you."

"I wasn't 'sleep. Andrew?"

"Yeah, Phoebe?" he asked as he unbuttoned his shirt.

"Thank you."

Andrew paused. "He ain't all I owe you."

Andrew stood to shuck off his pants.

"Andrew?"

"Yeah, Phoebe?"

"You wanna sleep 'side me and hold my hand?"

Still enough to hear their boy breathe. Still enough to hear a strike and crackle—the sparking of hope.

"Yeah, Phoebe. I do."

PART
THREE

Bless and Jack Crewe

Crewe's Way Station, Lower Norfolk
Colony of Virginia, 1703

Crewe attended the birth as he would have attended a foaling, his main concern that the mechanics go right, that the markings and weight and general health were recorded with care. The newborn was a boon. Already, he had a plan in the works with Jeffrey that would multiply the money earned from selling David. And, privately, Crewe congratulated himself for accomplishing in one go what David had failed over many months to do. With the new Negroes coming in and this child to boot, Crewe would be prepared to enter the market at an opportune time. Domestic slave prices were rising as the southerly territories clamored for hands. The natural increase of Negroes would become a cash cow.

As it turned out, Crewe had made only one miscalculation: Bless did not have a natural, maternal instinct. As with the stillborn child, she did not tell Crewe of her pregnancy. And she gave none of the signals slave women were supposed to. She did not stop braiding her hair. She did not ask for more or different food. She did not beg for less strenuous tasks. Bless did nothing to help nor hinder the development of the child.

Crewe himself finally took notice of her widening, slowing gait, of the darkening of her skin and the swelling of her hands and feet. She never even confirmed that she was, in fact, with child. Crewe ordered Bless to nod, to at least acknowledge that she heard him, when he ordered her to inform him when she felt labor begin. Bless did nod, but only so she could quickly return to the distance and numbness that had been her retreat since she'd said goodbye to David. She doubted any kind of feeling, even the pain of birth, could reach her, but if it did, she would tell Crewe.

The baby, however—like wild and wily creatures born with whatever is necessary to escape the dangers they are born into— arrived forearmed to save itself from the neglect of a traumatized and emotionless mother, from the schemes of a father who still tasted the hungers of his earliest years. The child was so game that Miss Patience startled and lost her grip on the blood-slick skin. For no sooner had she spurted from her mother's body than the baby girl punched the air, screwed up her face, and opened her eyes.

When Miss Patience fumbled, Crewe lunged forward to catch the child and felt himself falling into the same clamoring depths that had swallowed his mother. This child squinted at him with eyes as blue as that ocean, as blue as Crewe's own mother's eyes and identical to those of that bartered-away baby girl Lydia, her mother, had given her life for. He caught the baby in the snug cup of his hands. He felt tied to her even while the pulsing cord still fastened her to Bless.

Abashed but recovered, Miss Patience plucked the child from Crewe's hands. She used her fingers to clear the baby's airway, then deposited her on Bless's belly.

"Move now!" she ordered Crewe out of her way as she reached beneath the mattress for the knife positioned there to cut the birthing pain.

Bless felt the wet, warm weight of her baby. She felt the frantic beating of its heart against the frantic beating of her own. She registered the small-animal trembling, the reflexive clutch of the tiny fingers as the baby grasped for purchase in this world: Bless, the only firm footing for the newborn to find.

It was then—as Bless trailed her fingers over the pale torso, and lightly, so lightly, over the pulsing, egg-fragile head—that the part of herself sent all those months ago to slumber in the dark peace beneath the bed, roused to the needs of her child.

She pushed up onto her elbows. "What is it?" she demanded. But neither Miss Patience nor Crewe, in their distraction, told her.

Bless dragged that helpless, mewling creature over her body and felt the cord of love bind and twist between them.

• • •

Across the small cabin, forgotten on the table, lay the quill and parchment and scale Jack had brought for weighing and cataloging the child.

"Careful. Careful now," he said to Bless as she lifted the child to better see her in the smoky light.

"*Move,*" Miss Patience said again. With the knife in her hand, she motioned Jack out of the way. This time, he obeyed. But Crewe did not just step aside. He stumbled outside. He fled the cabin's stifling heat—the midwife had insisted on a fire—all of them sweating through woolen clothes and the smell of burning tallow and blood and birth fluids spilling onto the bedding, turning to brume in the close air.

Outside, the air flowed in fresh streams. Crewe's breath, however, grew short. Sweat prickled his brow. He felt the blood from the baby's skin turn sticky, tightening on the palms of his hands. Likewise, his lungs contracted. Mercifully, the thickets exhaled a breeze. But just as Crewe began to gain control over his own panicked inhalations, he heard his daughter's first, hungry cry.

It spooled in his brain. It vibrated his bones. It effortlessly unlaced the seams of a heart that had grown as leathery and misshapen as the handle of a whip.

It was a herald of comeuppance, a harbinger of retribution.

Tiny, birdlike—a trill—her cry sounded, almost, like laughter.

• • •

Inside the cabin, Miss Patience hovered and fussed, kneading and massaging Bless's belly, urging forth the reluctant afterbirth.

Enraptured as she was by the tiny girl rooting for her nipple, Bless barely registered this secondary pain. And the baby—a small conqueror who could not heft the weight of her own head—fed heartily, with gusto, from her mother's breast.

Bless

Though there was no other woman on the farm to guide and advise Bless, Miss Patience had to leave her on her own. All around the county, there were other babies to guide into the world. Patience stayed for the first few days of Bless's laying in, but the new mother had to complete all the "firsts" by herself.

Just that morning, around the fourth week, the dry little stump of umbilical cord had fallen off. Bless buried it, adding it to the hole where Miss Patience buried the placenta. And so, instead of a ritual that rightly should have been overseen by sisters and aunts and performed by Cassie, the grandmother, Bless prepared the baby's first real bath all on her own.

Bless held her newborn over a pan of water. The infant drew up her legs and turned those uncanny and wonderful eyes on her mother. Though the wriggling baby in her hands demanded all of her attention, Bless could not help thinking of the other, whose eyes she had never seen, lying still and unwashed beneath the stones. Bless had known with near certainty what kind of life awaited that little black girl. What assurance did she have that life would be any better for this fair-skinned, blue-eyed child?

She dipped the baby's feet and witnessed her kicks of confusion, the wrinkling of her little brow. The baby was making up her mind whether to trust or protest this new encounter. Bless was also deciding. She'd birthed two slavery-bound daughters. She loved them the same. Didn't that mean she owed them the same? Wouldn't it be kinder, as Cassie had said, to drown this child in the tub long before "slave" had any meaning for her? Could Bless again find the courage that Cassie never had, the courage to be unselfish?

Bless moved the baby to the crook of one arm. With the other hand, she dipped a palmful of water and let it fall over the tiny chest. The child squirmed but did not cry.

"See?" Bless said. "Nothing to worry about." She did not want the baby to be afraid. Bless scooped more water onto the baby's head. The infant jerked as liquid filled her ears. Then, just as the baby inhaled, Bless poured a palmful of water over her face. The baby stiffened. She gulped and sputtered and flailed, fighting for air.

Bless sprang away from the pan. With her free hand, she slapped the basin off the table. She pressed the child to her shoulder and frantically thumped the small back.

"Cough!" Bless begged. "Please cough! Please! Please! Please!"

Finally, the baby did. With tears spilling from her eyes and water running from her nose, she wailed.

"I'm sorry!" Bless said, "Forgive me! I am sorry! I am sorry," she said, over and over, rocking the baby.

Long after the baby eased from fearful to restful, even when she slept, Bless held the child in her arms and said it still, "I'm sorry. Forgive me. I am sorry."

It did not matter that the baby had calmed and probably forgotten. It did not matter that she did not hear her mother's plea. For Bless begged pardon not only from the daughter who slept in her arms but also from the one who slept in the earth.

She entreated both of her girls, because Bless was not sure then, nor would she ever be sure, which act needed forgiving.

Which daughter had she saved, and which had she failed, utterly, to protect?

Bless and Jack Crewe

When Crewe came into Bless's cabin that evening, the only evidence of the failed drowning was a spill on the earthen floor. The baby suckled at Bless's breast. Bless did not even glance up when the door opened. She brushed her lips over the baby's tiny, velvet fingers and inhaled the sweet scent that pulsed from the top of her head.

Crewe did not know how to ask to hold the baby. He hovered a few steps away. Hands in his pockets, he glanced around at the oily window coverings, the soot-stained walls, and the dank floor. The baby had a cradle, something rigged together by David, Crewe suspected. Bless had filled it with straw and rags. Crewe had seen the same set up in slaves' quarters before and had hardly registered the sight. Now, it appeared no better than the pile of chaff a new calf landed upon or a nest some mouse had scratched together.

He thought quickly. "The air in here ain't good for her. Sleep in the house 'til she's weaned."

Bless nodded, but her gaze never left the baby as the cobalt eyes opened in momentary wakefulness then drifted shut. Crewe would have been glad to hold the girl, to catch a glimpse of his past in her sleepy eyes, to stare into them as far back as he could see.

He could demand that Bless hand him the baby. He could ask that she allow him to hold the child for a while. Neither seemed right. Crewe turned to leave. Then, like a thing he'd just thought of, instead of the thing he had come to say, he abruptly turned back.

"Call her Lydia," he ordered.

The baby opened her eyes once more as the door shut behind her sire. Bless studied the blue and knowing gaze. She did not know where Crewe had gotten the name, but somehow it seemed to fit. She decided she did not mind it.

"Hello," she said. "Hello, my little Lydia."

David Cabarrus

Cabarrus & Co., Crossroads
Frontier of the Colony of Virginia, 1703

Bill winced, then straightened. He dug hard fingers into the small of his back. He and David had just loaded the last of his supplies—a heavy side of dried meat, a small caske of molasses, a bolt of winter wool, blankets, a new coil of rope, and a knife—into the wagon. Bill had arrived at Cabarrus & Co. to pick up the provisions for his next job and the sweet syrup his wife and daughters craved.

He caught David eyeing him, assessing the pain on his face. "You right," Bill said wryly. "I can't do this job forever. My back and knees won't have it. For that matter, neither will my wife."

David had not intended for his expression to betray his thoughts. Only, as Bill knuckled the small of his back and grimaced at the pain, David saw beyond the man's rugged and ruddy exterior and glimpsed a well-disguised vulnerability. Bill was not a young man. Silver roots peeked through the dye fading from his hair. When he'd climbed from the wagon, he had taken a moment to gingerly unfold himself. His first steps toward the store were tenderfooted.

"Not to worry," Bill joked. "I thaw out come spring."

David realized he had been staring. "When you heading out?"

"Soon as Adaline sew this wool into something to keep the chill off my bones." A smile arose as he spoke his wife's name. But it faded as he said, "Neighbor'a mine got word his sisters being sold to settle a debt. Going down to Isle of Wight to see if I can't make a deal before they go up on the block."

David nodded. Bill's plans fell in line with news customers shared. "I heard you helped a few people. Not just my ma and me."

Bill began to tie down his purchases. He glanced at David from the corner of his eye. "No, not just y'all."

"Folks say you even help the ones don't have money to pay."

Carefully, Bill fashioned a bowline knot. He gave the curves and loops his full attention. Tugged it tight. Only then did he look up at David. "Where you going with this, son?"

"Papa told me why you do it. I-I want to know *how*."

Bill snorted. "Why? You thinking 'bout joining up with me?"

David threw a guilty glance over his right shoulder, toward the open doorway of the store. Through the shadows, he could see his parents behind the counter, busy with tasks that allowed them to stand in touching distance of each other. He turned a forthright gaze on Bill.

"Uh-uh," Bill said. He shook his head. "No, sir." He waved his callused hands in the air as if to ward David off.

"You ought not go by yourself," David said.

"No."

"You just said—"

"*You* hardly been here a year!" Bill lowered his voice. He craned his neck to look over David's shoulder. Phoebe and Andrew remained behind the counter. "Your ma will think I'm leading you off. Isle of Wight is back in slave territory. Why you want to go anyway? You ain't even had a chance to settle—"

"That," David said. " 'Settling.' That's just the thing."

"What?"

"It don't feel right. Living *settled*, easy, comfortable when there's folks I love left behind."

"There's always gon' be folks left behind, David. What I do ain't no cure for slavery. Wish it was, but it ain't. So ain't no cause for you to go messing in it."

"You said you can't do this job forever," David answered. "Who gon' do it when you stop?"

Momentarily thrown, Bill tried a different tack. "What you said was right. Everybody *don't* pay. Every deal don't go to plan, David. That can make things—complicated."

"What that mean?"

Bill glanced around. The evening was cold, rapidly turning colder, the hour growing late. The only folks on the wide dirt avenue were packing up their wares, heading out of the crossroads town. No one would overhear them.

"It mean the only way you woulda stayed with Crewe is if you somehow convinced Andrew that's what *you* wanted. If the man refused to sell but you wanted to go—well, we wasn't leaving without you."

Bill pressed home the point. "That's how it will be with these women. And if we caught, it won't go easy for none of us, but you know they won't treat me and you the same. Lashes for us both, certainly, but it won't stop there for you." He let the unspoken threats hang in the air, the return to bondage, laws that sanctioned dismemberment or death. "Who worth that much to you, son? That girl, Bless? She wanted—"

Bless *was* worth it, and Celeste, too, and Cecil, if he was still alive, but most of all, "I could have a daughter," David confided. "There was a woman before Bless, a girl really. And she asked me to give her a child, and she said it would be a boy, but how she know? Here what *I* know. Slavery destroy a woman different than it do a man. You know that."

Bill thought again of Adaline. "I do know that."

"Boy or girl, I been thinking 'bout what that child's life is coming to."

In Bill's line of work, keen observation was the best way to stay alive. It was a hard skill to turn off. He had noticed signs even if he only now understood the meaning of them.

"You get this look about you," Bill said, "in the store when Phoebe and Andrew ain't watching. You get a look like the walls too close. But you ain't took Andrew up on his offer to set you up on a piece of land."

"If things had gone the way Papa hoped—if we had gone straight from Scarborough to Papa's land—that's the life I wanted. All the time before I got free, that's the life I wanted. But now—I can't walk away unless I bring somebody with me. I'll help you. In return, you help me find my child. *Then* I'll settle."

Bill exhaled into the cold. His breath crystallized along with understanding. There were people—not as many as he would have liked, but more than he would have thought—who could not helplessly abide slavery. Most of them were not like him, willing to risk their own flesh and property, but they were ready with small but risky gestures. They left food or a piece of old clothing behind an outhouse or packhouse, anywhere a harried fugitive might find it. Some hung a lantern or took one down. Lighted a wick or snuffed it to signal whether the way be clear or impeded. They turned weathervanes in the direction of safety.

When Bill stopped, seemingly, to water his horse or beg other hospitality, they passed on innocuous-sounding messages—"I heard the widow Shuler might receive a parcel from her relatives farther South a few days hence"—so that Bill would be in the right place, at the right time, to deliver that "parcel" on to some free haven.

People willing to help, in ways small or heroic, were not plentiful. Bill could not turn one away.

He wagged his head in defeat. "When she find out, your mama gon' stomp a mudhole in my ass." Annoyed, grateful, he asked, "You know that, don't you?"

David smiled, mischievously, happily. "I do know that."

Bless, Jack Crewe, and Lydia

Crewe's Way Station, Lower Norfolk
Colony of Virginia, 1707

Bless and Crewe could not avoid taking mutual joy in Lydia. A child is a wonder, humor, and delight in day after day of drudgery. Bless and Jack relished the changes in her with the pride of new parents. Grudgingly, they shared the delight, almost never addressing each other directly: "You smiled today, didn't you?" might be spoken to the baby but loudly enough for the other parent to overhear. But sometimes one or the other could not resist directly communicating a moment of astonishment, "Look!" came the command on the day Lydia lifted her head, just as it came when she turned her gaze toward Crewe's voice and tracked his movements with her eyes, when she responded to Bless's baby talk in nearly comprehensible babble, and on and on, all through the rolling over, sitting up, bouncing, scooting, crawling, and the first stumbling steps on her own two round, little feet.

Over almost two years of milestones, both Crewe and Bless were often surprised not only at the baby's growth and development, but also at the tenderness and great patience of which the other was capable. In fact, it should not have been a surprise. Bless had seen her mother forced to her knees. Jack had seen his mother washed off the face of the earth. Jack fed his sister from his own mouth. Bless fed his child from her breasts. Neither would refuse Lydia the marrow of their bones.

Only slavery blinded them to these tenuous connections. The arrival and departure of each slave coffle, that chained and fetid misery, brought back all the suspicion and animosity inherent between enslaved and enslaver. As soon the baby was weaned, Bless moved back to her cabin. Still there were days of ceasefire when Bless and Jack spoke of nothing but farmwork and Lydia.

In the toddler's third or fourth year, those whole days of unspoken truce began to dwindle first to hours, then to mere minutes. That was around the time John Jeffrey brought two of his slaves, Jonah and a woman, Nora, to live and serve at the farm. In one well-thought-out deal, Crewe took the money from the sale of David and "doubled it" in the form of two slaves. He had been distracted long enough, and the labor needs of the colonies around Virginia were changing. It was time to get back on track.

• • •

Jeffrey promised that the deal would serve all of their needs. Nora and Jonah came to Crewe's holding a young son, Kelsey, by the hand, with a daughter on the hip, and a baby in the belly. The couple were one of Jeffrey's most successful pairings.

Jonah and Nora were the type to multiply and grow industrious under the illusion of self-rule. Jack Crewe's would be the perfect place to settle them. Crewe had more than enough land and some money to invest, and he would benefit not just from the arrival of offspring, but also from the many years of field and household labor the pair still had in them. Jeffrey would benefit most of all. In exchange for his large infusion of cash, Jack would handle the day-to-day care, feeding, and raising of the slave family. The family's labor would be poured into an enterprise in which Jeffrey owned a large share, and Jeffrey would have, if he chose to exercise it, the right to buy—at a discounted rate—the first pick of any of Jonah and Nora's brood when they were ready for market.

Crewe and Jeffrey arranged the deal through letters posted back and forth. On parchment, they justified the enterprise in altruistic terms: well-raised, domestic-born slaves were best for all. Fewer Africans would be torn from their shores. Born and bred under the eye of their ultimate masters, there would be no need for the risky period of seasoning. Born into the climate and diseases of Virginia, there would be less attrition. These slaves would be raised in the language and customs they must serve. They would inherit their station with little discomfort or questioning. There would be little need for bounties on the heads of maroons or laws that condoned the killing of runaways. Raised right, slaves would know their place and be content to stay in it.

Crewe and Jeffrey settled the matter in their heads and hearts. They struck a deal. They solemnized the agreement with a handshake and signed it with iron gall ink. Jeffrey filed documents in the courthouse on his way south. And so came the day of delivery: Jonah, along with his young wife, Nora, and their children arrived at Crewe's.

A cream draft horse pulled the wagon. Jeffrey held the reins. A large black-skinned man, his face made darker by the shadow of a floppy hat, sat beside him. In the back, among a few barrels and other supplies, a young woman and two small children were wedged in.

Bless noticed the arrival from the window of the kitchen. Lydia played just outside, away from the heat wafting off the hearth, close enough to beg a scrap of dough for her play, or a taste of what was cooking, or to climb for just a bit, onto her mother's lap. At four, she was still babyish that way. At least twice a day, she took the notion to rest her head against Bless's breast while toying with the lobe of her mother's ear. Sometimes, after a few moments, she hopped down and went back to play. Sometimes, she drifted off to sleep. No matter how busy or hot, Bless stopped for those lulls. She knew they were numbered.

As the man pulled the brake, the woman began climbing out from among the crates and bags that had shifted during the journey. Bless forestalled her perusal of the men in favor of the children and the young woman who was, in fact, more of a girl. She still had the wispiness of a teenager, thin face, neck, and shoulders. The boy beside her could have been her younger brother, but Bless guessed that he was not. When the woman stood, Bless was certain.

Hefting the smallest child on her hip, the woman unlatched the tailgate and scooted to the ground. She reached back for the boy and helped him hop down. Jeffrey, who even from a distance looked diminished compared to the man Bless remembered, handed the reins to the black man who drove the wagon toward the barn. In their certainty that the woman could do without a helping hand, neither man went around to her and the children.

"Jack Crewe!" Jeffrey called.

"John Jeffrey, you old land pirate!" Jack called in return, and the two men strode toward each other.

Left in the yard like luggage, the boy stared around with curiosity while his mother, with a groundward gaze, seemed to be waiting for direction. She hitched the smaller child higher on her hip and kept a hand on the boy's shoulder to keep him from running after the wagon. Adjusting the child caused the loose-fitting top she wore to pull free from the band of her skirt. Bless would have to get closer to be sure if she really saw an already rounded middle, a protruding belly button.

What involuntary motion, or sense, or sound alerted the girl that she was being watched? With the ungainly beauty of a sunflower, she lifted her head in Bless's direction. Their gazes met, and Bless felt her future tie into the fate of this young woman whose name she could not divine, but whose story she already knew.

• • •

Bless knew her escape to be tied directly to the fact that Lydia loved her. Crewe loved Lydia. Therefore, he had decided, apparently, to spare from destruction anything that Lydia loved. In the same way that he avoided stepping on the marbles of hard-packed clay that Lydia loved to shoot and did not make good on his threat to run over the hoop and stick she abandoned in the cart path, he would spare Lydia's mother the griefs of the market and the tolls of breeding.

Bless looked across the distance at the young woman—at the burdens hoisted on her hip, led by the hand, and carried in her belly—

and felt ashamed. And felt relief. Crewe no longer intended to make commodities out of Bless and her child.

Looking up at his mother, the boy said something. The young woman looked down at him, and Bless was finally able to lower her gaze. She grabbed onto the first solid thing that came to hand, a coarsely woven kitchen towel. She spent a long time wiping each finger clean.

What, Bless wondered, had changed inside her, so much that she stood there giving silent assent, even gratitude, to the very circumstance she had sacrificed her first child to avoid?

"Mama! Mama!" Lydia screeched. She clattered up the steps and barreled through the kitchen door. "There's a little boy here! And a grown-up woman like you and a baby!" Lydia bounced on her toes. Excitement and delight radiated off her like heat, and Bless understood exactly when she'd changed and why.

Just as Lydia had altered Bless's body—widened her hips, elongated her breasts, stretched pale rivulets into the skin of her thighs—so the child had reshaped even her most resolute convictions.

Bless balled the towel, twisted it until she lost feeling in her fingers.

"Mama?" Lydia tugged her by the skirt.

Slowly, Bless set the towel aside. Her fingertips prickled as the blood made a rushing return. She smiled for her child.

"Let's go meet them," she said.

Jack Crewe

Up close, Crewe could see that his partner had been ill. Jeffrey carried at least twenty pounds less than a man of his height and frame should. A scattering of nearly healed scars blighted his face, and there was a new concentration when he walked, as though it took some effort to hold his long limbs together.

The men shook hands. "It is good to see you," Crewe said. Then, despite his intention, he asked, "How have you been?"

Jeffrey laughed. "Look like shit, do I?"

"No, it is just—"

Jeffrey waved a hand to dismiss his partner's discomfort. "You are right. This road is hard on a man, made worse by the quackery of barbers and surgeons with their lancing, inunctions, and sweat baths. I've been skewered, rubbed raw, and suffocated!"

"But you are well now?"

"Well enough. I shall be taking some time from the road as soon as Ethan returns from his travels."

"Travels? He is old enough for 'travels'?"

"He is all but a man now. He took some notion to see the trade from the castles of the Ivory Coast to the jails here in Norfolk. I see no use in it, but he has become quite strong-willed. Nothing at all like the boy you met."

Crewe recalled the boy, sentimental and ponderous, reluctant to raise a whip. He inclined a brow. "He will be your successor?"

"Someday, but not for a very long time," Jeffrey assured him.

"Lydia!"

The two men turned toward Bless as she called to the little girl who ran ahead of her. Though still young herself, Bless lacked the speed and agility of a four-year-old. Lydia ran straight toward Jack, unable to resist a twirl in his arms even as she dashed eagerly toward a potential playmate.

"Papa Jack!" she called as she catapulted herself at him. And just as he had from the very beginning, Crewe caught Lydia. He spun her once and set her down. She ran on toward the new arrivals.

Bless skirted the men. "Pardon, please," she said as she ran behind her daughter.

Jeffrey's gaze followed the child, trying to piece together startling bits from a fragmented glance. She trotted on, her auburn braids bouncing like rigging as she went.

"What an extraordinary little picaninny," Jeffrey murmured. "Are her eyes *blue*?" He turned back to Jack. This time, it was he who arched a brow. "*Papa Jack?*" he said. "I admit, my travels have kept me away since we signed our deal, but we accumulated quite the correspondence. Your letters neglected to inform me of how much I have missed."

Crewe met Jeffrey's speculative stare straight on. Despite his meager beginnings, he had grown, like other men of means, to believe his actions lay beyond scrutiny or censure. He was, before all, white, male, and monied.

"What of it?" Crewe said.

Jeffrey held up his hands as if to indicate he knew when a topic should not be touched. Still, he cautioned, "These kinds of things are usually not professed so openly, Jack."

Crewe stiffened at the familiar use of his boyhood name, but Jeffrey was a contemporary of his father. Jeffrey, too, trusted that Crewe would defer to him in respect for his age. "Thomas is not here to guide you, so I will offer this counsel: You mustn't be soft with her. See her for what she is."

Crewe's perpetual sunburn reddened. He opened his mouth. Whether in rebuke or protest, Jeffrey did not wish to know. Again, he held up a hand. "Offer me an ale," he said, "and we shall get down to business."

. . .

"They won't be any trouble," Jeffrey said.

The men had finished their beer and now walked about to see the improvements Jeffrey's investment had made in the farm. Crewe showed him the kitchen garden with its long straight poles ladened with growing beans, the bountiful heads of cabbage, the swelling corn and burgeoning carrot tops, enough to feed them all. As they walked farther, he pointed out a small pen of sheep, newly fenced, and planted acres of the expanding farm, the new tobacco barn, and the slave pens in good repair, and, lastly, the recently added storage building. Here they stopped to sip from bladders of water they carried and to allow Jeffrey to catch his breath.

"That little boy—Kelsey, he's named—he's six and may be the smartest little picaninny I ever seen. Show him something once and he got it. Keep growing like he do, and by next spring, I wager he'll be able to drive a cart for you.

"The girl? Nora. She's as fruitful as an apple tree! Can set my watch by her. Her littlest one, Irene, is only three, and just look! Every time Nora weans one, she comes up full with another one. She shall bear eight before she's thirty! They're just the kind you need for this place."

Jeffrey took a long drink from his waterskin. He stretched his neck to admire the storage structure. Crewe waited for him to say more.

"And the buck?" Jack finally prompted. "You've said nothing about him."

Jeffrey wiped his mouth. He sighed. "Jonah is a little more complicated."

"How so?"

"Do not give me that scowl," Jeffrey said. "He is not lesser goods. In fact, in his youth, he was one of my best stockmen."

"In his youth?"

"And now. It is just that a few years ago, right before I paired him with Nora, he began to go funny."

"Funny how?" Crewe asked, reminding himself of Lydia when she barraged him with question after question, each answer leading her to another inquiry. "We are partners. Must I beg you for clarification?"

"Funny in the head," Jeffrey finally said. "Weeping. Out of the blue. Weeping! Crying out in the night, fit to wake the whole damned slave quarter. Stopping children on the street when he accompanied me to town. Asking them, 'Ain't you mine?'"

He took another swallow from his waterskin. "He improved once I paired him with Nora, but—"

"But what, John?"

Jeffrey capped the waterskin and looked Jack directly in the eye. "He's said he will murder himself if he is not allowed to remain with Nora—only Nora—and their children." Crewe opened his mouth in protest. Jeffrey jumped into the gap. "*But* he will do no harm to himself, and he will continue to perform, if I do not force him to mate with other women." Jeffrey shook his head in wonder. "Not even a well laid-on whipping made him recant. I could not have him as an example among my other servants. And so, when you needed to replace your stud, I immediately saw this was the best way to serve all of our needs. Together they have been quite prolific," he said. "I've decided to let well-enough be."

"Well-enough for you. You are rid of a willful slave!"

"You are already agitated," Jeffrey said with yet another sigh. "I might as well tell you the rest."

• • •

Jonah begged only one privilege for his family: that they be allowed to live removed from the immediate reminders of slavery. The "stockman," as Jeffrey called him, did not want to open his cabin door each morning to captives shut up in the pens, to fall asleep to sounds of weeping.

Grudgingly allowed by Crewe, Jonah chose the location for his family's cabin with great care. He even built the cabin so it faced away from Crewe's house and the pens, a small but bracing attempt to set slavery at his back. The cabin's lot was not the prettiest spot, not the most fertile, nor the most convenient. Nora and Kelsey walked some ways to the creek where they took up water for the household until Jonah could dig a well. Still, he chose the most secluded, uncultivated nook on the farm. Oxen got loose and browsed there. Deer and bears trespassed but, thankfully, seldom anything human. Nora and Jonah cut a path with their own feet on the daily walk to the tasks they performed for Crewe.

The walk home was their favorite part of the day. As often as work would allow, they made the journey home together. Sometimes, they held hands. Nora reminded Jonah of those walks on the nights when he had the nightmare. Though the dream came less frequently now, it was the same each time: Jonah walked through a forest and from behind every tree came the call, *Papa!*

Jonah ran from tree to tree, from cry to cry, catching sight of the flash of a heel, the hem of a dress, never able to lay hands on any of his children. He woke up weeping.

Nora pressed his face to her breasts before his sobs could wake Kelsey. Whispering, she reminded Jonah of a different walk, *their walk*, through the woods: the stroke of the calf-high grass, the litanies of small chirping beasts, the rustling sound of whichever season's wind stirred in the underbrush, Kelsey and Irene's laughter guiding their parents home as they ran ahead, toward the cabin. Jonah could *hold* those children and the one soon to come. He could lay hands on them whenever he wanted to. Kelsey and Irene, Nora and the unborn child, all lived with him in a house turned away from sorrow. Jonah had seen to that.

Her words soothed him each time, but never before Jonah marveled, his words a mumble of sleep talk, "Don't seem real there's a world where men lay claim to other men's children."

Jack Crewe

For his part, Jack Crewe ignored the foolhardiness of trying to foster both slavery and an enslaved daughter. He ignored the contradictions within himself just as he ignored those all around him: In Virginia, it was settled law that children born to enslaved mothers and free white fathers were slaves, while any white woman who bore a Black man's child risked whipping and having her child cast into thirty years of servitude. Farther up the Chesapeake Bay, Maryland decreed the children born of white women and Black men to be free. As Virginia and North Carolina snatched away slaves' right to self-defense, Pennsylvania Quakers asserted the Negroes' right to "liberty of the body." Virginia took away a slave's right to own even livestock as Massachusetts decreed slaves and free whites should be governed by the same courts and procedures. White men in every colony wrestled with ways to curtail or unshackle the Negro.

Jack Crewe chose to be mute, as well as deaf and blind, when it came to the dilemma. He said not one word about Lydia's bondage or freedom. Yet it was clear that he did not want the girl raised to be a slave. When Lydia turned six years old, he bought her a hornbook and a primer. Though not a religious man, Crewe ordered a Bible so she would have a decent book to read. While Bless could have taught the child, it became a common occurrence to see him seated at the table with Lydia on his knees, guiding her finger over a tracing of words or numbers.

With Lydia, Crewe made an exception to the rule that farming and housekeeping should be the limits of an ideal slave's education. As Lydia sat on Papa Jack's knee and recited Scriptures and rhymes, the children of Jonah and Nora went unschooled, except in the most useful and salable tasks. Irene began to learn all a middling farm could teach about housekeeping and gardening, from collecting stray feathers for quilts to how to catch, kill, and scald feathers from a chicken. Kelsey walked by his father's side as Jonah taught him to drive an ox and plow straighter than a ruler's edge. When he was just strong enough to lift the tools, the boy learned to dig postholes deep and build fences strong. When they were old enough, Crewe intended to tutor Nora and Jonah's children in raising a fine grade of tobacco, from sowing seeds to prizing it into hogsheads. They would learn their role: to be whatever and whoever a slaveholder needed. But if pressed, if a pistol were held to his head, Jack Crewe could not have said who, or what, he was raising his daughter to be.

Bless, Jack Crewe, and Lydia

Fucking Jack Crewe had backfired. When she'd yanked off her dress and pressed herself against the man who meant to breed her like a sow, Bless had intended, once and for all, to accept her place as a slave, a farm implement. The degradation of Crewe rutting between her thighs would surely snuff the last living hope inside her.

It worked at first. For months Bless stood and dressed herself when light came through the window. She performed her work by rote and direction. She closed the cabin door and shut her eyes when the light went away. She thought of nothing, dreamed of nothing. For months she could not feel the accumulation of losses—beginning with Cassie and ending with David—as the numbness deadened all sensation from heart to womb. Bless barely felt the unborn life rooting and sparking within her until Miss Patience plopped it, naked, helpless, and shivering on her chest. A creature more powerless than herself.

If not for Lydia, Bless never would have awakened from her stupor. Bless loved Lydia more than she had ever loved anyone except for the baby girl buried beneath the stones. On the night she gave birth, within the oppressive heat of the cabin, Bless's body trembled at the irony: by giving birth, she had indeed fallen into bondage.

Whatever was copied down in Crewe's ledger, however many men had exchanged bills and coins for her flesh in all the time before, only *now* Bless was truly enslaved. Not to laws, not to bills of sale, not to violence, but to the love and duty she felt for Lydia. Bless would do anything, stand anything, for that child.

Her only solace, her only pleasure, came from the knowledge that Crewe suffered the same.

• • •

In different ways, Crewe and Bless gave Lydia latitude, perhaps too much, because it was a revelation to them to see what a child, one unencumbered by poverty or cast in the role of servant, would make of a day. They let her run and splash. They let her climb, jump, and hide.

Only the barns, full of forked and cutting edges, and the slave pens, an array of agonies, were forbidden. To the best of their ability, Crewe and Bless satisfied the needs and nourished the interests Lydia revealed to them. At least twice a day, they fed her much of what she needed and some of what she desired. In return, she offered them the vicarious magic of imaginary friends, a spectrum of questions neither had ever considered, and the staggering experience of wholehearted love.

Parenthood gave them many opportunities to marvel, but little time to hover. Care of the house, the garden, animals, fields, and the arrival and departure of captive Negroes meant that Crewe and Bless might work in the same vicinity, but separately at their own tasks. As long as Lydia stayed close enough to come running when one of them hollered, they did not keep her in their sights.

One summer's day, as Crewe was working inside the barn and Bless was on her knees in the kitchen garden, Lydia's scream summoned them.

Crewe reached her first. The topmost rail of a split rail fence, the one she liked to straddle and ride like a horse, had wrenched free. Lydia lay on the ground, screaming from shock and fear, her small arm bent at the wrong angle.

Crewe scooped Lydia from the ground and carried her into his house. Bless ran to keep up.

"Fetch water," Crewe barked. "Get cloth. Long pieces." He sat at the table with Lydia on his knee. "It's not so bad," he crooned to her. "Let me see," he said, coaxing the child with the soft sounds he made to the horses and oxen so they did not shy or rear when he needed to examine a wound. Lydia let him touch her arm, gently unbend it, and tear away the sleeve of her dress. Crewe probed the lumpy jut of her arm with his fingertips. The back of his hand was tanned and freckled, darker than Lydia's skin of heavy cream and brown sugar.

When Bless came with the kettle of water and a length of rough sacking, Lydia's shrill screams had quieted to hiccups, and Bless could hear Jack Crewe crooning to the child in a singsong Gaelic. For all Bless understood, it *might have* been a song. "Papa *beidh a shocrú tá sé, A mhuirnín." Papa will fix it, sweetheart.*

He looked up. "Hold her."

Bless took Lydia onto her lap. Crewe ripped the cloth and wet a piece. He stroked gently where Lydia's flesh had begun to swell. Again, he probed the break with his fingers. Lydia dug her head against her mother's breasts as the shock of the fall wore off and the pain of the break set in. She whimpered. Bless kissed Lydia's head. With her lips and cheeks, she swabbed the sweat from Lydia's brow. She was so intent upon comforting Lydia that it took her a moment to realize Crewe had gone still.

They had grown used to communicating without resorting to words. Bless looked up. She read his stricken face. He would have to wrench the bone back into place. He made no move to do so. Fixing Lydia's arm would hurt more than the initial break, and Crewe, physically stronger and more practiced, would have to cause the pain.

Bless was surprised by the reluctance and fear she saw in his eyes. She had seen Crewe hammer a boar between the eyes at hog-killing time. She had tended the raw evidence of what he had done to David's back.

Bless tightened her grip on Lydia. She wrapped the child's good arm and torso within her strong arms. She tucked the child's head beneath her chin. "Do it," Bless said.

Crewe took a breath. "Papa *beidh a shocrú tá sé, A mhuirnín,"* he murmured again. He tried a smile, but Lydia was not deceived. She leveled her frantic eyes on his and began to cry loudly again. She began to struggle.

Bless tightened her grip. Crewe faltered, his hands uselessly patting over Lydia instead of taking hold. "You have to do it," Bless said. "Now."

Crewe positioned one hand at the child's shoulder to secure her in place. With the other hand, he cupped the back of her arm. Cradling her elbow in his palm and holding her forearm within a long-fingered grip, he yanked.

Lydia screamed. She stopped inhaling. Her cry turned soundless. Fat, clear tears rained onto all of them as she thrashed and gasped for air, her gaze still riveted to Jack's.

Once. No, twice before had he seen such a look of betrayal.

Jack Crewe stepped backward. He turned away, but not before Bless saw his tears.

Lydia shuddered in her mother's arms. Bless shook too. Even as Lydia began to calm, her mother's shaking increased.

Bless told herself it was an after effect, a late reaction to her sudden fear for her child. But as she watched Crewe, pacing back and forth, then hurrying from the room, a fresh wave of shivers quaked through her again. She knew the feeling for what it was.

A thrill of triumph. Vengeance after all.

Bless, Jack Crewe, and Lydia

They soaked the corn husks. Bless's and Lydia's hands touched often in the warm water of the bowl. They gently overlapped the supple chaffs. They bound them tightly with twine to make the head and waist and hands. Lydia placed her finger *here* while Bless tied the string. The child giggled each time her finger got caught in a bow. As they worked, Bless told Lydia all about Cassie. She told her of hair-washing day, falling asleep across Cassie's knees, or sitting on her mother's crossed ankles until she got too big and had to sit in a chair.

"That's how you braid my hair!" Lydia said.

"That's how my mama taught me to do it," Bless answered. "That's how you will braid your daughter's hair," Bless said, hoping, when the time came, she would be near enough to see it. As they smoothed and rolled the corn-husk body, she told Lydia about the kitchen at Willow Oaks where Bless played with her own doll while Cassie cooked, about the extra dollop of cream.

They dressed the doll with scraps of cloth folded and stitched to look like the little dress and apron Lydia wore. Bless showed her daughter how to pull her fingers gently through the corn silk, parting the tangled threads into sections for the braids. They finished the doll by painting on her face with pigments—crushed red berries and such—from small pots Bless kept above the hearth.

The smile was crooked, and one eye sat higher than the other. Still, Lydia took the finished creation gently in hand. "I *love* her!" she said.

"What will you call her?" Bless asked as she began to clean away the stray silk, the husks that had torn, the thrums of thread.

Lydia thought for a moment, studying her doll in a comical, crinkled-brow way. Decisively, she said, "This is Love."

The doll-making implements dropped from Bless's fingers as the words, almost identical to Cassie's, echoed from Lydia's lips. This is *Love*. "This here is love." A doll. If only it were that simple. But it never could be for them. Bondage excluded love from all its calculations. In bondage, love was never the bottom line. Therefore, a slave simply decided to bear the anguish.

For the first time in many years, Bless allowed the hole, the space bereft of her mother's love, to open and ache inside her. She felt dizzied by the onrush of need for all she'd been deprived of when Cassie decided to protect her own heart instead of Bless's. Yet she understood the impulse that made Cassie pull away like a ship receding from the shore. Cassie hid from pain that she both anticipated and knew, the way she knew recipes and sewing stiches and the steps to a dance. Knowing how things would end, Cassie retreated into the absence of her daughter years before Bless had physically gone.

To succor her own pain, Cassie stopped loving her child. Perhaps Bless had done the same thing with Jeremiah's daughter. Bless would not withdraw now to suss out the answer, because the living child in front of her could not be starved of love. Bless would not do what Cassie had done. So that Lydia could have what she needed, so that Lydia would *never* believe herself deserving of the treatment she would endure, Bless would suffer through loving her child.

Bless squatted in front of Lydia. The child barely noticed as she fussed with the hair and skirt of her doll. Bless kissed one of Lydia's busy hands—still plump with the dimples of babyhood—then the other.

"I will do anything, anything," Bless said, vehemence making it hard to draw enough breath for the promise, "for you."

Lydia smiled distractedly. She tucked the doll against her chest. "May I go show Papa Jack?" she asked.

Bless nodded. Lydia jumped from her chair and darted out the door. Bless watched as her daughter ran, barefoot, propelled by joy, across the yard into her father's world.

• • •

It was the kind of toy Jack was used to seeing in the arms of picaninnies. The kind of plaything poor whites gave to their children. Made of crackling layers of corn husks, the doll had a tangle of corn-silk braids and a painted-on face. Her lips were red. Her eyes were blue. Likewise, her clothes were scraps of the same blue Negro cloth Jack's daughter wore. Lydia cradled the miniature slave doll in the crook of one arm.

"Her name is Love," the child said as she offered up the toy for approval. Jack's face tightened, though all Lydia noticed was the smile in that motion. Jack took the doll, and he was careful with it as he turned it over to examine how the little dress had been affixed with tiny, neat stitches. The braids were the lumpy, uneven work of a child's hand.

"I bet I know which part you did all by yourself," Jack said. He tugged Lydia's matching auburn braid, and the girl giggled. To please his daughter, Jack said, "She is beautiful." He glanced toward Bless's cabin. "Why don't you take her to visit Nora? Tell her I said let you have a piece of sweetbread."

Lydia bounced on the balls of her feet. "Kelsey too?" she asked.

"Yes," Jack said. "Kelsey too."

Bless and Jack Crewe

The door of Bless's cabin stood open, but even if it had been closed, Jack would not have knocked.

"I told you to inform me of her needs," he said.

Bless glanced up from the sewing on her lap. Lydia was ripping through dresses and growing out of them faster than Bless could make them. "I have done." Bless answered concisely. That way, she mostly avoided calling Crewe "Master," or anything at all for that matter.

"You did not tell me she wanted a doll. I could have gotten her a plaster doll on my last trip to Norfolk."

"The one we made is good enough."

"You do not say what is 'good enough' for her."

Bless paused in her sewing. "A slave girl with a plaster doll?"

Crewe ignored the exasperation in Bless's tone, but more importantly, he ignored her description of Lydia and the image that coalesced in his mind: a dirt-caked slave child holding a doll better dressed than herself. He insisted, "Throw that corn-husk thing in the burn heap."

"She loves it."

"I will buy her a doll."

Bless exhaled. She never willingly shared anything with her master. A child was more than enough. But she would have to tell him the truth so he would let this alone. She did not want Lydia exposed to fancy toys, as Bless herself had been, not if the child faced a lifetime of making do.

"She did not ask for a doll. She asked after my mama. When I told her how she used to make me corn-husk dolls, Lydia asked if we could make one."

Happy noises from across the yard suspended the tension between Bless and Crewe. Lydia and Kelsey erupted from the kitchen, each with a slice of sweetbread in hand. They played together like puppies from the same litter, happy now, but in moments they might be nipping and squabbling. They chased each other, somehow nibbling as they ran. Their feet were bare, legs coated in the same yard dust. Even their clothes matched, Kelsey's long shirt and Lydia's dress cut from the same bolt of blue cloth. Their laughter rolled across the yard like loose beads.

Crewe turned from the sight. "I do not want her running barefoot like some shoeless nigger. Make her a dress out of something besides that damn Negro cloth and stop filling her head with your damn slave stories."

He turned to go, but Bless checked his forward motion. "I beg your pardon, sir," she said. "You are right. It will be full enough of her own."

Crewe whipped around. Had Bless become more willful or was she simply hiding it less? Though barefoot and wearing an apron, she held her chin high. She had given up mobcaps for headwraps worn like turbans. She had grown into a womanhood of smooth walnut skin and discerning brown eyes. That look of hers, forthright but indifferent, was why he had never sought seconds between her thighs. Bless had worn that look when he was on top of her: Crewe had bought her; he had whipped the man she loved; he had fucked her; yet he elicited nothing from her. Not even fear. Bless remained indifferent and unimpressed. And now he saw that her connection to Lydia had made her bold.

"I will not tolerate sass. I will not have it taught to Lydia. You will show me respect, or you will be marching out of here with the next coffle."

A spasm of panic tightened Bless's face. It widened her eyes but cinched her lips.

"We are clear?" Crewe asked.

Bless swallowed. "Yes, sir," she said.

He waited.

"Yes, *Master*," Bless said.

Crewe did not gloat. He did not linger but left with a nod as if Bless's newly found humility were nothing more than his due.

• • •

Jack hurried from the cabin before Bless could see his satisfaction at having frightened her drop away. Her eyes had gone wide, her face and mouth slack.

Then everything had tightened as she seemed to summon all the strength she possessed to hold herself upright. The woman who had not stepped aside when an ox ran at her full bore looked ready to fold at Crewe's feet with one threat to sell her away from her daughter.

Bless was so afraid that she called him "Master," a word she'd found ingenious ways to avoid over the years. Best of all, perhaps, her voice trembled. From now on, Crewe felt certain she would parse her words before she spoke to him. Finally, Bless would avert her eyes from his face in the manner of a respectful servant.

He had almost crowed with triumph. He'd felt gratified, buoyant, until he noted how much Bless's fearful expression resembled that of a frightened child—*his* frightened child.

Lydia's eyes always widened at an unexpected hurt. Then came the trembling and clenching of her small body as she fought not to cry. In his mind's eye, it only took the time of an inhale, a blink, a thought for Lydia to become the enslaved woman on the receiving side of his threat.

He felt appalled at his own power.

Jack Crewe could do anything he wanted to Bless. He could make her walk around all day with an iron cuff around her neck. In life, he knew, any privation was possible. In slavery, most privations were likely. He could force her to wear a yoke. He could chain her to the plow and plod her like a mule. He could bed her any way he wanted. He need only think of his pleasure and never of her pain. He could mark her with the imprints of his palms, knuckles, and boots.

He could brand her with an iron. No man would say a mumbling word. And so it could be with Lydia.

Jack Crewe rushed from the cabin. He jogged into the yard. He turned in a full circle but did not see his daughter.

His voice trembled when he called out.

Jack Crewe, Lydia, and Kelsey

"You is too."

"No, I ain't."

"You is too!"

Crewe heard the shrill voices of Kelsey and Lydia when he was still ten paces away from the slave pen. His first reaction—anger that Lydia had disobeyed and gone inside the pen—was overtaken by curiosity. What could an eight-year-old and a six-year-old argue about so passionately? He put his hand on the door but did not open it.

"No, I *ain't*!" Lydia said.

"Yes, you *is*. I heard Mama say! She told Papa she never seen a white man do a slave child 'like he do Lydia.' She say, 'Maybe Master Crewe ain't *so bad* as Master Jeffrey.'"

Jack Crewe's hand clenched on the door.

"Papa Jack ain't bad," Lydia said.

"He is too. He shake hands with Master Jeffrey. That mean they friends. Master Jeffrey sold us from home, from Granny and all them, and he brung us here because Master Crewe help him sell niggers. That's how come they friends. They 'greed we got to stay here, and that's why we can't go home. Even if he ain't as worse as Master Jeffrey, Master Crewe still bad, and you still a slave."

Lydia said nothing. The silence filled with the siren call of insects, loud and throbbing, then gone. Crewe waited, as did Kelsey, to see if the boy would have the last word.

Jack Crewe did not know what he expected from his daughter. Tears of outrage because Lydia was a little girl? The sound of a blow because she was his child, and, in her place, he would have struck Kelsey in anger? But Lydia took a moment. Jack could imagine her brow furrowing like it did when she was busy over her slate or taken away by her world of pretend.

Finally, Lydia said, "I will ask him to stop."

"Stop what?" Kelsey asked.

"Stop making you all stay. Stop making us be slaves."

"He won't stop," Kelsey said softly, and it was odd to hear such certainty, such gravity, from the mouth of a child—until Lydia spoke.

"He will stop if I ask him," she said.

Jack took a long, deep breath. He forced his limbs to move. He yanked the door open. "Lydia! Kelsey! Come out of there right now," he demanded. He heard the scramble of feet, then Kelsey appeared in the doorway.

Towering over the boy, Crewe went on the attack. "Don't you know better than to play in there?"

"Yes, sir. We was just finding a cool place to eat our sweetbread," the boy explained.

"Get up there to your ma'am. Next time I find you here, I will take a strap to you, you hear?"

"Yes, sir," Kelsey said. His gaze darted toward the door of the pen, but he clamped his mouth shut. He seemed to know he had gotten off lightly.

His hunched shoulders began to lower until Crewe said, "Tell your ma'am I'll be up to see her about all this talking out of turn she been doing."

"Yes, sir," Kelsey repeated, and Crewe was certain the boy would gladly take the strap rather than face Nora. He felt the same about facing the child on the other side of this door.

He gripped the gate. "Lydia, come out here."

Only the light and shadows moved.

Jack Crewe would have to go into the slave pen to bring his daughter out.

• • •

A quarter of the way into the pen, the light rippling against the poles reminded Jack Crewe of the way sunlight and waves had rushed and receded against the portholes of *The Venture*. Halfway to Lydia, he caught the familiar smell of 'tween decks: filth from the overturned buckets, sickness, and sweat. If he stood still and waited, surely the sounds of weeping and cursing would come whistling out of the cinched poles and hollow bars. He scanned the gloom for his daughter. She sat in the center of the pen, fiddling with that poor-man's doll, on ground seeded with the flux and misery of slavery.

Crouching beside her, Crewe began with the point that was easiest to defend: "Lydia, you are not supposed to be in here."

Lydia looked up at him. She held his gaze so long that Crewe felt an unanticipated swell of pride. She did not cower. She hid nothing and expected openness in turn. If he lied to her, she would know, and that mattered.

Lydia did not dispute her father's point or defend her disobedience. Instead, she used the same wiliness, the same honest need, that forced Jack and Bless to love her in the first place.

"If Mr. Jonah and Miss Nora want to go home to Kelsey's granny," Lydia asked her papa, "will you let them?"

Jack Crewe sat on the ground. "No," he said.

"Why?"

"Because they have to stay here and work."

"Even if they don't want to?" Lydia asked.

"Even if they don't want to," Jack Crewe said.

"Why?"

"Because they are slaves," he said. "They are my slaves."

Lydia turned her attention from her father's face to the corn-husk doll in her lap. "Why are they slaves?" she asked.

Crewe knew his choices: Ignore the question. Grab the girl up and carry her from the pen. Tell her that some things are not for children to know or understand. Tell her that a father owes no explanation to a child. Use his hand or belt to make her afraid enough never to ask him such a thing again. He could blame her features, her color. For all her vivid blue eyes and the way her skin paled in the winter months, the Negro within Lydia appeared in the flare of her nose, the kink of her hair, the summertime darkening of her skin. Many justifications that Crewe had heard and repeated—from Ham to heathenism—came to mind, but he knew only one thing to be true, and he could only bring himself to tell his daughter that truth. Without the income from the pens and labor from slavery, he would be nothing. Vermin. Slavery made the house, the animals, the fields possible.

"They are slaves because men like me say they have to be."

"Kelsey is a slave?"

"Yes."

"Ma'am is a slave?"

"Yes."

"I am a slave?"

Jack nodded, and only through that motion did the words work free. "Yes, Lydia, you are a slave."

Still Lydia was not done. "Are you a bad man?" she asked.

Again, Jack found he could not lie to her. "Yes. I am a bad man. But I am also your papa, and I need you to come out of this place with me."

Jack stood. He reached down to his daughter.

Lydia looked up at her "Papa Jack," at his outstretched hand, the wiggle of his fingers beckoning her, and for the first time since she had taken her first wobbly steps, she did not reach toward him.

Lydia tucked the corn-husk doll under one arm. She scrabbled up on her own. Jack slowly withdrew his hand. His fingers clenched on the coarse material of his breeches instead of the softness of his daughter's hand.

Lydia wrapped both arms around the doll, and walked, with a dignity as inherent as her smile or her intelligence, toward the door of the slave pen.

Jack followed.

Bless

Bless sought out the only person she knew who had more to lose than she did. She heard the laughter of Nora's children and the squawk of chickens before she rounded a clump of trees and saw them. Nora stood in the yard with her hands on her hips ordering Kelsey and five-year-old Irene to, "Stop chasing them chickens! All that running make they meat tough!"

Excited to join the chase, Lydia bolted ahead. Kelsey's laughter faltered when he saw his friend. Lydia hesitated. The children watched each other, unnaturally shy and uncertain. Irene sprinted between them. She pressed her hand into Lydia's and pulled her into the fray. Before long, all three children were laughing, and the revelations of the slave pen, if not forgotten, were at least set aside. They abandoned Nora's harassed hens and ran to play in the woods. The mothers were left alone.

Bless held up a sack of string beans she'd brought along, a peace offering. "I came to see if y'all are all right."

• • •

Bless and Nora sat on the steps of the cabin—where they could speak without waking Nora's toddler, who napped inside—with a wooden bowl and the sack of beans between them. Green pods thudded into the vessel. Around the women's feet, chickens clucked and strutted as they pecked at the castaway bean ends. There was only that for a while—snap, thud, cluck—punctuated by the screeches and shrieks of their children in the distance.

"How she?" Nora asked.

"Quiet," Bless answered. "Him?"

"Quiet. Jonah whipped him."

"Oh, Nora!"

Nora shrugged as if readjusting an invisible load. "Jonah say he got to learn. He can't take what he hear and carry it back to white folks."

"He got a whipping for telling the truth," Bless said.

Nora sighed. "This started with me. I was speaking on what don't concern me, but she call him *Papa*. Never occurred to me she didn't know."

"He taught her that. I should have stopped it, but—he has never treated her like what she is."

"Treating her free don't make her free," Nora said. Her gaze wandered over the little cabin, off to itself but still on plantation land. "I try to tell Jonah the same thing. Master Crewe was quick enough to remind him."

"What did he say?"

"He say if we don't know what to talk about, he move us up front where he can keep a better eye and ear on us." Again, Nora's gaze traveled over the cabin, the wild field in which it sat, the woods of shade and beauty. The impression of privacy, the illusion of freedom, surrounded them like a rail fence. "Jonah can't live like that no more," Nora said. "This all that keep him from running or something worse," Nora said.

"Listen to that," Bless said. She inclined her head toward the high-spirited sounds floating from the nearby woods. Both women paused in the sound of the children's laughter, the way they halted sometimes in the scarlet of a sunset. "At least they are happy."

"They don't know no better," Nora said, and the huskiness of her voice that rarely, but sometimes, intensified with weariness or impatience, deepened to bitterness.

"I-I thought—" Bless began.

"You thought I was a fool who don't know no better than to grin and make babies for these men to put in they pockets."

Bless glanced away. She snapped the ends off the beans in her hands, but she didn't throw them in the bowl. She gripped them tightly. She looked back at Nora. "Then why?"

"You talk like I got a choice."

Bless thought of her own choices. "There are things a woman can do," she said softly.

"You want to know what choice Master Jeffrey give me? Here the *choice* he give me: Settle down with Jonah. Give him eight live births. Raise them right. After that, I be free." Nora snapped beans and threw the pods into the bowl as she spoke. Each snap sounded like the crack of a small bone. "Or he pass me around. Sell me when he done. One way or another, he getting eight babies off'a me."

Nora raised her gaze to the trees where the children dashed in and out of view.

"But who know what might happen in between Kelsey and number eight? And if I do get free, who know if I might not live long enough to buy some of my own children and see them buy a few of their brothers and sisters free?"

Bless did not say anything.

"I sound like a fool, don't I? And you wondering what's to make Jeffrey free me in the end?" Nora shrugged. "Nothing. Be more consequence if he break his word to his horse. But that's all the hope I got, Bless. Meantime, one man come to me in the evening. One man. I feed him. Rub his back. He play with the children. We sleep all under one roof, and we don't tell the children it's all pretend."

Bless said nothing.

"Now you can't decide if I'm a fool or a beast," Nora said.

Bless thrust her hand into the bag of beans. She filled her lap and snapped two, three, four, before she said, "I will tell you when I decide which one I am."

"Mmm," Nora said.

And they sat there snapping beans and listening to the laughter of children hidden by the woods. The sound waxed and waned. Already it was as if the three of them—Lydia and Kelsey and Irene—were memories or gone off somewhere to live out their mothers' choices.

Kelsey and Lydia

Crewe's Way Station, Lower Norfolk
Colony of Virginia, 1710

As he rode into the yard, the young man took in Jack Crewe's place with the dispassionate, calculating eyes of an assessor. The fences and outbuildings looked to be in good order. The nearby kitchen garden and the fields fanning behind the house and barn were neatly cultivated. The henhouse and corrals could not be faulted, no sagging or broken boards and, at a glance, the animals looked healthy. From the height of his horse, he saw two hatted heads bobbing in a far field. The young man could not deny the relief he felt at finding the place in good repair and the inhabitants occupied with work.

He dismounted in front of the house, but the greeting he set to call out was forestalled by the shrill cry of a young child. It came from the direction of the cookhouse. He reckoned the women were occupied there. If they had not already heard the clop-clop of his approach, they certainly would not hear it over those robust cries. Only a boy popped out of the barn to greet him.

"Help you, sir?"

"Where is your master, boy?" the young man asked.

"He in the field yonder with my pa. You want me to fetch him, sir?"

The man settled his appraiser's gaze on the boy. Sturdy looking. Long in the legs. Eager to please. He looked to be about nine, maybe ten years of age. The man declined. "He'll be in soon enough, I reckon."

"My ma's in the kitchen. I can fetch her or Miss Bless."

The man cocked his head toward the noise of the bawling child. "Sounds like they got their hands full."

"That's my brother," the boy said with a grimace. "Ma say he won't always be so worrisome."

The man added wit to the child's list of attributes. "How about you just show me where I can put up my horse while I wait for your master."

"I take care of the animals when Pa ain't here," the boy said eagerly.

"Are you sure you can handle him?" the man asked. The boy looked strong, not weakened by rickets or any other childhood infirmity, but the horse was broad and many hands taller than him.

"Yes, sir," the boy said. "Pa learned me." He took the reins in a steady hand and began to lead the animal toward the barn. The man added "confident" to the list.

He looked around. No one from the kitchen seemed to notice his arrival, and he could still make out the two workers in the field. He recognized an opportunity he might not have had otherwise. Instead of following the little stable hand, he took the opportunity to make an unaccompanied inspection of Crewe's farm.

Wandering from structure to structure, he found the cellar and dug around in the straw and ice to unearth fruits, cream, potatoes. He entered the servant's quarters. He saw a spare dress hanging on a nail, a spinning wheel by the hearth. The usual cobbled-together mess of table, chairs, a bed. Sewing a child's dress, unfinished. Nothing but slaves' things.

From there, he walked to the packhouse where he rocked a few hogshead barrels and sniffed to try to ascertain the contents. He pried the top from one and found it stuffed with sweet, golden tobacco. In the smithy, he held his hand to the hearth to determine how long since it had been fired. Cold. He calculated the cost of such disuse. He opened cabinets and cataloged the chains, shackles, nails. As he inspected, the young man created an itemized list in his head. Each thing he saw and touched shaped itself into a numerical value. With the beginnings of a solid idea of the place's worth forming in his head, he headed back toward the barn to make sure his prized animal was indeed in capable hands.

His approach was so stealthy that he startled the boy. "You pick his hooves first?" he asked. The child turned suddenly. The currying brush flew from his hand.

"Yes, sir!" the boy said. He hopped up from his haunches, where he had squatted to brush dirt from the animal's flanks and legs and went to retrieve the tool.

The man was pleased to find that not only had the boy picked stones from the hooves straightaway, but he had also hung the tack and tied a feed bag on the animal. The boy was a quarter way through brushing the detritus of the road from the horse's hide. The young man watched. He liked the boy's comportment, the pert, "Yes, sir!" and the way he dove into work. He liked the form of him—strong, the man guessed, from tending animals and pitching hay. He'd bet anything the boy would be tall but not lanky. Just the type to make a good hostler or footman. "What's your name, boy?"

"Kelsey, sir," the boy replied, glancing respectfully over his shoulder as he brushed.

"How old are you?"

"Almost nine, sir."

The place the traveler had in mind would be glad to get the boy so young, before he learned many bad habits, while he could quickly unlearn the ones he already knew. The man took a coin from inside his vest. He flipped it between his fingers. The boy's gaze got hooked on the dazzle.

"What else can you do except tend horses, Kelsey?"

Watching the coin, the boy took a breath and began to answer, but a small voice interrupted from the open archway of the barn. "Who are you?"

Both man and boy glanced toward the voice. The boy looked annoyed. He'd been about to earn that coin. The man faltered. He struck the coin with his fingers instead of catching it in his palm. It bounced toward Kelsey, who picked it up, rubbed it against his shirt, and reluctantly handed it back. He might have gotten away with keeping it because the man's gaze fastened on the little girl.

If he had ever seen a prettier creature, the young man could not remember where or when. "Who are *you*?" he asked.

"Lydia," she answered. She crossed the floor of the barn to stand beside the boy.

"Oh!" the man said. "You must be the pretty little girl I heard about."

To her credit, the little girl gave him a suspicious scowl. Her world was small. She was not allowed to interact with anyone who came to use the pens. Everyone else she knew lived on this farm. Who could have told this man about her? She slipped her hand into Kelsey's.

"My father saw you once. He said you were the prettiest little girl he had ever seen."

The description had not done her justice. Her skin put him in mind of fresh milk sprinkled with a hint of India spice. Someone had tried to hide her braided hair beneath a kerchief, but what was visible was fired with reds and golds enough to shame the wares of any fur trader.

Lydia blushed under the man's stare. "You didn't say your name," she said.

"How about I tell you a story first? Yes? Okay. When I was a boy, not much older than Kelsey here, I met Mr. Jack Crewe, *Papa Jack*, you call him, right?" Lydia nodded. "Well, your Papa Jack saw that I'd had me some trouble, and he covered me, head to foot, I swear, in a salve that smelled worse than this horse's shit!"

Lydia and Kelsey grimaced. They knew that salve. Despite the threat and delivery—once Jonah caught him—of a whipping, Kelsey ran from the ointment every time.

"If I get a sore," Lydia confided, "Papa Jack puts it on me, but Mama makes me wash it off before she let me in the bed!"

The man nodded in camaraderie. He squatted low and flipped the silver coin again. Lydia and Kelsey tracked it as it spangled the sunlight. It landed in the center of the man's palm. Both children stepped closer.

The man smiled.

Jack Crewe and Jonah

Hoes on their shoulders and still mopping sweat from their brows, Jack and Jonah walked into the barn to find their children entertaining a stranger. Kelsey had just landed a flip, and Lydia had taken off her kerchief. She had dismantled one long braid to show the man that she could plait it back together.

"Now," the man said, "show me who is the tallest!" The children knocked into each other as they scrambled to line up.

Jonah was the first to recognize the stranger, John Jeffrey's son. "Mr. Ethan?"

"Jonah!" Ethan Jeffrey said. "You don't look so glad to see me, old boy."

He did not. Crewe turned his uncertain gaze to Jonah's face. Jonah, who did the dirtiest work without comment or complaint, who never smiled nor frowned, fought for blankness. The muscles around his mouth, in his forehead, jumped and quivered. He finally summoned his voice. "Always glad to see you well, Mr. Ethan."

"How is Nora?" Ethan asked.

"She fine, sir," Jonah said.

"That her young'un I heard squalling?"

Another spasm passed over Jonah's face. "Yes, sir," he answered.

"What does that make? Three?" Ethan Jeffrey asked with eager interest.

"Yes, sir," Jonah answered.

"Good, good. We are getting there, aren't we?"

Jonah's nervous gaze fell on Kelsey before returning to Ethan. "I reckon, sir." He turned to Crewe. "Sir, if you don't mind, Kelsey and me best be getting on. Nora be calling us to supper soon. She get mad as a wet hen we come to the table without washing first."

Crewe studied the strain on Jonah's face a few seconds more. "Go on," he said. "Take Lydia with you."

"Y'all come on," Jonah ordered. The children, always eager for supper, forgot their tricks for silver and ran to him. Jonah left the barn so quickly that he forgot to hang the hoe he carried, leaving with it still resting against his shoulder.

Crewe turned to the young man. He was dressed more like a Williamsburg merchant than a slave stringer. He wore a bespoke pleated frock coat over a waistcoat and breeches, both of fine linen. His brown leggings and black boots, all of leather, were protected by spatterdashes that kept off the far-flying muck of his business. The uncertain, boxy boy had grown stout, broad, with the muscularity of a cottonmouth and, Crewe sensed, the same poise, the same patience.

"Ethan?" he asked. "You are the boy, Ethan?"

"I am."

"You are a young man now! Last I heard, you were traveling, learning the business."

"I returned some months ago. Summoned home due to my father's illness. We did not have much time together. Word must not have reached you," Ethan said. "My father is dead."

Jack took the hoe from his shoulder. He removed the hat from his head and mopped his face with the brim as he absorbed the news of John Jeffrey's death.

"I am truly sorry to hear that. Your father—much of my good fortune is owed to him."

"Yes, well, he has gone on to his reward." Ethan's mouth curved into a faint smile. "I am sure the devil had something quite worthy of my father's generosity in store for him."

"I-I," Jack stammered. His shock at Ethan's words was such that, not knowing what to say, he turned to parsing the last time he'd received a letter from John Jeffrey. Some months—six? eight?—had passed. Jack had not worried. Letters were posted with hope rather than assurance of delivery. "When I last heard from him, he told me he was on the mend. He expected to travel again soon."

"One does not 'mend' from syphilis. But, of course, men like my father do not think the laws of nature apply to them."

Something, the snakelike narrowing of Ethan's eyes, the directness of the young man's gaze, told Crewe that he was classed among the *men like my father*. Instinctively, he understood that, despite their accomplishments, the alchemy of making fortunes out of nothing, Ethan did not hold this class of men in high esteem.

Crewe blinked once, twice, a third time as he waited for the sudden pounding of his heart to slow. "You must be tired and hungry," he said. He put away his tool and led the way out of the barn.

Crewe personally saw Ethan settled in the drovers' cabin with wash water, linens, and food. Then he set off to talk to Bless.

Bless and Jack Crewe

Bless stood in the center of the small cabin looking around. Nothing seemed out of place. Even the shoes that Lydia hated, so much that she sometimes hid them, were lined up beside the door. Still, the cabin did not feel quite right. When Crewe barreled in, demanding, "Where is Lydia?" Bless knew there was a message in her sense of unease, no different from the warnings animals sniffed in the wind.

"Following behind Kelsey, I would guess," she said, though she also knew that bit of information would not please Lydia's father. He had not cared much for Kelsey since the boy told Lydia she was a slave. Something between father and daughter had changed that day. Even Bless felt it. Lydia loved him still, but she did not dog his heels or launch herself into his arms the way she used to. She didn't find excuses to visit with him past her bedtime, and when Bless called her to the cabin she came running. On some evenings, the child did not visit Crewe's house at all. Lydia would hug her father, but the contact was fleeting and, almost always, initiated by him. For all those reasons, and the unflagging mischief of children, Crewe had little fondness for Kelsey.

"They've caused some trouble?" Bless asked. It wasn't that long ago that the children had enraged one of the sows by "borrowing" her piglets. Kelsey and Lydia had grown tired of inanimate corn-husk dolls. Jonah had to repair a breach in the fence.

Crewe shook his head. "Not like you think. But I want you to keep her under a tight rein. We have a visitor."

"A visitor?"

"John Jeffrey is dead. His son, Ethan, has come."

Bless did not know the extent of the dealings between her owner and John Jeffrey, but she knew there were business ties, and such ties could be tried or broken by death. And all enslaved people knew that a will—a dead man's directives on what should be done with the destinies of the living—could dismantle slaves' lives, butchering and parceling them out, like a hog killing.

Crewe had come with one concern. He didn't want the visitor to see Lydia. Bless's knees suddenly felt weak. She crossed to a chair. Here was the other thing he did not have to say: All slaves were vulnerable, women more than men, children more than women, little girls more than all the rest. Bless wanted to scream, "Too soon! Too soon!" but she knew it was not.

Calmly, she asked, "He's looking at her?"

Crewe nodded. He gripped the doorpost. It was his turn to feel weak with shock as he realized that Bless was not surprised. For her, this menacing day had always been on the horizon. All that had been wanting was the date.

Crewe looked coldcocked. Bless was certain he would sway, stagger on his feet if he stepped away from the lintel. She took no pity on him. "Men like that are going to be after her all her life," Bless said.

She stood. She pushed her chair neatly beneath the table. "Excuse me, sir. I have to get back to helping Nora."

Bless skirted past Crewe and out the door. She left him standing there, holding tightly to the solid post of the slave cabin.

Jack Crewe, Ethan Jeffrey, and Jonah

Jack Crew had the women prepare an unusually luxurious dinner for Jeffrey. He convinced himself that rich food and a convivial atmosphere could forge with Ethan the bond Jack had forged with John. It could allow the two men to come to an understanding, to construct and erect boundaries of mutual respect upon which they could build their business dealings. But, first, Crewe would have to get to know the boy.

"Tell me about your travels," he said. "You were just a boy the last time I saw you."

"Oh," Ethan said, "I have been all up and down this coast since we last met. Colony to colony. I have seen all caliber of Negro from prime to refuse. I can tell just by looking that you are raising some of the best."

Crewe cleared his throat. He had not been ready to steer the conversation toward business, but he nodded and said, "That is the deal I made with your father. Raise them right. Raise them to know their place. When importation ends, buyers will come to us."

Ethan leaned forward. "They are already coming. That is why I am here, in addition to inspecting my holdings. Before his death, he told me about the extraordinary little picaninny you are raising here."

"Your father *was* quite impressed with Kelsey. He made that clear when he brought the family—"

Ethan gave a sigh. He sat back in his chair and sipped his drink as if to give himself a moment for his exasperation to pass. He chided, "You know that I do not mean the boy, though I do think I have a ready buyer for him too."

"You cannot mean Lydia."

"Of course I do."

Crewe sipped from his drink as he tried to swallow back annoyance. His conversation with John Jeffrey should have been the end of it. "As I told your father, Lydia is not for sale."

"She is a slave, isn't she?" Ethan persisted.

Jack Crewe could not tell if the sudden flush that heated him was from the spirits or from anger. He set down his glass. "Yes. She is a slave."

"Then she *is* for sale, Jack," Ethan said as if explaining the business to a newcomer.

Crewe leaned forward, resting his forearms on the table, meeting the younger man's steady gaze. "And isn't that my decision to make?"

"Is it?" Ethan asked, a taunting lilt in his voice.

"*Indeed*, according to the agreement I made with your father, it is. No matter, you should be embarrassed to broach this with me. But you are new to the business. You don't yet understand how some things—"

"On the contrary, sir. I believe I know this business better than you. *I* have been to the Slave Coast. *I* have walked through the castles and gone belowdecks on the ships. Since I was a child, I have been going to auctions, visiting the jails, watching my father buy and sell slaves all up and down the King's Highway. There is *nothing* about this filthy business that I don't understand." Ethan cocked his head. "You, on the other hand, might need to learn a thing or two."

Jack leaned heavily into the back of his seat. The last person to speak to him like that was Thomas Crewe.

Ethan stood. He brushed the crumbs and flakes of dinner from his breeches. "If you will excuse me, this has been a long and tiring day."

Ethan showed himself out. The door closed behind him. Crewe recognized his own lapse in manners. Courtesy called for him to stand when Ethan stood. He should have seen his guest to the stringer's quarters.

But he could not move. Crewe remained in his seat, astonished.

• • •

Jack Crewe had no idea where he was going until he found himself in front of Jonah and Nora's cabin. The dwelling was dark, but the yard was lit by the serene white light of a half-moon. As if by prearrangement, Jonah sat alone on the steps while his family slept inside. He appeared to have just crawled out of bed. His long, narrow feet were bare. He wore breeches but no shirt. He did not seem surprised that his master had come.

"What do he want?" Jonah asked.

"The children," Jack answered.

The night, alive with its animal and insect sounds, was not loud enough to cover Jonah's indrawn breath. "Both of 'em? Kelsey and Irene both?"

"Kelsey and Lydia," Jack said.

Nor his sigh of relief. "He want—he want Lydia?"

Jack nodded, the motion jerky like the handle on a rusty water pump. "I need to know how to get around him."

A sound, something between a sob and a chuckle, escaped Jonah. "No disrespect, sir, but if I knowed how to get around men like y'all, I wouldn't be sitting here."

A splash of moonlight revealed the surprise on his master's face. Jonah jolted too: Had the man imagined that, given a real choice, Jonah would want nothing more than this animal life, robbed of everything he loved, dragged to and fro on a lead?

"I need to know—I need to know anything you can tell me about him," Crewe said.

It was not wise to talk about white people with other white people. That was a good way to end up with a horse bridle in your mouth. "I can't tell you nothing you don't already know, sir."

Crewe pressed. "He is so different from the boy I met years ago. That boy didn't even want to be in this business."

This business. A colorless description of a bloody system that stripped his life from him again and again. Jonah began to rise. "I ought to go in—" he said before he could say or do something that would hasten—even more than Jeffrey's arrival—the loss of this temporary reprieve.

Crewe stopped him. "Did you live on Jeffrey's place when Ethan was a child? Did you know him?"

"I knowed him."

"What was he like?"

Jonah did not answer right away. Instead, he walked into the moonlight. He stopped in arm's reach of his master.

Crewe stepped backward, but he could not deny what proximity revealed: A mirror could not have given back a truer likeness. In the way that mattered most at that moment, he and Jonah were identical. The same worried eyes and drawn mouth. The same hunched shoulders and bunched fists. A father afraid of what would become of his child.

"I'll tell you what I know," Jonah said, "but I want something."

"What?"

Mentally, Crewe toted up the amount of silver secreted in his house, the number of hams in the storehouse, reams of cloth, extra shoes, furniture, lengths of lumber that could improve the Negro's house. But Jonah did not ask for any of the things Jack Crewe might have asked for in the other man's place.

"Kelsey," Jonah said. "Get him to spare Kelsey too."

"Jonah, I—"

"You *feel* how it is, don't you?"

"I do," Crewe admitted, "but I-I can't promise that."

"Goodnight, sir." Jonah turned to go inside. Crewe studied the scars, fat and twisty like tobacco worms, bulging on the man's back. Not many more years would pass before Kelsey's back began to look like his father's.

"I could try," Jack Crewe said.

Not a promise, but more than might have been expected. A little hope. Jonah sat heavily on the step.

Jack Crewe and Jonah

Resting his forearms on his knees, Jonah leaned forward. Jack could almost see him picking through memories, like the women sifting through peas, discarding what he did not feel was fit or safe to share.

"He used to always like to be with the people," Jonah said. He glanced up to make sure Crewe took his meaning. "When he was a boy, wasn't no other children up to the main house. They say his mama almost died birthing him. She stayed poorly after. So Mr. Ethan was always chasing round with our young'uns too young to help in the fields. Where they went, he went. What they ate, he ate. He knowed all they songs and games. Won sometime too. He run in and out of the cabins like the other young'uns. And we fed him, and tended him, and chastised him just like we did the rest.

"But truth is, if Master Jeffrey hadn't been away so much, shifting and shuffling people like playing cards, Mr. Ethan never woulda been among us so much. His ma'am had been too sick to nurse him. One of our women, Fannie, did it. He ate at her table, played with her young'uns and come to see her for years. His ma couldn't make him stay up to the house with her. I reckon he even slept in the quarters sometime, or he come mighty early.

"Well, when he turned about ten, old enough to keep his seat in the saddle, Master Jeffrey put a stop to all that mingling. *We* all knowed it would happen, but it seemed hurtful for the boy. Mr. Ethan didn't want to go with his daddy. Was scared of him. With good reason. Master Jeffrey don't make no whole lotta difference between a woman, a child, and a slave. Treat them all to his fist and his boot.

"I don't believe Mr. Ethan wanted to mistreat nobody. Not at first. But every time he come back, he were different. Last time he come, he sliced a quirt right 'cross the face of one'a Fannie's young'uns. The boy greeted him like he always did, 'Ethan' instead'a *Mister* Ethan. Almost took his eye. They was 'bout the same age. Sucked from the same teats. Napped together wherever Fannie laid 'em down. But that lick 'cross the face told us folk all we need to know.

"After that, Mister Ethan ain't come back no more. But Fannie, she lived long enough to see him sell away some of her young'uns. Some of mine too. Chil'ren he was brought up with. What else you need to know about 'im, sir?"

Jack Crewe looked down at his own hands. He felt again the weight and the heat of the pot of mush he had thrown at Shango, but what mired him in the memory was not the African's bewildered look of pain—a look not dissimilar from the one Jonah wore now— but the recollection of his own anger, how it had swelled inside of the boy he'd been until there had been room for nothing else.

"Nothing," he said. "There's nothing else I need to know."

Jonah placed his hands flat upon his knees. In the manner of a much older man or one twisted by the rigors of the fields, he pushed to his feet. "Well, sir, morning won't tarry. Don't reckon I ought to neither."

Crewe nodded. He turned to leave but spoke again. "Jonah, did you—"

Jonah paused on the top step. "Did I what, sir?"

Jack Crewe's own voice betrayed him. His words came out as truth, stark, not cloaked in the guise of a question. "You left behind family—I mean, other children, when Jeffrey brought you here."

And Jonah's voice did not disguise his grief. "I did, sir."

He bade Crewe goodnight and shut the door to the cabin built around all he had left.

Jack Crewe and Ethan Jeffrey

Early the next day, Crewe and Ethan completed their tour of the farm. Ethan had peered into every building and trough. He tasted the sweet water of the creek that irrigated the fields. He checked the teeth and hooves of the livestock. He plucked from the crops that were coming ripe. Lastly, the men only had to review the books to calculate the income from the slaves jailed on the property. Then, with a better understanding of his father's investment and the profit to come, Ethan could pack and be ready to leave at first light.

All day, as they had walked the fields and examined the farm's structures, the laughter and squabbles of Lydia, Kelsey, and Irene reached the men on the odd breeze, but Ethan made no mention of the children. Jack Crewe decided he must have panicked, read too much into Ethan's interest in the young ones. Jonah must have reached the same conclusion because, after dinner, Nora was brisk but not ill at ease as she poured chicory coffee first into Ethan's cup then Jack's. Her gaze remained downcast, as was proper, but her hands did not tremble. Jack concluded that Jonah had not told her of their fears.

"If they's nothing else for now, sir," Nora said, "I'll go set the kitchen to right."

"Nothing else," Jack said. "You can fetch the rest of this in the morning," he indicated the coffee service and the saucers of sweetmeats with a flick of his fingers. He retrieved the ledger from his desk.

"Dinner was excellent, Nora," Ethan said as his gaze slid over the young woman's breasts, her thickened waist, and broad hips. "Delicious."

Nora nodded. She backed from the room until she was forced to turn at the doorway. Ethan watched until her backside disappeared from view, then informed his host, "She used to be as skinny as a rail. Childbearing has done her good."

Jack Crewe cocked a brow as he carefully cleared space for the ledger. "Your father said they were not to be interfered with as long as they uphold their part in the bargain."

Ethan shrugged. "And the devil's own bargain it is." His gaze wandered around the house, modest, but due to the telltale signs of a child, not cheerless. Solid, with some comforts. "They think they are gaining something," Ethan murmured. "Just the kind of agreement my father would make."

Crewe opened the cover of the ledger. He wanted this night done. He wanted to show Ethan the expected profit on the Jeffreys' investment and send him on his way before another word could be said about Lydia—and Kelsey too.

With a dismissive wave of his hand, Ethan indicated that there was no need to open the book. "I can see the place is thriving. You have done well with the capital my father loaned you."

"Thank you," Crewe said, and he could not deny that he felt buoyed by the praise even if it came from this impudent younger man.

"But tell me, what of the interest accrued on the late payments?"

The rush of pride drained away like the drawback of the sea before a tidal wave. Alarm filled the suddenly empty space. Still, Crewe managed to keep his voice level. "'Interest accrued on late payments?'"

"Yes, of course." Ethan opened his jacket. He reached into a pocket hidden in the silken lining and extracted a small, fine-grained leather book. "I call this my father's 'little book of leverage.' Things he wanted to keep track of—off ledger, mind you."

"*I* am in that book?"

"Oh, yes!" Ethan said. "Here he noted each favor, legal or illicit, that he ever did for anyone he met. Names, dates, actions, amounts. Bits of information that could be used to smoothly grease the wheels of his enterprise." He thumbed the book open. "Would you like to see?"

With a twist of Ethan's wrist, Jack Crewe found himself staring down at a page that bore his own name in heavy block letters. That page and the one that followed were divided into columns: payment due on; payment received on; the amount of interest charged each time the funds arrived beyond the due date.

Baffled, Jack said, "I always paid."

"Indeed, you did. The record does not say otherwise. These penalties accrued for paying behind time."

Jack Crewe shook his head to clear his confusion, to deny what was becoming clear. "Your father said he would forbear. He said he would allow me grace."

"I assure you the word 'grace' does not appear anywhere in your contract," Ethan said, his tone amused.

"We *spoke* of it. John said there would be leniency. He said he would treat me as he would have my father, his friend."

"I assure you, he did! This is exactly how my father treated his *friends*. He kept track of every shilling they owed him."

"He said—"

Unlike Jonah had just the night before, Ethan did not smother his derision nor hide his disbelief. He snorted. "Sir! You are not naive. You surely know it is not what the man *says* but what the signed document *stipulates* that holds sway." Ethan sat back. He spread his hands and smiled, a brief, tight flexing of the lips. "How do you think we came to possess this glorious land in the first place?"

Jack Crewe did not laugh at the dark joke. His gaze traveled the column of numbers. Over the years, John Jeffrey had tracked each time Jack remitted a late payment. Jack recalled some of the notations. A season when the slave pens did not fill as expected. Weather delays. The inoperability of a much-needed tool. Impassable roads to market. An animal that could not haul or plow. His own stretch of injury or illness. Nothing outside of what usually befalls a man who makes his living from the land. Yet and still, Jack always managed to pay.

The "behind schedule" fees, however, were extortionate. The interest, compounded. The final sum, sizable. Worse than that, however, was the realization that John Jeffrey had made Jack complicit in his own ruination.

Jack's voice lowered to a disbelieving whisper. "He said the fees were customary and implied they would not be enforced. It would have taken time to amend the contract. We wanted to get on with the deal."

"You met my father how many times over a span of ten years, Mr. Crewe? Three? Four? You did not know him well enough to distrust him," Ethan said, as if comfort could be found in ineptness. Then, he turned thoughtful. "But perhaps you are the one who is right. Mayhap he liked your father well enough to treat you better than all the other men he cheated. He *was* a land pirate to his putrid soul," Ethan mused. "Perhaps he kept your record because he simply could not help himself."

Jack seized on that. "You will honor your father's words then? His intentions?"

That constricted smile convulsed Ethan's lips again. "And how am I to know what those were?" He shook his head. The smile hardened into a grimace of determination. "Rather, I will do as I have done since boyhood: I will follow my father's example."

He leaned forward, took a swig of coffee, scowled, and removed a flask from his pocket. Ethan poured as he spoke, his words as singeing as the liquor flowing into the dark coffee. "Late fees were to be remitted with your payments. Since that was not done, the fees have, of course, accumulated interest. As my father's heir, I am within my rights to call in the debt you owe his estate. I would like to leave with the funds."

Jack shook his head. "I don't have that amount of money—"

"On hand?"

"Anywhere!"

"The place appears to be thriving."

"The margins are thin. Enough to pay the loan. To buy what we cannot produce."

"Ah." Ethan said, and Jack Crewe knew that everything had been coming to this. "Well, lamentably, I see only three paths open to you:

You can produce the funds. You can vacate the premises, or—" he said, pity in both look and tone.

Anger swelled in Jack. His heart and lungs hurt from the pressure. He wanted to bash the false sympathy from Ethan's face.

"Or you can indenture yourself to me until you've paid me what you owe. Due to my interest in your holdings, it is only reasonable that I would administer your property until the debt is paid. Any sensible judge would agree to that—"

"And you will end up with her anyway," Jack whispered.

Just like that, Jack was drowning in the inescapable reality of Jonah, of Nora, of Bless.

Before his opponent could even gasp for air, Ethan continued.

"I will make you a deal, Mr. Jack Crewe, a better deal than my father would ever offer. No strings. No secret books. No fancy lawyers needed." He waited for Jack to indicate that he listened.

Jack shuddered as he gulped for air. Ethan had his full attention.

Ethan cupped the coffee in his large hands. He inhaled deeply of the aroma, then said, "The late fees and accumulated interest forgotten, the payments done, the debt forgiven, every blade of grass free and clear," Ethan sipped the spiked coffee, settled back, and smiled, "all for one little blue-eyed picaninny."

Ethan Jeffrey

When Ethan Jeffrey capitulated, when he accepted slavery into his heart and gave himself over to his father's dream of a slave-trading empire, he did not conduct himself as most sons would have, relying on his father's knowledge, parroting John Jeffrey's every maxim. Instead, Ethan set himself the task of learning the business for himself.

By sixteen, he'd traveled from the Chesapeake Bay to the Slave Coast of Africa. He'd ventured into both the holding forts of Benin and the holds of vessels where slaves were packed in sludge and misery. He'd witnessed their bewilderment and their fury. He saw them die by violence, by suicide, by grief. He saw the survivors—slaves touted as "tamed and degraded"—and knew they had been uncoupled from something more vital than home and kin.

Ruination begat ruination. Ethan changed.

Every debasement, every humiliating act Ethan watched, condoned, and committed, estranged him from the boy he'd been and made him the man his father wanted. This son who earned his father's approval hated the enslaved for their wretchedness. He hated the slavers for their atrocities. He hated himself—pathetic enough to become what he loathed and feared—most of all. He struck Fannie's son not for forgetting his place, but because Ethan could no longer tolerate the people's grace, their willingness to believe he differed from John Jeffrey, when, in fact, Ethan lacked the courage to be even a whit less than what his father demanded.

With one exception. Ethan could not traffic in the rhetoric—of his father, of Jack—that painted slavery in a redeeming light. He knew that souls, his own among them, were lost, not saved, in the coastal cells of West Africa and the rice fields of the Carolina Colony. Slavery was not "training," not "making niggers fit," as John Jeffrey said. Slavery was business, profit-making, a voracious quest to plant, pluck, and boil the sugar cane, to top the tobacco, to harvest the cotton, indigo, and rice. And every aspect of the business depended on one enshrined rule: A slave was simply a slave. Chattel. Property to be bought and sold.

If there were allowances, if there were degrees, everyone—from the ships' captains and the speculators to the lawyers, the middling farmers and rich plantation owners, the overseers, the merchants, and the jailers—would have to reconsider the whole enterprise.

Early on, Ethan had tired of men like Crewe and his own father, who wanted to dress what they did in shades of gray, who wanted moral leeway, loopholes, and gradations they could use to skirt the truth and, so, sleep easy in their featherbeds.

Ethan had infinitely more respect for men like himself: the men who slept in featherbeds but did not rest; the ones who savored smooth rum but accepted as their due the taste of blood at the bottom of the cup. He walked about all day with the tang of copper and salt in his mouth. Without a doubt, Ethan knew what kind of man he had become. The kind who built accounts, credit, and reputation on the backs of men who, for the first ten years of his life, had been like brothers to him. Why on Earth would he spare Jack Crewe when he had not spared Fannie, the woman whose breastmilk fortified his very bones?

Call it vengeance or call it principle: Ethan would make no difference between the selling of Fannie's children, or Jonah's child, and the selling of Crewe's.

Jack Crewe and Ethan Jeffrey

"On top of everything else, I'll pay you four hundred pounds for her," Ethan said. "That will solve your problems of 'tight margins' and 'cash on hand.'"

"That is a very large sum for a child," Jack said. He concealed his trembling fists in the pockets of his waistcoat.

"Damn right!" Ethan laughed. "What is more, you'll be spared the expense of feeding her." He sobered. "In all seriousness, you are keeping that little mulatto better than most white children I've seen."

"What of it?"

Ethan shook his head. "It is not wise to harbor tender feelings toward them, Jack. They are commodities, not pets."

Jack Crewe felt the same fearful lurching that six years ago drove him to rescue his newborn from the slippery hands of a startled midwife. He braced his body against any sudden, forward movement. He could not be certain what that feeling would drive him to.

"There is a market for her kind," Ethan continued, "so lucrative that folks are willing to take them young. Train them up. Teach them the graces."

"Graces for what?" Crewe asked.

"The same thing all pretty Negro women are trained for."

"A-a bordello?"

"Doesn't have to be," Ethan said. "I know a man who keeps one. Put her in her own house in the back of his yard."

"Lydia for a whorehouse or kenneled in some debauched man's backyard? She is my *daughter*."

"I don't give two pins about her sire!" Ethan exclaimed, mystified that Jack even considered paternity an issue. "A slave is a slave, Mr. Crewe."

"Lydia is not— Not Lydia," Jack said.

Ethan set his drink aside. He leaned forward, elbows on the table, fingers steepled—a judge absorbed in the evidence of a case.

"Was Lydia's mammy free when she birthed her?"

"No."

"Lydia got free papers in her little apron?"

"No."

"You filed manumission papers down at the courthouse?" Ethan waved away Jack's repetitive response. "No. Because if you file them, you well know she has to leave this colony.

"Perhaps, to you, Mr. Crewe, she is a child. To everyone else, she is a slave. How long do you think you can protect her? You'd be doing what is best for her. I'll make sure she lands easy." He leaned farther onto the table. "There is a place in Charles Town that only takes the ones that look like her. They pamper those girls. Raise them like blooded horses. They only let them out to men who can care for them and keep them as well as they keep their wives! No better outcome for her in this world. Her kind don't make good field hands, Jack," Ethan said.

"No better 'outcome,'" Jack Crewe repeated, "than I sell my daughter for a whore?"

Ethan drew back. He studied the man across the table from him. Flared nostrils. Rapid breathing. Red face. Righteous indignation.

"Tell me, Jack," Ethan asked, "what did you have planned for her? Before, I mean. Before you saw those eyes? When she was just another calf falling from between her mammy's legs into the straw?"

Crewe's fists clenched. Ethan smirked. "Selling that girl is no worse than anything else we have done in this excremental business."

"You must see that this is different," Crewe said tightly.

Ethan sighed. "How do you think my father contracted syphilis?"

Confusion and annoyance whipped through Crewe "What? Your

father's conquests have nothing to do with what is to become of my daughter."

Ethan smiled again. "He would like the word 'conquests.' A rather heroic euphemism for the things he did. And you *do* know what he did." He held up a finger to stifle the denial trembling on Crewe's lips. "But do you know how many times I pretended not to hear? Not to see? Would you like to hear about the first time I—"

"No!" Crewe struck the table with his fist. Plates and drinking vessels shook.

He did not need to hear. He did not need to imagine. "Is you like them? Don't let them, please!"

Ethan looked mildly surprised, mildly amused, at Crewe's reaction. The younger man shrugged. "I came around to my father's way. To your way. 'Brutes,' you called them. Do you remember that? Brutes. He waited for a response, but none came because Jack Crewe was waylaid by the memory of the waving grass and wagon ruts, watching the Jeffreys and their coffle of boy slaves march away.

"I repeated it to myself. Brute. No different from an ox. Man, woman, or child. Brute. Use an ox to haul. Use a nigger for what a nigger is made for. That's what my daddy did. Especially when it came to the women."

There was nothing Crewe could say. It was not at all uncommon. He had, quite clearly, done it himself.

Ethan leaned forward again. Shoulders hitched and clasped hands dangling between his knees, his tone was confidential. "I have brothers and sisters in the indigo fields, Mr. Crewe. My own issue are strapped to their mothers' backs as they wade through the rice fields."

Had there been a mirror nearby, Jack Crewe would have startled at the replica of his father's face on his own. Not the face of Thomas Crewe, but the face Rowan Dane wore the day he searched adolescent Jack for some likeness to the little boy who'd slept with a newborn sister swaddled upon his chest. Some remnant of that sweet, wise boy in the angry youth who'd dashed hot mush upon Shango.

Just like Rowan Dane, Jack Crewe found nary a trace. Where was the boy who had so solemnly said, "What we do is wrong," in the young man who sat across from him?

"I regret what I said to you," Jack said haltingly. "I regretted it that very day. I came after you—"

All traces of condescending amusement drained from Ethan, leaving him pale and shaking. His words hissed as if escaping from the pressure of a garrot.

"Don't you dare," he said.

"Since she has been born, I am a better man," Jack insisted. "Not a good one yet—"

"Yet?" Ethan scoffed. "You don't understand, do you? You think, because you have misgivings over selling one mulatto picaninny into whoredom, you can become a good man? That prospect was lost the moment you joined this barbarism, Mr. Crewe. What you are is a charlatan, but the only person you fool is yourself." Ethan shook his head. "I will not allow you that comfort. You want the profits of this filthy trade, the benefits? Then do the thing you never thought you would do—just like the rest of us. You are not exempt. Your little blue-eyed brute, is not exempt."

Jack surged to his feet. Despite his seething fury and bold talk, Ethan flinched, a reflex learned in childhood.

Jack did not strike.

When no blows fell, Ethan glanced up. Something boyish and sad surfaced in his face. As if flicking away a tear, he thumbed his cheek where the pale trace of a scar remained.

"There is no salve for the truth, is there, sir?"

Jack Crewe glared at him. "Give up the land, the legacy Thomas Crewe entrusted to me in exchange for my child?"

Ethan stood and phrased it another way. "Give up slavery or give up the slave."

The men stared at each other. Jack looked away first.

Ethan looked away too. He glanced around the room until he spotted his hat. "You will understand my decision not to further impose on your hospitality," Ethan said as he settled the hat on his head and adjusted the brim. He paused at the door. "Tomorrow I will return with the sheriff. Then I will depart with my merchandise or my money."

"She is not what you want," Jack said, embarrassed by the note of pleading in his voice. "What is it you want?"

Ethan cracked an enigmatic smile. He shrugged. "Perhaps all I want is to do for you what you and my father did not do for me."

• • •

Jack stared down at the leftovers on his table—meats with sauce, fresh bread, and honeyed things—but he remembered hunger. It was a fist clenching and twisting his guts. He remembered the humiliations of poverty: dozing and waking surrounded by the mingled smells of human shit and sickness; the bite of body lice; his horror the first time he saw wiggling maggots in the food he'd been given. He remembered the shame he felt as he picked and chewed and swallowed. He remembered cowering on the deck of *The Venture*, waiting for a kick from the merchant to whom, days later, Jack would surrender his sister.

Years gone since such deprivation and abuse, yet he could readily recall the aching shame.

To keep Lydia and surrender the land was to reverse the gains of all that suffering. It meant starting again, no better off than when he and Rowan walked, grieving and destitute, off *The Venture* and into the world of Thomas Crewe.

Across the yard, Ethan gathered his belongings from the slave drovers' cabin. Jack heard his footsteps, then the faint jangling of his horse's harness as the young man mounted the animal and cantered out of the yard.

The staccato pounding of hooves faded.

Jack dropped into a chair at the table. He did not know if Ethan's ultimatum was the punishment he deserved or an unmerited gift.

• • •

Jack peered through the cutout window of Bless's cabin and saw Lydia and her mother sitting cross-legged on the floor in front of the hearth. A banked fire smoldered behind them, offering warmth in the form of light. The two were playing with the corn-husk doll Jack had ordered Bless to toss onto the burn heap. They laughed as they took turns making it prance and talk. As he watched, it struck Jack that Bless was correct: a plaster doll would not have made Lydia a bit happier. Children needed more than Jack had been given as a child, but perhaps not much more.

Bless, Jack Crewe, and Lydia

Near first light, Jack rapped on the cabin door. He had spent the night gathering, packing, preparing. Money, warm clothes, food for a few days, documents of manumission—the ink finally dry beneath smatterings of sand. He had left, of course, this sundering to last. He loaded everything onto his horse and then went to fetch his daughter.

When she opened the door, Bless looked more confused than sleepy. She had risen early as always, but no one, certainly not Crewe paid the courtesy of knocking.

"Come out here a moment," he said.

"Sir?" Bless whispered trying not to wake the sleeping child.

"I've come for Lydia," Crewe said.

Bless glanced over her shoulder. Holding her doll in one hand and rubbing her eyes with the other, Lydia stood beside the cot. Bless had been hoping for a few minutes of quiet before Lydia's eyes popped open and the girl bounced out of bed. Then came the knock. Bless tried to keep the irritation out of her voice.

"Sir, I haven't even washed her face—"

She turned back to find Crewe looking at her, a long, penetrating stare meant to divulge what he lacked the courage to confess.

"No," Bless said. "No." She tried with all the strength in her body to slam the door.

Crewe forced his way in. "He offered me a choice."

Acquainted with the choices offered by the Jeffrey men, Bless used her forearms, her thighs, all of the power in her hips to shove Jack Crewe backward, toward the door.

"Freedom!" Jack said as he grappled with Bless. "He offered freedom, for her, for me."

Bless stopped.

"Lydia, come here," Jack said.

"No!" Bless said, turning to the child. "Don't you move."

Lydia stayed put. Her blue eyes were the greater part of her brown face. She hugged the corn-husk doll to her chest as her gaze darted from Bless to Jack. From mother to father.

"We have to leave right now," Jack said to Bless. "Ethan is coming back for her today."

"Ly-Lydia," Bless said, the name faltering, stuttering, shuddering like her heart. "Don't you move."

Jack held out his hand. "Come, Lydia. Now!"

Lydia shifted from one foot to the other. She did not run to her mother. She did not reach for Jack. Between her bare feet, a puddle formed on the floor.

Jack turned to Bless. His gaze was fearful, imploring. "He'll make a wh-whore out of her," he said, his voice breaking.

The look of hatred that Bless leveled on Jack was breathtaking. Illuminating.

Jack had never owned Bless, nor had he owned David. And do with them what he might, Ethan did not own Nora or Jonah or any of their children.

The enslaved were bound to their love for one another and that alone. For the sake of that love, they would do anything—run or stay, fight or surrender—withstand *anything*.

Bless charged across the room. Roughly, she lifted Lydia and thrust her into Jack's arms. She shoved them, her enslaver and her child, toward the door, toward freedom.

• • •

Wailing filled the silence left by Jack's galloping horse. Bless knelt on the dampened floor, the corn-husk doll clutched to her chest.

This here is love.

Jack

It took weeks, but Jack finally arrived in the backcountry of the Virginia Colony with—as he was coming to think of the two—*his children*, Lydia and Kelsey.

Along with the supplies that filled his saddlebags, the two were all he took in forfeit for all of Crewe's—acres of farmland, animals, and human capital. His actions, Jack knew, were not praiseworthy. What he surrendered in no way compared to the sacrifices of Bless, Nora, and Jonah. Jack had galloped away with their beating hearts.

But now, together, where the land buckled and rose beneath the overhang of the Blue Ridge Mountains, Jack, Lydia, and Kelsey pieced together a humble dwelling, a humble life.

In this backcountry settlement, they found people like themselves, those who had been mixed and matched by circumstance and the complex machinations of the heart. Some folks had come on their own. Others had been driven away by people and conditions they could not abide. None owned slaves, and few bothered themselves with who had been a slave, or an enslaver. Jack resolved to bring up his children there among the German and English traders, who brought back wives from among the Overhill Cherokee, the maroons and Protestants and unbelievers, and whoever else minded matters of their own home and left everyone else to do the same.

In that place, Lydia and Kelsey sat in a schoolroom with other brown and black and white children, then returned home to work beside their Papa Jack in the fields and garden and kitchen. It was not an easy life. Born as he was into different skin and less likely than a mother to soothe and coddle, Jack sometimes failed them. There were comforts the children had to do without.

One thing, however, Jack was determined to provide. He kept them together, Lydia and Kelsey, sister and brother of a kind, to foster each other through their boundless new world.

Bless

Ethan sold Jack Crewe's people in the time of the azaleas, spring-time, when leaves—tender strokes of color—and cascades of sassy pink blossoms mocked the wretchedness of the enslaved. Ethan sold them at planting time, when crops and people turn their attention to putting down roots—when filaments grasp the soil and babies are born. He sold them quickly, at a loss, out of spite, so Jack would not have time to outrun the news of his homeplace split asunder. And so, Bless found herself trekking south.

Days away from Lower Norfolk, somewhere on the other side of Portsmouth, Bless, like the strangers to whom she was chained, grieved what was left behind: a grave she would never visit again; a living daughter sent off into a motherless future. She closed her mind against memories of the other loves—Cassie, Jeremiah, and David—lest she crumple. Even if she did, the coffle would not stop. She would simply become another weight for them to drag. Bless kept moving, and her mourning stretched over the miles. She felt her life being pulled away like strips of skin. No wonder then that for days she counted the stinging and burning in her thigh as just one more pain on this forced march into a lower colony.

The speculator who bought Bless and this slapdash string of captives was taking them to a growing settlement situated on the Pasquotank River. There, where every skill was wanting, they would be dispersed among tobacco growers, oystermen, and households.

When they had covered forty miles, Bless's feet and legs numbed to the daily trudge toward this unwelcome fate, but the stinging in her thigh only grew more persistent. Only when she finally reached down to knead the ache, did Bless finally realize the source of her pain. Jeremiah's map. Burning as it had not burned since he'd carved it into her. It was the sensation of being scored with ice. The strange pain drew Bless from her grief long enough to look around. *We are headed south.*

Through the worn fabric of her dress, she traced the scars. What had Jeremiah said? What signs had he said to look for? "When the dark grains of earth beneath your feet firm up to a solid, sturdy clay." She had not noticed when the soft tobacco-rolling roads became hard-packed, impermeable, but here she stood.

When the air begins to turn warm, like a June night with no breeze, and the mosquitoes bite though it is not their time. When you smell the earth itself on fire. It is the smell of lightning-struck peat guiding you in. Look up. You will see jessamine vines tangled high up in the pines. If you run in spring, the hanging golden blooms will point the way. In another season, listen for warblers, a choir of them. They will lead you aright. There are bears and bobcats and panthers. They will give you wide berth. They are hunted too. Rather, mind the snakes and biting, stinging critters. For your wounds, break off a piece of the devil's walking stick. Know it by its thorns. Bind it to the wound. When you see the blue-green spires of cedars, you are not far. Wade through the switch cane. The water will rise to your chest, but level ground lies beneath. Listen. The wind will make music rise from the reeds. That is us, the fugitives, the defiant ones, the Cimarrons, calling to you. You are not lost. You are tired, but see how the cypress rise out of the ground and shape walls from their roots? Rest there. You are hungry. Look for muscadine. Even if you have missed the fruits, there will be fresh water in the vine. Rest and rise and keep coming.

Bless looked around her. The terrain was unfamiliar, pathless, but all around her were signs, portents.

She felt a change in her sorrow. It did not lift but rather shifted—the way she used to move Lydia from chest to hip—it became a weight more easily carried.

It might take years of detours and delays. Certainly, it would cost the last of her daring. Not everyone she loved would be there, perhaps only the one, and so much of her heart would be left behind in this wilderness.

Still, Bless was freedom bound.

Acknowledgments

My gratitude:

To Mama, thank you for each Little Golden Book and for answering all of my questions about tobacco farming—over and over again. To Ma Ruth, who sang my great-great-grandmother's song, "Hark! The black bird said to the crow!" I heard. I remembered. I wrote it down. To my sisters, Loretta Perry Shuler and Tammy Perry Spruill, for each time you stepped into the breach. Loretta, Sugar Plum-Plum, special thanks because you told me I was smart. To Matilda Cox and Remica Bingham-Risher, Road Dawgs, thank you for writing retreats, best-friendship, and poetry. Where are we going next? To Judy Mercier and Temple West, our workshop is wonderful; our friendship is indispensable. Farideh Goldin, thank you for years of quiet writing in coffee shops. Janet Peery, author and mentor, whenever I call, you tell me how to fix it. There are not enough thank-yous. Timothy Seibles, you surprised me with wonderful books and reminded me to write. Sheri Reynolds, your door was always open. Janis Smith, for tuna sandwiches on the back porch. Doris Bingham and Doris V. Gaskins, thank you for your patience. You waited longer than anyone, and here it is! Thomas Shuler Sr. and Thomas Shuler Jr., thank you for the emergency pictures, car repairs, counsel, and that trip to the zoo. Jennifer Natalie Fish, thank you for allowing me to see myself through your lens. Kelly Morse, we are officemates and feral cats forever! Laura Pegram, you believed before I did. Thank you. Mary Parker, thank you for lending Cassie your name. Amy Cherry and all the employee-owners at W. W. Norton, I so admire your history, and I am grateful to be a part of your present. Thank you all for choosing me. Amy, thank you for looking at the pages and seeing what I could not see. Jodi Hughes, thank you for your sharp eye. To Victoria Sanders, Bernadette Baugham-Baker, Christine Kelder, and the team at Victoria Sanders & Associates, it took years of patience and revisions, but you got me to the finish line! Thank you for sticking with me.

I imagined the characters in this book but not the suffering and not the overcoming. My wholehearted thanks to the Lord who has brought us thus far.